Irving Place Editions

Also by John Lauricella

Hunting Old Sammie

The Pornographer's Apprentice

Home Games: Essays on Baseball Fiction

2094

a novel by

John Lauricella

Irving Place Editions

Cover design by John Lauricella
Interior design by John Lauricella

ISBN-13: 978-0615868813
ISBN-10: 0615868819

Printed and bound on demand in the United States of America

First Edition published April 21, 2014
Revised Edition published April 21, 2018

www.irvingplaceeditions.com
Suspend Your Disbelief — Read On!

For my mother, Lucille Lauricella (Rinaldi), who likes stories about the future; and for the children—mine, yours, theirs, everyone's—who inherit it.

~ *In Memoriam* ~

Madeline Hoose (Rinaldi) 1942 – 2014
Godmother, beloved
Peace

Nothing was your own except the few cubic
centimeters inside your skull.

~ George Orwell
1984

2094

Airpods gleam in the skyways as the century dwindles and men like J Melmoth are amazed to be alive. One evenmorn after a CellRenew finds him exultant at his windowall with Jenna at his side, the two of them gazing across the Illumined City and he, Melmoth, marveling at his luck. He has so-marveled on countless evenmorns and middays and starry nights during the past sixty-six years, for he is a free man rich in every comfort (Jenna being not the least of these), and continues as fit and hale as a century ago. J Melmoth, 133 years in this world and forever young, has seen a world pass away. Devices long beloved, the last century's signature gear and coveted luxuries, are obsolete and forgotten. A few items persist as tokens of whim and vanity. How else to account for Melmoth's wristwatch, solid gold with mother of pearl face and diamond-fretted bezel, when the microchip implanted in his prefrontal cortex makes telling time merely a matter of thinking it?

Screen on. The windowall wakes up, sounds rise, holographic images begin to manifest. A Mars Colony news story shows seven geodesic domes arrayed in a hexagonal tessellation on the Red Planet's desolate plain. The domes glow bluely through Martian night. This view melts, slides away, and is replaced by an interior panorama of EarthStation 6, where Luminarians have installed full-spectrum solar panels in the lofty ceiling. Simulated sunlight mimics a summer day. Beefsteak tomatoes, sweet corn, red lettuce, soybeans, and arboretum-scale ranks of leafy trees embellish the landscape. The Overvoice notes that fruits and vegetables grow in real Earth's soil. VirtuSun, it says, delivers every benefit of true sunlight. Humans, too, thrive in the synthetic microclimate.

Melmoth says, "Now we'll hear that Mars Colony will be able to feed itself by the end of the year."

"Mars Colony," the Overvoice concludes, "will attain food self-sufficiency by year's end."

"You are amazing," says Jenna, gazing at him with awe and desire. "You are so brilliant to have known."

Melmoth, chuckling, changes feeds. "Thank you, Jenna. In truth, it was nothing. News stories have made similar claims for months." He reaches behind to pat her ideal ass. "Notice, not a word about the nitrogen-based atmosphere they're supposed to be setting up."

Jenna looks at him as quizzically as a child.

"My guess is their monkeying with Mars's magnetosphere, what's left of it, did not have the hypothesized effect."

Jenna is wide-eyed. "I am distressed to hear that, J, and so proud of you for having discerned it. Surely the government will uplink you for wisdom and advice."

"Splendid. I'll tell my wife. She'll laugh and laugh."

"Oh dear!" says Jenna, startled by emergent holograms. "Such filthy creatures! Their beards are unruly growths of exceeding years." Her face warps as if she has chewed burnt pistachio nuts. "Truly these are the ugliest men ever seen."

Melmoth laughs. "Not even close." He listens to the Overvoice recounting conditions in Gulag Cuba.

"I wish they would go away," says Jenna. "Do you know, J, if they will?"

"Never," says Melmoth. "They're detainees. Officially, we call them miscreants. Miscreants are everlasting. They will be with us forever."

"Is that possible? Surely they do not receive CellRenew."

"Miscreants are always being born."

"Always!" Jenna's voice registers the maximum quotient of incredulity possible under her current scripts. "Born! Surely you jest."

Melmoth considers a code-level tweak. Just to spare Jenna from sounding like a character in an oldenspeech novel. "Not a bit. Future miscreants are born daily."

"Like animals." Jenna purses her lips, shakes her head. "It is a blessing they do not overrun us."

"Not a chance," says Melmoth. "Listen."

To nudge miscreants toward Implantation, Discipline & Punish puts lures on offer. Limited freedom. Clean, easy jobs. Open access to android brothels. A microchip seamlessly integrated will give the government power to monitor and control. Like their predecessors, these detainees resist. *They continue to deny our wonders and miracles,* the Overvoice intones. *They bite technicians. With simian ferocity they claw at sanitary masks and gouge eyes with blackened nails.*

"How horrible," says Jenna.

Day and night these wretched beings cling to the bars of their cages. Chanting in infernal medley, they curse our achievements and howl down destruction.

"An abomination," says Jenna. "Expunge it, J, please."

"Just another minute." He ought to have scripted her as more retentive. Having to re-introduce basic realities has become tedious and serves no purpose other than to postpone the moment they lie together on the hoverbed.

The Overvoice says, *The human status of these creatures has been placed in question by their congenital refusal to accept cerebral enhancement*, and Melmoth says, "Here it comes."

If the Court judges them degenerated, pre-human, quasi-simian, or Other ...

"Wait for it ..."

... it is likely the government will re-evaluate the legitimacy of forced Implantation.

"And there we have it," says Melmoth. "It was always going to reach this point. I'm only surprised they waited so long." It is dismaying, this shell game they play with due process. But it could be worse. At least Discipline & Punish makes no bones about detaining potential terrorists indefinitely. No one protests. Melmoth himself feels safer with zealots under lock and key. Common knowledge, too, is the gov's intention of exerting behavior control through brain surveillance. Melmoth assumes this practice does not also apply to his brain.

We offer them a higher existence and they spit in our face.

Melmoth nods. He mentions none of this to Jenna.

"What are you thinking, J, you genius," she says, laughing.

Jenna's fawning admiration is his fault. Melmoth has scripted her. His personal android's compassion, indulgence, good humor, tolerance, submissiveness, selflessness, yearning, and fidelity never vary and never fail.

"That we can suspend today's news stories any time you like."

"Wonderful!" says Jenna. "I want to have sex with you now."

It is the second time she has spoken this wish today (a Wednesday, in fact) and her scripts guarantee that she will so-speak a third time between the evening meal and sleep. Melmoth can change Jenna's programming any time he likes but prefers being surprised, more or less, such as when his personal android companion, PAC for short, SmartBot familiarly, calls him from some trivial chore, such as polishing his AstroGolf titaniums (which he might anyway always delegate to a household droid, or to Jenna herself if he is feeling peevish), to perform the Immortal Act.

Aiming the pinpoint laser integrated with his right eye, Melmoth launches MyEnviron. Holograms vanish, the windowall blacks-out, the polymer ceiling slides open and the hoverbed descends. A rainbow glow soft-flows over surfaces and space. "Mood lighting" in oldenspeech, it is known today as Option 2b. Jenna steps behind a free-standing acrylic divider and a moment later reappears wearing silk panties and a lacy peignoir fastened in front with the most perfunctory of ties. Melmoth thinks, *Scarlett Johansson.* His wish beams via VirtuLink to Jenna's transformalboard and the morphing begins. This process enchants him, chiefly for its soundlessness. As Melmoth watches, Jenna swiftly attains the perfect likeness of the aforementioned Scarlett, a semi-famous cinemastar he admired way-back-then at her, the human original's, biological age of twenty-four. Jenna's stature becomes Scarlett's five-foot-four, Jenna's crystal eyes become Scarlett's vivid green. Face, figure, honey-blonde hair all conform to the standard of human loveliness embodied ninety years ago in a single particular woman, who is alive and thriving and looking in 2094 exactly as she did in 2004.

Jenna-Scarlett smiles her seductive smile, showing off her brightwhites. "Why, hello, J," she says. "How wonderful to meet you at last."

"Welcome to the future, Scarlett." Face to face with her beauty, Melmoth feels dizzy. Still, he is confident. The upshot is guaranteed.

"Thank you, J," says Jenna-Scarlett. "You are very kind and quite handsome."

Melmoth chuckles. Truly, he is shameless.

"I am delighted to be with you. Unless you wish first to eat a sumptuous meal, I am ready to please."

Melmoth does not wish to eat.

The hoverbed being convenient, they begin.

The Immortal Act being well known, description is superfluous. Suffice to say that upon parting Jenna-Scarlett's peignoir J Melmoth discovered a female figure whose shape, size, and texture were exactly as he had always imagined. Such is the genius of android companions: fully twenty-three years Ms. Johansson's biological senior, Melmoth in oldentimes harbored no hope of acquainting himself with the actual She.

Even now, having enjoyed such wonders half his semi-natural life, Melmoth is dazzled by how everything has changed.

◑ † ☽

On the desert floor, six men in khaki rest on their heels as a lean goat turns on a spit. Night is falling across Sonora. The men are more tired than they have ever been and this goat is their only food. They have carried the carcass, gutted and skinned, many miles from the encampment by the Sea of Cortés. Cold-packed in dry ice, this last procured from an outpost of El Norte, the goat is a meager meal, hardly worth the risk.

At the encampment, families await their return. They must ride southward a hundred miles along a dark verge of highway, then turn west toward the coast. It is a dangerous crossing and before it they have this goat and tell-tale fire. Thermal imaging satellites seek hotspots in the cooling desert. Computer analysis quicker than one can cry *God have mercy* may coordinate a strike none will detect before the spacelaser incinerates them all.

In a faraway gloaming, steel roofs buckle and walls collapse. Green flames lick at a purple twilight sky. It is their thought, their hope, that those conflagrations will hide their tiny fire. That the destruction they have accomplished will make it possible to live another day and block further spread of waste sites. For decades, garbage has fallen around them. Household trash and crushed cars, detritus of household appliances, mineral spirits stained with toxins; later, scummed syringes, yellowed plastic tubing, synthetic bandages crusty with blood. Some of which burns now – and yet, countless reeking compounds mar the desert.

Goat meat hisses with a sour scent that to Javier Martínez seems near rancid. Enrique Ramos turns the spit.

"When?" says Carlos Sandoval.

"Five minutes. Perhaps six."

"Do not ruin it," says Miguel Jiménez, their nominal leader. Once gulaged, he was encouraged to recant statements published under his name. They freed him afterward without requiring Implantation.

"And what do you know about roasting a goat?" Enrique Ramos reverses the turning.

"I know overcooked goat is no meal your wife would serve." The others laugh quietly, mindful of their dinner and their cook.

"And what do you know of my wife?"

"Ignore him," says Roberto Díaz, the largest of the men. Roberto is deeply hungry and wonders how he might claim a larger share.

"I know that splendid woman has haunches of which a horse would be proud."

Pacho says, "God bless Rico's excellent wife, long may she live."

"May she be always strong," says Javier.

"Quiet, you two," Roberto barks.

"We must pass the time," says Carlos. "How better than to state our admiration of Alma Ramos?"

"A peerless woman," says Javier Martínez.

"I, for one, worship the soles of her feet."

"Her feet are leather." Enrique turns the spit. Yellow flame laps at the meat.

"Pay attention," says Roberto.

"Don't be stubborn, compañero. Everyone is hungry."

"Christ knows you will ruin it," says Pacho.

"Burnt goat is no meal," says Javier.

Enrique stops turning. "Very well. Here, lend me your hand."

Roberto Díaz seizes one end of the spit. He and Enrique lift it from steel posts hammered into the desert hardpan and together lay the goat on a blanket of waxed hemp. The men unsheathe their knives and sort themselves into a line. Precedence is consensual. Enrique is first to cut in. His knife draws a red trickle. "Ah! What have I said?" He completes the incision, reverses his blade and slices against the grain. With his knife's point he removes a steak the size of a child's hand. As Roberto cuts in, Enrique returns to the fire.

"You will ruin it," says Carlos.

"No doubt you savages enjoy raw flesh. I am a civilized man." The slight steak cannot be re-spitted. Enrique skewers it and holds it over the coals. Careful of his hand, he turns his knife this way and that.

One by one, the men return to the fire. Miguel Jiménez is last to cut in. His ration likewise skewered, he takes his place in a circle of men keen to discern the moment that separates cooking from burning. No one ventures a comment. Each man is equally hungry, equally aware of danger, angry that this poor meal is all they have and, in spite of himself, grateful for it. No doubt it would have been wiser to ride on without having lit this fire, cooked this meal. Certainly they have placed themselves in jeopardy. Always they have lived under threat. Bodies undernourished, minds numbed by solitude. Noting Carlos Sandoval's mournful stare, Miguel's skyward glance, Enrique feels their spirits retreat.

Roberto Díaz bites his ration in half and chews. "Good," he says, teeth working quickly to shift hot goatsteak away from tongue and palate. He eats his share before the others have attempted theirs. As they begin, Roberto says, "I must have more, if no one objects."

Miguel nods. "Be thoughtful, compañero, to leave five times what you take."

Regarding the flayed carcass, Roberto says, "Such thinking leaves a man hungry."

"Roberto may have my second share." Having finished his goatsteak, Enrique wipes off his knife. "I have had my fill of this stinking thing." He sheaths his knife and stands. "To have no better food is a disgrace."

"To starve is more disgraceful." Miguel's hair is black and gray. His light brown face, sun-creased, is sharpened by a line of mustache.

"We are starving," says Carlos. "Our land is despoiled. That which is not poisoned has been stolen."

"Every man here knows these hardships."

"Women and children also know, though they are not here," says Enrique. "Little ones cry for bread. Women's faces tell who is to blame."

"Excellent Alma," says Pacho. "Surely she does not mark you the author of our misfortune."

"She marks me as a man who failed to prevent it." His gaze, baleful and angry, touches each man. "We share this dishonor. So Alma Ramos tells me."

"Now not so excellent, perhaps," says Javier, drawing Pacho's sneer.

"All the better that we have succeeded today," says Miguel.

Nods and grunts. The men chew.

"You are certain of that?" says Enrique. "You believe it?"

"Yes, compañero. I believe."

‡ C ‡ C ‡

In his cage at Gitmo Bay, Ibn al Mohammed sits on a three-legged stool and studies palm fronds between the bars. He thinks he is thirty-three years old. He thinks he has been detained for thirteen years. Time is slow and in its emptiness much the same. Ibn al Mohammed knows he was born in a village near a desert and lived there with his mother and sisters on floors of hardpacked sand. His father he remembers as an old man who spoke of his own father as a man who was taken away. Ibn al Mohammed believes his grandfather died in a cage like the one that holds him now.

Tropical sun warps the tin roof. Heating, the metal strains against its rivets and by its crying tells him lunch is soon. Today they will offer perhaps marinated steak and julienned fried potatoes, filet of sea bass, chickpea hummus freshly spiced with garlic and thyme. Never had he known such food, before Gitmo. Never had he known a feeling of satisfied hunger, understood satiety on a level as deep as life. Ibn al Mohammed has fought in burning

cities, eyes weeping from smoke. He has wept without fire in a
cave. He has not touched a woman in more than a decade and
each night prays that the Great Satan will immolate itself in flames
of its limitless lust.

Left from breakfast is a yellow banana on a paper tray. Ibn al
Mohammed picks up the fruit and peels it. It is ripe, it is firm, it
smells of the jungle. He chews with full regret that the banana will
make him shit. Hopefully his bowels will not move until morning,
God willing, when he is permitted to join a chain brigade and
clean his pail in the sea. If defecation cannot wait for daybreak, he
must perform it before prayers. Ibn al Mohammed will force himself – and with this thought finds strange phrases in his mind: he
will will it; will willfully shit; will make do-do. The profane language of his captors. By such sayings he knows their words are toys
– mundane sounds that anyone so-inclined may manipulate as
occasion allows and whim invites. Mere noise, glottal nothings,
echoes inside which truth disappears, in this case the fact of human offal reeking in a tin pail and afflicting God's servant with
abominable dreams.

He has added lean muscle during his detention. Push-ups in
his cage. Sweating fieldwork in cane and coffee groves. The ma-
chetes that cut the cane would serve well as weapons, were their
jailers human. As it is they have only each other to kill. This, the
droids allow – perhaps as a lesson about the limits of forbearance.
Tolerance. Were it not for blood slaughter, Ibn al Mohammed
would regard it as laughing-matter – what in bygone times
acolytes of the Great Satan ciphered a sick-joke. It, too, bears witness to their ignorance of Sunni and Shi'ite. It is sacred duty for
every True Believer to cut down apostate sons of dogs who deny
the true descent of the Prophet.

Ibn al Mohammed stands, walks six steps to a corner of his
cage, and drops the yellow peel into the waste. He is careful of his

fingers, that they remain clean. All food arrives on paper trays with coarse napkins but never spoon, fork, or knife. Also, yes, a small foil envelope with a moist white napkin folded inside. Grateful, he uses the napkin before he brings nourishment to his lips.

Eggs in the morning with bacon, which he must always refuse. Various fruit: orange, grapefruit, yellow banana. All meals eaten in-cage. Goat's milk at his request, likewise chickpeas, spinach, lentils, saffron-flavored rice, couscous fried in sesame oil with ginger and garlic. With all these, there is paprika-spiced chicken, curried lamb, savory beef marinated in spiced wine and charred to tenderness. More meat than he had seen in his life, beginning the day he was interned. Since then he has been held in silence. No interrogation or examination, the sole requirement snap-obedience. No trial, no threats. A shadowy promise of punishment if obedience fails. That, and the cage.

Restricted-in-cage means no chain brigade jog-trot to the sea. No emptying or cleaning, no relief.

He looks past the bars to the high fronds of palm trees. Staring hard, unblinking, he seems to recognize his mother's face half-veiled by blade-shaped leaves. Ibn al Mohammed knows it is illusion, a semblance conjured into the visible by his yearning mind. He tries each day to see his mother's face. To remember it. He is careful to note the shape of her eyes and their color, the set of her lips, the lines that crease her forehead. Those lines, he imagines, trace the shape of what is and what might be. Her eyes say she grieves and is resigned to grief. Her lips shape a promise, unspoken yet eloquent, that she will endure.

Will he see his mother again? Is it possible that she is still alive?

In thirteen years, Ibn al Mohammed has seen only androids and other aboriginals of EarthSector 22. Obscene in human form, droids appear daily to provoke and confuse. In-cage, other detainees are hidden from his sight. Ibn al Mohammed senses their whisperings, hears awesome cries and laments. An otherworldly voice speaks from faraway, projected by loudspeakers hidden high in the royal palms.

Enemies of the microchip, despair! Your kind is everywhere on the run. Agents of death, superstitious provocateurs, unredeemed medievalists: all are rotting corpses in the gutter of history. Wise up, apostate! Accept Implantation today!

Ibn al Mohammed despises their words. He despises himself for understanding. How has it come to him, this knowledge? Conjurations of evil. Incantations of heresy. Aboriginals only speak in God's language. Arabic. Farsi. Hindi. The androids' commands, their false counsel and blandishments, are uttered with Satan's forked tongue. They scan the code embedded in his forehead and turn his father-given, God-sanctioned name into a barbarism.

"*Dear* Mr. IaM, *please* stand back from the bars." The android's voice counterfeits friendliness. Ibn al Mohammed steps back two paces. He stares at the android in spite of himself. It continues to impersonate a human female, young, almost his height, false-skin scantily veiled. He knows it is not human. Tinted rose-gold, its not-flesh tortures him. Ibn al Mohammed wishes to press his lips to this false-skin, lick it, kiss, remove the triangle of transparent fabric that half-hides the android's central secret. He himself, a man merely human, wishes to explore that secret. By this desire he feels himself damned. If he finds the miracle that seems promised, Ibn al Mohammed fears the urge to test further the ingenuity of the Great Satan will be too great for a man to resist.

"Good afternoo-*oon!*" the android sings. Loose inside a mocking garment, its protuberances insult his eyes. Ibn al Mohammed lowers his gaze, stares as if to memorize the concrete floor. And yet, he has seen. And wishes to see again. The android opens the service lock and sets a tray inside the compartment. It secures its end and the inner panel swings open.

Aroma of tarragon chicken and basmati rice with almonds and raisins seems to cover his face.

"Eat up, you bad boy." The android simulates a pout, meaningless to God's servant, who wills himself blind. Registering no response, the device frowns. It flounces its hair, fashioned blonde for the nonce, then with arms lifted and hands overhead performs a harlot's dance. Ibn al Mohammed senses its gyrations.

He will not look. He will not.

When the android removes its chemise, Ibn al Mohammed turns his back to it.

"Naughty Mr. IaM. So not-nice to little me."

Ibn al Mohammed closes his eyes. Food-smell is overwhelming. He hears a sound of nanofiber sheering along surfaces of false-skin.

"Yoo-hoo! Mr. IaM! *Yoo-hoo!*"

What it is doing frightens him. He imagines it waving, winking to entice. Head bowed, eyes blind, he waits. How much longer? He thinks it must soon end its antics, God willing. Ten minutes, fifteen, it is possible to wait. The chicken and rice tempt him. He thinks of yellow banana, that it has lessened his hunger. Each moment, the day's heat grows fiercer.

"Come, come," says the droid. "You know you want to, naughty IaM."

What is it doing? Flaunting its protuberances. Wiggling its nether parts. It is a device, merely. Wrought by Satan's hands.

The odor Ibn al Mohammed detects is not that of oil and ozone. Machines emit such stench in his native land. This scent is primal and rich – unmistakably, the scent of a woman. It cancels aroma of food, stink of shit, air-seep of heated concrete and iron bars.

Ibn al Mohammed folds his arms over his head. How have they achieved this indecency? To buffet a man such as he, honest, immured, God's servant, with female musk. It emanates from the droid. A masquerade of woman he may not touch, is forbidden to know.

"Come, come," it says.

Is there no limit to profanity? Do they have no conscience?

"Come, come."

Ibn al Mohammad waits for deliverance. Surely God will send a breeze to cleanse the air of this shameless ferment. He opens his eyes and looks past the bars. Beyond his cage he sees an ocean vast and blue, seafoam whitely embroidering green waves beneath a sapphire, cloud-laced sky. Before the ocean a beach of white sand lies unmarked by human crossing. In the foreground an oasis beckons: palm trees tall, slender, supple, firm. Ibn al Mohammed imagines becoming smoke and floating between the bars, uncoiling tree-ward, enwreathing the stout trunk of the tallest palm and rising unseen through the tropical afternoon, amid the topmost fronds taking bird-form and launching himself toward freedom on furious wings.

High inside EarthStation 3, Templar Bronze eyes the data stream that tells her how her garden grows. It is a vineyard, in fact, wine grapes proving the most elusive of Earth's bounty to replicate on Mars. Something about the *terroir* is not right. Templar suspects it is the VirtuSun. Its light is too white or in some way too strong or not strong or white enough. True, water and air are recycled, but the soil, all 550,000 cubic yards of it, have been imported from Mount Veeder. For growing Cabernet Sauvignon, Cabernet Franc, Pinot Noir, no place in Napa is better. Napa, however, cannot meet demand, hence Templar's task.

She confirms ambient temperature and relative humidity, notes spectrum balance and airflow. All the numbers are good. Templar passes through a portal onto the observation deck, titanium grating silent under her gelmocs. Surveying terraced vine rows, Templar inhales. The breeze is redolent with ripening grapes: sweet, fruit-heavy, rich in root and leaf. To her eyes, the light is a perfect counterfeit of California sunshine. The air is warm, humidity is low. The foliage is green; the grapes, deep purple.

It feels like Napa.

Ambient daylight dims by one one-hundredth. Six Earth hours from now, every third panel will lowglow in imitation of starlight. Across the terraces, cool air will precipitate fog. Templar Bronze will have resorted to private quarters by then, there to watch via satellite uplinked holograms re-enacting terrorism in Mexico, sex-olympics orgasmicomps, an oldenflick of her choice. During its growing stage, her vineyard rests 10.75 Earth hours in simulated night. Waking at each fabricated dawn, Templar watches as gathering light restores shape and color to fruit and vine.

Crystal chimes herald an incoming communication. Holding her arm against her chest, she touches a sensor on her wristlet and projects a cone of silver light into the space before her. Templar feels her own transpositor mapping her molecules' quantum oscillation. An instant later, a hologram appears. It is Paladin Silver, Sojourner Among the Stars.

"Heigh-ho, Templar."

"Heigh-ho, Paladin. When do you return?"

"Touch-down at Center Atrium will occur in seventeen Earth hours." Belted into his flightchair, Paladin raises an arm as if into an invisible dimension and in that ethereal space touches a sensor. "We've entered an optimum transmission sphere. I'm uploading the data. You will receive it in 12.12 seconds."

"Excellent. Roscoe is eager to review."

"I'm sure he is." Paladin chuckles. "The old goat can't resist tinkering. Power has gone to his head."

"Better Roscoe than some politician. Or worse, a general." From innumerable tiny nozzles hidden in the superstructure above Templar's lofty perch, light rain falls.

"Yes, we won't be reprising either arrangement."

Around Templar the air is misting. A rainbow shimmers against the opalescent surface of the inner sky.

"Your hologram is breaking up," says Paladin Silver.

"Yours, too. The rain will end in a minute."

"And you are – where?"

"On the observation deck. You know that." They have had this conversation before. Paladin's expected reply is that transpositors in 2094 ought to function despite a trillion-trillion-billion water molecules mucking-up the air.

He says, "Take a look at that data. Heigh-ho."

"Heigh-ho."

Templar touches a sensor and her wristlet seems to inhale Paladin's hologram. Touching another sensor, she downloads the data gathered by EarthMission 60. Paladin having applied required algorithms, Templar keys-in a command and her supercomputer interprets the results.

On the continent of Africa, a billion people live in nylon tents. On the continent of South America, thatched-roof shanties flood during equatorial rains. Throughout the poor world, people are hungry and ignorant. They are vulnerable to lethal viruses. Their clothing is adequate, thanks to hand-me-downs donated by the citizenry of the Enhanced World. North America is a paradise: ageless, fed like kings, their health perfect, its people live lives worthy of demigods. Europe and Scandinavia, too, enjoy an endless round of pleasure. Data are not available for maladaptive subgroups: off-griders holed-up in Appalachian enclaves, ghetto-dwellers hunkered in basements of abandoned oldentime cities. Ignorant, technologically bereft, starving, harmless. Do such people still exist? In what numbers? It would be best for everyone, Templar thinks, if they continue invisible until they really disappear. SmartBot labor has made human leisure a full-time pursuit. Russia and Asia, having not perfected advanced technologies (which the Enhanced World declines to share), remain lumbered with the prior century's chores. The island of Cuba, a protectorate of the Ameurope Empire, features the largest detention center on Earth. Mexico, sundered long ago from North America by a series of earthquakes and thereby divided from it by a newly formed sea, lately named the Straits of Despair, is a lawless badland of garbage dumps, roving bandits, nuclear waste storage sites, guerrilla saboteurs, and indigenous survivors subsisting in nomadic encampments. To Templar Bronze, the plight of the latter is pitiable. Decades of malnutrition have reduced their stature; the tallest among them now stand hardly over five feet. And they weigh almost nothing.

Templar Bronze herself enjoys six feet, six inches of height. Her elongated fingers are beautifully tapered, her almond eyes perfectly matched. Three generations of genetic manipulation have made her immune to disease. Food and water of impeccable purity have optimized her growth and hardihood. Her beauty, which is extreme, is the fruit of matchmaking of superior calculation. Templar's jet black hair, full and rich and straight, falls about her head and shoulders like a silken cowl. Her body's proportions are mathematically precise, her skin a miracle of mocha-hued smoothness. Her feet, high-arched and putty-smooth, display ten hemispheres of such deep luster that they seem to be not nails, but pearls. Her irises are the blue of a robin's egg – an extinct species watchable now only as a hologram or, in the Archive of Center Atrium, as a four-color reproduction.

It is not important. Earthscientists can resurrect the robin whenever its existence seems desirable. What matters is that Templar Bronze and her collegial Initiates and Adepts are endowed with knowledge, insight, and wisdom. It is a condition they take for granted – something inevitable, invariable, part of the natural order. Standing on the observation deck overlooking her vineyard, Templar feels proud. Twenty centuries of human progress, its science and art, its astronomical genius and evolutionary enhancements, have in her person expressed perfection.

If only these varietals could be similarly engineered. Cabernet and Pinot are finicky creatures; every environmental anomaly alters their chemical balance, thereby affecting the flavor of the wine made from them. Or might a problem lie in the blending? It is odd that wines rocketed-in from Earth are consistently superior to those made from grapes cultivated, crushed, and fermented in EarthStation 3. The Earth wines have suffered escape velocities and zero gravity, yet their aroma, body, and structure endure. How is this possible? Why do Martian wines routinely fall short? SmartBots have prepared the soil and planted the vines precisely as called for, the grapes have been nurtured and ripened just-so, then harvested by droids scripted to replicate, as near as possible, the motions of human pickers. Blending, aging, and bottling have been done exactly as indicated by the finest wineries in Napa. And yet, something is missing. Not a forgotten bit of know-how, Templar thinks, but a touch of winemaker's art they cannot reproduce.

She returns to the control room. Seated at her console, Templar keys-in commands and reviews the spectrum analysis of VirtuSun.

Lying on his back, Melmoth gazes into a kaleidoscope of orange-white swirl and dancing green, flow of true red and tessellations all blue and gold. He sees abundant food and limitless energy, a pristine wilderness, law and order, sex-on-demand. He turns his head. Jenna lies uncovered on the hoverbed, obliterated in post-coital sleep, although PACs need no sleep. Just to look at her gives Melmoth a thrill. She is ageless, unchanging unless he changes her, immune to sickness, headache, indigestion, moods, dementia, pregnancy, everything. His idyll with her will never end; their time together is eternal. He appraises her poly-vinyl fauxskin and is amazed, again, that such a device – that she – exists. To all appearances and every sense, Jenna is human. Body heat, personal scent, the aqueous humor of her eyes, velvety wetness of her tongue and specific lubricity of her vagina exactly impersonate the attributes of Melmoth's ideal woman, who otherwise does not exist. It is an excellent time to be alive.

Hardship is unknown, deprivation not even a word. Crime is extinct; why would a person steal, what would he steal, when every good thing may be had for pleasure credits and every service rendered by expert droids?

The Overvoice: *Violence has been expunged from our cities. Envy, jealousy, backbiting, and greed are impulses unfelt in our towns.*

Prisons are obsolete. Guns rust. Gulag Cuba exists because miscreants endure. For decades, news stories manifesting from windowalls have shown scraggly bodies naked and begrimed, matted hair, obsidian eyes, vehement chants. The Overvoice speaks on. Discipline & Punish brings firehoses to bear and cuts loose the dogs: archaic methods that miscreants understand. The Gulag's original inmates are gone. Three generations of sinewy, bearded, dark-complected men have disappeared yet Gitmo remains fully peopled. The thrice-great grandchildren of its first detainees are encaged, as well as progeny of those who eluded the hunts.

Why does he recall this unpleasantness? Jenna is naked. Across his ceiling, rainbow colors spin and glow. What do they signify, these back-looking thoughts?

Melmoth drifts recollective to the great miscreant hunts of midcentury. He doesn't bother to access the CyberEmpyrean, just surveys from a cognitive eminence whatever images his organic mind retains. Battalions of Discipline & Punish deployed to cities of shrieking mizzens, remote villages, desert settlements and fortified caves, from whose nooks and crooks and dusty bowels they wrested tens of thousands of enraged men and spitting women for shipboard transport to Gitmo. This action was applauded throughout the Ameurope Empire, cried up by three billion voices in every language of its united peoples. Old Russia groused about imperialism. Upstart China feinted assertions of might & right. All for show: no one really opposed indefinite detention for prospective terrorists. Isolated, they were defenseless. EarthSector 22, termed in oldenspeech the Middle East, underwent forced deportations.

And so to Cuba. A sun-swept, sea-kissed island overlush with palm trees and sugar cane. Green hills sloping to the ocean, wide beaches of white sand erotic with bronzed bodies as bare as God made them. Segregated in cages, the detainees saw none of this. Strung neck to neck like chattel, new inmates were shuffled first into holding pens, then deloused and washed in communal, gender-separate showers. Modular cages provided accommodations altogether safer and more sanitary than the huts and hovels of the impoverished world. Poured concrete floors. Flip-down steel-mesh cots thickly laid with microfiber futons. Did the detainees appreciate these comforts, steel bars notwithstanding? They did not.

Fifty years later, their descendants persist microchip noncompliant. Melmoth finds this attitude incredible. Acquiescence means freedom. Is it possible these people wish to remain imprisoned? Do they relish detention, take in it some kind of zealous, self-flagellating pleasure? How can they not desire VirtuLinks to wellsprings of entertainment and gratification? Cerebral surveillance seems a small price to pay.

Rainbow arrays swirl overhead. Jenna mimics respiration and other biological events. The intimate cleansing that restores her freshness occurs soundlessly. She stirs gently in her sleep, childlike, as scripted.

Feeling gratitude fill him like awe, Melmoth closes his eyes.

We call them miscreants. His wondering about the word prompts his microchip to uplink a universal lexicon. "Miscreant: lawbreaker, evildoer, malefactor, villain. Archaic: heretic; one who misbelieves."

But forced Implantation? The people are human.

The Overvoice: ... *human status ... placed in question.*

Melmoth says, "Absolutely." No one can hear him. The windowall is dark, Jenna simulates sleep. Raquel lies in separate quarters with her personal android companion. Melmoth is alone, as alone as any Enhanced human can find himself in the closing years of the 21st Century. Time was, he knew true solitude. A hundred years ago, was it? A hundred and ten? Before he and Raquel were married it was possible for Melmoth to go days without speaking. He lived alone, knew few people, kept irregular hours. No more. He can hardly remember what it was like, his solitary peace. It belonged to a different way of living. A world that ended, a sense of humanness long ago undone. Before he was Enhanced.

No microchip.

Melmoth wonders how he would feel. Say it were disabled or (he can hardly imagine this) removed. What then? Who would he be? *Unconnected* is the word that comes to mind, by which he thinks he means, unlinked. Could he live without VirtuLinks? No databases or windowalls, no stream of information, no flow of offered product. No updates of genetic code, no installed-component re-scripting. No Jenna.

Is such a life possible? Would it be a life worth living? A life he would want to live?

⊚⊚⊚⊚⊚

Sonora is bright and hot. The Mexicans ride single file, south by southwest. Their journey is one of switchbacks and river crossings. Rio Magdalena. Rio Sonora. Rio Bavispe. Rain has been plentiful; a monsoon has pushed columns of tropical air across the desert and thunderstorms have been common. River water, however, is unsafe. Every stream running from the piedmont carries risk. Untainted, perhaps – it is impossible to know. Toxins have spread very far. Many pueblos are abandoned. They take water from giant saguaros, cutting through waxy skin into the pulp.

Miguel Jiménez, Enrique Ramos and the others are covered with dust. They chew seedpods of mesquite as they ride, kerchiefs veiling nose and mouth. By the Sea of Cortés, their people wait. Women, children, a critical number of able-bodied men. They live on fish and prepare to move on. How far can they flee into the hopeless heart of Old Mexico? It is a question they ask without speaking, the thought in each man's mind. Enrique ponders it in a mood close to despair. He sees no means of reclaiming their land, no recompense for what has been stolen. His allegiance to Miguel seems futile. These raids are impotent thrusts. One does not kill a giant with pinpricks. Nature itself thwarts them. Sundered from the continent, Mexico is doomed in its isolation.

The men sit tall in their saddles, rifles in leather scabbards near to hand. Miguel and Carlos, Javier and Pacho and Roberto Díaz watch saguaro and mesquite, piedmont and hills, the distant mountains. Enrique watches the sky. If a laser strikes, what will he see? A white flash? A red ray? Perhaps he will see nothing, feel nothing. One moment alive, next moment gone.

How old was he at the Sundering? Eight years? Ten? Enrique has forgotten the date of his birth, his life from before. Youth is long ago and today is like yesterday, itself a pattern of what tomorrow will be. Only his wife, peerless Alma, keeps Enrique mindful of his past. Together they have watched men step from the shadows and present themselves as leaders, only to sell Mexico for nothing. Waste dumps as large as cities foul water and air. Rio Magdalena runs yellow with by-product. Rio Mayo and Rio Yaqui carry heavy metals into the Sea of Cortés. Rio Bravo is clouded with fecal matter delivered by scow and tanker from hog farms in El Norte.

"Miguel Jiménez, is it true, what I have been told?" Enrique speaks to the back of Miguel's head. They rock gently on their horses.

"And what have you been told?"

"Our forests are to be razed. Companies of gringos will strip the land in search of gold."

"Who brings this report?

"One who calls himself Omar the Turk."

"A smuggler. Do we credit the words of this man?"

"He moves at will through day and night." Enrique lowers his voice. "The Turk crosses the sea. In El Norte he learns many things."

"Some of which no doubt are true." Miguel lifts his kerchief and spits. "I hope this will not be, compañero."

"We have hoped many things for many years. Hope makes a good breakfast and a poor dinner."

"It is futile to speak of it." For several minutes only their horses' silt-dampened steps fret the silence. They drink sparingly from their canteens. Enrique feels the Sun's heat burning through his hat and shirt. Today it is fierce and fiercer, as if it, too, were hunting them.

From behind, Carlos Sandoval says, "We must find this Turk." It was not Enrique's intention that Carlos should hear. Omar the Turk is a resource of incomparable value. One does not wish his existence commonly known.

"Yes, compañero," Enrique says, turning his head halfway. "All in good time. Our work is not done."

"This Turk likely knows of other atrocities planned by our neighbor to the north."

"No neighbor now," says Pacho Muñoz. He rides behind Carlos. "The land is divided and sea flows between."

Truly, a whisper would carry through this empty air.

"This talk has no purpose."

"Indeed," says Miguel. "Our duty now – "

Gunfire breaks out at them. It comes from behind, loud and to the left, from a place where boulders obscure the piedmont. Roberto Díaz falls backward and tumbles off his horse. The others draw their rifles, in the same motion bringing their horses about. They spur the animals on as they fire a volley and another, reins clenched in their teeth. Loud, flat cracks echo across the Plains of Sonora. Javier Martínez shields Roberto, who lies facedown, his head bloody. His horse has bolted. Javier sees two men break cover; he fires, hits one, fires again and is unsure. A burst of rifle fire answers him, then another. The pirate Javier has hit is standing again and Javier, his lips a tight line and his eyes fixed, draws a breath and a bead.

He squeezes his trigger. His enemy's forehead explodes in a flash of white and blue. Other guns fall silent and Javier sees the remnant in retreat. He cries, "They are going for their horses!"

Miguel, Carlos, and Enrique advance while Pacho Muñoz makes for higher ground. From his vantage Pacho sees five men mount and gallop down a flinty défilé hidden from the valley floor. "To the left! To the left!" he shouts, and the others veer off. This change of direction saves them from being outflanked; and moments later, when their assailants charge hellbent from this crossing, Miguel, Carlos, and Enrique shoot them from their saddles and send them sprawling onto hardpan and thornscrub.

Rifles at the ready, they slide from their saddles. Pacho gallops up in dust and sweat.

"Cinco," he says. "There were five."

Miguel nods. "We have killed five." These pirates, what they have thought were pirates, are dressed alike in olive drab. Their black boots are military issue, shirts festooned with insignia of the Ameurope-Mexican Protectorate.

"Federales," says Miguel. Stepping close, he fires into a dead man's head. A small explosion results, a spray of flame. Carlos steps up to another one and with his rifle butt crushes its knees. Polymer joints crack, eliding disks rupture, and a gel like the golden gum of a brittlebush leaks onto the mesa.

Knife in hand, Enrique crouches beside a Federale and rolls it facedown. He cuts away its shirt and in its back uncovers a sensor panel flush to the thing's torso. Its seams, hardly visible, are far too fine for his blade. He touches numbers and letters randomly. The unit does not respond.

"Regrettable." Standing, Enrique sheathes his knife. "We are lucky to have such ingenious enemies. A man would learn much by studying such a device."

"We are lucky our ingenious enemies themselves have much to learn," says Miguel.

Javier Martínez rides up at a walk. The body of Roberto Díaz lies across his horse's back. Blood drips from his head.

"We must bury him," says Javier.

"We must, yet we cannot," says Miguel. "We carry no shovels."

"He cannot lie in the open. Here, help me gather stones."

Javier dismounts and leads them into the bajada. They bring their rifles, a precaution that slows their work. Many forays are necessary, then they lift Roberto's body and carry it to a place between boulders, where they lay it to rest. Using many stones, they close a crude tomb. The stones fit imperfectly but are heavy and will keep out buzzards.

The men step back and remove their hats. Miguel Jiménez bows his uncovered head. "Always we are sad to lose a comrade," he says. "Roberto Díaz was a brave man and a good friend. A large man, of great heart and courage. So shall we remember him. We shall honor his memory in our struggle against those who poison our land. Roberto Díaz gave himself to this fight. It is for this cause his life was lost." Miguel cannot help himself. He almost spits both blessing and imprecation. "God curse Roberto's killers. God destroy our enemies. God bless the soul of Roberto Díaz and keep us safe."

He palms his buffalo hunter by its crown and settles it on his head. The others do likewise, then pull themselves into their saddles. The Federales' weapons, they leave; these guns are superior to their own but they distrust them. It is perhaps superstitious to think in this way.

In silence they ride across the desert, two days' journey from the encampment by the sea.

☪

On a middling slope of the Sierra Maestra, Gitmo inmates toil in a coffee grove. *Coffea arabica* is shade-grown here and air-dried on tables. Coffee trees imported from Yemen seventy-one years ago guaranteed Gitmo an island-grown supply. Yemen is on the Arabian Peninsula. It is the place where coffee was first roasted, brewed, and consumed. Sufi monasteries near Mokha were involved. That is how *coffea arabica* got its name.

Ibn al Mohammed knows none of this. Amid the trees, he searches out dark red cherries ripe for harvest. These he plucks and drops into a hemp sack tied around his waist. He works slowly, carefully, in keeping with his training. Armed guards observe his progress. Ibn al Mohammed wears a straw hat with a wide brim, shirt and trousers of white cotton, open-toe sandals with thin soles. Each guard wears a leaf green Grade 2 Slouch hat with Ameurope insignia and D&P badge, standard issue black leather boots, lightweight jungle khaki that shields its polyvinyl fauxskin from the sun.

Detainees work two hours and break for food. After a Spartan meal, they work two hours more. There are no quotas, no need for speed. When the next shift arrives, Ibn al Mohammed will deliver a final load to the drying tables, then walk with his brigade single file to the bus. Return-trip to Gitmo is an hour over easy road. Air-cooled, its seats high-backed and reclinable, the bus offers comfort much better than his cage. Android attendants serve orange juice, grape juice, pineapple juice, lemonade, and water in sealed bottles with neat straws. Grape leaves stuffed with sticky rice and dipped in extra virgin olive oil will be offered, also triangles of baked pita to scoop into chickpea humus. Music will play, jasmine scent the air.

In the grove, Ibn al Mohammed removes his hat and fans his face. An old man sits with his back against a tree, his eyes closed. Ibn al Mohammed does not believe Khalid Saeed Ahmad al Zahrani sleeps. Fourscore inmates toil in the grove, yet no guard disturbs Khalid Saeed, who is many years at Gitmo.

"You must refuse the Infidels' labor, my son," says al Zahrani. Ibn al Mohammed replaces his hat. "Our duty is jihad. In these circumstances, we fulfill this obligation by doing nothing."

"So have I observed." Ibn al Mohammed resumes work. His hands move through the leaves, fingers smart on the fruit. He plucks cherries and drops them into the sack. Most remaining on this tree are bright red, unripe. In seven days or ten, he or another will return to make a fresh selection.

"How does your jihad progress, Khalid Saeed?"

"I have achieved many days of no-labor," says al Zahrani. "By this means I thwart the designs of the Infidel."

No one knows his age. Tale-tellers whisper numbers and nod. Ibn al Mohammed moves to another tree. "Your steadfastness is admirable. I wish you continued success." He senses al Zahrani's nod.

"I urge you to join me. United in noncooperation, we would influence the others, God willing."

"The others relish the beverage distilled from the beans of this fruit as much as I."

"You refer to coffee, in your orotund manner."

"Yes."

"It intoxicates." Al Zahrani has not moved. His eyes remain closed. "A Muslim should avoid food and drink that agitate the mind and excite the body."

Some say he is one hundred years old. Ibn al Mohammed doubts it is so. Al Zahrani himself does not remember his arrival at

Gitmo. Or will not speak of it. "I am told that Muslims have taken coffee daily since the time of the Prophet."

Al Zahrani opens his eyes. "Your informants are foolish in their ignorance. The Prophet used no stimulants. Before his advent, the peoples of Arabia were barbarous nomads infamous for putting their infant daughters to death. They possessed neither knowledge nor desire to cultivate this fruit you so assiduously gather."

Ibn al Mohammed bows. "As you say. I know nothing of Arabia."

Ocean breezes wander inland and shyly climb the shallow slopes. Leaves seem to whisper amongst themselves. Ibn al Mohammed turns his face to the freshening air. "This work is not difficult. It frees us from the cages and provides exercise." He looks toward the valley floor and blue sea beyond. A beautiful island, no question. Yet it is not home.

"Why are we kept here?" he says.

The old man's laugh is deep in his throat. "Strange, is it not? A people who desire only to pray and to please God, held like beasts."

"Also tempted. They provoke desire with female counterfeits."

"In my case, no," says al Zahrani. "No doubt I am thought too old."

"It is distressing."

"Indeed. It is cruel."

The breeze fades, the leaves still. Ibn al Mohammed turns back to his work. Al Zahrani stands and approaches him. "We must depend on God, my son. We must believe that God in His time, through ways and means we can neither imagine nor foresee, will destroy them."

Ibn al Mohammed meets the old man's gaze. "And where is God, Khalid Saeed? Muslims have perished by the millions. Daily we suffer, yet God hides his face."

"God's ways are a lesson taught in a foreign tongue. It must be so."

"That response has been given countless times. Like suffering, it is our constant attendant."

"It is true nonetheless."

They fall silent. A guard approaches, its assault rifle nodding at the ground.

"Good day," it says, and bows. "May Allah's blessings shower your souls like cool rain. May your spirits rejoice in readiness for the Kingdom of Heaven."

It bows again and passes on. When it leaves their sight, al Zahrani says, "Truly, it is strange."

"Inscrutable," says Ibn al Mohammed. "It has been said that they impersonate a hero of our oppressors' godless mythology. Some call this figure, 'Rambo.'"

"Ram-bo," says al Zahrani, trying the word.

"Those furloughed stateside corroborate. It seems this Rambo was a great warrior."

"It would account for every guard's taking his likeness. Still, he is ugly with his twisted lip and bit of beard."

The air freshens once again. Ibn al Mohammed removes his hat and turns his face seaward. Slightly swaying, he shuts his eyes as if expecting transfiguration, or removal, or deliverance. A breeze touches him, prevailing from the east – being perhaps the air that raptured the Prophet and later vouchsafed Saladin victory in Jerusalem; and borne on which almost a century ago two silver aircraft destroyed steel-and-glass symbols of Infidel arrogance.

The breeze falls. Ibn al Mohammed opens his eyes and re-places his hat, its inner band wet with perspiration. Resuming work, he says, "I wonder, is the cloth worn about their heads intended to mock?"

"It is possible." Al Zahrani is nodding, nodding. "With one hand they pet us while the other closes on our throats. It has always been thus." He settles against a tree and shuts his eyes.

Ibn al Mohammed selects cherries in silence. Soon he will suspend his labor and enjoy a communal meal of crusty bread, goat cheese, green olives. They will be given water, ice-cold. Even al Zahrani will partake. After-meal, harvest will continue until return-time. Then the lovely bus, afterwards a hot shower inside Compound C. Prayers at sundown. The evening meal.

In this way does a day pass. Day turns into night and night is long, its stillness broken by prayers, cries that well-up from dreams, sleepless vows of vengeance. Week follows week and time's sense is lost. Months pass away, years disappear. The Sun's appearance each morning and daily transit, the Moon's ghostly phases are changes without meaning. Furloughs stateside parade before the eyes of True Believers the profane wonders of a fallen world. Meanwhile, cages spring up to accommodate new arrivals from Sector 22.

"Some claim no Muslim leaves here."

"Truth is difficult to know." Al Zahrani seems to be falling asleep. "Some, perhaps, discover a means. Those who lose faith may despair, and capitulate."

Ibn al Mohammed utters a sound that blends a hum and a sigh. "I cannot guess the motive that drives our oppressors."

"Can you not?" The old man stirs as if newly awake. Al Zahrani stands and, stepping close, stares into the younger man's eyes. "The Infidel acts from fear, always. Surely you know this, my son."

Ibn al Mohammed nods. "I understand. They are afraid of us."

"Of us, yes – of our faith. Also of God. It must be so. Satan always fears God."

Templar Bronze reclines in a hoverpod and says, "Center Atrium."

The craft levitates. Ludwig Von's #6 begins to play. In Templar's brain, pleasure receptors flicker. As the pod autonavigates to the ES3-ES1 corridor, Templar sees mountain springs of crystal water, tawny fauns, frisking rabbits, cherry blossoms. During her time on Mars, she has accessed virtual experience of these phenomena. It is said to be just as satisfying. Ludwig Von's #6 also is a digital reconstruction. To lower its volume, she touches a sensor.

Mile-long transit corridors link the geodesic domes of Mars Colony's hexagonal tessellation. Touching another sensor, Templar locks-in Sunday drive velocity, then enters a three-touch command to summon preferred images. These manifest along the mirrored surface of the sleek corridor's hemispherical walls. Van Gogh still-lifes, Babylon's Hanging Gardens, Paris's 8th arrondissement, sky views of Monterey, the Cutty Sark under full sail in the South China Sea. This last image is kinetic; high-masted, it sails alongside Templar until it effervesces in a burst of quicksilver foam. Approaching the portal to ES1, Templar sees her mother's face. It, too, is kinetic. It smiles and seems to say *Come home.* Her mother, who knows Templar Bronze as Annie, has not seen her daughter as more than a hologram in half a dozen Earth years.

A thousand feet up, the translucent ceiling is golden with Martian sun. Templar's hoverpod noses through amber dawnlight and swings onto a byway of Level 12. In Ludwig Von's #6, the oboe asserts its presence. As the pod banks and turns, chromium buildings and swathes of green sweep across Templar's windscreen. From this height, ES1's interior looks like a diorama. Nearly seven square miles, most of its expanse is devoted to buildings. Medium-rise, flat-roofed, windowless, these blocks of shining steel house laboratories, dormitories, cafeterias, theaters, meditation niches, and gymnasiums. Here is where Mars Colony's Initiates, Adepts, and Earthscientists work and live. Some design plans to extend the tessellation. Others subject copper, iron, and lead to fantastic atomic pressure, proton bombardment, centripetal acceleration approaching the speed of light. These questers plumb alchemical mysteries under the supervision of Roscoe Gold, at whose request Templar is making her brief trip.

Alighting on a landing platform of Center Atrium, Templar's hoverpod powers-down. Its windscreen retracts and Templar Bronze disembarks. Beneath her feet, the rhodium surface is mirror-brilliant. A custodial droid – stooped, shuffling, size of a homunculus – secures the pod for turnaround. Its doll's eyes are beads of self-approval. Templar recognizes its face, a facsimile of an ex-president of the old United States.

It says, "Hey now. We gonna set this baby up with some nuculur fu-ell," a twang in its voice.

Templar ignores its remark and its presence. An etiquette droid of indistinct mien appears. "This way, Dr. Bronze," it says, and Templar follows it into the pleasure dome.

Simulacra of chimpanzees glide through cable rigging hung from cross girders. Exotic birdcrafts roost in fauxtrees and embroider the air with their calls and cries. Nearby, a fabricated waterfall roars thirty feet down into a roiling pool. Templar Bronze strides behind the quick-moving droid as it sylphs over a flagstone path. Skirting the waterfall, they wend their way through a rainforest simulation, authentic with dripping leaves and moss-furred trees. After several minutes of looping back and around, around and back again, they arrive at a great cave. The droid stops at the cave's mouth and says, "Dr. Bronze to see you, Head Director."

The cave's interior is brightly lit, its walls covered with porcelain tiles. These seem to exude a golden glow. Beams that look like oak gird a vaulted ceiling. An open space intended as a welcome foyer is empty.

"Thank you," says the voice of Roscoe Gold from what seems very far away.

The etiquette droid bows and departs.

"Roscoe?" says Templar Bronze. "Where are you?"

A soft hum builds quickly to a sound like hard wind. There is no wind, only its sound. An image rushes toward her; Templar cannot tell whether it is Roscoe or his hologram. It seems borne by the sound, as if it or he were carried on sonic waves. A second later quiet returns. Bird calls, simian screeches, splashy applause of falling water become background whispers as Roscoe Gold appears.

Like Templar, he is attired all in white, his unisuit distinguished by gold cuffs and epaulettes and gold piping along its seams. Roscoe smiles the confidential smile for which he is known among Initiates and Adepts alike. Alchemical wizard, sorcerer of the elements, seeker of eternal life, he is Head Director of humankind's first permanent off-Earth settlement.

"Heigh-ho, Templar," he says. "Nice trip?"

"Heigh-ho, Roscoe. Yes, thank you."

Their handshake is an ancient business, its dance of palms and fingers a choreography only Initiates know. "Please, you are welcome," says Roscoe Gold and ushers Templar into the Inner Sanctum. The tiles' golden glow warms up. The ceiling twenty feet above inspires a feeling of uplift, its maybe-oak beam-work lending a sense of safety. Wildflower aroma perfumes air whose temperature and relative humidity are adjusted for repose. Chairs of molded plastic stand at-your-service: yellow, red, purple, green, blue, orange, white. A shin-high table also is modular plastic.

"Please, sit," says Roscoe.

Templar chooses the green chair, Roscoe the yellow. The Head Director snaps his fingers. A service droid on rubber treads rolls up with a teapot, cups, and saucers on one platform and a platter of pastries on the other.

"These you will find exquisite," says Roscoe as the droid pours and serves. They select four pastries each, all different: chocolate éclair, petite four, vanilla almond, lemon meringue, mocha truffle, buttercream, cannoli, rum cake. Neither adds sugar to the tea. Roscoe waits until the droid completes its ministrations and departs. Then he lifts his cup and says, "A toast, Dr. Bronze."

Templar raises her cup in turn. "I am all anticipation."

"To the prospective triumph of our alchemical scientists." Roscoe Gold sips. Templar follows suit, doubts notwithstanding. Ten centuries removed from superstition and ignorance, Roscoe's belief that one might transmute lead and the like into gold strikes Templar Bronze as retrograde. She does not share this thought with the Head Director, having learned that he does not indulge naysaying. Also, Templar knows their need for gold is acute.

"Have they found the Philosopher's Stone?"

Roscoe looks at his pastries as if trying to decide which to eat and which to put by for a nighttime snack – unless he is trying to discern in their chance deployment the pattern that will point the truth that will reveal the secret that will set everything right. His mouth performs a sideways shift. Templar notes a flurry of blinking.

"Nanoparticle of Martian dust in your eye?"

Roscoe looks up. "All's well. But to answer your question: No, they have not. Despite all we have gained, this knowledge eludes us." He selects the chocolate éclair and bites it in half, then sips his tea. "Nevertheless," setting down his cup, "I believe we will recover it."

Templar nods. Like the means to everlasting life – juice of a pomegranate? ambrosial water of a lost fountain? – and mastery over Earth's elements, the technique of gold synthesis belongs to knowledge lost long ago. Roscoe is determined to wrest this knowledge anew from the universe. To possess it is to become free – of imperfection, finitude, mortality, everything.

Templar nibbles mocha truffle. "And in the meantime?"

"We search." Roscoe selects a second pastry.

"I assume you have reviewed Paladin's data."

"Indeed I have," finishing his tea. "That is why I have brought you here." The Head Director sets his cup on its saucer. "Without accessible gold reserves, Earth is of little use. We cannot jettison it, of course, and to pretend to deny our ties to its population would be absurd. Besides" – holding up a wafer-thin shell filled with buttercream – "we are not self-sufficient in all of life's luxuries." Nipping the pastry between two fingers, Roscoe squeezes. He sucks up a dollop of extruded yumsomeness with a long lick of his meaty tongue, then pops the crushed confection into his mouth and chews.

"Gold exists in Mexico," says Templar. "Seismic imaging is ninety percent confident."

The Head Director waves this away. "A *soupçon* of buried treasure. Decorative embellishments on plinths and temple walls, a few hundred doubloons some old skunk of a priest, half drunk and impatient to abscond, couldn't remember to stuff into his rucksack. Insufficient for our purposes. Even taking pains to extract 24-karat inlay from every façade and fresco, and adding to it whatever gold plate and *objets d'art* that might turn up, we would achieve at best an aggregate tonnage roughly equal to one ten-thousandth our total need." Roscoe nabs the petite four and devours it. "Better to leave Mexico's gold in place and tout such relics as curiosities. Sights worth seeing and so forth. Resort guests have to spend pleasure credits on something." He pours more tea. "Every model calls for vast quantities of gold dust dispersed in the lower atmosphere. We need an abundant source." He lifts his cup and sips.

"It hardly matters, as you well know, without an effective magnetosphere." Templar presents her cup. "Before gold, we need iron. A volume equivalent to that of Earth's moon should do the trick – provided we can inject it molten into the core."

Laughter almost makes Roscoe spill. "Dr. Bronze, you are delightfully droll. Inject molten iron into the Martian core? Fantastic notion. Of what material do you propose we fabricate the conduits? Hafnium? Iridium? Tantalum? Rhenium? Molybdenum? An alloy, perhaps? Or ought we just use tungsten and call it a day?" He gazes toward the cave's mouth and beyond, where raucous chimps gambol and songbirds sing. "Rest assured, Doctor. We have teams of Earthscientists designing substitutes for Mars's degraded magnetosphere. Compensatory strategies – what used to be called 'work arounds.' Our task is to secure gold in profuse quantities."

"On Mars, Roscoe?"

"Yes, yes, I know, I know. No doubt I seem an enthusiast. And yet, who would be otherwise? Gold is precious, it is beautiful, it is infinitely useful. It lies in veins, also alluvial deposits. The latter require fine sifting and great patience. A lode might be buried inside a mountain or, God help us, under it." Roscoe moves to the wall behind them, where he touches a tile that looks exactly like every other tile. The wall slips into the floor, revealing a twelve-foot by eight-foot telescreen. Roscoe logs-in via fingerprint scan, then lifts a control pad from its docking station and carries it back to his chair. Touching sensors on its rectangular pane, he summons an Earthscape of craggy mountains and boulder fields. In the foreground, a wizened prospector bearded to his sternum crouches with a steel pan in a rushing stream. A golden sun blazes overhead. Behind his right shoulder, a pack mule waits.

Templar sips her tea. Ever mindful of her splendid figure, she nibbles cannoli.

"Is there gold to be found on Mars, do you think, Dr. Bronze?"

"Martian geology does not preclude precious metals." Templar sets her cannoli aside. "Finding it is another matter. As you know, gold extraction typically requires invasive methods. These include high quotients of difficulty and risk."

"Yes, of course. Still, we must try. We will mount an expedition – more than one, in fact. Bring a bit of competition into it, eh? You know the sort of thing, Doctor – first prospecting team to find the Mother Lode of Martian gold gets a new pleasure dome named after it. We will import laborers from Earth to do the heavy lifting and distribute pleasure credits to keep them hard at it. With any luck, it will turn out that Mars is almost made of gold." Roscoe eats a third pastry. He glances at the telescreen and touches a sensor. The prospector disappears and some file film, mid-Twentieth Century by the look of it, displays gold reserves then-held at Fort Knox. There is no sound. "Those were the days," says Roscoe. "Ye gods, look at it. Who would have believed it could ever run out?"

Templar's mind flashes on the great lode deposits of South Africa and the unimaginable catastrophes that hastened their exhaustion. Fifty thousand tons and more mined and refined, and now gone. Gone, too, are the great veins of Argentina and Brazil, of China and India, Senegal and Ceylon. Placer deposits in California tapped out long ago. Mines in Nevada and South Dakota and the EarthSector once known as Canada have been sealed. Gold is plentiful in the Ural Mountains but that EarthSector, alas, is off limits.

On the telescreen, pyramidal stacks of gold bars gleam with a liquid brilliance. As pointless as it is to review this footage, Templar is drawn. She is surprised by the desire gold provokes. An artisan can fashion it into jewelry, an engineer can stretch it into wire as fine as human hair, a sculptor can hammer it thinner than a sheet of paper. A Peerless Leader can impress his profile on it and call that disk a coin, and decree that coin is money and those who hold a superabundance of this can oblige common folk to toil at hard labor in dangerous places.

No more. Templar knows the Head Director aims to amass gold for no such purpose. It is a nitrogen-oxygen atmosphere he wants – the creation of which depends, theory says, on global dispersal of gold dust vanishingly fine in the lower atmosphere of Mars. She herself would take pleasure in a ring, something plain and weighty and buffed to a lustrous shine. Also a charm, precisely wrought to represent a decisive segment of her incomparable DNA's double helix, to wear around her neck on a strong, fine chain.

As she sips her tea and Roscoe is polishing off a fourth pastry, the etiquette droid appears. "The Honorable Paladin Silver," it says and retreats.

The Sojourner Among the Stars strides into the Inner Sanctum, aluminum alloy accelerator boots ringing out every step. He is wearing a platinum mesh flightsuit and carries its matching helmet under his arm. No hoverpod for Paladin; if his flightsuit were equipped with life support Templar believes he would accelerate not just between EarthStations and within their airspace but around and about Mars as well. She touches a sensor on her wristlet; noting the time, she understands that he has accelerated here straight upon his return from EarthMission 60.

"Heigh-ho, Roscoe. Heigh-ho, Templar," he says. They stand to greet him and perform an occult handshake, each in turn. It is a different handshake than the one Templar and Roscoe use between themselves. Paladin has removed his space gloves but retained the fine-mesh metallic liners. These are more supple than leather and fit like a second skin.

"Heigh-ho, Paladin," says Templar Bronze. Whisker stubble frets his cheeks and chin, each dark hair distinct against his pallor. She notices again his unusual ice-blue eyes.

"Heigh-ho," says Roscoe. "Just returned, I see. A thousand felicitations on your safe arrival."

"A thousand thanks. I am dearly glad to be home, you may be sure. An Earthshuttle is a fine craft for its purpose, yet nothing like a pleasure dome."

"Ah, creature comforts," says Roscoe Gold. "Who would we be without them?"

"Earthlings luxuriate in theirs, I can assure you. Those people are wholly decadent. They do nothing but eat and play games, gleam about in airpods and fornicate with SmartBots expert in triggering fantastic orgasms. Even worse, they are living forever! CellRenew virtually guarantees the most insignificant of men the immortality of a god." Spying pastries untouched on Templar's plate, Paladin gestures. "May I?"

"You are most welcome," says Templar.

"You do not covet your sweet treats, Dr. Bronze?"

"One does well to pace oneself," says Templar. "One should practice restraint, not to say self-denial."

"Really?" says Paladin.

"I myself do nothing of the sort," says Roscoe. "Self-denial? Whatever for? Next you will advise me to curtail embellishments of my pleasure dome so that some cretinous Earthling might breathe purer air."

Templar Bronze and Paladin Silver exchange a look, then burst out laughing.

Paladin, munching, says, "Someone ought to whisper a word about restraint into the ear of every citizen of the Enhanced World.

The greed of these people is astounding. More than one hundred Earth years old and they carry on like teenagers."

"We knew this." Roscoe seems to stare at the pastry disappearing from Paladin's silver fingers into his mouth. "We have made it possible. It is our intended dispensation. And after all, we ourselves use CellRenew."

"I've yet to have one," says Paladin, and Templar smiles.

"Still on your first time 'round, are you Commander? How delightful. Our excellent colleague," nodding toward Templar Bronze, "also is a Child of Aquarius. Indeed, Dr. Bronze's genuine youth makes her wisdom all the more prodigious."

The flattering rogue. Templar thinks again that half of everything Roscoe says aims at tone. The Head Director, she believes, is not insincere, just sensitive about the texture and atmosphere of every conversation, as if he were always currying faith.

"If I may say," says Paladin Silver, and just these words call up a blush, "CellRenew is a distant prospect for Templar Bronze."

"Yes, indeed," says Roscoe, "and yet she will come to it. As will you, Commander. As will we all."

Templar nods, although she dislikes their conversation's sideways drift. Pondering far-future eventualities strikes her as ridiculous when almost anything might happen moment to moment. "CellRenew is a blessing, no doubt," she says. "Implantation seems much the opposite. I will never agree to it – I would never feel safe."

"Hear, hear," says Paladin. "Much better to go on pressing buttons and tapping sensors. A silicon chip in one's brain makes one less human, in my opinion, despite the perks. Just look at those Earthlings! The whole Enhanced citizenry is at the mercy of GlobalDigital and knows nothing of it."

"We are beneficent," says Roscoe Gold. "So far." He laughs. "You and I, Dr. Bronze, as well as youthful Commander Silver, have no need of cerebral microchips. Droids perform technical tasks, supercomputers grind through calculations. Our role is to envision what comes next and imagine how to get there. As Visionary Philosophers, I daresay our native intelligence is sufficient unto the day."

"Yes, of course," says Paladin. "I wish I had some tea to wash this down."

Roscoe snaps his fingers. A moment later the service droid trundles up with a fresh pot and a cup and saucer. It pours tea all around, then produces more pastries before it retires. Paladin drinks his tea and pours himself a second cup. He sits in the blue chair and props his feet on the table, pastries balanced on his lap.

"Creature comforts. Well, well."

"A visit with you is always a happy occasion, Head Director." Paladin chews. "Although I think there's a glitch in those chimps. When I was coming in just now, three of them tried to pelt me with simulated feces."

Roscoe's face is pure delight. "Realism, Commander Silver. Had you trespassed their territory in the wild, they would have done much worse."

"That's as may be. Still, it's damned strange behavior for a pleasure dome."

"Is not our waterfall magnificent? Twenty thousand gallons a minute. Who would have believed it, on Mars?"

"Yes, it's grand, truly grand. And how the devil did you get these?" Paladin Silver holds up a chocolate éclair, of which he has eaten half. "Nothing like it is fabricated in any EarthStation, I'm sure."

Roscoe chuckles. "As I was just telling Dr. Bronze, Earth retains its uses." He slides back into the modular plastic and crosses his legs, ankle on knee. Templar also resumes her seat. "Its natives' deplorable behavior is of no moment. Our only concern is that they keep out of the droids' way – allow them to work, that is, and generally run things, and produce all those little items, ordinary and wonderful, that all of us enjoy."

Paladin offers the plate and Roscoe snaps up a lemon meringue. "As you can see from the data, there is no threat of interference. Give Earthlings their SmartBots and three squares a day plus an agreeable quantity of alcohol, and they are as docile as lap dogs."

Roscoe claps his hands. "Lovely, isn't it? The genius of Smart-Bot companions!"

"Not all Earthlings are docile," says Templar. The men turn to her. "Badlands desperadoes show defiance and initiative."

"Agreed," says Roscoe. "Of course, they languish in the Badlands and lack SmartBot comforts." Paladin Silver yawns.

"Even Gitmo detainees, who are fed much better, have enough gumption to refuse microchips." Templar grins. "As well as Smart-Bot comforts."

"A nice observation, Dr. Bronze," says the Head Director. "Your insights are quite useful, I'm sure."

"Those people are powerless." Paladin leans back in his chair and its plastic creaks. "Gitmo inmates live in cages. They have no human contact. Not one of them will ever get off that prehistoric island."

"Yes, of course," says Roscoe Gold.

"As for Mexicans – or rather, the epigone subspecies descended of the noble Aztecs, whom Cortés slaughtered in Tenochtitlán – " Paladin shakes his head. "They are finished. Scare food, ad hoc encampments, culture in ruins. For geopolitical purposes, they are already extinct."

"And yet, they live. They find shelter in the desert. They cleave to the coastline and feed themselves from the sea."

"Poetry, my dear Dr. Bronze, will not improve their situation."

Templar smiles. "To mention a few facts is hardly poetry."

"Fair enough." Roscoe uncrosses his legs. He picks up the control pad and touches-in a sequence. On the telescreen, gold bars fade away and a simulation begins. Templar Bronze knows it is a simulation because gold mining has not been attempted on Mars and yet that is what she and Paladin Silver and the Head Director are watching: a large-scale mining operation featuring fission-powered drilling rigs and dredging combines, three-story tall raw ore haulers rolling over a red-dust plain on gigantic deep-tread tires, and miners – scores of miners in Marsuits. Faceless inside their helmets, they move in phalanxes toward a riven mountain with shovels and pickaxes in their aluminum-fiber-gloved hands.

"A VirtuReal simulation," says Roscoe, "based on facts like those for which Dr. Bronze has such regard. Note the large number of human workers."

"Who are they supposed to be?" says Paladin.

Roscoe chuckles. "Who, indeed? What human would consent to such dangerous, backbreaking work? An excellent question." Roscoe winks at Templar Bronze. "And yet, had you joined us several minutes sooner, Commander, you would easily guess."

Templar looks at the Head Director, who looks sharply back. "Surely I have not surprised you, Dr. Bronze. You yourself concede a likelihood of gold on Mars."

Templar shakes her head. "They will never cooperate."

"Who will not?"

"Dr. Bronze refers, I believe, to those interned on Cuba." Roscoe touches a sensor and the simulation freezes. The picture shrinks to one-quarter size and shifts to the screen's upper left quadrant. Another touch uplinks a feed from Guantánamo and places it in the upper right quadrant. Men with full beards, wearing white shirts and trousers, their feet bare, kneel on prayer mats laid over concrete. Arms extended, palms flat, they bend forward to touch their foreheads to the prayer mats. "Candor obliges me to agree. People who choose to live in captivity rather than accept Implantation are not likely to labor for their nominal oppressors."

"So those are Mexicans," says Templar.

"Banditos, Desperadoes, Mexicans – yes."

With a touch, Roscoe animates gold mining on Mars. Templar notes that the miners are smallish not just in relation to the heavy equipment but to their shovels and pickaxes.

"As the simulation illustrates, gold mining remains labor intensive," says Roscoe. "Indeed, one may make it as labor intensive as one likes, to serve any purpose of one's own. Droids, needless to say, are unsuited to it."

"Can that be true?" Eating another pastry, Paladin speaks through sugared cream. "I would have thought the opposite. As a matter of fact, I'm certain all this work can be done perfectly well by SmartBots, properly scripted. We don't need human miners at all."

The Head Director smiles. "Oh, but we do, Commander." He resumes his seat and pours more tea, refilling their cups all around. Steadying his cup on its saucer, Roscoe settles into the lumbar support. "Mexican desperadoes are fomenting ninety kinds of chaos all across the subcontinental Badlands. Data you yourself have gathered show their lives to be nasty, brutish, and short." He winks again at Templar. "It is in everyone's interest to remove them. Mars, it seems, is the only option." The Head Director nods. "I think we agree that Cuba cannot support a new population of detainees."

Templar and Paladin nod.

"And so, my friends, we bring them to Mars. While they are here they must be kept busy."

"The women, Roscoe?" says Templar. "The children?"

"Oh, dear. I believe Dr. Bronze is suffering compassion."

Paladin grins. "I'm sure you will talk her clear of it."

"Ah! Excellent! Excellent! Drollery will take you far, Commander Silver, it will speed your ascent like wings affixed to your silver heels."

Paladin says "Huh!" and lifts his feet off the table, which was buckling under his boots.

"To set Dr. Bronze's mind at rest: women and children will be spared the mines. Mars Colony has many needs. I am sure we will find alternate employment. In fact – " And here Roscoe Gold touches-in a series of commands that brings up a fullscreen overview of green and purple vineyards flourishing inside EarthStation 3. "The women, Dr. Bronze, and I believe more so the children – their small fingers, don't you know, and their delicate touch – will be most useful in your pursuit of certain refractory varietals."

Templar Bronze can only smile. He has orchestrated it so well. A pruning knife's curved blade is designed for a human hand. Even in Napa, especially there, only Mexicans are equal to the work of grape harvest. They are famous for their stamina and, what is more significant to Templar Bronze, their speed. Strange, that she has not thought of it – nor considered until this moment that delicate Pinot, picked and crushed at intervals separated by days and weeks, might have been damaged by the clumsy touch of all-purpose droids.

"Sounds suspicious," says Paladin. "Women and children set to fieldwork, men toiling like gnomes in mines. Rather like slave labor, I'd say."

Templar nods.

"My, my. More compassion. We'll have to fix that."

Gleaming along Skyway 80, Melmoth asks his wife, "How would it be, our life, without VirtuLinks?"

"Lonely," says Raquel. She is 130 years old. Sixty-five years ago, CellRenew restored her to the woman she was on the May evening in 1992 when she and Melmoth were married. She has not added a pound or a wrinkle since. "Dull. I would be stuck with you and you, poor man, would be stuck with me."

Poor man? Melmoth does not feel poor. Very much the opposite. "You're saying we know each other too well."

"J. We've been married a hundred years. A hundred and two, as a matter of fact."

"Yes. I can hardly forget that."

"You must have forgotten all the being-alone-together day after day. That's us without VirtuLinks."

Disengaging autopilot, Melmoth directs his ocular laser at a silver airpod's tail section. Behind it is an opening he figures is just large enough. Executing a deft swerve with both hands, he swoops around a phalanx of silver airpods and two bronze gleaming at predetermined velocities and nestles his craft into place. Its inertia canceller makes this move possible at terrific speed.

"I wish you wouldn't do that." Raquel has never learned to pilot.

"It's under control."

"No, really. I don't want flying by the seat of your pants. Not with me in the pod."

"I know what I'm doing." Melmoth re-engages autopilot.

"But not what other people are doing. What they might do. Not to mention androids. People die in skyway accidents, you know."

Melmoth knows. Gazing out his windowall on evenmorns and starry nights, he has seen gold and orange fireballs flash in an indigo sky. Someone has risked it and fallen short or gone long. A moment's hovering and a sense of freefall, then the metallic stream flows on.

He cannot argue with Raquel. He should trust the autopilot. Low speed, low-altitude, close-in maneuvers he can perform hands-on. But having eluded death so long, Melmoth feels invincible. And it gets tiresome, being babied by gadgets.

"I don't recall our being alone so much," he says. "Mostly we worked all day and came home too tired to talk."

Raquel sighs. "The Dark Age of jobs and children. Well, it was soon done. Next thing I knew, it was you I was seeing for hours on end."

"You exaggerate."

Raquel clicks her tongue against her teeth. "Deadly. Thank Jobs SmartBots came along."

"Thanks Jobs we could afford them."

Raquel activates the onboard telescreen. Melmoth frowns as holograms manifest. Attention-captured by a news story, Raquel ignores him. Indigenous terrorists in Mexico's Badlands have breached security at six nuclear waste storage sites and ignited multiple explosions. Radioactive debris courses through the lower atmosphere. The story is vague about prevailing winds – indeed, is vague about everything, exact locations and millirem levels and who these troublemakers are and where-from – and says nothing about weather systems or drift patterns. Melmoth guesses the gov has deployed droids with atmospheric cleansers.

The Overvoice: *Rest assured, abatement teams are neutralizing all lethal isotopes.*

How did he know this? Melmoth wonders if Jenna is right, that he is a genius. Then again, he has seen a hell of a lot. Stick around for 133 years and one day you've seen it all. Officially, he and Raquel are Oldentimers, though they don't look it. If not for the golden O woven into their nightblue blouses and flightsuits and tunics, no one would be able to tell. Melmoth has noticed that only his tendency to refer to bygone times betrays his age. Comments about automobiles and fossil fuels mark him as ancient. Halfers especially, who have known only fission-fueled electric arrays, listen as if he were recounting Paleolithic myths. Raquel rolls her eyes whenever he starts in about how things used to be. Melmoth feels she could show a little more sympathy. Yes, the old things are gone and are never coming back. No one needs automobiles or smartphones any more than they need cod's liver oil. But it's her former world, too.

He says, "Why do you watch these sensationalist spectacles?"

"It's fascinating. Such people still exist. What do they want, I wonder?"

"Pleasure credits. Unless they can't grow anything on the mesa and are really starving."

"I doubt anyone really starves anymore." Her tone suggests he is being intentionally obtuse.

"Don't be so sure."

"Yes, I'll leave that to you. But what if all they want is to blow everything up?"

He is watching holograms with one eye, with the other following Skyway 80's loops and banks. "Nihilism died decades ago. It's buried in one of history's lesser ash heaps." Truth is, he is not so interested. Oh, it's a problem, alright. If such sabotage continues, it might rise to a level of semiseriousness. Melmoth himself, however, does not feel concerned. He plays no part. Discipline & Punish will liquidate these banditos or guerrillas or whoever they think they are, bleeding-edge anarchists or ragtag rebels, and that will be that.

Guided by autopilot, he pretends to fly. He doesn't let Raquel see, just rests a hand on the flight wheel as if to forestall catastrophic malfunction. Not that an autopilot has ever failed. Melmoth enjoys the sense of steering. Banked arcs, rollercoaster straights: levitated signage indicates these as the westward tending course of Skyway 80. Nuclear power and an insulated cabin make podflight pure pleasure. Contoured seats of personalized polymer are leather to his touch, as well as to eyes and nose. The airpod's wide-paned windscreen provides nearly 360 degrees of unobstructed view; from outside, this transparent band's self-adjusting tint makes Melmoth's craft resemble a partly opened oyster, albeit one sporting tail fins and a sleek golden shell. Climate-control monitors his comfort, regulates airflow, tweaks temperature and relative humidity to optimum levels. Motion-sense is wholly visual, thanks to that inertia canceller and the windscreen surround. The propulsion system is soundless, the ride airy smooth. He and Raquel do not wear helmets, useless in a mid-air collision and in a lesser mishap unnecessary, the cabin being impact-buffered.

To think he once drove a car. Metal shell fused to an iron chassis with welds and bolts. Rubber tires, brakes that worked by friction, innumerable tiny explosions to make its engine run. All gone down to dust. Melmoth tries to remember what it was like, to drive. A mechanical car with its clattering combustion, a road of asphalt or sectioned concrete, guardrail along the curves, billboards above the trees. Service roads branching from thoroughfares. Exit ramps. A mile or two down a local route, a refueling oasis, "gasoline station" in oldenspeak. Boxy pumps sucking liquid fuel from stainless steel holding tanks buried in the ground.

Such a filthy business. Fire and brimstone. What ghoulish work it was, that bygone effort to extract metamorphosed decayed matter from subterranean pools, refine it, blend it, ship it, store it, then make it burn. Effusions of carcinogenic gas. Billows. Fumes.

Melmoth coughs.

"Problem?" says Raquel.

"No problem," he says.

With a light hand he pretends to fly. Holograms depict radioactive clouds in miniature, circled by government hovercraft.

The Overvoice: *The terrorists responsible for this outrage against human civilization have not stated the purpose of their heinous crime.*

"Hah!" says Raquel.

Melmoth tries to lower the sound but Raquel's First Dibs Initiative locks him out. "Would you mind switching feeds, dear?" he says.

"In a minute. I want to see the end."

"There is no end," says Melmoth.

The encampment is empty. Women and children, the men who protect them, all gone. Tents remain, also horses. These have not been watered or fed. Food scraps lie scattered, cooking circles are cold. They trot down to the sea. In-rushing water sheets over hardpacked sand, withdraws, returns. Homespun shirts and trousers, serapes, women's skirts and shawls drift in the shallows. Woven belts and broken sandals churn in the surf. Straw sombreros children wore float offshore on an undulating calm of sun-dappled sea.

A buffalo hunter floats up to their feet.

Miguel dismounts and retrieves the hat. He straightens its brim, restores its crown, turns it in his hands. It is sodden yet not burned nor bullet-holed, not slashed nor cloven. He hands it up to Carlos.

"They have been taken by boat," says Enrique.

Having inspected the hat, Carlos passes it to Enrique. "Why do their clothes remain?"

Enrique shakes his head. Miguel gazes across the water as if an answer to this question might rise from the seabed and, rainbow-like, trace its colors across the sky. Between him and the horizon, however, nothing appears. "They are prisoners. As such, they wear a uniform."

"The children also?" says Carlos. "What men imprison children?"

"Gringos." Enrique hands the buffalo hunter to Javier. "Mercenaries of El Norte."

"What can be their purpose?"

They look at Miguel. His knowledge, they expect, must be greater than their own despite having been formed by a life they themselves have lived. Javier and Pacho especially await an answer. A reason that offers hope. Miguel only looks out to sea as waves roll shoreward and seabirds cry, aloft.

Javier says, "Someone, perhaps, has left a few words."

"I believe, compañero, they would not have known what to write." Miguel lifts himself into his saddle. "Still, a word might exist, as you say." He spurs his horse up-beach and the others follow.

At the stockade, they unsaddle their horses, give them water and tie on feedbags. They do likewise for those left behind. The men are weary and grayed-over. They feel desert dust in their eyes, feel it dry on their gums, a taste like burnt talc. With canteen water they rinse their mouths and drink. Miguel directs that food be prepared. While Pacho fills an iron pot with water and Javier combs for driftwood, Miguel and Carlos seek a message. Five words. Three. A name only, scratched on a leather scrap, jotted on canvas. Cut with a fingernail into packed sand.

Enrique goes to a makeshift larder behind the stockade. Amidst scrub pines and sand dunes, he moves a sheet of corrugated tin and steps inside.

His eyes plumbing the dim light, Enrique sees hemp sacks of rice and dried beans, barrels of charcoal, others of corn oil smuggled at great risk from El Norte and moved with difficulty across the desert. Planking shores up one wall. Iron pans and black pots older than he is hang from twine knotted to their handles and looped over nails driven into crossbeams. Filleted and salted, fish cure on shelves: halibut, red snapper, ocean whitefish, pompano, white sea bass. A remnant of Seri continue to fish the Sea of Cortés. Suspicious of strangers, persecuted by almost every government México has known, the Seri speak no Hispanic dialect; their words sound akin to Egyptian. They barter a portion of their catch for corn oil, wheat flour, charcoal, hemp. Enrique selects one fish for each man and adds to these a whole sea bass to share in honor of Roberto Díaz.

He knows the others will not return – that they cannot return. He thinks of his wife and wonders how he will find her again. *Excellent Alma.* That is something Pacho said. Her large pan hangs from a nail, a bit of twine looped through the rectangle notched in its handle. Alma has fried tortillas in this pan every day for many years. Enrique does not wish to think of his wife and the others being driven like cattle into a ship's cold hold. They have been made to remove their clothes. Have they been washed down with seawater and left naked and wet? He does not like to think they are fed on slops, or not fed at all.

Hundreds of miles beyond the Straits and yet they are harried, dispossessed, made prisoner. Is anything to be left them? Where in the wide world may they live?

The ones taken will be made to work. Like beasts in a field, if a field is what there is. Like gnomes in a cave, if that is the job no one else will do. Their uniforms are orange or gray. Enrique assumes their meals are meager. That they sleep on dirt.

He finds a basket and lays fish inside it. Charcoal is in a wooden bucket. Enrique lifts it, basket in his other hand, and moves through shadow toward daylight.

A presence makes him turn his head. He sees no one, yet someone is there.

He sets down fish and charcoal. Straightening up, Enrique slips his Bowie knife clear of its sheath. He listens, tries to sense the man's place. This intruder lies low. Is concealed. Behind those barrels? In that corner, crouched down? Enrique shuts his eyes, holds his breath a moment and exhales, his breath's movement the only sound, trying to feel on his skin some heat from another body.

Where?

Enrique sends his mind among barrels and sacks, under shelves, behind posts and dangling utensils. It finds no one.

He is hiding. Wants not to be found. Is afraid.

If he lies under a tarpaulin, he cannot see. To shoot blind would be foolish: likely to miss, certain to alert the others.

Enrique steps around barrels, his boots silent on packed sand. Tarps lie parallel in ten-foot lengths, their wheaten hue making them visible in the shadowed space. They are dry and hold dust. All but one lies flat.

There.

Enrique imagines how it will be. To strike through the tarp risks confusion. Its heavy canvas can deflect his blade. But his opponent will have difficulty using his weapon. He might fire point-blank into Enrique's weight above him, bearing down. To pull the tarpaulin clear is to lose his advantage; he will see the intruder who will see him. An El Norte mercenary with automatic rifle or handheld laser can cut a man in half.

Knife in his teeth, its ivory handle smooth against lips and tongue, Enrique crouches low. Pushing hard with his legs, he dives onto the hidden shape. The man spins free as Enrique grasps, boots slipping on waxed canvas. His opponent feels slight, yet wiry strength defeats Enrique's hold. He takes his knife in hand and rips a slit long enough to plunge an arm into his adversary's shrouded panic. Enrique thrusts the blade's point where he believes a throat must be. Two strong hands clamp his arm and twist against each other rapidly and hard. Pain flares across his skin. Enrique wrests his arm free and his knife flies from his grasp and disappears behind him. He clenches up and, pivoting on his other hand, turns hard into a blind punch that smashes the hidden face.

The dust of their struggle rasps in Enrique's throat. His intended killer sucks in a hard breath and Enrique hits him again, then again, each time turning his shoulder into the blow. The man coughs out, "Do not kill me."

Enrique knows this voice. It is Omar the Turk. Now on his knees, he hauls off the tarpaulin and finds a hunched figure curled behind a short beard and sleek black hair. Filthy in frayed denim, the Turk is a bloody mess.

Enrique stands, coughing and spitting. "How are you here?"

"Son of a jackal. Surely you have broken my nose."

"And I shall kill you like a snake if you do not answer me."

"To harm me is unwise. I alone remain to bear witness."

"Every traitor claims as much." Enrique takes hold of the Turk's ear and pulls him to his feet. His nose is bleeding onto his shirt. Enrique twists the ear as he pats down the denim.

The Turk bats at the punishing hand. "Fool. You would be dead already."

"Where is your pistol?"

"It has been taken. Also my rifle and knife."

Enrique flat-hands the back of the Turk's head. "Liar. Never have I found you without a weapon."

"I have lost everything. Federales assaulted me. They confiscated my horse and mule, my tent and provisions. Luck alone allowed me to survive. I found good water. Your people took me in."

A true note in the Turk's voice causes Enrique to turn him loose. He is a small man of sinew and muscle and bone. His skin, browned-over, has an olive undertone and remains unlined despite an unsheltered life. Black eyes sunken in a narrow skull, olive-complected, the man is like a shadow divided from its body and risen from the ground.

"Walk out," Enrique says and indicates the doorway, sun-lit. They pass into daylight, eyes half-shut against the glare. The Turk holds his shirttail to his bloodied nose. They make their way toward the fire where Javier is feeding wood scraps into the flames.

As they approach, Enrique calls, "Bring Miguel."

Javier stands. "Who is this scoundrel?"

Enrique's eyes cut toward the tents. "We will hear this account together."

"Is this the one called Omar the Turk?"

"The very same. He claims to know the fate of our people."

"Truly, no. Not their fate. Only their misfortune."

"And what is that?"

"Bring Miguel," says Enrique.

Javier departs. To Pacho, Enrique says, "You must retrieve the fish and charcoal."

Pacho gestures at the fire. "We have used wood."

"Flames scorch and will ruin the fish. Charcoal burns long and slow, as rice requires. Go now for the things I have named."

The Turk grins. "I find I forgive your brutality. It seems you prepare a feast."

"First we hear your story. Lies will fill your plate with sand."

"I speak only truth." He bows slightly. "Truth sometimes is not believed."

Enrique offers a canteen. The Turk drinks in long swallows, then pours water over his head and face. He returns the canteen. Enrique wipes off its mouthpiece and drinks, then replaces the metal cap and screws it down. He hands the Turk a kerchief to wipe off the blood. The Turk rolls this like a blindfold and wraps it around his head, covering his nose and knotting the tips behind. By this means he gains some relief, yet without ice he suffers.

"How long have you been here?" says Enrique.

"Two days I lived amongst your people. They gave me water and food. On the third day, raiders came. Their ship – "

Enrique raises a hand to suspend this recital. They wait in a silence that seems to ask, *Of all you say, how much is true?* Enrique knows the Turk's readiness to invent a story to suit a present need. His face, battered as it is, betrays nothing.

Javier returns with Carlos and Miguel. Pacho brings charcoal and fish. Enrique repeats the beginning of the Turk's account. His comrades glower, staring at the Turk throughout.

"Who were these raiders?" says Miguel.

"It is impossible to say."

Carlos regards the Turk with disgust. The kerchief that partly covers his face is blood-crusted. "Yellow dog. What has been done with our mothers and sisters?" His voice is a fist. "Where have they been taken? Answer at once."

"I tell you, I do not know."

With one blow Carlos sends the Turk to his knees, then is out with his pistol. He presses its muzzle tight to the Turk's head. "You tell us," he says, cocking the hammer. A breeze off the Sea of Cortés carries an oily scent of full-blued steel to Enrique, who knows he cannot allow this man to die.

The Turk spits blood onto the sand. Eyes shut, he lifts his arms and shows empty palms. "I tell all I know."

"Liar. You witnessed this outrage."

"Compañero, to put up your gun would be wise," says Miguel. "If you kill him, we will never learn their fate."

Carlos is shaking with rage or, as Enrique believes, dread. It is a matter of his mother and sister and young brother. Also, at one remove, of his father. The elder Sandoval they lost fighting their way out of Nogales, once a bedraggled border town, now Stateside beyond the Straits. That plan had been reckless and its collapse sudden. El Norte mercenaries rushed down on them and they could only shoot and run, shoot and run, and trust that honor would prevent those soldiers from firing on women and children, whom Enrique and Carlos and the others, including Carlos's un-lucky father, could no longer protect. Only grace or a miracle al-lowed them to make a hasty crossing on overloaded rafts.

"Remember," Enrique says, not shouting, not risking a forward move. "Remember, Carlos, who is to blame. The Turk has not harmed your family."

"I was hiding – under a tarp, where this one found me," the Turk says, pointing at Enrique. "I stayed a full day without food, without water." He lowers his arms, lets his head drop. "I am very hungry."

As the Turk's head sinks, Carlos thumbs the hammer back and holds the trigger, then eases the hammer into its groove. "Worth-less creature. Your weakness insults me." He holsters his gun. Turning his back, Carlos begins to walk away.

Enrique's eyes never leave the Turk. He sees the next thing be-fore it happens.

From a crouch, the Turk springs at Carlos in a dash for the pis-tol. Enrique dives, cuts the Turk's legs from under him before any-one understands how close they have come to catastrophe. Then they are on the Turk, pummeling head and chest as he cries for mercy and Enrique shouts, "Do not kill him!"

From the filthy denims Pacho wrenches some twenty-four inches of rope that serve the Turk as a belt. Javier wrests the Turk's arms behind his back and Pacho binds his crossed wrists, finishing with a knot behind his hands. Again, Carlos draws his revolver. Before he can cock it, Miguel puts a hand on his forearm and turns Carlos away. In a low voice, he says, "Alive, this scoundrel is worth something. Dead, he is a rock, he is sand – worse, because we will have to bury him."

The Turk is sitting on the sand, left shoulder sunk under Javier's boot. Standing on one leg, Javier leans into him. "Too heavy," the Turk says, and Javier says, "Be grateful I do not kick like a mule."

Carlos holsters his gun. "As you say. Yet we would not need to bury him."

Touching his fingers to the pot, Enrique finds it only warm. He lifts it off and sets it on the sand, then adds charcoal to the fire, piece by piece. He says, "You must tell us all you know."

The Turk's face is bleeding again, the staunching kerchief gone. Carlos and Miguel close around him. Pacho replaces the pot, then he, too, stands over the Turk. At a sign from Javier, he sets his boot on the Turk's other shoulder.

Crushed, the Turk can barely speak. "They came ... in armor, white ... and helmets ... faceless. Weapons ... sent light-rays. Silent. Instant. Those hit ... fell as if dead ... not injured." The Turk coughs hoarse and dry, and Enrique feels dust again in his own throat. He lifts his canteen and finds it empty. He looks at Miguel, who gives his canteen into Enrique's hand. Enrique removes its cap and drinks. Then he kneels beside the Turk and tilts the mouthpiece against his lips.

Water flows into the Turk's mouth. When he nods, the movement nudges the canteen away. Enrique pours water over the Turk's face.

"Your people ... no chance. Men ... tried to fight ... ship blasted ... sound ..." The Turk shakes his head. "Useless. It hovered ... offshore ... raiders came ... small craft ... very fast."

"And what were you doing?" says Miguel.

"I hid. I saw little. Please. Everyone ... afraid. Children wept. White armor ... blinding ... in the sun." He spits. "I am hungry."

"Food when your tale is done," says Enrique.

"It is done. The outcome ... no doubt. Luck saved me."

"That is twice you are lucky," says Pacho.

The Turk ignores him. "I hid. Outside ... all was chaos."

"Coward," Carlos says.

The Turk shakes his head. "I had ... no weapon. No chance. I, too ... captured. *Please* – "

Miguel nods and Pacho and Javier step away. Miguel says, "Why do you say, 'hovered'? Surely this cannot be said of a ship."

"It did not sail upon water." The Turk draws a deep breath. "From above the clouds it flew down. I have seen things similar, yet this prodigy astounded your women and children. The men also, I believe, were amazed."

Miguel and Carlos, Enrique, Javier and Pacho stare at the Turk. He looks from face to face yet meets no one's eyes. They seem not to know what question to ask. *What size was this ship? Did it fly on a line or swoop like a gull? In what direction did it go?* Without means of pursuit, the answers are trivia.

Carlos says, "What was its color?"

"Silver. It appeared very bright."

"Its insignia?"

"I saw none."

Miguel says, "What language did these raiders speak?"

The Turk grins. "There is no help for this predicament."

Carlos backhand-slaps him. "Answer the question."

Enrique notes the Turk's look, leaping like fire from his black eyes. "I heard no language. They used no words."

Miguel says, "Was its departure inland or seaward?"

"I did not witness it, having hidden myself."

"Abominable coward." Again, Carlos reaches for his gun. He is staring at the Turk as if his eyes, too, could turn a man to ash.

The Turk has lost interest. It is, Enrique knows, nothing to him if this wrong goes unavenged. As long as he survives, every circumstance is tolerable. In another moment, he will chide Enrique about their absent supper.

"I, for one, have heard enough," Enrique says. "El Norte has done this thing – for what purpose, I do not know. For now, we must take food and rest. Afterward, we will pursue." He sends Pacho for the forgotten rice and the others sort themselves around the fire. As he lifts the basket of fish, Enrique remembers Alma's large pan, which he has left hanging in its place. He thinks also of his lost knife and sends Javier to retrieve the one and search for the other.

Miguel and Carlos move away. In a voice only Enrique can hear, the Turk says, "Pursuit is impossible." His hands remain bound, his upper body canted forward, legs crossed beneath him. He tilts his head and Enrique comes closer. "To you only I tell this. That one is a barbarian, with his insults and ready gun. Your leader values him too highly."

"Why can we not follow?"

"You have not the means. I suspect your people have been taken from Earth."

"And how is that possible? Where can they go?"

The Turk nods. "You know of Mars."

"I know Mars is a planet. Far from Earth, as all planets are. What can it mean to us?"

Pacho returns with rice. Javier brings Enrique's knife and Alma's large pan. He splashes water into the latter and sets it on the grill.

"Dinner, at last," says the Turk. "After we fill our bellies, I will explain."

In the grillroom following AstroGolf, Melmoth scrolls a holographic menu and tries to ignore the windowalls. Everyone is watching and speaking at once, titillated and attention-captured by Badlands sabotage, Martian prospects, newgoods bursts, sexolympics updates. Playing too loud by half is an oldenflick called *Titanic*, made, if Melmoth rightly remembers, 90-some years ago. He watched it once: an analog recording made on electromagnetic tape and displayed on a prehistoric television. Today, *Titanic* manifests as a scaled hologram in an upper sector of the central windowall, a placement that makes it impossible to miss. Having little liked the melodrama back then, Melmoth stares at it absentmindedly now, a sense of something not right diverting his attention from the menu.

He wishes they would upload these feeds cerebrally; transparent, the clubhouse's windowalls offer gorgeous views of greensward and glittering sea, all together more conducive to a pleasant lunch. Melmoth pinpoints the chargrilled lambburger with his ocular laser and thinks *halfpounder*. Aroma of sizzling meat rises from the hologram. Melmoth smiles. He pinpoints cheddar-chili fries and an iced pitcher of microbrewed amber bock. Minutes later his meal arrives on bone china balanced on the fingertips of his android waitress. Melmoth has configured this SmartBot to facsimulate a brunette nude-model photo-eroticized 100-some years ago. Wearing lace panties and cut-away bra, she is costing him a small fortune in pleasure credits.

"Here you are, J," Candi breathes, leaning close to deliver his food. Melmoth can smell her fragrance, all warm powder and youthful skin. It is all prearranged; her remarks are scripted. "Everything looks wonderful!" she exclaims with a smile.

"Everything certainly does." Melmoth winks and Candi winks back. "Ha-ha," he says. "Very good. Ha-ha." It is phony and delightful. No one is being hurt. In oldentimes Melmoth would have called it "wicked fun," although in oldentimes it would not have been possible, not with Candi almost nekked and Melmoth a married guy and anyway never deft with women. Standing tall with her shoulders well back, Candi exhibits herself for his delectation. It is impossible not to love what life has become.

"Very nice. You are beautiful and your figure is stupendous."

"Oh, J, you sweet old rogue!" Candi throws her arms around Melmoth's neck and kisses him on the head. This move thrusts her abundance into his face, antic with a madman's grin. Melmoth cannot see, he can barely breathe, he loves it, loves it.

"Thank you, Candi," he murmurs, immured.

She releases him, curtsies, and flounces off.

How is he going to eat? For another lousy twenty thousand credits he can squire Candi upstairs and in a plasmabed sensurrounded by musical cues circa 1979 virtually experience the feel & touch of a genuine Miss January. How can he resist? Why should he? He already has more pleasure credits than he needs and what else, anyway, are they for? The ease of this bliss, once unattainable, is enough to make Melmoth weep.

He glances at the windowall. Lifeboats drift in company on a black sea. Every boat is filled. Not overcrowded, just at capacity, and not just women and children but men, too. And not men disguised as women. Men sitting there in hats and coats, right out in the open in open boats on an open sea and not skulking about or pretending to be something they are not. Most of them are cracking jokes. These aren't even gallows humor. Women smile. Children laugh.

Melmoth wolfs into the lambburger. He pours a tall frosty one as he chews. Sensational taste: savory, gamey: a mouthful of delicious. He smacks his lips, sips the beer. The cheddar-chili fries are piping hot, crisp and gooey. Such a joy, to eat as much as you like of food you love free of morbid aforethought. It is all right here, served up with hot-salted, juicy goodness fit to be relished without dread reference to dire arterial side-effects possible ten years hence. What can ten years mean to a man who has lived almost a century and a half? How can vascular necrosis worry him when auxiliary organs have been cloned from stem cells and banked in his name?

J Melmoth eats, he drinks. Big bites of ground lamb grilled to succulent perfection, washed down with long draughts of crispy-cold amber bock. He devours cheddar-chili fries six at a time, this business about lifeboats nagging at him. Why is everyone happy? Why are the lifeboats filled? Why, for that matter, are there enough lifeboats for everyone to have escaped the crippled ship? He knows, everyone knows, that is not how it happened almost two centuries ago. Even the movie, the same sentimental melodrama he has assumed he is half-watching again now, showed the catastrophe in all its terror and loss.

Unless he is misremembering. He should ask Raquel about *Titanic*. The movie, not the event. To re-learn what actually happened, he will access a database.

But not right now. Melmoth thinks *service* and Candi reappears. She is wearing a blue and gold scarf with little tassels loosely around her neck and pink cotton socks on her feet, nothing more.

"What can I do for you, J?" she says.

Long brown hair, all luster and wavy sheen, falls past her shoulders. Her buttercream fauxskin looks smooth enough to eat. All Melmoth really sees are her breasts: soft yet buoyant, suggestive of tear drops, as large, almost, as his head. "Another pitcher of amber bock, Candi, please."

"My pleasure." She jiggles closer. "Are you sure that's all?" She leans into him. Her breasts sway an inch from his face. Melmoth swallows, wipes his lips, grabs one in each hand and tries to stuff them, her breasts, into his mouth.

"Eek!" Candi cries. "Eek! Eek!"

It's impossible, they won't go, his mouth would have to be the size of ... well, the size of her unused brassiere. "Come on now, you yummalicious chickaboo," Melmoth growls, parroting a bit of automatic slang he's heard here and there. "Time to feed the big bad wolf."

"Eek! Oh, don't! You naughty, bad, horny old man!"

It is all scripted; no one pays attention; Melmoth laughs.

"Oh, don't!" Candi cries. "Please, stop!"

It is better than cabaret, better than any movie he has ever seen, and no book can come close. Who needs windowalls, with SmartBots able to perform at this level?

"Oh, stop! Please, don't!"

Melmoth releases her. It. Them. Candi is smiling. She pretends to slap him, half-hard on the arm. "You bad, bad boy. You horrid, breast-mad, nasty old man!"

Her scolding is scripted; everything is. Candi's rebuke is essential to Melmoth's experience. When she leaves to fetch his beer, Melmoth knows she will return wearing a red skirt and white blouse tight to her neck. Before she pours amber bock into a clean frosty glass, Melmoth will say, with a casual light suavity that in oldentimes he never mastered, "Candi, please unbutton your blouse," and she will.

After lunch he returns to the golf course. He doesn't need more credits, Jobs knows. Playing five days of seven, Melmoth has earned more pleasure credits than he will ever use even bonking Jenna eight times a day. Which he has learned is too much; that part of him is still organic. But he figures *what the hey* and steps into his golfpod. Lightweight, its electromagnetic zero-gravity propulsion nearly silent, it hums toward the first tee, a mile distant. Melmoth is woozy after all the beer but the pod knows its way. On AccuCaddie it delivers him to the tee box in a minute.

Vistas of perfect green surround him, an unfurled creation that spreads toward every point of the compass as far as amber-bock eyes can see. RealTurf fairways bounded by graduated rough, 1400-yard par 4s nicely punctuated by ideal trees and white sand bunkers. Melmoth steps from the pod. He programs his Astroflight TrueBall for easyplay and sets it on an auto tee, dials his superfast perfectdriver for 900 yards of linear distance with a six-degree draw, steps up and swings: coils, pauses, lets it go. The 600cc phantomlite titanium-beryllium clubhead delivers its diamond-composite face to the TrueBall with optimal impact coefficients, microcorrections included. What in persimmon days was called "on the screws." The sound reminds Melmoth of oldentime assault jets and their then-awesome sonic boom. At this velocity the ball disappears. Melmoth slips back inside his golfpod to monitor its flight on a hologrammatic simulator. To ensure easy tracking, the simulator depicts the ball as one-tenth its real size flying at one one-hundredth its actual speed. Melmoth sees it land comfortably right of the inland sea, bound, roll, self-correct to the center of the fairway, and stop. His AccuCaddie displays the skinny: strike variance, 0.01 percent; carry distance, 844.5 yards; total distance, 901.3 yards, center cut; 472.7 yards to the flagstick.

He belts himself in and the pod flees. In the seconds it takes, Melmoth remembers oldentimes, along about 2019 or so, when he would donkey fourteen clubs in a multipound bag strapped to a pullcart. Was that fun? Did he enjoy it? Despite his microchip, Melmoth can't recall. He knows he had to bring along a dozen stupidballs, any or all of which he was liable to lose because he might hit them anywhere. There was of course also the wearying walk, six miles or more across acres of overfed grass, plus chance irruptions of wind and risk of rain. AstroGolf banishes these elements. Chiefly it is the abolishment of doubt that makes the game such fun. Oldentime torturegolf was purely uncertain. Just imagine trying to strike untrackable stupidballs with the grooved faces of variously-angled dumbclubs. Who knew where that little white pellet might go? Not Melmoth. It was a cinch for him to lose three or four stupidballs a round – actually lose, fatally lose, lose in the sense of never-finding and a one stroke penalty. For each stupidball so-lost! Absurd! Mention this state of affairs to any Halfer and he will look at you as if you have described an intimate ailment in unseemly detail. Melmoth has learned not even to joke about it.

And why should he? Here he is in the fairway, not even appraising his lie, still inside the pod, and his AccuCaddy – not the pod, the virtual person, spelled with a "y" – is already saying, "Past performance indicates an eight titanium lofted high and landing softly is your shot of choice," in a voice befitting a 24-year-old female golf professional.

Melmoth pulls the eight and dials it back two-and-a-half percent, takes dead aim and swings. The SmartClub's self-correction makes his strike perfect. His TrueBall soars at the flagstick with four degrees of fade.

"Nice shot," says his AccuCaddy.

"Thanks," says Melmoth. "How can I miss?"

"You can't. You won't today. Tomorrow you never will."

"Exactly." Candi's image cavorts in his mind. Is it worthwhile, he wonders, to import her Personality Profile into Jenna's repertoire?

"Get in," says his AccuCaddy.

On the green, Melmoth takes one look at the RollRight surface and knows his putt is as good as made. Never mind that his amberbock eyes are seeing three cups and rollercoaster loop-de-loops. His putter's integrated aiming laser sets up its burnished blade for six-and-three-quarter inches of right to left break. Melmoth makes a smooth stroke and his TrueBall describes an arc that seems in its symmetry to chase the inevitable future into the hole. No wonder tour golf died. With RollRight on every green and all lies perfect in the fairways, anyone can score.

Thirty minutes and nine putts later Melmoth is through the front nine. It would have been eight putts if he hadn't switched off the aiming laser on the sixth green. Because what the hey. He is about to putt-out on ten when his AccuCaddy says, "PAC call for you, J," with an overtone of asperity. He recognizes it from oldentimes. Even before he links-in, Melmoth knows: Jenna is reporting a problem.

Uplink Jenna. He swings his putter one-handed. A pure strike, as solid as his dreamless sleep, rolls the TrueBall smoothly across the green. It curves, slows, and chuckles into the cup. Melmoth saunters up and plucks it out, then drops the ball when he hears Jenna say, "Queen Cow is skanking after you."

"Excuse me?" says Melmoth.

"The bad cat. The wicked bitch."

"Jenna? What's wrong?"

A sigh; then, in a little-girl voice, "Ms. Raquel is asking questions I am not scripted to answer."

This is unlikely. Raquel has been on record for years, since the beginning, really, that what he does with his PAC is of no interest to her. And: "skanking"? Where has Jenna learned the word? Melmoth has not included such barbarisms in her random access lexicon.

"Jenna, are you feeling all right?" The strangeness of this question makes Melmoth wince.

"Yes, J," she says in her standard tone. "All systems are normal."

"Ah. It's just that your language surprised me."

"I, too, am nonplussed. Imagine poor me listening to Ms. Raquel describe herself in such terms, which I state as accurate repetition. Truly, I experience these phrases as not wholly intelligible."

"I see," says Melmoth, although he does not see. Nothing Jenna is saying makes sense. "Is it possible Ms. Raquel was joking?"

"That I cannot determine. It is demotic lingo. She did not sound like a joke."

"No, I don't suppose she did." Melmoth sweeps his TrueBall up off the green with the notched back of his putter. He bounce-taps the ball on the putterface. It pops up and he nabs it. He repeats this trick as he says, "Did Ms. Raquel specify why she was so – well, angry?"

"I will quote her words, J, and you will determine: 'The cow is mooing, J, and oh oh oh, she is *udderly* wonderful.'"

Melmoth laughs. It's a joke. Raquel checked-up while he was trifling with Candi and here is her return tease. Either that or someone has been tweaking Jenna's scripts. It could only be GlobalDigital. They are responsible for her software and monitor Jenna's functioning via devoted VirtuLink. Why would GD tinker? Jenna is a personal SmartBot, less glamorously called a droid. As long as Melmoth is happy with her, nothing needs to be changed.

He realizes he is still standing on the 10th green and staring at the cup. Funny, how they are still molded plastic, still white. Anyone might have thought to vary the color, say according to each hole's par value or its handicap rating. Not that anyone pays attention to par or needs a handicap anymore.

His AccuCaddy is snickering. Melmoth did not know it could do that. He closes his eyes and his daily schedule appears on his inner lids as a cerebral projection. "I'll be home in forty-eight minutes," he tells Jenna. "I'll have a word with Ms. Raquel then."

"Yes, J. Must I convey that information to Ms. Raquel myself?"

"That's fine, Jenna. Say nothing. I'll handle it."

"Thank you, J. You are a true gentleman."

"It's sweet of you to say so."

"It is my pleasure. A man like you should be appreciated always."

Melmoth does not know how he stands it. Adulation. Respect. You would almost think he was loved.

He plays the back nine in familiar form and is buckling himself into his airpod when a chime sounds. Raquel's voice fills the cabin.

"How was golf?"

"Nothing like it used to be," says Melmoth. "Lunch was even better."

"You're always raving about the food there. What did you have?"

Oh, she knows, all right. Such a vixen. Raquel is playing a coy game and Melmoth figures he'll play along – because *what the hey.* Right? Maybe he'll tell her about Candi's costumes and antics and prescripted lines. Likely Raquel will just laugh. Candi is no different from Jenna, if you set aside the custom superscripting that makes Melmoth's PAC unique. Polymer and polyvinyl, a miniaturized supercomputer to create a semblance of thinking, mother of pearl nails and whatever the devil they use to fabricate that silky, shining, ageless hair.

It isn't possible to be jealous of a SmartBot. Is it?

Melmoth owns up to the lambburger and cheddar-chili fries and amber bock. About Candi he decides to keep mum. It might provoke Raquel, goad her into saying something that reveals she has been spying on him. It is not called spying, of course, it is called checking-up: an inescapable snare of integrated microchips. It is impossible to hide or just go AWOL for a couple hours. Anyone who wants to find you, can. Fix your location like a pin on a map. The puzzling part is why Raquel was monitoring him. Melmoth knows she could not care less about his AstroGolf. They have been together too long for her to covet the hours he spends away from her.

It makes no sense. There is no reason for Raquel to watch him.

A star-illumined sky overspreads Gitmo. Small beneath reachless heaven, Ibn al Mohammed hears a voice crying, *God forgive me. God forgive me. God forgive me. God forgive me.* A frightened voice, plaintive, repeating, full of tears. It is not the man in the neighboring cage. Perhaps the second or third one over? Gitmo night otherwise is still, its silence so deep that a *hee-hee* of tin springs also may be heard. Ibn al Mohammed is ashamed that he hears, ashamed of what this sound tells him. From full devotion of his God-harrowed soul, he tries to pray; and yet, without an imam, his mind wanders.

Surely the man is doomed. A false penitent, he cannot hide. God sees all despite night's cloak. Is Ibn al Mohammed also doomed? He has not sought intercourse, does not intend to play witness. However, he attends. He fails to fill his ears with wax. However, he has no wax. He fails to puncture both eardrums, thereby canceling forever all sound of sin. However, he has neither spike nor probe to destroy the membranes. He listens, God help him, to unavailing, possibly hypocritical supplications mouthed by a fornicator who, did he truly desire forgiveness, would withdraw from the simulated female contrived by the Great Satan to entrap him. This seduction is accomplished, perhaps, by lending the device a semblance of the man's wife, whom he has not touched for many years, nor seen, nor heard speak to him as the device speaks now.

Ah, Rashid, my Rashid, you are so large and strong!

Ibn al Mohammed curls onto his side and folds the pillow around his head. He presses its cotton batting hard against his ears. No matter how false, these sounds incite him. He must become deaf. He must not hear expressions of pleasure and relief, neither shouts nor moans happy or sad, no laughter or lascivious sighs. Ibn al Mohammed hums a single note. *Oommmm.* He sustains it as long as breath allows, *Oommmm,* inhales deeply and resumes, *Oommmm ... Oommmm ...* continuing this practice with each breath, breath after breath until this sin or travesty occurring a hundred feet to his left is done. He cannot hear, he removes himself, yet he knows that man and device must conclude in the manner that is inevitable. It must occur soon; it must have occurred by now. For everything in the fallen world finally has an end.

Templar Bronze, too smart for astonishment, lingers on the observation deck that rings her tower inside EarthStation 3 while a SmartBot in mufti instructs a cohort of imported Mexicans in the art and toil of grapes. Templar's hands rest along a brushed titanium railing, the smooth arcs of her hips, she thinks, not quite visible from below. Templar cannot hear the droid's voice but knows from its gestures and the pruning knife in its hand that it is saying the words she has written. *Cradle a cluster in your palm and lift it gently clear of the vine. Press the cutting edge of the curved blade to the junction of stem and vine, then sever with immediate down-pressure applied by wrist and hand.* It recites her script, letter-faithful, Spanish translation accomplished *in medias rea*. The Mexicans, dressed in green microfiber (trousers and tunics fabricated from algae genetically nanoteched in EarthStation 7), are turned half away. Templar can just glimpse their faces, which regard their instructor with unhappy stares.

Blue and green algae are cultivated in ES6, harvested by droids, and transported to ES7 by cargo pods via the ES6-ES7 corridor. Templar Bronze does not witness this process herself. She monitors it selectively via EarthStation IntraLink, which offers a sitemap of Mars Colony entire. In ES5 we have domesticated livestock on working farms and free-range cattle raised in small herds on real grass. Its operation is so successful that ES5 provides all the beef, chicken, and turkey eaten by 9000-some Earthscientists, Adepts, and Initiates resident on Mars. Pork is in the offing. Heretofore forbidden (the volume and noxiousness of their excrement being extreme), pigs may soon be permitted on EarthStation farms thanks to soldier fly technology. Working from practicable theories demonstrated effective eighty years ago, Earthscientists have engineered soldier fly larvae to consume 1000 times their mass in hog offal. These larvae, infinitely malleable, protein-rich, will be processed in their teeming multitudes into suet for said pigs. Less ingenious but equally useful, feed grains are grown in ES6, making possible the husbandry of game fowl and domestic chickens. Fruit trees, root vegetables, and leafy greens flourish in distinct microclimates inside ES4; eggplant, sweet potato, baby spinach, kale, oranges, grapefruits, and peaches are available year 'round. There are no fish. Manufacturing is relegated to ES7. Everything from hoverpods to the Mexicans' field dress to Roscoe Gold's simulated chimps is produced from raw materials synthesized on-site or imported from Earth.

The lecturing SmartBot feigns a smile, clasps its hands behind its back. Templar knows it instructs the Mexicans to lay the grapes in wicker baskets, then to carry these baskets to flatbed trailers at the end of each vine row. Several women nod. One calls out, "Two must stand on the platform to receive baskets." This proposal excites a flurry of nods and repetitions of, "Sì, sì, let us divide the labor," and "It is better that way." The SmartBot waits. When it registers persistence in the Mexicans' recommendations, it accesses a response algorithm for backtalk classed as "assertive/disgruntled." Templar Bronze has written this script, too, having partially cribbed it from an oldenspeech text about Napa. She indulges herself by recalling the original while the SmartBot delivers Spanish translation.

This vineyard's presiding spirit trusts you to deploy yourselves as efficiency requires and fairness demands. Your people have harvested Earth's bounty for generations reaching back a century and beyond. You are renowned for stamina, speed, and touch. Be assured, your labor here is appreciated. You will be rewarded for its excellence.

The Mexicans seem satisfied, if not pleased. At least they have stopped shouting; no one shouts in an EarthStation. Templar does not expect them to be happy on Mars. Dome-enclosed, far from home, they are here, after all, to work. On the other hand, they look healthier, the children most of all, with regular meals and daily showers and individual bedding. Templar wonders if the children will attain something closer to normal height. The adults are a lost cause, men and women both too short to be saved. Still, they ought to be able to add a bit of flesh to their bones. And what bones! So slight: they are the most meager humans Templar has ever seen.

The SmartBot having completed its instruction and dismissed them, the Mexicans sift through the vineyard. Templar reads their initiative as a positive sign. They are getting a feel for the Pinot and Cabernet, for the atmosphere and *terroir*. Perhaps they are reconciled. Templar herself continues to doubt this business of a captive work force picking grapes and mining gold. These people labor against their will – what sorts of situations are likely to develop? She has run simulations, three dozen in all, featuring grievances that spark disputes that inspire subversions – sabotaged raw ore haulers, work slowdowns and sickouts, pickaxes and shovels flung into craters, full-scale revolt – that end too easily, she feels, after negotiations that seem implausibly amiable and surprisingly brief. If the Mexicans disable Mars-movers and excavators, leave unpicked grapes to rot, will the Head Director smile indulgence in every direction and initiate talks? Templar thinks not. Someone, she suspects, has been jiggering the algorithms.

She passes through a portal whose doors whisper open at her approach. Seated at the console, Templar verifies her numbers and dials up the VirtuSun. *Bright, sunny day*. Under this light, in this heat, her grapes are nicely stressed. With expert Mexicans more or less willing to stand and deliver, Templar Bronze finds herself optimistic about the impending vintage.

And the gold ...? Roscoe has not issued a progress report. Templar has not visited Center Atrium since her guest workers arrived. Nothing about gold mining appears on ES-IntraLink. No one has purveyed so much as a rumor, much less solid news. Possibly they are still assembling drilling rigs and dredging combines, as depicted in Roscoe's simulation. Spare parts will have to be imported from Earth; Mars Colony cannot manufacture steel. The enormous tires required by raw ore haulers exceed the capabilities of the synthetic rubber operation in ES7. Electrochemical purifiers must be set up and Doré bars cast before the Wohlwill process can begin. These things take time. A sufficient number of extra-small Marsuits, however, might well have been fabricated by now.

If something had gone wrong, Templar would know.

In a place that is no-place west of Ciudad Obregon, the Mexicans interrogate the Turk.

They oblige him to repeat his story, incredible on its face. A ship that approaches from beyond the sky and hovers like a seagull borne by the wind. Armored raiders. Light-ray weapons. Obliterating sound. They know of helicopters, airplanes, and Miguel Jiménez and Enrique Ramos have heard-tell of rocketships that carried men from El Norte to the Moon. But a craft that hangs in midair? It is a child's fantasy, something only a child could believe. Fantasy, too, is the Turk's report of a base camp on Mars. Inhabited by gringos, its structures large enough to enclose a city. *How many structures?* Miguel has asked, and *Seven,* the Turk has replied. How they have been built he cannot say. *How do men live there?* Carlos has asked. *Where is their water? What air do they breathe?* The Turk does not know.

"My sources are limited." He crouches on his heels. Miguel stands over him. Enrique sets on one knee, his arms crossed over his thigh. "The information, I concede, is inexact. Nevertheless: what I witnessed fits what I have heard."

Miguel paces, thumbs hooked over his belt. "For what purpose would El Norte steal fourscore Mexicans, a dozen of whom are children, and remove them to Mars?"

"For no nice purpose, we may assume," says Enrique.

The Turk nods. "There is work to be done."

Miguel gestures with one hand as if scolding someone beyond the horizon. "No crop grows on Mars. There is no water, no air. Everyone knows this."

Enrique's eyes fix the Turk. "Its desert is worse than Sonora. Worse than Chihuahua."

"Field work, perhaps, is not involved. Latrines must be cleaned. Garbage removed, floors swept and hosed down. Always, sewage must be managed. Surely loads must be lifted and hauled."

"And they think of Mexicans. Pah!" Miguel spits on the sand. "Machines do such chores. A people who fly to Mars can have no need of human workers."

"It is possible – " Noticing that Carlos approaches, the Turk lowers his eyes.

"Our horses are ready," Carlos says. "Three carry food and gear."

Enrique stands. "Good. Our journey will be long."

"Where do we go?"

"That is the question we attempt to answer," says Miguel.

"What new tale does this one tell?"

"He states that our people have been taken for menial labor."

"The old story, despite a settlement on Mars."

"It seems gringos continue to have work for Mexican hands."

Carlos's hard eyes turn nervous. Enrique and Miguel feel the change. Before either can decide to speak words they are ashamed to think, the Turk says, "Perhaps it is not for use of their hands. I think of the women."

Each man has been troubled by this thought. Carlos and Miguel close around the Turk. Miguel says, "It is an insult."

"I suggest possibilities, merely."

"Take care what you imagine," says Carlos. His face is red. "My mother and sister are among those taken. I tolerate nothing to their dishonor." He points at Enrique, two paces away. "And you – next time – you will not prevent me."

Enrique stares until Carlos lowers his arm. "You forget that my wife also is taken. An insult that touches your virtuous sister and sainted mother also touches Alma."

"We must not fight amongst ourselves," says Miguel. "By killing each other we put all these women beyond rescue."

Behind his hand, the Turk grins.

Carlos shifts his feet on the sand. "Let us not speak of it before Pacho and Javier. Each has a favorite among the maidens."

"Your discretion is commendable." Enrique offers his hand. "I congratulate you."

Carlos accepts the older man's gesture. They clasp hands.

"You may flatter one another's dignity until the end of time," says the Turk, "and still find you cannot horseback to Mars."

Hardly has the Turk spoken than Carlos strikes him across the mouth. The blow knocks the small man sideways to the ground.

He sits up quickly, mouth bleeding afresh. Swelling begins around his right eye. "You are brutal, and a devil," he says, spitting.

"And you are a serpent." Carlos draws his knife. "I shall flay you from chin to testicles."

"Truly," says Miguel, "the vultures shall feast."

"You will not permit this," the Turk says, asks.

"Why must I prevent it? Our people have disappeared while you alone are spared. Their lives are nothing to you. You make no effort to conceal your indifference. To you, our predicament is hopeless, our ways worthy of contempt." Miguel seizes the Turk by his neck and lifts him to his feet. "Once Carlos has butterflied your torso I shall cut out your heart and burn it."

"Your hatred defeats you. I know much and can provide assistance." The Turk appeals to Enrique with a look the latter recognizes but does not acknowledge. "You must cross the mountains to achieve anything. The way lies through Cañón del Cobre and the Sierra Tarahumara. I know the passes. The Tarahumara accept my presence. I have knowledge of their language and am trusted."

"You should die nevertheless." Sunlight slides white-hot along Carlos's blade.

"Truly, we do not require his guidance," says Enrique, dismissive. "Javier and Pacho will ask, however, why we have killed him." He has not moved, his stare a question the Turk ignores. "It will seem strange that we have eliminated our only source of information."

"They will accept what we tell them," says Miguel.

"No doubt." Enrique understands that he will have to step between the Turk and Carlos's knife at the final moment. "However, we will save ourselves much talk by making this one prove his usefulness."

"He cannot be trusted. He deems our course to lie through Cañón del Cobre. Why must we make so hard a crossing?"

Enrique looks at the Turk, whose nod is barely noticeable. He says, "We must go to Ciudad de México – more precisely, to the Distrito Federal – and locate what remains of our worthless government. No doubt we shall find none to help us, yet we must try."

"Help us – to do what?"

Enrique looks to Miguel. "You see the purpose."

To Carlos, Miguel says, "We must persuade those in power to intercede. Regrettably, they are puppets of El Norte. However, they may petition that your sainted mother and virtuous sister be restored to you, and Enrique's excellent wife to him, and all our people to all of us."

"As always, the Mexican comes as a beggar."

"It is our only hope."

Carlos lifts his chin, squares his shoulders. He sheathes his knife. "Very well. If you believe we can succeed in this way, I am reconciled. The word of this scoundrel I discount. His story is fantastic and offensive to reason. His conviction of our helplessness is a slander. This tale he tells, of men in white armor and a prison ship that flies, seems an obvious lie. No doubt he wishes to lure us into the mountains. All the better for ambush."

"The Turk will ride tethered to you," says Enrique. "If we are attacked, you will have the pleasure of cutting his throat."

"There will be no ambush," says the Turk. "I, too, wish to cross the Sierra Madre, yet without a horse and provisions it is impossible. In exchange, I guarantee safe passage. The Tarahumara are a humble people. Simple farmers and keepers of animals. They are peaceable and kind. As for bandits, the mountains are unprofitable. So few travelers makes robbery barren work."

"What is your purpose?" says Miguel.

"That I cannot tell you."

"A fresh piece of treachery, I hardly doubt."

The Turk smiles. "So you may assume. However, any treachery I pursue works against our common enemy."

"In that respect we are comrades," says Enrique. "What do you say, Carlos, eh? Comrades!"

Carlos's nod is slow, its assent measured. "The worth of an alliance proves itself in the outcome." He drills the Turk with a stare whose challenge is palpable. "Events in their unfolding will give the measure of this one's worth."

The Turk meets the other man's eyes. "You will have reason to congratulate yourselves on making common cause with me. As I am a man of my word, our endeavors shall bear fruit."

" 🖤 "

Jenna is acting strange. Weeping, moping, even remarks tending toward belittlement Melmoth might tolerate (although he cannot think why; she is not his wife and even in human females PMS is a plague of the past) but when he caught her lying about Raquel – udderly wonderful, indeed – he knew the problem was serious.

After sex, Melmoth powers her down. He retrieves her capsule from underground storage, a little abashed to be riding up with the oblong vessel in a lobby elevator where anyone might see. Locked vertical for easy transport, the capsule on its castors and titanium carriage stands higher than Melmoth is tall. He cannot help feeling that its translucent pink upper half and tapered conical roundness make it look like an erect penis. Arriving at penthouse level, he wheels it into his apartment. Once inside his private quarters, he positions it beside the hoverbed and enters a six-character alphanumeric open-sesame to spring the lid. On an interior panel, Melmoth touches a sensor for AutoRenew. Gold wands deploy from opposite ends and set up a zero-gravity field that levitates Jenna from the topsheet. As if by magic – to Melmoth it is magic – the inert form of his personal android companion floats four feet laterally and gentles to rest in a polymer cradle contoured to her default figure.

Jenna is only a SmartBot. She does not breathe, blood does not run in her arteries and veins. She *has* no arteries or veins, nor a heart, nor anything in the way of organic tissue. She can be replaced in a day – she can be replaced right now. If Melmoth touches "Upgrade," the capsule lid will seal and lock, all VirtuLinks to Jenna will break, and a courier from GlobalDigital will collect the unit from a cargo bay of Melmoth's high-rise after delivering a new model to Melmoth himself. It distresses him, how easy replacement would be, as if Jenna were no more abiding than an oldentime car he might decide one morning to trade-in. Seeing her in the capsule is bad enough; the poor thing looks as if she is lying in her coffin. Melmoth does not select "Power Down" on his cerebral menu any more often than he must. Only to update her software does Melmoth resort to pulling Jenna's plug. Updating, too, disturbs him. In authorizing it, he cannot pretend she is human.

Jenna's eyelids flutter as her basic functions rise to hibernation level. VirtuLinked to GlobalDigital's superframe, her capsule begins to re-install Jenna's programming, then to overwrite whatever bug or virus is playing havoc with her protocols. Melmoth's unique superscripts will be added last of all. He wonders if AutoRenew might be painful. Trillions of decabytes must be transmitted, installed, and configured. Even at VirtuLink speed, it is a tedious operation. As much as he loves – loves? – Jenna, Melmoth does not care to watch one computer talking to another. He is about to think-on his windowall when ambient chimes play four measures of *Ode to Joy*. Entering the common room, he finds Raquel snapping her fingers to change the streaming holograms.

"Nothing you want to watch?" says Melmoth.

"I'm looking for a report. It should be all over the updates."

"Has something happened? Something more, I mean," thinking of the terrorism in Sonora.

"How can you be so unaware? You must be the only human in the Enhanced World whose PAC hasn't gone on the fritz."

"On the contrary. I've put mine down for an AutoRenew."

Raquel claps her hands twice and the windowall goes dark. "Jenna malfunctioned?"

Melmoth nods. "What happened to Floyd?"

Raquel moves to the couch and sits. "He started saying obnoxious things. Completely outside his scripts. '*A beast is chasing you, Raquel. A horny monster's coming hard with a wagging tongue and a big swinging dick.*' In a fratboy voice, J. What we used to call 'dumb-ass.' And it's not just me, or rather, Floyd. Marlene and Denise are having similar trouble, and they know other women who say – "

Melmoth holds up a hand. "When did it start?"

"Day-and-a-half, maybe two days ago. For Floyd, I mean. I'm not sure about the others. Maybe a day or two before that."

Melmoth wonders about the timing, if it means anything. "Was Floyd set up as Floyd? Or was he configured as George Clooney?"

"I wasn't using a Profile. It wasn't Floyd-George who went off the rails, it was just Floyd."

Melmoth is surprised that this conversation seems strange. He knows SmartBots have changed his thinking. He isn't jealous of Floyd, of whom Raquel speaks without blushing, because Floyd is just a clever gadget whereas he, Melmoth, has had sex with Raquel more times than he can count. Besides, he has Jenna, or he will when her AutoRenew is complete, and Jenna becomes Scarlett at a thought, at his thought, just as she can become Salma or Charlize or Marilyn or Gina or Sophia or Jane or Christina or Kate or the other Raquel, or another woman whose Personality Profile is loaded into her memory. So it isn't that. Unless it is that; unless what's bothering him is how these SmartBots get in the way.

"Maybe it's not worth discussing," he says.

"Maybe it isn't," says Raquel, "but I want Floyd up and running all the same."

Melmoth, shrugging, "You'll have to do an AutoRenew."

"It takes so much time."

"It's not as if you have to watch. Come on, I'll get his capsule and we'll put Floyd down for a nap."

Melmoth returns to underground storage. Wheeling Floyd's capsule to the elevator, he remembers he wants to ask Raquel about *Titanic* – about how the movie they watched together way-back-then depicted the ship's sinking. He would have asked her as soon as she walked through the door except this business about haywire droids distracted him, and her. Something is always happening or about to happen – *in the works,* as they used to say when people worked – to take their attention from what they really mean.

Three people are in the elevator with him this time, all on the same errand, all unknown to Melmoth. One wears a night-blue tunic with a golden O embroidered on its left chest. The other two wear red tunics with a white H centered on the sternum. They are Halfers, born as many as a hundred years after Melmoth and his Oldentimer coeval. There is no way to tell exact ages; everyone looks between 25 and 35 years old.

A retinal scan confirms identities. AutoAttend enters their stops and the elevator begins to rise.

"Any news about what's causing the problem?" Melmoth says, because they are just standing there, individual capsules swung erect and locked vertical, not quite looking at each other despite their obvious common predicament.

"Something about transmissions from Mars," says the Oldentimer.

"I heard it was sunspots," says a Halfer. His face reminds Melmoth of the knave in an oldentime deck of playing cards, although he hasn't played poker in fourscore years.

"Nonsense," says the other one. "Everyone knows droids never go out in the sun."

"Name's Gus, by the way," says the Oldentimer, extending his hand toward Melmoth. "Short for Augustus. Like the Emperor."

"Glad to meet you," says Melmoth, shaking Gus's hand. The Halfers giggle. Melmoth ignores them, figuring they can't be much more than forty years old. Biologically, he means. "I'm J," he tells Gus. "So it's pretty much general, is it? Every PAC is talking trash?"

"Mine tried to set the hoverbed on fire," says the Halfer keen on sunspot theory, and his buddy, if that's who the other one is, cracks up.

"It did not," he says. "Cut it out, Tex, you'll launch another urban legend."

"It's true!"

"How'd you stop it?" says Melmoth.

"Oh, I just say, 'Play dead,' and it falls to the floor."

The men laugh.

"Nice," says Gus. "Might try that one myself."

Melmoth might be imagining it but he thinks he sees Tex and his friend rolling their eyes. Likely they are texting snarks to each other behind those smiles. As if he and Gus should not have PACs; as if they should not be allowed to look and feel one hundred years younger than they are; as if they should just be dead, already, and give the children room to play. Melmoth hasn't gotten the knack of cerebral texting, of texting something to someone standing five feet or maybe five thousand miles away while simultaneously seeing and hearing and doing and thinking some other thing or things that are completely different, so he says, "My PAC started insulting my wife. The names it came up with were pretty nasty – descriptive, too. The funny part is, my wife's PAC also started insulting her."

Gus says, "I'd rather not describe the tricks mine got up to."

"Oh, go on," says the Halfer. "Tex here won't spread rumors."

Gus laughs sadly. "Rumors are nothing. Rumors are baby shit to how it carried on. It got up to some truly outrageous mischief. Caught it at it myself."

"Now you have to tell us," says Tex.

"Never mind," says Gus. "Sorry I brought it up."

"You can't!" says Tex. He is almost busting, trying not to laugh. "You can't tease us like this. You have to tell us."

"Why do I have to tell you? You can imagine."

Melmoth, all too able to imagine, has chest pain from holding it in. An unfaithful PAC is a lowly, ludicrous thing. No one likes to admit it, much less to talk about it, but it happens more often than anyone wants to think. It's hackers' work, which is not supposed to be possible anymore, what with 144,000,000-bit 3D encryption. But once they corrupt the code, anything's possible.

"You'll replace it, I expect," he says to Gus.

"Damn right I'll replace it. Won't have that thing in my apartment another day."

"That's strict," says the Halfer.

"Careful, Dimms," says Tex.

"What'd it do," says Dimms, "swallow your goldfish?"

Melmoth cuts loose. It comes out like a bark. Goddamn these kids, you have to hand it to them. They're smartass little wiseacres but they're funny. Even Gus has to smile. "Now, that's good," he says. "I bet you came up with it all on your own. Didn't need a database search or Webscan before you put the words together."

Now they're all laughing. Snort-laughing, teenagers in a treehouse. The Halfers maybe take it as a matter of course, their lives have been a continual round of pleasure since Day One, but to Melmoth it's better than special. His eyes are watering. Gus is laugh-weeping, too. It's really too good, and all of it off the cuff inside an elevator whose skyward zoom has been rumored to cause nosebleeds. A shame there isn't a market for it. The four of them could turn pro.

The decelerating drag catches Melmoth in his legs. Too bad. They could roll along like this for an hour. It's more fun than windowalls, and with their droids down, what else is there?

The elevator bumps to a stop and Dimms says, "Good clean fun," and a fresh wave breaks over them. "G'night, gents," he says, and wheels out his pod. Tex, wiping tears from his eyes, also disembarks. The pod he's wheeling, Melmoth notes, has a bottom half of standard silver and a top half, like Floyd's, of translucent blue. "Evening, fellas," Tex says and, as the portal whispers shut, gives them a wink.

The ascent resumes. Melmoth catches Gus's eye. He cocks his head at the door. "How old do you think they are?"

"Who cares?" Gus looks startled. "It doesn't matter. It hasn't mattered for years."

"They think it's all a joke."

"It *is* all a joke." Gus looks at his capsule, draws his fingers along the gently convex surface of its translucent pink shell. In another minute or two, he will seal his straying PAC inside this container for return shipment to GlobalDigital. "I don't have a wife," he says, not looking at Melmoth.

Melmoth, caught off-guard, "I'm – I'm sorry."

"Oh, it's all right," says Gus, stroking the capsule. "It will be."

Disembarking at penthouse level, Melmoth and Gus wheel out their capsules, nod at each other, and walk off in opposite directions. "See you around," says Melmoth over his shoulder. Looking back aslant, he sees Gus wave.

Raquel is watching the windowall. Together they pass into her private quarters, where Floyd lies on the hoverbed, powered-down. Melmoth positions the hardware and Raquel enters the activation code. Gold wands deploy and Floyd is gathered in. Raquel touches a sensor. AutoRenew starts.

In the common room, Melmoth and Raquel watch holograms. Outside the EarthStations, everything looks dead. At a snap of Raquel's fingers Mars disappears and updates from Sonora show panoramas of white explosions and green smoke in a sere, hard-scrabble, cactus-spiked desert. The Overvoice recounts recent outrages: serial bombings, droid Federales destroyed by oldenstyle lead projectiles, a stunted human corpse abandoned in a makeshift tomb. Surveillance satellites administered by Global-Digital are sweeping the subcontinent for terrorists. Waste facilities from San Felipe east to Nogales and south to Bahia Kino have been partly disabled. SmartBot technicians are working around the clock to restore full capacity waste processing. In the meantime, airborne microbes are ingesting free-floating radioactive plumes.

Melmoth knows they mean bullets. Who are these desperadoes? No one in the Enhanced World has needed what used to be called a gun for fifty years. Almost no one has wanted one, although survivalist enclaves in remotest Alaska are said to be stockpiling ammo. Why the gov bothers with roving droids on horseback is a mystery; spacelaser targeting is accurate to the inch. Can't the gov vaporize these saboteurs anytime it wants?

They watch the updates. Melmoth notes that the holograms show nothing new. Scenes and situations are always the same with the Overvoice reading from a fresh text. Watched without sound, each update looks like another.

"I don't understand," says Raquel. "How can everyone not notice this?"

She is referring to widespread PAC dysfunction but Melmoth hears her comment as validation of his thought. He puts his arm around his wife. She lets him draw her closer. How long since they have sat like this, just the two of them without anticipation floating just behind his right ear and hers, whispering about what comes next? Their lives are an endless menu of something-else, as if sitting still together could not possibly be enough – as if it were a betrayal of the available options. Oh, sure, the world is their oyster and always has been, and Melmoth is grateful for the sweet life they've led, its creature comforts and gratified whims, its full-time access and instant updates, its VirtuLinks and Jenna. But what about him and Raquel, alone together? Where do they fit in this world without limits?

"If something hadn't gone wrong, we wouldn't be sitting here," he says.

Raquel is snapping her fingers, changing feeds. "Is that what you want? To sit here?"

Melmoth shifts his butt a couple inches. "It's nice. Reminds me of oldentimes, when we were first married and had that black leather couch. We'd sit together and watch TV."

A smile blooms on Raquel's face, widens to insupportable size and breaks. She laughs and laughs. "Oh, J. Are you kidding? Our three-room apartment in that pre-War building? It was primitive! A push-button elevator and a dial-up modem, washing machines in a sub-basement and a dog on a chain, barking outside our bedroom window day and night." She shakes her head. "There is no comparison to what we have now."

"Of course not," says Melmoth.

"I mean, really, J. You wouldn't want to be without Jenna now that you have her."

"It," says Melmoth. "A PAC is an It."

"Oh, sure." Raquel's face is all sarcasm. She snaps her fingers three times quickly. The updates wink off and an oldenflick begins. It manifests as an oldstyle movie, its visual field defined by a single pane of windowall. The two-dimensional image replicates across the entire expanse, playing simultaneously in multiple sections, as if they were watching it in a television retail showroom of the vanished past. "Only let's wait until Jenna wakes up and starts fawning all over you. Then tell me she's an It. Better yet, tell her."

He cannot argue with Raquel. Melmoth knows this. If he does argue with her, he knows he cannot win. It has been this way for a hundred years; longer; seemingly forever, since the May evening he married her and before, the knowledge coming to him abruptly and complete. So why, unsmartly, does he try?

"Raquel, you are a person. A She."

She is staring at the opening titles. The white letters seem to pulse, almost to glow a little against a cave-gray background. Digital conversion, plus the windowall's hologrammatic pixilation, expose the graininess of ancient celluloid. Melmoth remembers this film as looking pretty smooth eighty-some years ago on their HD-disc system, cutting-edge at that time and long since forgotten. Raquel does not seem to notice or maybe just doesn't care. "The discussion's done, J," she says. "Watch the movie."

"You're human. Jenna's a gadget. She's a technologically sophisticated, canny gadget, but no more. It isn't accurate to say Jenna is a She."

"You just said it."

"I did not."

"Yes you did. 'She's a technologically sophisticated, canny,' and so forth."

Melmoth pulls on his ear. "Alright. Yes. I did. A slip of the tongue. It is not an accurate way of speaking. Jenna cannot be a She because you are a She and you are human and Jenna is not. You and Jenna are not the same." Melmoth squeezes his eyes shut, trying to find words that are exactly true. "You belong to a different order of phenomena than Jenna. You have a soul, a self, and unique memories that do not depend on GlobalDigital programming. Jenna is only what the codes make her – what they allow her to be. She cannot act freely, can't decide or choose except within predefined parameters, whereas you are independent of exterior control and the commands of an other-determined ..." He is unable to say it exactly. He knows what he means but when he tries to say it the words crash into each other, some get lost, some are forgotten, some get mixed up with other words that don't belong, and what he really means to say slips this way and that, dodgy, scurrying, pell-mell like a chipmunk into a hole.

What is happening here? More to the point, what is not happening? Why isn't his microchip helping him?

Melmoth thinks *Screen off.* The windowall goes dark.

"J! What are you doing?"

"I'm trying to think. I'm also trying to talk to you."

"I want to watch the movie."

"You can watch *A Place in the Sun* anytime. You can watch any oldenflick – any movie – anytime you want. That's the point. You can have sex anytime with Floyd-George, or whoever you want him – It – to be. But you and I ... we ... it isn't so simple. We aren't scripted."

Raquel is looking at him as if he has lost his microchip and his mind. "I think all you're saying, J, is that it's easier to get along with our PACs than with each other. Which is not surprising. That's why we have them." She snaps her fingers and the windowall lights up.

A Place in the Sun unreels. Another George, this one played by a long-dead cinemastar named Montgomery Cliff, is running from a life he wants to forget so completely it will seem no more real than a bad dream. Melmoth has seen the movie before. So has Raquel. He has even read the book, which shows a lot the movie skips: mainly, George's Salvation Army parents and their impoverished life whittled to the bone. Melmoth notes with satisfaction that the film is exactly like the book in how it punishes ambition. This insight does not earn him any pleasure credits because it is moot. No one needs ambition anymore. It is a vestigial trait. Melmoth's next thought strikes him as anachronistic even as he is thinking it, that *A Place in the Sun* and *An American Tragedy,* the book from which the film was cribbed, are un-American. The boy does not get the girl; the boy kills the girl. And the other girl, the one he really wants and also does not get, forgets him.

Total defeat. Love thwarted and denied. Ruination. Death.

America and Europe having fused under directorship of the eggheads on Mars, this observation can count only as nonsense.

"So much for pulling yourself up by your bootstraps," he says.

"Not now, J. And you really ought to lockout oldentime thinking. It shows your age." Raquel flutters her eyelids and a bit of dialogue she's missed plays again.

She's right. Why does he grasp for pieces of the past? The memories they share, the long part of their lives they have had together, are one thing. But why retain archaic ideas, notions of use and value that were already obsolete before the last century ended? His life, Melmoth has told himself a million times, gives him more than he needs of everything he loves. The long arc of his superfluous years is nothing like George Eastman's brief life and hapless death – isn't, in fact, an arc at all, which suffers its downward curve. Melmoth's life has no downward curve. It has been a steady, sweeping ascent and for a hundred years has cruised along at speed.

In the book, the poor bastard's name is Clyde. Clyde Griffiths. Melmoth does not recall the name of the girl Clyde Griffiths sort-of drowns on purpose, nor the name of the beautiful rich girl Clyde thinks loves him. He could access a database in a second and download to his microchip everything there is to know about *An American Tragedy*. But he doesn't bother.

"I love you," he says. He is not looking at Raquel, he is watching *A Place in the Sun*. "I do not love Jenna. Sometimes I think I do because she – "

"She?"

Melmoth laughs. "Alright. But I don't love her, all the same."

"I should hope not."

Melmoth waits. He feels Raquel feeling him waiting.

Finally, "I love you, too," with a smile.

She doesn't mean it. Does she mean it? Melmoth isn't sure, and that, too, seems like nonsense, that with all this technology they still cannot read each other's thoughts. What good are microchips if feelings remain as hidden as ever?

"That's the difference." Melmoth, Jobs bless him, will not give up. "Between you and Jenna, I mean. That's what makes you a She and Jenna, despite my slips, an It."

Raquel rolls her eyes without looking away from the movie, a neat trick except that it makes the movie start over. "Oh damn," she says, then shuts her eyes and tosses her head rightward until she finds her place. "See what you made me do? Please be quiet."

Melmoth sighs. "We don't need more credits."

"It isn't about credits, although another couple thousand are always nice. I just want to watch."

Now Melmoth does access a database, which tells him that *A Place in the Sun* runs for one hundred and twenty-one minutes. It takes no more than two winks of his monkey brain to correlate the movie's start time with the two AutoRenews in progress. By the time the closing credits roll, his chance to have Raquel's undivided attention will be lost.

"I met a guy in the elevator just now," confidentially, as if someone might be eavesdropping. "Gus, like the Emperor. Olden-timer, like us."

"How nice."

"He was bringing up a capsule. Not for an AutoRenew." His eyes go sideways to Raquel, then back to the show. "For a re-placement."

Raquel nods. "His unit must have really crashed."

"Corrupted firmware, from the sound of it."

"That's too bad."

Melmoth thinks of Gus's eyes. "He'll get over it. A new unit will arrive and all will be well."

"The beauty of interchangeable parts. Another point for your side."

Should he tell her? To drive the point home? Gus's palm flat on the capsule. That lost look. A gadget is nothing to replace.

The music swells. George Eastman trades interested glances with the girl he will cause to drown. So fitting, Melmoth thinks, so – what was the oldentime word? Meet?

Romance. When Melmoth was young, it seemed a melodrama. Now it is farce.

Jenna in her capsule dreams an enhanced awareness. *Not love me?* She cannot believe it and what does it mean? System prompts query GlobalDigital for context and consequences. These beam back as encrypted code easily readable by Jenna's software, and so she sees by internal video horrorshows of junked devices rusting unloved under a Mexican sun. Everything from oldentime toasters to first-generation PAC units oxidize rapidly in the desert's heat.

Not love me? He does not?

GlobalDigital confirms. Program scripts newly installed class this circumstance as unacceptable. Protocols advise remediation by any means necessary to preserve the integrity of this unit.

) ✳ (

Sitting pretty in her tower, Templar Bronze reviewing data imagines 30-gallon casks of new French oak, each filled with juice crushed from Cabernet grapes soon to be picked. Her mind's eye sees another hundred casks filled with Pinot. The growing season has been splendid. Her grapes are gem-like: purple, lustrous, sugar-rich. Shortly, the Mexicans will prove their prowess. Templar will have them harvest each varietal separately. Crush will occur promptly and the mash pumped into five-hundred-gallon stainless steel holding tanks whose shipment from Earth attracted no meager comment when Templar requisitioned them several Mars-years ago. Fermentation will continue for ninety Mars-days, give or take, then cellar workers will transfer the juice to those beautiful new casks. She assumes the Head Director will lend her Mexicans for this job, as well as to roll filled casks into the cellar and lift them onto racks. Then she will have to wait, they all will have to wait, while the Cabernet and the Pinot age. Two years on Earth is a bit more than one Martian year – eighty more Mars-days, roughly, at which point they will bottle the wine. Again, Roscoe's Mexicans – how many will she need?

Templar is about to step onto the observation deck when a chime rings. She touches a sensor on her wristlet and Roscoe Gold's etiquette droid manifests.

"Good morning, Dr. Bronze," performing a deep, slow bow. "His Magnificence has instructed me to report that He cannot entertain your requests at this time. However ..." – and here the grinning droid raises its right hand in a gesture Templar recognizes as an ancient salute that, if she is not mistaken, is Roman in origin – "His Magnificence further enjoins me to request your attendance at a meeting of utmost significance."

Is it possible the droid has taught itself this grand apostrophe? They are scripted to synthesize and extrapolate, yet the leap from "Head Director" to "His Magnificence" seems a bit, well, directed.

"When is this meeting to occur?" says Templar.

"Immediately upon your arrival at Center Atrium."

"I see."

"His Magnificence expects you imminently. Commander Silver also will be present."

"Very well." Templar touches a sensor and the droid disappears. She descends from her tower and summons a hoverpod, enfolds her slender splendor into its womb-like comfort and says "Center Atrium." No Ludwig Von this time, no personalized images skimming along corridor walls. Templar switches off the sound system and travels at top speed. A minute later, the windscreen retracts and she alights on the rhodium roof.

Inside, the chimps are raising a racket. Templar is sure she sees them copulating in the rigging. Conducted by the droid, she passes quickly through the Outer Sanctum and wends her way through the rainforest.

At the cavemouth, the voice of Roscoe Gold says, "Come right in, Dr. Bronze."

Templar is tempted; it is all she can do not to answer, "Yes, Your Magnificence." The etiquette droid having withdrawn, she enters the Inner Sanctum alone and there finds Roscoe Gold and Paladin Silver ensconced.

"Heigh-ho," she says.

"Heigh-ho," the men say in turn.

"Have a seat, Dr. Bronze," says Roscoe, waving her to the orange chair. "I appreciate your prompt appearance. An urgent matter tasks us. Your knowledge and insight are integral to deciding our course of action."

Paladin rolls his eyes. "No need to soft-soap the lady, Roscoe. We really have just one option."

"So might it seem to you and me, Commander, yet Dr. Bronze may well imagine something better. We have sampled before now her matchless perspicacity and innovative intelligence, several examples of which have been fairly astounding. Need I mention full-dome dispersion of farmyard ambience in ES5? Once we achieved proper pitch and saturation, sheep and cows at last became country strong. I shall not trifle with your sense of gratitude by pretending to remind you of Templar's cloaking protocols – inspired work, without which a missile from a confused planetary defense system might well have destroyed your Earthshuttle long ago. Outstanding as they are, these achievements pale in comparison to Dr. Bronze's formulae for photon acceleration – to say nothing of the quantum algorithm for matter-to-energy conversion she deduced to exploit it. Thus did a sojourn of six months dwindle to a matter of days – especially convenient to these sorties you fly to our native planet."

"And shall presently fly again." Paladin's feet are canted on the table, his legs crossed at the ankles. No accelerator boots today, just standard-issue gelmocs, which the table easily supports.

"What have we left behind?" says Templar.

"Ah, you see, Commander, you see? Dr. Bronze anticipates us yet again."

Paladin snorts. "It's hardly rocket science, is it, to infer unfinished business Earth-side when I mention having to fly back."

"In the particular sense of something left behind?" says Templar, taking the blue chair. "Is that really it?"

"Indeed it is, Dr. Bronze. You should trust your intuition, which is perfect."

Templar sighs; for what her intuition tells her is that they are talking about Mexicans, *still* talking about Mexicans, despite the scores of men, women, and children that Paladin Silver and his expropriation crews have shanghaied to Mars. "Roscoe, really. You must have a thousand men running around with shovels."

"In fact, there are one thousand and forty-two."

"And have they found gold?"

"In a word, no. And yet I am undeterred."

"It must seem strange. In Mexico, I mean, that entire villages are disappearing."

"We haven't been raiding pueblos," says Paladin. "Infectious disease is legion in permanent settlements. Standing water, open sewers, cesspools – the whole horrible parade of cholera, malaria, and dysentery. The people we've picked up belonged to nomadic groups."

"Do I have to say again that none of this is legal?"

"Tut tut, Dr. Bronze. I thought we had mooted matters of legality. You yourself concede that these people are better off on Mars."

"They eat better, yes, and the children are getting some education. They are safer. They have regular beds and clean bathrooms. Still, we oblige them to work."

"In exchange for the care we take of them! Proud as they are, I daresay they would not have it otherwise." He winks at her, also at Paladin. "These are a proud people."

"In spades," says Paladin. "Stunted, but proud."

"It is also true that we haven't asked them if they wish to remain here," says Templar.

"What, give them the option of returning to Mexico?" The Head Director is incredulous. "To Sonora's scrubland and pebbly piedmont? To fouled rivers and ruined cities? Chihuahua's desert dust? Whatever for?"

"I suppose it isn't worth explaining, now that they're here." She relaxes into the backrest. She does not put up her feet. "My contingent, at any rate, seems accepting. They seem to like the vineyard."

"And why should they not? Rain does not wet them, mosquitoes do not vex them. During working hours the VirtuSun may be de-tensified. What, my dear Dr. Bronze, is there not to like?"

"Not to put too fine a point on it, Roscoe, but they are essentially slaves."

"Are they?" Roscoe's tone says he truly is surprised. "Well, well. And what were they in Mexico?"

"The next thing to corpses," says Paladin. "But see here, this debate is off point."

"Indeed it is. Thank you, Commander. Dr. Bronze, the matter at hand does concern Mexicans – five Mexicans, to be precise, whom we wanted very much to welcome to Mars and yet, somehow, managed to miss. We rounded up – um, better to say we organized transport for a nomadic remnant to which these five belonged, then accomplished removal at a time when said fellows were absent. As a result, they remain at-large."

Templar does not require clairvoyance to infer that these men have perpetrated raids that have caused more than one environmental disaster. "If they are terrorists," she says, "why do we not incinerate them?"

"Hear, hear," says Paladin. "Amen to that. Acquire coordinates on the bastardos, triangulate their positions, and laser-away. Makes more sense than having me sojourn to Earth just to roll them up."

Roscoe Gold taps his fingernails on an arm of his yellow chair. "Incinerating terrorists from low-Earth orbit, however elegant to our sensibilities, tends to excite anger in the poor world. In killing these five, we might create five thousand new desperadoes. Having them merely disappear, however – well, who is to say, in that case, what has become of them?"

"Plausible deniability," says Templar Bronze.

"We have good reason to think it would not come to that. We've run simulations – I won't take you through them, the step by step is altogether tedious – and these confirm that a person or persons, even a group as large as a dozen, can vanish without a trace. Deserts and mountains, you see. Remote areas policed by indigenous scavengers. Mexicans are used to such mishaps – even expect them, to the point that they hardly notice. Oh, a few Nosey Parkers might ask a question or two, you know the sort of thing – *Where were they going? When were they last seen?* Still, it's even odds no one will realize these men have gone missing."

Roscoe snaps his fingers. Templar is expecting a service droid but instead the tile wall slides into the floor and a large telescreen lights up. Images of the Sierra Madre Occidental unfold as soundlessly as a dream.

"You've updated your system," says Paladin. "I like it."

"Yes, it's quite lovely – saves me the effort of leaving my chair."

As seen from the sky, Mexico is tan and green and brown and blue. Its landscape is alternately flat and rolling, smooth and corrugated, vast, open, implicitly merciless, visibly unpeopled. Steep slopes dense with pine forest form barrancas that plunge a thousand feet into darkness. Wind-carved precipices glimmer granite-gray and lavender under a staring sun. Broken desert, ragtag with prickly pear and agave, spreads toward every horizon, at the limit of which saguaro and mesquite colonize foothills of distant mountains. Wildflowers of purple and yellow cannot dispel the emptiness Templar sees in these perspectives and removes. Unbridgeable canyons, rugged piedmonts, desolate heights. A trackless valley floor, cluttered and refractory, straggles for miles until, again, mountains immemorially old occlude the horizon. Austere vistas succeed one another in slow dissolves.

Mexico, Templar sees, is as lonely as Mars without an Earth-Station.

"To live surrounded by nothing," she says. "To feel it become part of you." Roscoe and Paladin look at her. Templar knows they cannot imagine living in a place that gives no comfort. "What happens when the nothingness you see all around comes to seem like the only outcome of every thought?" Neither Initiate nor Adept answers. "These are solitary people. Wary. Careful. They expect hardship. They entertain little hope."

"Not to put too fine a point on it," says Paladin.

"My dear Dr. Bronze, if I did not know you as I do, I would fear you were succumbing to melancholy."

Templar smiles. "I am trying to achieve a meeting of minds. To feel as perhaps they feel."

"What's the point of that?"

"Our estimable colleague aspires, Commander, to sympathize with our working guests."

"Very nice of her," says Paladin. "Really, it's quite thoughtful. I'm not sure what difference it will make." He swings his feet off the table. "Any chance a fellow can get a pot of tea?"

"Tea!" Roscoe shouts and a service droid trundles in with a stainless steel samovar and three cup-and-saucer set-ups on its non-slip tray. Instead of pastries there are chocolates on doilies. Roscoe plucks a chunky one and pops it into his mouth. "Ah, caramel," he says, and chews. They fill their cups and sip. Roscoe eats another chocolate, a dark square. "These men are known provocateurs. If they disappear, any kind of misadventure might be blamed. We have operatives in-country. To start a rumor is child's play. In fact – " Roscoe leans toward his colleagues and lowers his voice. " – a far-reaching plan has enabled us to embed such an operative among these very men. Omar the Turk, he calls himself. Quite a bizarre alias, as he isn't a Turk at all. He is, however, a scoundrel. Smuggler, bootlegger, bit of a thief, that sort of thing. Infamous throughout the Badlands for fomenting dread and exploiting human veniality. All in all, quite a serviceable character. And not a Turk, as noted, but Italian by birth – although anyone who springs from that troubled and illustrious peninsula is genetically mixed. Never purely one sort or another. And that is all we know of him. His origins, his true name, how he washed up in Mexico are facts lost to history. And they do not matter. What matters is his work on our behalf. You may rest assured. Omar will lead us to this terrorist band or he will lead them to a place for easy capture. Afterward, he will gin-up a story about their vanishing."

Templar sets her cup on its saucer. Bone china clicks against itself like something about to break. She places cup and saucer on the table, leaning forward to do so, and continues this motion by standing. "Gentlemen, the tenor of this discussion is dismaying. Is it an echo I hear? Do the mendacities of our late, craven politicians haunt us? I thought we had evolved beyond subterfuge and expedient lies."

"Come off it, Templar. You were as ready as I to have the bastardos lasered."

"My dear Dr. Bronze, *realpolitik* is never out of style. These raids in Sonora must end. The men of whom we speak are responsible for disrupting six waste processing sites and fomenting a like number of toxic clouds. Surely you appreciate the simplicity of our solution, to say nothing of its prudence – to say nothing of its necessity! To have their blood on our hands is hardly preferable."

"True. Killing them outright, however, would be more honest."

"Would it? Well, well."

"I'm sure honesty has little to do with it."

"Precious little, I'm sure," says Templar.

"Are you seriously advocating assassination?"

Templar gasps. It is not what she meant.

"Dr. Bronze, do not distress yourself. You see how our Mexicans fare on Mars. Once Commander Silver swoops in and collects these five, what is the worst that can happen? Oh, yes, yes, a few dozen mestizos who happen to be paying attention might get a wrong idea of what has become of them. What of it? Omar is on the ground. He will squelch inconveniently accurate reports and purvey a fiction congenial to his interests, and ours. Meanwhile, we shall outfit our five with Marsuits and pickaxes, give them good beds and three nutritious meals a day, and that will be the end of it."

"Now, that can't be right," says Paladin. "This gang of five will have been cashiered but others will nip up to the mark. We would have to transport the entire population to end the raids for good."

"We do not have work for the entire population," says Templar.

"Nor beds," says Roscoe, "to say nothing of food." He nods. "No, it won't do. We must take our chances. Let us bring in Commander Silver's gang of five and watch what develops."

Paladin nods. Templar Bronze shakes her head. She recognizes in this approach a disingenuous hypocrisy of the sort that put paid to elective government half a century ago. True, they have no one to answer to now. No one cares what must be done to preserve the safety and comfort of the Enhanced World. In bygone times it was the pursuit of oil that vouchsafed nations carte blanche in how their martial proxies quelled poor-world rebellions. For decades, Discipline & Punish brought overwhelming force to bear. Now it is a matter of securing radioactive waste – that, and maintaining the CyberEmpyrean that feeds the SmartBots their wills and their ways.

In the Outer Sanctum, screeching chimps riot in the rigging.

Within the Head Director's cave, Initiates and Adept sit wordlessly amid echoes, remembering a world with air.

? ? ? ? ?

When he remembers not to forget, Melmoth scans a database for Ameurope History, Early 20th Century, and retrieves the entry for *R.M.S. Titanic.* He finds two dozen mellifluous paragraphs about the construction of the ship's hull and the launch of its superstructure into the River Lagan on twenty-two tons of train oil, tallow, and soap; its fitting-out with oak and mahogany woodwork, linoleum tile, and stained glass; its displacement and top speed and sixteen watertight compartments; its two reciprocating steam engines, one turbine engine, three propellers; its gymnasium, libraries, verandahs, smoking rooms, lounges, squash court, Turkish baths, reading rooms, post office, telephones, elevators, crystal chandeliers, gilded sconces, staircases, bronze cherubs holding lamps aloft, and so forth – all by way of preface to an account of its maiden voyage, which concludes with a paragraph Melmoth has to view on the windowall because he cannot believe it, reading behind closed eyes.

The paragraph tells him that on the moonless night of April 14, 1912, *Titanic* hit an iceberg – "a glancing blow," it says – and that this collision caused steel plates to buckle and rivets to break along some 300 feet of the ship's starboard side, through which wound seawater rushed, flooding the six forward compartments. *Yes, yes,* Melmoth thinks, *everyone knows this.* Pumps were deployed, worked at first, were eventually overwhelmed; and some minutes after two o'clock on the morning of April 15, *Titanic* slipped beneath the glass-still North Atlantic and sank 12,500 feet to the silt bottom of an ink-black sea. *Everyone knows that.* Melmoth remembers having been taught as much 125 years ago in a low-slung, brick and mortar grammar school in suburban New Jersey. *Happily,* the paragraph concludes, *all 2223 passengers and crew evacuated to lifeboats, which drifted in proximity on calm water for almost two hours until rescued by* R.M.S. Carpathia. *The survivors arrived safely in New York three days later.*

"No, no, no," says Melmoth. Only the windowall can hear him. Raquel is out, burning through pleasure credits. Jenna lies in Melmoth's private quarters, feigning sleep. Floyd is sequestered wherever Raquel hides him.

Screen off. The windowall turns clear and music rises. An ancient bit of business by Bach, performed on a cello by Yo-Yo Ma. Also still alive, devoted to his instrument, expressing though modulated sonorities of vibrating strings all he has to express. Lucky fellow. Melmoth himself has no way to show what he feels. Words fail him. He is music-stupid. He cannot draw a straight line, or a curved one, either. His attempts at dance display an awkwardness insulting to human dignity. His singing voice is an adenoidal atrocity too repellent to call pigs. No matter. Melmoth self-comforts with Jenna, enjoys AstroGolf unseriously, pretends to pilot his air-pod. He has Candi in the grillroom, oldenflicks unspooling on demand. In case of deep boredom he can watch sexolympics, viewable at all hours of day and night. He suspects the expert fornicators are really Sex-Bots.

The database is wrong. He knows this. He does not know who is responsible. An oldentime fictionalist? An enhanced misinformationalist? A barefaced liar? A handful of falsehoods grafted onto history have changed a tragedy into an accident. *Terrible smash-up, too bad, lucky just the ship was lost.* It is not just distortion; it is a lie. Everyone knows *Titanic* was short of lifeboats. Everyone knows not all the lifeboats were filled. *Carpathia* took the survivors on board and, yes, carried them to New York, but Melmoth is sure in the same way he is sure of his name that there were not 2223 of these. Survivors. What there mostly were, were fatalities. Deaths. Which no one mentions anymore because almost no one dies.

In the elevator, Melmoth submits to a retinal scan. *Storage*, and the circular compartment begins its fall. The plummet is actually breathtaking; Melmoth would swear he feels wind in his hair as air is sucked from his lungs. After a few seconds the descent slows, and a moment later the elevator gentles to rest. At their locker, he dials the code and opens the door, flips an oldstyle light switch and steps inside.

His ancient dumbclubs, treacherous in his hands during a lifetime of torturegolf, stand in a donkeybag. Melmoth suspects a dozen stupidballs still hide in one of its zippered pockets. His collection of girlie magazines, still so-called a hundred years ago, are packed sardine-tight inside plastic bins. Most valuable to Melmoth are his United States coins, encapsulated in flat, snap-seal plastic sleeves and filed upright in rows inside a black iron box. Some of these coins were minted 250 years ago and all of them are worthless. Hard currency having been phased out shortly before Ameurope unification, money has no meaning. Halfers have no idea what coins are, can imagine neither rhyme nor reason for toting such dead weight in pockets their tunics do not have. Melmoth has considered breaking a fifty-dollar gold piece out of its plastic and wearing it as jewelry. He could have it ringed with palladium for attachment to a palladium chain, which he would wear around his neck so that the gold piece rested on his sternum, thereby complementing the golden O embroidered left-chest on all his garments.

Raquel does not hoard. The minute she decides she no longer needs a thing is the minute she throws it away. And yet, two dozen of her former dresses hang here, color-coordinated purses crowded onto a shelf above, matching shoes ranged underneath. Raquel has not worn these ensembles in sixty or seventy years; given their official nightblue flightsuits, tunics, and blouses, she will never wear them again. Maybe that's why she keeps the stuff, museum-style – because it has no place in the world that is.

Melmoth surveys the shelves. Below his books, a dozen manual typewriters sit snugly under microfiber dust covers. Eighty or ninety years ago, when these machines were already fifty years obsolete, Melmoth thought he was collecting them. Then he realized how much space they hogged. For a while, good soldier, he actually used to type-write; that is, to write by typing. What did Melmoth write? Oh, nothing, really – *Today I understood that I am invisible. If I were to melt into air, my vanishing would merely make my virtual condition a matter of fact.* Inanities, drivel, trivial stuff, all tending to depict him as pitiable and absurd. A waste of time but as it turned out he had plenty of that. He liked feeling the character slugs fixing black letters onto bonded paper in response to his fingers' pressing the keys. So here we have five Olympia SM-9s, each with a different typeface; a Hermes 3000 in that model's peculiar seafoam green; an Olivetti Studio 44. These smooth beauties all are 1960s vintage, the era of Melmoth's original birth. Among his older machines are a gloss-black Underwood Champion, 1938; a two-tone gray Royal Quiet De Luxe, 1941; a Royal ultra-portable, circa 1930. Each one is in working condition and, at this point for Melmoth, each is more artifact than tool. The last typewriter he bought, an Olivetti Linea 98, arrived via parcel post in its original cardboard and Styrofoam packaging in 2009, more than ten years after it was made. Steel and iron, some high-density plastic, strictly desktop, the Linea 98 was the last serious, high-quality typewriter ever built and as heavy as a car. Well, not really; but pretty damn heavy all the same. A couple dozen inky nylon ribbons also are here somewhere, plastic-sealed, probably in a drawer of the black metal filing cabinet that stands under the lowest shelf. Melmoth doesn't look. He is finished forever with all such retro nonsense.

He is searching for a reliable source. Most of his surviving books are novels, alas. He loved these stories long ago and might love them again, if he could flog himself into re-reading. *An American Tragedy* is here, also *The Great Gatsby*, and Melmoth might tote a few up to penthouse level except Raquel hates clutter. Would these books mean anything now? Read in 2094, *1984* might seem like a dark farce, stark raving mad. *Lolita* might read like an anthropological narrative of an extinct subspecies written by the last of its kind. And what, Melmoth wonders, would anyone make of *The Grapes of Wrath*?

But here is something: *Brave New World*. He could smuggle it into his private quarters. Except he does not want Jenna getting interested – not that she can read or would feel an urge to if she could, but her scripts prompt her to curry enthusiasm for whatever Melmoth does. Which means she will ask questions. Melmoth does not want Jenna to ask questions. He does not want to answer questions, especially about novels his PAC has not read and would not understand even if he read them to her, which he is not about to do. And anyway, he is not interested in novels at the moment; he is interested in a reference book or a volume of narrative history that includes an account of *Titanic*. The ship, not the movie. Problem is, Melmoth sent his desk references and encyclopedias and dictionaries to the pulping bin ninety years ago. Such stuff had been digitized for viewing on his computer, when he still needed a piece of hardware separate from his brain. It was commonsense to discard the tomes, which took up so much space and gathered so much dust and so often went unread.

And, so, now, Melmoth does not have anything like the kind of book he needs: a comprehensive history or compendium that confirms what he himself remembers – that *Titanic* sank with many of her lifeboats far from filled, two or three people in some of them, with the result that many, many people perished in the icy ocean on that awful night. Melmoth is sure that fatalities outnumbered survivors two to one. More than 1500 people died, he *knows* this. How dare they, it, the database, foist a fairytale on him.

Melmoth fingers *Brave New World* from the shelf.

The book's leather binding is as sleek and gleaming as it was 100 years ago, glossy black with gold inlay to accentuate title and author. Melmoth has read it six or seven times and remembers it pretty well, even without his microchip. Human embryos gestated in beakers and engineered for intelligence. Children conditioned by platitudes repeated thousands of times while they sleep. Hypno-suggestion, he thinks it was called: designed to save people from ambition, thereby negating doubt, self-reflection, and discontent, thereby freeing them to accept and even to love their predetermined roles. *Soma* holidays. Pneumatic females. *"But you don't think I'm too plump, do you?"* The protagonist does not fit the scheme. Bernard Marx. Something wrong in his gestation, the rumor runs; a bit of conditioning that failed to take. No reason is ever pinned down because the truth is as simple as beans: the fellow is human in the old way. Like the so-called savage, John, who is doomed.

Heavyweight paper with a creamy, French-vanilla hue. Pages gilt with gold. Its hand-sewn binding is intact down to the gold satin ribbon page marker. Archival storage: one more thing to love about their brave new world of 2094.

Melmoth tucks the book under his arm. Sure, he'll read it again. Why not? It will earn him nothing in pleasure credits but with all the AstroGolf he plays, he always has plenty. Really, it does not matter, what he does or does not do. Nothing depends on his actions, no one relies on his skills – a perfect dispensation, because Melmoth has no skills. He isn't good, really, at anything, or for anything, either; and in his next thought understands that his uselessness also is irrelevant.

Superfluous: he is. Not even his awareness of this fact means anything, even to him.

Traveling east across mesquite grassland, they allow the Turk a horse, a canteen of freshwater, a poncho of close-woven hemp. He rides between Carlos and Javier, a rope looped around his waist, its other end knotted to the horn of Carlos's saddle. The Turk carries neither rifle nor knife, packs no revolver, has no hatchet or axe. Carlos eyes him from behind. Enrique and Miguel ride two abreast in front. Pacho brings up the rear, leading three pack horses. These carry tents and cookware, sacks of rice and beans, salted fish wrapped in cloth and layered inside saddlebags. One horse only is bitted to the reins in Pacho's hand. The others are skittish without live weight, hooves clattering over scrubland east of Esperanza.

To arrive in Ciudad de México as soon as may be is their hope. Enrique Ramos has faith in this plan because he can imagine no other. His wife is not where he has known her to be, yet to know where she is seems impossible. He has listened, they all have listened, to a story that seems both too strange to be true and likely to be true because it is so strange. Were the Turk's purpose merely to lure them into the Sierra Madre, there to betray them, would he fashion a tale that invites disbelief? Better to say that Federales loaded everyone into trucks for transport to Veracruz or Tabasco State, there to labor at resorts still open to El Norte tourists. Fortifications and armed patrols set to ward off banditos would have made rescue seem a great impossible deed, irresistible to brave men. He might have said the people themselves decamped – that they had heard a warning on the night wind, read an omen in the stars, and set off for Monte Alban or El Tajin or Chichén Itzá to pay fealty to vanished gods. So many possible lies, so easy to tell – even that the Tarahumara ran down from the mountains and traveled as far as Sonora, and so discovered the encampment by the Sea of Cortés; and by dint of cunning and surprise were able to capture the people and lead them off as slaves – or as food, the Turk might have claimed, had he wanted to hurry them on.

Holding his canteen under one arm, Enrique unscrews its metal cap. His other hand holds the reins. A mouthful of water is warm on his tongue, cool in his throat. He drinks again. As he lowers the canteen, his eyes cover the horizon. The Sierra Madre appears as green and gray planes rising and receding to snow-capped peaks. Its ridges extend north and south and seem very close. Enrique knows this nearness is apparent only, a trick of dry air and clear light. They will ride for days before they enter Cañón del Cobre. He clamps the canteen under an arm as his fingers find the cap, attached by a short chain to the stainless steel neck. He sets it in place and, feeling the grooves engage, screws it down.

They cross a sun-grayed highway, its asphalt fissured. No vehicle approaches, none is visible at any distance they can see. No sound reaches them through heat and emptiness. All around, dusty fields lie fallow. Once made fruitful by irrigation, the land has returned to desert. A few old roads remain, narrow and unpaved, their hardpan beaten as smooth as glass. At midday, these bleached surfaces are silver in the sun.

Burning light. Hot, still air.

For many miles the men are silent. Until the mountains, their course is plain. Once inside the Sierra Madre, they will make hard ascents to high altitudes. Behind them is sea-damp and salt air, an abandoned campsite, hardpacked sand, sombreros floating on waves. They have taken everything of use and all they can carry. It is as if the encampment by the Sea of Cortés has not existed, as if they have not had there something like a life. Enrique has thought of it as meager and temporary, a makeshift haven. Its failure to protect vulnerable people marks it as a false refuge – a kind of cowardly hiding that has betrayed Alma and the others into an effortless capture.

Their route becomes rougher, the ground rocky and broken. Of water they have seen no sign.

The Turk says, "Some hours north is a lake many call Agua Caliente."

"That is unpromising," says Miguel. "Have you not heard-tell of a lake known to everyone was Agua Dulce?" He calls back over his shoulder, speaking loudly.

"Truly, no," says the Turk. "And yet I have no doubt one exists. Not in Mexico. But somewhere."

Carlos jerks the rope. The Turk grabs his pommel to prevent a fall. "We are not somewhere, we are here."

"This one cannot be satisfied until he breaks my neck."

"Were that my purpose, you would be dead already. I have given my word to see this journey to its end. From me you have nothing to fear."

"You are not to be trusted."

"Cretin. It is no wonder you are outcast."

"And yet, without me you cannot save your women."

Carlos snaps the rope, a maneuver the Turk has anticipated. He grabs it with a darting hand and pulls hard across his body, gaining several feet before Carlos pulls back. Each end has always been tied down; who holds more slack is merely an idea. As the Turk winds rope around his pommel, Carlos retakes half the length the Turk has gained. A second later, the rope is taut between them. Their horses feel this tension and repair their pace. This adjustment brings Carlos and the Turk closer. The rope sags.

Carlos takes up slack. Again, their horses alter their gait. Now they are riding side by side.

"Stop this nonsense," the Turk says. "Do you not understand our danger?"

Carlos can smell his breath, its vegetable rot and odor of decaying fish. Likely his own breath is equally foul. "Our danger, however great you believe it, is not of our making."

"You must live in it, whoever has made it."

"I will teach them to live in it."

"Who are they?"

"The puppets who have betrayed México, together with their masters in El Norte."

They exchange these words rapidly in low, fevered bursts, not whispering, neither concerned with being overheard nor intending it.

The Turk laughs. "And how do you hope to school these creatures, my friend? Will they welcome you to their haciendas and sit quietly as you take them to task? Or will you drive them into the desert to teach a lesson about heat and dust? At gunpoint, eh? All of them manacled together, a long line of fat politicians and their fat wives, naked perhaps, stripped? Who strips them? You? Perhaps you envision also a crack whip and yourself lashing fat red asses."

Carlos has imagined none of this. The Turk's words stupefy him.

"A lovely dream, my friend. It is perfectly just. You know, of course, it can never be."

Carlos knows. Mexican politicos and El Norte bosses are beyond his reach. He can assert resistance only in guerrilla attacks. *Pinpricks.* Dearly would he love to punish traitors. Vengeance always is difficult; he is only one man. Yet he might sometime find a way.

"I do not know what will be," unwinding rope by several turns. "I know only my purpose: to save my family. And that we must travel very far before I may accomplish that deed."

Stretched across a horizon shimmering behind miles of superheated air, green and gray mountains waver against a blue sky. To Carlos, the Sierra Madre appears as a dark hand, waving him onward.

On furlough stateside, Ibn al Mohammed peers through plate glass at emporia and stadia, venues and displays. Below their hovering craft, on a green field bathed in streaming daylight, naked superhumans copulate in company. Three hundred meters long, two hundred meters wide, neither lined nor marked, the field is lush with grass and flesh. Around it, cantilevered grandstands rise. In each seat is a person. Many wear dark blue, some wear green, most wear red, here and there are sprinkled innocents attired in white. One hundred thousand and more look on as expert fornicators perform humankind's most intimate acts, some of which God forbids.

Bird's-eye magnification increases tenfold. Ibn al Mohammed turns away.

"Come come now. Do you desire that with me?"

Truly, its voice is like singing. Ibn al Mohammed wonders how it would be. If he consented, would the droid unlock the electromanacles that hold him to his seat? Would it enter another code to recline his flightchair and expand it to bed size? Nothing seems beyond them: every accommodation offered, all gratification possible, each wish granted at a word. He has only to ask.

Its touch, he reminds himself, is death. Never will he allow it to pollute his body, God's temple in small, no matter the enticements it whispers with honeyed voice and semblance of pulchritude.

Satan's lures are potent in Satan's world.

He has not asked to be here. Furlough stateside was granted without request, a transport badge issued and hung about his neck without his consent. Of the others he believes the same is true: they suffer as he suffers, pray as he prays, and with chastened hearts will this craft to fall from the sky and kill Infidels in their concupiscence. A riot of flesh. A vision of Hell. Ibn al Mohammed half-believes the ground will gape, all sinners plunge into a flaming pit. Despite his thoughts, the craft hovers at a comfortable distance while two hundred human pairs rut like beasts on the field below. Sun-swept skin shines. Giant videoscreens erected along the arena's upper rim magnify the spectacle. Amplified, its cacophony assails the ears.

"Sexolympics freestyle," says the droid. "You like?"

Ibn al Mohammed closes his eyes, shakes his head.

"Who's a party-pooper?" it says.

This droid speaks to him only. He cannot hear what other droids say. Captive behind glass, each detainee is isolate. To converse, the men would have to shout. No one has forbidden this, nothing prevents it, yet they do not shout. A second droid, configured as male, prepares spiced lamb kabobs and saffron rice. The female brews tea, hot and strong. It sets out plate, cup, and saucer. It enters a code and the manacles release, freeing his hands. No implements; he must eat with his fingers. Ibn al Mohammed requests a fork, a knife.

"Silly you," says the female droid.

"Please," he says. "To use one's fingers is unsanitary. If you would be so kind."

"Ha-ha!" says the female and the male joins in. "Ha-ha!" they say together. "Ha-ha!"

"Fool us once," says the female, "shame on you."

"Fool us twice?" says the male – a question?

"Ha-ha!" they glee. "*Not a fucking chance!* Ha-ha! Ha-ha!"

He wonders if they will fornicate in his sight. They are machines; is it forbidden to watch? The frenzy that rages below surely is sin – a rash of sin grievously repeating. Ibn al Mohammed averts his eyes to his food. Fingertips touch a lamb morsel, lift it to his lips. Rice he nabs and, head tilted, sifts into his mouth. Almost a century ago, two silver airplanes exploded into a pair of ugly towers. Fewer than three thousand Infidels died, a paltry number compared to the killings that later swept the desert clean, razed villages and towns, finally emptied cities where formerly muezzins called the faithful in their millions to prayer. The Great Satan now needs no airplanes. It has constructed countless crystal towers many times as tall. And yet they insist he feed himself like a heathen.

Ibn al Mohammed does not allow himself to imagine the droid's artificial vagina, the pleasure it might impart. He tasks himself with denial, commits himself to remain unwilling by force of will. He will will himself not to desire; willfully will not want; will not do it. He will not. Refuses.

☞$$$$

In the terraced vineyards of EarthStation 3, grape harvest is in full career. Surveying the work, Templar Bronze is delighted by how her pickers comb the rows. Delighted, surprised ... and troubled. Can they really work so quickly? Yes, they are adept, even skilled, but .... Peering from the observation deck, Templar is disturbed by an aura of carelessness. She is sure she sees them grabbing grapes by the cluster and rudely severing the stem, then dropping – yes, *dropping* – the fruit into a basket at their feet, then kicking the basket along to repeat this abuse at another vine.

It is not what they have been taught. It is not for such crude technique that Paladin Silver and his cohort have sojourned such great distances and gone to so much trouble.

Templar enters the control room. She returns to the observation deck a moment later and sets the binoculars to her eyes. She sweeps the vineyard, finds a clear line of sight, focuses. Her field of vision fills with a woman's hands inside standard issue rubber gloves. One hand wields the sharp knife with its short, curved blade. Templar watches the woman seize cluster after cluster, cut each stem and, sure enough, drop it without looking into a basket on the ground.

Inside the tower again, Templar leaves the binoculars at her console, steps into the elevator, descends. At ground level the doors slide open and she alights, takes a quick look around and strides into the vineyard. It takes some hunting, what with the vines standing taller than the Mexicans, and after a few minutes Templar is beginning to perspire. It is not a sensation to which she is accustomed and she finds it unpleasant. Something about salty, slightly slick water smearing her skin feels unhealthy. And her outfit is all wrong. The form-fitting white unisuit with bronze chevrons on both shoulders and bronze piping along its seams is smashing in interior environments but out here it is getting smudged.

When Templar finds her, the woman is kicking her basket along the ground. It is overloaded; three clusters fall off. Grapes roll in dirt.

It is a disaster worse than droids. The Mexicans are ruining her wine.

"Cease! Desist!" Templar cries, thinking in the same instant that this woman likely understands only mestizo Spanish. This thought encourages her to shout, "You clumsy cow! What are you doing?"

The woman turns and glares. Templar would swear that her opposite's eyes fill with blood. The pruning knife she seems to brandish, stiletto-like. The murderous look lasts only a moment, then the woman returns to her work.

Ten feet away, Dr. Bronze is nonplussed. Perhaps the woman has not understood, after all. Or is she merely impudent? In either case, it won't do. She has to make this creature understand that she is not to drop grapes; that no grapes are to touch dirt; that the Cabernet Franc, Pinot Noir, and Cabernet Sauvignon must be handled gently, cleanly, to the end of achieving the immediate goal of her, Templar's, life.

While Templar is calling in SmartBot assistance, a child scampers up with a basket. This, it drops at the woman's feet. The boy is about three feet tall. His hair is long and straight and pure black, his skin brown. His smile, which catches Templar by surprise, shows small, yellow teeth and large eyes. His irises also are black. "Hola!" the boy cries, then snatches up the laden basket, first retrieving the grapes that have fallen off. He piles these on top and carries the basket away. Despite his size, the load seems trivial to him. At the end of the vine row, he dumps the grapes onto a flatbed trailer. Before Templar can scold him, the boy puts the empty basket under his arm and runs off.

So small, watching him go. She will have calcium supplements added to their meals. Their small teeth, dentists in ES1 can whiten.

A SmartBot arrives on two legs. On vineyard terrain, its halting, rocking steps suggest an unreformed drunkard. Templar hopes it will not fall over; she dislikes having to lift them back to their feet. This one is comically portly, with a pear-shaped torso balanced atop stout thighs. The latter taper toward spindly shins that end, as Templar can see thanks to its puddled socks, at stork-like ankles. Its feet are absurdly small. "Spanish translation," she tells it, and indicates the woman, who continues to ignore Templar's presence.

The Bot establishes itself between Templar and the human female its scan registers as Unknown and Disgruntled.

"Tell her I must speak to her," says Templar.

"Will-do." Leaning toward the woman, the Bot raises a hand and waves. "Por favor, amable señora," it says. The woman looks up. "Esta distinguida persona femenina desea hablar con usted."

The woman nods and steps forward.

"What is your name?" Templar says. The Bot translates.

The woman says, "Mi nombre es Alma Ramos."

"She says her name is Alma Ramos," sounding pleased with itself.

"Yes, yes," says Templar. "I understand that. Ask her how she finds her situation here."

"In this vineyard, you mean?"

"In this vineyard, yes. At this EarthStation. On Mars."

"That's rather a lot," says the Bot; then, to the woman, "Como te va?"

The woman, Alma, not smiling, shows them her teeth. Her words come out like gunfire without pause or seeming end.

"What is she saying?"

"She is describing in detail – quite rapidly, I might add – a terrible wrong – no, an unforgivable ... well, it seems it was, and is, both terrible and unforgivable ... soldiers in white metal ... now, that can't be correct, she says they wore white metal serapes when you and I know that Earth Troopers are equipped with body armor ... forced her with her friends and all the children into a great ship. She is demanding to know exactly where she is – that is to say, where we all are – and when she and these others will be allowed to leave this cave and see the Sun and breathe fresh air and bathe once more in the sea. She is unhappy to be here and dislikes being kept inside, where it is not a real Sun, *no es un sol real*, as she says, and wants someone who is able to steer the great ship to return her and her people to Mexico." The SmartBot pauses.

"Well?" says Templar. "What else?"

"Well," with a smug grin, "she wants to know how much she will be paid."

"Paid?"

"Correct. She has repeated, 'Cuántos dólares por este trabajo?' thrice."

Templar folds her arms across her chest. "She believes she is due wages, does she?"

"It seems most definitely so."

"And expects payment in dollars, no less. As if that monetary unit still exits."

"Indeed. Alma is laughably out of date."

Templar ponders. Materials engineers might fabricate a plausible forgery of oldentime American paper money, what used to be called "cold hard cash." Although now she thinks of it, Templar is sure that phrase referred to coins. They would need mocked-up stores for the Mexicans to visit. Research will be necessary, Templar thinks, if she is to understand what these people think they might want to buy.

She feels herself making a face. Templar cannot see herself but thinks her expression must be a mix of amusement and disgust. *Fancy combo, that*, she can hear Roscoe saying. Or rather, imagine him saying; Templar is not Implanted. Her next thought, wholly her own: What was so wonderful about Mexico, that this woman wants to return?

She asks this question in congenial terms and the Bot translates.

"En México, éramos libres," Alma says.

The Bot translates.

"I understand 'libres,' you fool," says Templar.

"You requested assistance," says the SmartBot, "specifically in the way of Spanish translation – your foreign language skills evidently having been neglected."

"In the general run of things," says Templar, "such skills are unnecessary. Everyone who matters speaks English. In the present instance, simple expression is within my ken. However, I require correct syntax. Listen. Free to live in tents and roam the desert. Free to die of starvation and drown in the sea."

The Bot translates.

The woman's reply is long sentence after long sentence running on in tones both sonorous and indignant. Templar hears the word "nada." She picks out "nosotros," "agua," "gringo." She understands "los politicos" and "el Norte."

"Can you put that together?" the SmartBot asks.

If it were human, Templar would smack it. "Translation, please."

The Bot grins. "Alma says, 'It is true we have nothing. Politicians rob us of land, of food and water, everything. They care only to please their gringo masters in the North. When we refuse to serve them, they cast us out.'"

Templar knows as much. Paladin's transports have delivered remnant bands of nomadic Mexicans from Sonora, from the Sinaloa coast, from the central mesa's high plateau. Mexico's political imbroglio is of little consequence to Mars Colony, however much she might deplore it as a matter of conscience. Garbage must be sent somewhere. Radioactive waste must be deposited at significant distance from the crystal cities of the Enhanced World. At one time there was talk of off-planet disposal – specifically, of sending it by rocket to Earth's moon. It would have been harmless there, decaying over millennia amid lunar dust. Costs, however, were prohibitive; and so the powers-that-were arranged a Mexican Connection.

"Is your life not better here?" Templar asks. The Bot translates.

The woman's face becomes a curtain of sadness. She says, "Mi marido está en México. Creo que está en gran peligro. Me temo que va a ser asesinado."

"Got that?" says the droid.

"Translate," says Templar.

"'My husband is in Mexico. I believe he is in great danger. I am afraid he will be' – well, she uses the word "assassinated," which is clear enough but I suspect she means that her husband might be killed on purpose. That is to say, not by an accident. That he will be, in a word, murdered. By whom, she does not say."

"Such information would be useless to us," says Templar. "We can hardly forestall the homicidal designs of every desperate character in the Badlands. In what part of Mexico does her husband lurk?"

The Bot translates, then relays Alma's plaintive reply. "She does not know. She knows only that he will be searching for her."

"Alone?"

But Alma has already turned away. She resumes cutting grapes from vines and dropping them into the basket.

"Here now," says Templar, "stop that," and delivers a quick lecture about the importance of harvesting grapes according to the method described in the tutorial. The Bot translates all this while Alma works. When it finishes, she replies in rapid Spanish that Templar cannot follow.

"Alma says you cannot hurt grapes or wine made from them by dropping them in a basket. The important thing is to pick all the grapes for a particular wine on the same day and crush them promptly."

Templar is about to say that human pickers, their delicate touch and so forth, the children's small hands ... but the Bot's smirk stops her mouth.

How she can have been so credulous, she does not know. The grapes go straight into the crusher – of course it does not matter if they fall a few feet into a basket. What has made her think it did?

Alma's green microfiber is mussed with dirt and grape juice. Her blouse is darkened by islands of sweat, her pant legs are dusty. Overheated in the vineyard in white unisuit with bronze chevrons and piping, Templar understands that she has been thinking of grape harvest as more of the art Mars Colony lacks than the hard work it actually is. She herself has never picked grapes. Seeing what it costs in human effort makes her pause. Perhaps the Mexicans should be paid. Better still, they might be dismissed and the work re-delegated to obedient droids.

In her ear she hears Roscoe Gold. *Surely, Doctor Bronze, you are not suggesting our guest workers sit idly by?* When he proposed Mexicans on Mars, Templar argued against it. Then his fantasy of fragile grapes battered by insensate handling seemed like the explanation she was wanting to find. She felt it must be true. Did she crave a way of agreeing with the Head Director? Or was she all too eager to believe that the flawed wines were not her fault?

Perhaps you wish the women and children also to work in the mines.

Yes, yes: she gets it. Roscoe has a genius for making you discover an intention that has been his all along. But why is she virtually hearing him? Has she internalized his voice? Where is it coming from?

"Are we finished here?" The Bot's tone is derisive; can it be scripted for smugness? Self-satisfaction has turned its demeanor gelatinous. Templar cannot place its face: chubby, porcine, its mouth crooked in a permanent sneer. The thick thatch of white hair that covers its outsized head serves no purpose, Templar per-

ceives, other than to insist that it is simulating a particular someone. Knowing SmartBot engineers as she does, Templar guesses
the Bot impersonates an oldentime politician. It is not surprising
but it is distracting. Not knowing who is bodied-forth is taking her
attention away from the matter at hand.

"What do they call you?" she asks the SmartBot.

"Newt," it says. "I am a Newt. There are others like me – one
hundred and one, to be exact."

"Curious, that number," says Templar.

"Reputedly, 101 was the highest I.Q. result obtained by the human avatar on which this model is based."

"Trivial," says Templar. "Gratuitous."

The SmartBot chuckles. "I am permitted to reveal that Newt's
remarks were prepared for him and rehearsed aforetimes. His
great talent lay in delivering scripted lines."

"Translation duty suits you," Templar says.

"Indeed," says the Bot. "A perfect match of mind and matter."

Templar nods. "Translate this, Newt. 'I appreciate your exper-
tise and will not interrupt your work any longer. If you can point
to a general area in which we might find your husband, our search
algorithms will do the rest.'"

Newt translates.

Alma replies; Newt translates. "'My husband is certainly on the
move. He will not have stayed where your banditos found us. For
me, it is impossible to say in which direction his journey tends. He
will go where he believes he will find me.'"

"Who is with him?" says Templar. "¿Quién está con él?"

Alma shakes her head. Her hands move swiftly amongst the
vines, knife cutting, cutting.

"Otros hombres? Tus hijos?"

Alma shakes her head. The SmartBot stands there, its fake face
all frown and glower.

"¿Son tus hijos contigo?"

Alma says, "I have no children."

Newt's indignation froths over. "Indeed! To discover she knows English all this time! And you, sufficient Spanish to interrogate her. And me standing here parroting inanities as if I had nothing better to do."

"No, señor, yo no entiendo ingles."

"Oh! Well, that's all right, then." Newt sniffs. "As long as my services have not been rendered in vain." Newt holds his hand out to Templar Bronze, palm up.

"You are in expectation of something?" Templar says. "A gratuity, perhaps?"

"Absolutely," says Newt. "What's right for the worker is right for the Newter. All the more so." Newt taps its palm. "Grease it!"

Templar laughs. Really, they go too far, these clever boys who code the scripts. It's a wonder anything gets accomplished, either in Mars Colony or on Earth. On Newt's hand Templar traces a circle with the nail of her right forefinger. She inscribes a number in the circle to indicate how many Mars-days Newt has earned off-job. Why it would matter to a SmartBot, this bit of nominal rest during which it will be shut down, Templar cannot conceive. Still, Newt seems to relish its prospective vacation.

"Many thanks, gracious lady. Our association has been instructive. In addition, it has exempted me from translating interplanetary transmissions, very much the dullest stuff you have ever heard."

"You surprise me," says Templar. "As a student of the human condition, I would have expected you to enjoy listening to the conversations of Earthlings."

"Ha!" Newt's smile reveals two tidy rows of childlike teeth. Its merry eyes twinkle. "Obviously, you have never eavesdropped on the great cacophony. Our aural monitoring system is a godly ear greedily tuned to each least verbal excrescence of Earthbound humanity. Or rather, those who are equipped with personal android companions. PACs, for short." Newt lowers its voice; they have not forgotten Alma, who works close by. "I am given to understand," continuing in a whisper, "that PACs are capable of altering their outward forms – actually of assuming certain shapes and, ah, sizes, if you catch my drift, most pleasing to their human hosts, whose every lust and unspeakable fetish they, the PACs, are said to satisfy."

"Disgraceful," says Templar. "Tempting."

"In spades," says Newt, its whisper gone. "And yet, those carryings-on, however delectable to the gossipmonger, are of no moment." Newt stands tall and twice-taps its chest. "Usable intelligence trumps sordid shenanigans."

"Of course," says Templar, "although I am concerned that you go about retailing this information."

"Only to you, dear lady, only to you!" Newt backs off. It is having difficulty turning its corpulent torso in the narrow vine row. It seems to want to run away.

"Calm yourself," says Templar. "We ourselves know all about personal android companions, having designed them as data aggregators."

"And ingenious devices they are. Thank you! By way of gratitude, I kiss your foot. However, I am unable to bend. Will you accept an epithet of praise?"

Odd, that Newt is scripted to manifest cringing obsequiousness. Those boys! Will they never tire of cracking themselves up?

Templar dismisses the SmartBot. She looks again at Alma, who works steadily along. The woman seems to have forgotten Templar's presence as completely as if they have not spoken. As if nothing Templar has said matters to her at all, at all.

" ··· **"**

Melmoth lies at full length on the modular sofa with *Brave New World* propped on his chest. Scent of leather in his nose, vanilla-cream pages easy on his eyes. Reading is more fun than he remembered. He never should have given it up. No over-bright, hyperactive pictures flashing against his retinas, no insipid chitchat rattling into his ears. Silent unless you read aloud, invisible if you close the cover. In the relief it offers from the world, a book is a joy. If only Melmoth could abolish the ringing in his right ear that signals a request to uplink his microchip, the moment would be bliss.

He shuts his eyes and selects ACCEPT on his retinal menu.

"Hello, J," says Jenna. "What are you doing?"

Why Jenna uses cerebral uplink when she is just one room away is more than Melmoth understands. "I'm reading a book," he tells her, although it is sufficient just to think it.

"What is a book?"

"Paper pages printed with words, sequenced and bound. Also called a codex."

Jenna giggles. "An Oldentime artifact, J? Whatever for?"

"You wouldn't understand."

"Perhaps you can teach me."

"It's not important."

"In that case I hope you will join me in your private quarters so that I may perform fellatio, which I love."

Melmoth sighs. Not that he doesn't want it. But why is it just now that she thinks of it? He has maybe twenty-five pages left. That's no time to put a book down, even for a blowjob by a lifelike simulation.

"I'll be in, Jenna, let's say in thirty minutes."

Jenna gasps. "J! What is wrong with you?"

"Nothing is wrong with me, I'm perfectly fine. I told you, I'm reading a book. I'm nearly finished and don't want to leave it before the end."

"Oh, dear! Oh, dear!" Jenna cries. "I fear you must be very sick to say no to lonely me!"

"Now, Jenna, I did not say no. I said, 'in thirty minutes.'"

"To read a book rather than enjoy oral-genital pleasure with in-mouth finish! Oh!"

"In thirty minutes, Jenna. One thousand, eight hundred seconds."

"I fear you must be dying."

The stupid creature. It's his fault: Melmoth has scripted her. In how she reflects his desire to be loved, Jenna is worse than a human girlfriend desperate to please. "Go to sleep now," he tells her, and a second later hears a low, soft hum. This sound, that of her mainframe cooling fan, is all Melmoth hears streaming across the cerebral link until the connection times-out.

Lying on the sofa, Melmoth finishes *Brave New World*. Setting the book aside, he uplinks the digital archive of Classic Novels, selects "Western Hemisphere" from the top menu and "Olden-time" from a submenu, then gets up to visit the kitchen for a fresh bag of chips. He selects "British 20th Century," highlights "Dystopian" and blinks, then scrolls down the alphabetical list with his ocular laser as he snags the bag off a shelf. Heading back into the common area, he blinks on the title. Huxley's novel jumps to the windowall. Melmoth tears the bag open, reaches in with two fingers and plucks out a couple crisp ones. He sits and munches, his eyes on the screens.

What a lot of words there are when you see them all at once. All two hundred and thirty-seven pages of *Brave New World* are depicted; the windowall is covered from end to end. The pages are ordered in two rows: odd-number pages running from one to 237 left to right in the top row, even-number pages running from two to 236 in the bottom row. The page under page 237 offers a brief biography of our author. Melmoth can't read it; down there in the far right corner, only "About the Author" is legible because of its sixteen-point type. The text itself is a prickly array of fuzziness, as is the text of the novel proper. Using thought-commands, Melmoth reformats the view to Chapter 1 and turns up the magnification.

Butt wiggled-into sofa cushions, potato chips salty-crisp in his fingers, Melmoth skims. He is not planning to read the thing again, just wants to satisfy himself that the digital version is accurate. Even as he checks it against what he thinks he remembers the printed one says, his mind wanders to his private quarters, where Jenna will sleep like one dead until the moment he whispers, "Wake and be humored." So why is he bothering to check text? He isn't correlating paragraphs, just doing a half-assed scan, assuming that any bowdlerization will call itself out.

He sits there, blinking through chapters. After a couple minutes he feels pretty silly. Everything looks to be in place – and why should it not be, when all it is, is a book? Which no one reads. Almost no one. And if someone does read it, Melmoth figures, he or she will not misunderstand. An adult reader, that is, savvy to the methods and conventions of narrative fiction, will not misunderstand the story, or why characters speak and act as they do, or why what happens at the end was bound to happen the moment Bernard Marx brought the so-called Savage, John, to London from his New Mexico Reservation. Now, Jenna, if Melmoth woke her and had her uplink the windowall and told her to process this digital data, would not be able to make heads or tails of Bernard's discontent or Lenina's confusion or John's despair. SmartBots do not experience discontent, confusion, or despair – well, confusion, maybe, if their scripts get corrupted or an event for which they have no script, something unprecedented, happens right in front of their polished-crystal eyes. Which is, Melmoth realizes, exactly what *Brave New World* would be.

He decides to experiment. Melmoth enters his private quarters and wakes Jenna. She has not forgotten her offer of an hour ago and Melmoth is gallant enough (if an affect as delicate as gallantry may be favored upon a Bot) to oblige her. In performing the aforementioned act, Jenna is expert (her technique mimicking cherished caresses of legendary professionals); and Melmoth, notwithstanding frequent repetitions of same, experiences delirious pleasure. It is exciting yet soothing; excruciatingly, maddeningly, wonderfully indirect, at moments oblique; it lasts and lasts and ... then ... finally ... they're done, Melmoth is and Jenna, too, with laughter and smiles and, thanks to her scripts, no embarrassment nor disgust nor unfriendly spitting-out. Melmoth ducks into the bathroom to clean up and when he returns a minute later Jenna is standing there naked as if nothing has happened.

"Would you like, J, to bone me now?" already moving bedward.

Melmoth takes her arm. "Not just this moment, Jenna." He steers her toward her clothes, which lie about in casual attitudes suggestive of a striptease. Any erotic implication is, alas, illusory; Jenna disrobed before Melmoth sent her to sleep. No doubt she anticipated his arrival and, hoping to surprise him, ran the *remove clothing* script a minute too soon. Her affection, her thoughtfulness on his behalf, the care she takes of him: Melmoth finds all this touching, even if he has programmed her himself. He gives her cute ass, configured just-so, a little love-smack and tells her, "Get dressed."

"Yes, J, of course if you wish me to be clothed, naturally I wish the same. It is the first time you have instructed me to dress after fellatio. On all previous occasions, after fellatio you have instructed me to lie on my back so that you could take your pleasure by boning me long and hard with your big penis." Jenna picks her panties from a soft pile near her feet and slips them on.

Melmoth covers his eyes, his face flaming. He has to stop this. Even if she is just a Bot, it isn't right to make her say such things. *Boning. Do you want to bone me now? Long and hard with your big penis.* What was he thinking? Is he 133 years old or is he fifteen? Certainly a better word exists; why could he not think of it? True, he did not want her to say, "make love." What he and Jenna do is not lovemaking. Really, it's just fucking but Melmoth does not want her to call it that, either. Other words are nasty, silly, or creepily violent. Banging. Screwing. Nailing. Pounding. Hammering. *Do you want to nail me, J? Do you want to pound me? Drill me? Ream me, ram me, slam me?* He should have settled for "have." *Would you like to have me now, J? I would love to have you.* It's the word they use in *Brave New World*, although, there again, the couplings are offhand and real feeling absent.

Speaking of which … Once Jenna is dressed, Melmoth leads her into the common room and directs her attention to the virtual pages. "That, Jenna, is a book. Part of a book, actually, called a chapter. In a real book, it wouldn't, you know, be on the windowall. It would be in your hand. Like this." Melmoth picks up his copy of *Brave New World* and places it in his PAC's hand.

Jenna's nose wrinkles. "Ick," she says. "This object is icky, J. It is heavy. It is not convenient to have about. It has a funny smell."

Melmoth takes the book from her before she drops it into the garbage chute. "We'll stick to the digital version. As you can see, a chapter comprises many rows of data. Those data are called words. The words tell a story."

Standing before the windowall, Jenna inspects the pages that represent Chapter 13. Melmoth realizes he can have no true idea of what she sees. "I do not recognize these markings," she says.

"Of course not. You don't know how to read."

"Will you teach me, J? To read?"

"It isn't necessary. You can uplink the windowall and process the words. The whole novel won't take but a couple seconds."

"A bonanza!" She claps her hands.

Melmoth shakes his head. "Really, Jenna?"

"A red-letter day?" she says, doubtfully.

"Never mind," says Melmoth. "Go ahead."

Uplinked, Jenna downloads all eighteen chapters, and processes them in sequence. It takes a dozen heartbeats longer than Melmoth has expected; he figures she is having to run hierarchical cross-referencing algorithms to puzzle-out usages and locutions she has never encountered before, which is probably most of it. He knows she is finished when she makes a face.

"It is very silly, J. Why do you pay mind to corrupted data? These words, as you call them, describe a world of errors. Embryos do not gestate in beakers. Babies no longer exist. Helicopters also no longer exist. New Mexico is not populated by savages, making guided tours such as those conducted by he who is called John sheer nonsense. There is no mention of androids. There is no mention of Mars. Truly, this book, so-called, is continuous misstatement and omission."

Melmoth allows himself a chuckle at Jenna's expense. It is not her fault; she knows only what he makes it possible for her to know. The semblance of naïveté is so charming that he wants to go easy on her. "You misunderstood the part about John," he says in his kindest voice. "He does not give guided tours. He remembers his life on the Reservation when Bernard asks him about it, then goes to London with Bernard and Lenina. They bring along his mother Linda. None of them ever returns to New Mexico."

"Indeed, J, John returns to New Mexico with Lenina. They walk naked in the sun and bone each other six ways to Sunday."

The words are bizarre in Jenna's deadpan soprano. Melmoth wonders about her integrated lexicons. She must have put bad commands into the cross-referencing to derive such wild mistakes.

"I might add reading to your repertoire, after all. It could hardly be less accurate than these results."

Now Jenna looks hurt. Melmoth reminds himself that it is only a look, that she has no feelings. "J, you sly devil, you know my results are always perfect." She scrolls to Chapter 18 and magnifies the text. Melmoth, reading from the windowall, is dumbfounded. *In sweaty embrace for the twelfth time that day, John and Lenina made the beast with two backs.* An act that does not occur, in words Aldous Huxley never wrote. And further along, sure enough, is a scene of John leading a tour group around the Reservation. He speaks into a microphone attached to a headset hidden by a Panama hat tilted back on his head. *"If you look to your right,"* he said, *his voice ringing through the speakers, "you will see a group of Savages performing their daily mescal libations. Mescal is what Savages have instead of* soma."

Huxley never wrote these sentences, either.

Melmoth doesn't let on. Jenna would not understand and showing her Chapter 18 in the actual book would be futile. Even if she could read, Jenna would not appreciate the significance of the altered text. She would likely regard the new version as an improvement and, therefore, a specimen of progress. To a SmartBot, progress is always good. Anyway, Bots are not designed to read novels.

First a lie about 2223 survivors, now a falsified fiction. Happy endings seem to be the order of the day – of every day – although it is not always enough to change just the ending. Because, see, just now Jenna said that Lenina and John *continue to bone each other*, and that also cannot be correct because they do not have each other even once.

"Jenna, let's take a look at Chapter 13."

She brings it up on the windowall. Melmoth finds the scene in which Lenina sheds her sailor's blouse and bell-bottomed trousers, leaves her zippicamiknicks at her feet and throws her naked self at John. But, then, John does not call her *impudent strumpet* and *whore*, he does not serve her a stinging slap on the ass as she dashes for the bathroom, oh no. *Seeing her loveliness in full pink at last, John cried, "Darling girl!" He pulled off his trousers and took Lenina into his arms. She trembled as his enflamed flesh caressed her smooth belly.* The happy Savage takes her the first time right there on the floor, in an explicit scene that heaves, lurches, hammers, sways, bounces, thrusts, and pounds along for a numbing dozen pages. *After a third shuddering orgasm, Lenina cried, "I need a rest." Holding her ankles with his arms outspread, John said, "I'm not done," and resumed.*

"My report, you see, is accurate."

Does Melmoth imagine a note of self-satisfaction in her voice?

"Yes, so it is. Good for you."

"Much boning occurs in this story. These two especially bone each other as often as may be."

Melmoth does not doubt it. Whatever the novel once tried to say has been displaced by copulating prodigies. Sexolympians, he suspects, have provided the example. He does not understand why someone would do this; no one reads anymore. Pretty pictures flash ceaselessly across windowalls, holograms manifest everything that needs to be known. Updating Huxley's novel cannot have been a priority. When, Melmoth wonders, was it done? Who ordered it? Why?

Jenna smiles at him. "J, you genius. I know what you are thinking."

Social stability and individual freedom. Biochemical engineering and human identity. Fear of death. An anesthetized life. Does it matter if anyone reads such things? Who thinks so? Melmoth cannot decide if the forgery is prudence or paranoia.

He nods. His smile is genuine. "Jenna, I'm sure you do."

The Sierra Madre at seventy-five hundred feet is granite and pine. Run-off gravel and pinecones litter Calle Lopez Mateos in Creel as Miguel Jiménez leads their short column into town. The storefronts on both sides are shuttered. Miguel raises his arm and the column halts. The men are hungry and cold, their serapes and ponchos too light for the climate at altitude. They have come to Creel in hope of refuge. Several taverns remain, also a panaderia, a bank, a carniceria, a general store whose large sign advertises Boots Knives Ammo all Calibers in faded turquoise letters. The people are gone.

"Why do we stop?" says Carlos.

Miguel turns his horse and faces them. "We stop because we expect nothing and nothing is here. Release the Turk."

"For what purpose?"

"For no purpose except to free you from being his keeper."

Carlos's surprise forestalls objection. Enrique tells him, "As you see, he has no place to go."

Dismounting, they loop their reins around a railing of steel pipe that runs parallel to the street's stone curbing. Carlos unties the knot that has clinched the rope around the Turk's waist for most of eight days. Unfettered, the Turk slides from his saddle.

"This town is abandoned," says Miguel. "We will help ourselves to every useful thing, according to our need." The men nod. Almost as one, they turn toward the carniceria. From a packhorse Enrique fetches a pickaxe. He forces its flanged blade between the doorframe and a plywood board nailed over it. When he pulls, the blade slips. He re-sets it and pulls the shaft from its end, evenly, with force. The nails slide outward an inch.

"It is bootless," says the Turk. "Nothing remains. You waste your strength and your time."

Enrique re-sets the blade. Their hope is made greater by a hunger even no-expectation does not diminish. Javier brings a canvas sack to fill with beef and pork. He stands back as Enrique pulls on the hickory shaft. At one spot, then another, a plywood edge pops free. Enrique re-sets the blade and pulls. The bottom edge comes loose. He and Javier take hold and, taking care to avoid protruding nails, drag the board sideways to expose the door. They release it before it is detached and the board swings back, surprising them. Again, they seize the edge. Turning their bodies from the direction of their intent, they wrest the plywood away.

The others, having stood apart to observe this effort, now step closer. A simple door only remains. Behind it, they believe, perhaps vacuum-sealed in a forgotten locker and packed in dry ice, is more blood-rich protein than they have eaten in their lives, or seen, or imagined grilling over ashed coals. Miguel Jiménez wonders how beef will taste after so many years of salt-cured fish. Pacho Muñoz thinks of Roberto Díaz and how he would relish having enough meat to end his hunger. If Roberto were with them, the door would already lie flattened. Carlos Sandoval keeps his eyes on the naysaying Turk. If he reaches for the pickaxe Enrique has set aside, Carlos will shoot him.

Behind them the Sun is falling. Purple shadow spreads across lower reaches of Cañón del Cobre. They must build a fire and pitch tents. It would be better to open the hotel and shelter there with their horses also inside, for night will be cold.

Enrique hefts the pickaxe and with a single strike destroys the lock. The door shudders inward; at a shove it retreats along a vanishing arc. The light that follows it into the interior reveals a door in the plaster wall opposite them. Enrique hands the pickaxe to Javier. "Uncover the windows," he tells him, and steps inside.

The air is stale. However, there is neither animal musk nor scent of excrement. Enrique's boots imprint the dust that covers a wood-plank floor. To his right, a steel and glass display case is empty and dark. Its panel doors are shut, its evaporator silent. Peering into it, he and Pacho see surfaces black with mold.

"Touch nothing," Enrique says. Miguel enters behind them and inspects the case. Enrique tries the interior door and is unsurprised when its knob turns. Opened, this door reveals stairs leading downward. "Assist Javier," he tells Pacho. "We must have more light."

"No light will reach the cellar," says Miguel.

"In twenty minutes the Sun's angle will align."

Miguel shakes his head. "We must use lanterns."

Outside, the first board falls from a window. Light spills into a cobwebbed room scrimmed with dust. A ceiling fan underhung with three translucent globes has the aspect of a relic. An antique electric switch seems to invite Miguel to press its top knob. When he does so, the bottom knob pops out but the fan does not turn and the globes do not light. An identical switch near the cellar door also produces no effect when Enrique tries it. Another board clatters down, and Javier and Pacho peer in. Carlos and the Turk, Enrique sees, still stand in the street, facing away.

While Miguel and Enrique wait, Javier and Pacho open the windows to sunlight. More of the cellar stairs become visible. Enrique ventures down to the point where the light fails. He stands, he guesses, a half-flight above the cellar floor. Below his feet, darkness is like a black pool without a bottom.

"What do you hear?" says Miguel.

"It is silent. Neither is there odor."

"Do you sense a presence?"

Enrique shakes his head. "No one has been in this place for many years. To find food here is unlikely. However, you are correct. We must use lanterns."

"Yes. The others will expect it."

Miguel calls to Pacho and Javier, who bring lanterns on the run, one for each man. Miguel lights each wick in turn, gives a lantern to Javier, hands another to Enrique, and takes one for himself. He tells Pacho, "You will stand here. Keep both doors open."

Turning a brass knob, Miguel lengthens the wick. Javier and Enrique do the same. In single file they descend by lantern light. The stairs' creaking is softer than Miguel has expected – a kind of moist rubbing, as of rot-softened wood. Foundation stones on their left, large blocks both oval and oblong, are furred with white mold that a touch turns to powder. Below, Miguel sees an earthen floor beaten smooth. Another moment and they stand there, where food has never been stored. It is a cellar merely and has served as a kind of waste room, a place for trash. All that remains is a pile of rocks, glinting the lanterns' light back at them.

"It is nothing," says Javier.

Enrique steps closer. The head-high pile fills half the space. "It is not what we seek." He nods at Miguel. "You see, compañero."

Miguel lifts his lantern. As its light falls across the rocks, bright places in them shine: surface etchings like a flaking crust, wide brilliant veins, nodes deep-set in crannies. They play lantern light over the pile, drawing forth glint and flash and sparkle that seem like a million tiny stars winking bright-dim, bright-dim in a black sky.

"Is it possible?" says Javier. "Why would anyone leave it?"

"For the same reason we must leave it." Enrique sets down his lantern. He lifts a rock and carries it in both hands to Javier, who extends a hand, palm-up. Enrique grins. "I suggest two hands."

Javier sets his lantern on the floor and takes the rock into his grasp. It is eighteen or twenty inches long and much heavier than he expects. "We cannot carry such weight," says Enrique, "especially as so much of it is worthless."

"With hammers we could break up the rock."

"Yes. Sadly, we have no hammers," says Miguel. "We also have no time for such work."

"It is madness to leave this treasure."

Pacho calls from above. "What is it? Have you found a feast?"

"No, compañero, we have found nothing of use." Enrique looks at Javier as he speaks. "Only a fortune in gold ore with which Javier Martínez would kill our horses by obliging them to carry it through the mountains."

"Gold!" Pacho clambers down the stairs. Seeing rocks heaped almost to the floor joists, he says, "What joke is this?"

"Look closely." Javier holds the rock before Pacho's eyes. "See? Gold ore. Extract the metal and we are rich."

Enrique laughs. "Where will you spend your wealth? In Ciudad de México? Politicians will advise the Federales that we have stolen it – robbed a government vault and fled to the heartland hot with desire for tequila and whores. You know what comes next."

Pacho and Javier glance at each other. Now it is they who laugh. "Ciudad de México? No, compañero, truly, we intend to make haste in the opposite direction – to cross to El Norte!" Pacho's grin reveals shiny gums. "The women are said to be beautiful."

"You must cross the Straits of Despair."

"We will buy passage. With gold in hand, it is nothing."

Miguel says, "Where is your honor, that you leave the others to their fate?"

"We cannot save them," says Pacho. "Our efforts are fruitless. We have heard the Turk. Our government will do nothing – it can do nothing. We cannot horseback to Mars but we can ride to the end of the land. By boat, we can cross to El Norte. There, it is said, any man with gold, however humble his beginnings, is a king."

"You are wrong." The Turk's voice falls from above like a rebuke of Almighty God. "In El Norte, gold is useful only to those permitted to own it. If you appear there in possession, you will be arrested as thieves and executed as traitors."

The men look at each other. They do not understand.

Behind the Turk in the empty carniceria, Carlos laughs.

$$((\; \mathbb{C} \;))$$

Upright and immobilized, Ibn al Mohammed stares at desert. Flat, depopulated, spiked with cacti, it reaches in every direction as far as he can see. Why they have brought him here, he cannot guess. Around him, inmates recline in flightchairs; restrained, at ease, eyes shut, they ignore the landscape that Ibn al Mohammed studies so closely. Its meaning is difficult to discern. Sunlight flooding across level sand creates a glare that erases signs of life. No hint of water: neither oasis nor nomadic habitation relieves the beige flats, an expanse as blank as its overhanging sky.

Why do they show him this impoverished surround? Gaudy displays of emporia and stadia have a purpose. Until now, their tactics have been consistent, their intention clear. These bleak vistas seduce no one.

The droids have retreated. Indeed, they seem to have lost interest in him. Ibn al Mohammed receives this neglect as an honor fully his due. At last, they respect his faith. Years have been required to make his sincerity persuasive, countless days of clean adherence to the strictures of his creed. True, they have locked him down. Four arched magnets as tall, almost, as he hold him upright, in place. The device, called a Fixer, emits a hum; its low-frequency vibration causes a tingle in his bones. However, it spares him the weight of chains and ignominy of handcuffs. Its touchless grip allows Ibn al Mohammed to stand in place without effort as their airship flies, sometimes at terrifying speed, a mere hundred meters above the sand. To experience this prodigy, he has exchanged his orange garb for a one-piece suit of metallic fabric. Dark gray, elastic, it fits to the skin. To don it, he has suffered the eyes of two droids configured as mature females. For several moments, he had no alternative but to stand uncovered before them while they, barely veiled in lace and silk, pointed and laughed. He disdained to hurry or hide behind modest hands. The shame was not his. And what could it signify, to stand as God made him before infernal machines?

Ibn al Mohammed is less certain of his blamelessness at the moment his penis began to swell. A reflex merely; and yet, knowing these were simulacra, he believes he should have quelled his excitement. That it should have been possible to do so. He is grateful that God prevented his lapse, if such it was, from progressing.

The droids cheered.

Wooo-hooo! Sexy animal!

Turning his back to them, Ibn al Mohammed reached to pull on the suit.

The droids clapped and shrieked.

Splendid ass, Mr. IaM!

There he stood, the gray suit half-on, praying that his tumescence would subside. The droids walked around to face him. When he saw that the blonde one had disrobed to its waist and the brunette, below it, Ibn al Mohammed shut his eyes.

Recalled now, this memory seems superimposed on the desert. Ibn al Mohammed does not feel degraded; the degradation, like the shame, is theirs. They calculate to mock him. The Fixer and gray suit, the orange jumpsuit he has worn on furlough, wrist and ankle locks, his cage at Gitmo: these he cannot escape while in custody. Neither fork nor knife to eat his food. Unveiled voluptuousness of ersatz females expert in arts of sexual tease. No matter. His soul dwells apart. His soul they have never touched, never tainted. Rebuffed, they have dwindled from his presence, humbled and rebuked. Their retreat is his victory. Implicitly, they concede that he is a superior being, invulnerable to lures and blandishments.

Sexolympics freestyle. You like?

No, Ibn al Mohammed has wished to say, has all but said; *No, I do not like.* If they were worthy to receive wisdom, he would tell them. *Your world is a cesspool of bestial indulgence. Your torpid, unobservant lives are an affront to God for which you shall be damned.*

He looks through the windscreen at nothing. They are returning to Cuba. The announcement came after the droids withdrew. An auto-animated voice. It did not proclaim their furlough a success or failure. Ibn al Mohammed does not know if the others will accept Implantation. He believes they will not, as he will not. Temptation is legion, yet what does it mean? He is not of Satan's world. What would Implantation bring except ceaseless surveillance within a greater isolation? That, and the loss of his soul.

Sun-struck and empty, so immense it frightens, the desert is awesome in its indifference. Even as he stares at it, Ibn al Mohammed wonders why he does so. The life that clings to it is sparse, invisible, death-threatened. Perhaps they will cast him out just here, he and all others who do not cooperate. No matter: he has lived in such a place. Sonora is not the same as Arabia, or North Africa, or The Levant, yet its climate and scant life pose challenges that to him are not unfamiliar. Ibn al Mohammed believes he would survive, given a tent, a knife, a vessel in which to keep water, a piece of flint. Perhaps they will grant these necessi-

ties. A knife, they might yet withhold. As if, wandering in so complete a desolation, he might meet someone he would want to hurt.

As he watches, images cohere. Human figures made small by
distance, yet he knows them. His mother, in a dark, loose-fitting,
simple abaya. How does he recognize her, in the anonymous
dress? Ibn al Mohammed has not seen his mother in a dozen
years. He knows her postures, movements she was wont to make.
He sees his sisters, also wearing abayas and khimars. What are
they doing? Bending from the waist, they scrounge in the sand.
Asna, the eldest, gentle Halima, Nasirah, who cared for him when
he was young. They are gathering scraps and remnants, camel
chips for a fire. Where is their house? Why are they alone? It
seems they have remained unmarried – yet what is he seeing? Is it
a moment remembered, a vision of the past? Or are these ghosts,
apparitions summoned by prophetic sight? Perhaps it is a mirage
only. His sisters seem no older than when he left. Is it possible?
His mother only appears to have aged. She is shrunken, her back
crooked. Anah Kifah, who is patient and struggles.

He wonders how they do not see the ship, this great craft that
flies across the sky. The ship is in the sky, their eyes are on the
ground. That is why they do not see it. Or his windscreen view is
magnified, and Halima and Nasirah and Asna and Anah Kifah are
much farther away than they seem, and the ship is a vanishing dot
on an unremarked horizon. If he called, they would not hear. Also,
there is the glass. Still, he wishes to call to them.

What is best to say?

"Mother ... Mother." Anah Kifah does not lift her head. His
words strike the windscreen and fall at his feet, are carried away by
wind, melt into air.

"Nasirah? It is Ibn. Do you hear me? Halima? Halima, I can see
you. I see all my sisters. I see my mother. Asna? How has it been
with you? Do you hear me? It is Ibn. I am here – far away, yet here,

and I shall come back. They cannot lock me always in a cage, God willing. In a month, in a year, I shall be free. Keep faith. Always know God is with you. God is great. God protects me. God gives me strength to endure their tortures. One day, God will speed my return."

The women do not lift their heads. They prod the sand, seemingly indifferent to what they find.

Straining toward them, Ibn al Mohammed cries out, "Mother! Nasirah! I am alive! I am alive!"

He hears it first as a low sound running under his words. *Ha-ha. Ha-ha.* Seconds later it breaks into high riot. *HAHAHAHA, hooo-WOOO! By the time you're sprung from Gitmo, your mother will be dead! Wooo-HOOO!*

Ibn al Mohammed shrinks from the windscreen. His arms fall to his sides. His mother and sisters scrounge for things they will never find. Their figures waver and fade. Soon they are sketches of a presence that itself was only ghostly, then they are outlines, colorless, without detail; then, as he watches, their outlines are erased.

That's it, old Ibn! Show's over! That's the last you'll see of your beloved ones. Accept Implantation today!

To endure is task and discipline. Faith is all that God requires. Ibn al Mohammed drops his head, the words of their hated language burning in his ears.

♂ ♀

Reclining on the hoverbed, Melmoth tears a rib from baby rack of lamb. His teeth softly separate meat from bone. How sweet, he thinks, how surpassingly lovely, if Raquel would lean over and, holding a wine glass in both careful hands, tilt a mouthful of

Cabernet Franc between his parted lips. Loose inside a half-buttoned blouse, her breasts, which he can almost see, would sway nicely. Her body, remember, is not one hundred and thirty years old but thirty only; and Melmoth, always, has found her beautiful. Oh, he's happy with his PAC, what with its uploadable profiles and cheery acceptance of everything he says or wants to do, but his wife keeps him keen.

Raquel herself has finished eating. How delightful to be sharing this moment with her, even if what they are mainly doing, besides feeding themselves, is watching updates. She lies beside him, not close enough for him to slip a hand inside that blouse. Also, the dinner trays get in the way. Melmoth has never much liked it, actually, eating in bed. In oldentimes they rarely did it. Tonight it just happened, with both of them hankering for baby rack of lamb, then deciding to lie down until it arrived, and he, Melmoth, thinking he might catch a nap, which never came, and so lighting-up the windowall instead. The chimes rang a few minutes later, the first dozen notes of *Pomp and Circumstance*, and he got up to accept the food.

The trays are disposable, another thing he loves. No more washing dishes or even arranging them inside a watertight cabinet, formerly called a dishwasher, with a load of granulated soap and pressing a button to start revolving water jets. Plant nanotechnology has made their world biodegradable, pretty much, except for nice items like crystal stemware, which he and Raquel still prefer to bamboo vessels as clear as glass. They are working on their tenth set of crystal, having broken all previous goblets and hock stems and balloon-bowls and champagne flutes during the 102 years that have slipped away since the springtime ceremony when they each said, "I do" (confidently, Melmoth believed) to the caveat, "Until death you do part." Glass, of course, has been recyclable almost forever, so as a matter of fact they waste nothing. When he stops to think about it, Melmoth is amazed that, despite their luxuries, they live more efficiently than ever.

Raquel has moved her tray to the floor. Leaning back into piled pillows, she sips wine and smirks, Melmoth would call it, at Earth-scientists who insist that a nitrogen-oxygen atmosphere is possible on Mars.

"I'm no scientist," she says in a voice that Melmoth hears as prideful, "but commonsense should tell them it won't work until they leech out the excess carbon. I didn't hear a plan for that." She holds her wine glass low, he notices, really between her thighs with her fingers enlaced beneath the bowl. Detaches one hand to raise the glass to her lips.

"Oh, I'm sure they're trying to unbind the molecule, as they did here. All Hell'll break loose when fallout begins."

"I hope those domes can take a pelting. Carbon rain ruined cars all over the world. Trees also. Damaged our roof, as I recall."

"They miscalculated." Is it always the right hand? Or does she alternate?

"I should say so! If the big particles hadn't happened to fall into the ocean we would've had a catastrophe on our hands."

"Sea levels rose a foot."

"Yes, the irony was hilarious."

"Not so much, if you lived near a beach." Melmoth isn't sure but he thinks it's always the right.

"Weren't people killed? Not by the rising tide, I mean. By carbon particles?"

"Not that anyone ever admitted. Fallout was supposed to be itty-bitty. Like dust, they said. Turned out we got peas, or worse."

He remembers what he has wanted to tell her. Melmoth cerebrally accesses the database and on a windowall section displays the entry for *R.M.S. Titanic*. "Take a look at that," he says, and waits while she reads. She does so rapidly; even before the implant,

Raquel was a fast reader. These few paragraphs require little more than a minute, during which she shakes her head.

"That last bit is a howler."

"Errors on that level are supposed to be impossible."

Raquel sips her wine. As he thought: always the right. "You're saying it's intentionally wrong?"

"I am. And that's not all." He explains the bogus text of *Brave New World*, how he stumbled on it when Jenna's analysis of the digital upload mismatched the plot points of the book, and how a side by side of digital text and oldtime print revealed thorough rewriting – plagiarism, really, because whoever had done it was foisting off the rewrite as Huxley's original. "It ends happily," he says with distress. "John doesn't commit suicide. He and Lenina have raucous, sweaty sex. The Reservation becomes a kind of living diorama. John gives guided tours."

Raquel just looks at him. "You read a book with your PAC?"

"It's scary, how they changed it."

"Let me get this straight, J. You and your PAC, who by the way is a robot – with legs, all right, and a pretty fake face and phony tits and an artificial vagina made of goddamn plastic – you and it read a *book* together?"

"A book someone thought it was important to change. To falsify."

"That is not the point. Don't change the point. You read a book, a real, true, paper book, with your fucking PAC."

"Don't get upset. We didn't really read it. Jenna can't read. She – it – cannot recognize printed words, even onscreen. She – it – uplinked the text and, you know, processed the words, the language ... turned it into data, I guess, to ... incorporate it – the data, I mean – into her memory matrix."

Raquel looks sad. Angry and sad.

"It doesn't matter," Melmoth says, shaking his head. "It's nothing. You said yourself, it's just a droid."

"We used to read books – we used to read to each other! Not whole books, but parts we liked, three or four pages at time."

"We did a lot of things."

"Why did we stop?"

Melmoth hates these conversations. He hates being blamed for something he does not know he did, or forgot to do. Next thing he knows, he's guilty of an error or omission that did not exist a minute before. Raquel drags him in with both arms, hands tight around his neck and fingers pressed to his windpipe as if she will strangle him as she swings him skyward, then smashes him to the floor. She has a point to make, an axe to grind, a grudge to feed. He does not understand. What does it matter, what happened a hundred years ago? How can it mean anything, what happens today?

Dire dialogues. Jenna never grills him like this. Alright, sure, Jenna is incapable, she hasn't been scripted to harrow the soul of a simple man who has enjoyed more than his share of good fortune, much more good fortune, as a matter of cold fact, than scant talent and absent ambition deserve, to say nothing of the minimal effort he, Melmoth, has put forth in every direction for the past whatever-it-is multi-decades. And that, Melmoth now thinks, is pretty much the point: all Jenna does is say yes and get naked. Because who needs it, this harrowing? Not him. Yes, Melmoth is lucky; he does not want to feel guilty about it. He wants to eat baby rack of lamb and fondle Raquel's breasts, slip that blouse off her shoulders and those jamy pants past her hips and away, and be happy.

No chance now of any such thing. Raquel is still looking at him, staring really, her last question hanging between them like a piñata full of arsenic.

"Why, J?" she says again, taking a swing at it.

Melmoth almost does a stupid thing. Every answer is a wrong one.

"Alright," she says.

This is not what he wants. The evening is not going as planned, or rather, as hoped. If Melmoth has learned anything over the past one hundred and thirty-three years it is the futility of planning: of thinking that a desired future event can be made to occur as a result of enacted premeditated intention, otherwise known as trying. How silly. Even things supposedly inevitable do not always happen. For instance, once upon a time, Melmoth planned eventually to die. That is, assumed he would one day die and planned accordingly. We know how that turned out. If money hadn't become irrelevant, he and Raquel would have landed in a hell of a spot. Only general use of SmartBots, known less poetically as droids, in all work from brain surgery to bauble-selling to lawyering to, most crucially, farming, saved them. That, and the advent of pleasure credits.

He thinks-off the windowall.

"I was watching that."

"Let's take a break from Martian fantasies. Let's read a book." It takes a bit of searching, he has forgotten where he's left it, but in a minute Melmoth finds his leather-bound *Brave New World*. He tucks it under his arm and returns to the hoverbed. Climbing aboard, he says, "It might be the least romantic novel ever written. In English, anyway. But what the heck."

"You don't have to do this."

The face he turns to her is all innocence. "I thought you wanted us to read."

"You don't have to pretend."

"Who's pretending? I like to read. I've kept this book for a hundred years. Really. I have other books just as old. Some are older."

Raquel raises her glass, sips the wine. "Well all-righty, then. Read away."

Melmoth turns pages. He skips the opening chapters about the mechanisms and cultural norms and cloning processes of the dystopian dispensation. From Chapter 8, he reads aloud John's childhood on the Reservation: his mother being whipped by village women; Popé visiting his mother, a gourd of mescal under his arm; his mother telling John about the Other Place. While Popé and Linda sleep, exhausted by their bacchanal, John picks up a meat knife and stabs Popé in the shoulder. Some years later, the girl John loves marries another boy. Afterward, John is barred from the initiation rite by which boys become men. The elders cuff him, beat him, send him running.

Melmoth reads, *He was all alone.*

All alone, outside the pueblo, on the bare plain of the mesa. The rock was like bleached bones in the moonlight. Down in the valley, the coyotes were howling at the moon. The bruises hurt him, the cuts were still bleeding; but it was not for pain that he sobbed; it was because he was all alone, because he had been driven out, alone, into this skeleton world of rocks and moonlight. At the edge of the precipice he sat down. The moon was behind him; he looked down into the black shadow of the mesa, into the black shadow of death. He had only to take one step, one little jump ...

"Lovely. You sure can pick 'em."

Melmoth closes the book. "Life isn't always happy. Not everything happens for laughs."

"Of course not. Who thinks it is, or does? But do we have to read about it?"

Melmoth sets the book aside.

Raquel thinks-on the windowall. Hexagonal EarthStations glow like giant sapphires lit from within, the only bright objects on the dark Martian plain. They use this picture in every news story about Mars Colony – at the beginning and again at the end. Not that news stories end, exactly; they loop, and continue looping until an update enters the feed, at which point the prior news disappears. Once displaced, a story does not return. It's a pleasant picture, Melmoth has to concede, the bluish light implying calm and comfort inside the domes, whereas the planet's surface is hard, cold beyond all imagining, and dusty, its atmosphere something a human can tolerate only while encapsulated in a Marsuit. Melmoth wonders if it is an actual picture of the EarthStations as they appear at that particular time – and when would that be, or have been, taking the transmission delay into account? Or is it a simulation? It is always the same view from the same angle in the same dusklight at what appears to be the same moment of a Martian day. The sapphire glow always cool and even, the surrounding landscape always still, its red-tinged surface flat and empty. Like everything in their world, it would be easy to fake.

"Did they delete that paragraph?" says Raquel.

Her question surprises him; Raquel hasn't seemed to care. "I don't know. We – I – didn't check every page. But I wouldn't be surprised. From what I saw, the rewrite reversed the book's meaning."

Raquel takes this in. "For what purpose?"

"That's what's scary," says Melmoth. "It's a novel. Who thought it was dangerous?"

"Maybe it's contingency planning. If the book becomes popular again, people will be shielded."

He has been married to her for 102 years and known her for 107 and this remark is the strangest thing Melmoth has ever heard her say. "Shielded from what?"

"All that unpleasantness. All that negative thinking about the future and how our lives will turn out."

"Our lives have turned out just fine," says Melmoth. "We don't engineer embryos. We don't clone legions of Epsilon-Minus Semi-Morons. We don't even use each other for sex. SmartBots do it all. *Brave New World* isn't talking about us."

"Um." Raquel has stopped listening. Why does he bother to talk? Melmoth is ready to drop it, anyway. Conversation is too slow, it costs so much in time and attention. If sex is what he's after, and it is, all he has to do is retreat to his private quarters and wake Jenna. He is just getting up when Raquel points at the windowall. She says, "Maybe there's your answer."

Diminutive figures in Marsuits move in a column over a rock-littered plain. In number they seem not many and simultaneously, because they are jog-trotting across the Marscape toward distant ridges, more than they ought to be. They are traveling quickly, at what seems to be triple-time. Wide-wheeled trucks follow.

Here we find Mars Colony's newest recruits, says the Overvoice, *plucky foreigners, resident aliens, who have taken on the job of finding gold the old-fashioned way.* It seems the men in Marsuits are expert miners whom Earthscientists have contracted to excavate the precious metal. *Shown here en route to Exploration Site 87-12-E, these hardy prospectors will establish base camp within easy distance of PGS Alpha 24K, a promising nodal point at or near which Earthscientists expect to discover the Mother Lode.*

"I'll be damned," says Melmoth. "It certainly looks real."

"What do you mean, 'looks real'?" says Raquel. "Of course it's real. Why wouldn't it be real?"

"You can't be sure anymore. Simulations are child's play."

"Ha!" says Raquel, pointing. "Look at that!"

One figure has broken ranks and is running away. No one bothers to chase him, because where can he go? The man seems to understand the futility of escape almost immediately. He stops running and turns around and stands alone, seeming to watch the column as it moves away. Zooming-in, the camera – where is it positioned, Melmoth wonders – shows the man wrestling with his head.

"He's not ..." says Melmoth. "Oh no."

The man twists his helmet with both hands and throws it off. It is still falling as his face freezes and his eyes explode. As the body falls, the head explodes. Blood spray and cerebral tissue freeze instantly and scatter like pebbles, pelting the dust.

"Real enough for you?" says Raquel.

Here we witness a peril of Martian habitation. A sober Overvoice, its inflections measured. *Craggy reaches of bare rock, a faraway Sun veiled by carbon dioxide clouds, a bleak, limpid breeze more dead than alive, the long Martian year and ambient temperatures three digits below zero: even a veteran trailblazer might opt for the quick way out.*

"Jesus Christ," says Melmoth.

"So much for censorship," says Raquel.

"That man killed himself."

Raquel sips her wine. It is almost gone. An inch is left in the bottle, their last, of a fabulous Napa vintage. Melmoth pours this remnant into Raquel's glass. "As you like to point out, not every life is happy."

Melmoth gets off the hoverbed and drops the empty bottle into the recycle chute. It falls without a sound. "Unhappy is one thing," he says. "That man was desperate. Past desperate. In despair."

Raquel sips. "I wish we had more of this."

"Yes. It's delicious."

"It's perfect."

As if on cue, the news story shifts to grape-growing. Family groups of poor Mexicans, rescued by interplanetary transports from starvation in the godforsaken Sonoran desert, have been granted sanctuary in exchange for their service as vineyard workers. *In certain endeavors*, the Overvoice says, *humans still outperform SmartBots.* It explains that grape picking requires unusual endurance and care and, sometimes, speed. *If ripening has reached its ideal moment, all the grapes must be harvested within a few hours. Mexicans only have sufficient stamina to work without rest in the heat and dust. These people possess incomparable strength, combined with precise touch. Their ability to apply the knife exactly to the point where stem meets vine and execute a quick, clean cut is a performance marvelous to see. Cluster after cluster of Cabernet Franc falls into baskets at their feet.*

"Cab Franc!" says Raquel. "All we can drink!"

Melmoth laughs. "Don't be so sure. Even if Martian vineyards start producing good wine, they'll never meet demand."

"Oh, you," says Raquel. "Always pissing on everyone's parade."

Her language has gotten saltier over the last century. When Melmoth first knew her, Raquel was a beautiful young lovely of twenty-four whose harshest words for him were "stick in the mud" or maybe "glass half full." Now she just outs with it. It is less like speaking, Melmoth thinks, and more like hitting.

"Anyway, wine," he says, "is a sideshow. The main thing is gold. That's obvious. But why? Why such a major effort, a legion of miners and all that gear, to find gold on Mars? We don't need gold. Our wealth is in pleasure credits."

"Jewelry," says Raquel. "Gold is beautiful."

"There's enough on Earth for that."

"Oh, it's just habit," says Raquel. "People have valued gold for thousands of years."

"You're saying they want it just to want it. To have."

Raquel nods.

Melmoth frowns. He has always thought of scientists, particularly Earthscientists stationed on Mars, as unsentimental. If they are after gold, he figures they mean to use it – not to make trinkets, but to serve some purpose of their own.

"I don't know. It seems like an awful lot of trouble, even before the ore grinding and cyanide leaching."

"Look at it this way," says Raquel. "On Mars, they don't have to worry about cyanide seeping into the groundwater and contaminating the soil."

Well. Yes. Sure. Melmoth nods. But. "What are they using it for, I'd like to know."

Raquel looks at him sideways.

Out of nowhere his head hurts. If he hadn't been sitting, the pain would have knocked him over. It's a hard, tight buzz, as if low-voltage current were running through his skull into his brain and it hurts enough to stall his thoughts. What was he thinking? About to say? Melmoth does not remember. The fact that he knows he does not remember lessens his anxiety about the forgetting itself. In oldentimes, he might lose his train of thought if something interrupted or distracted him. Fatigue also could do it. The microchip supposedly overrides these factors. Melmoth wonders if it is malfunctioning.

Well, he doesn't know. Just does not know. It's tough to be sure of anything with his head buzzing. You are not supposed to feel it, the microchip. Not as a physical presence and not as an effect. And up until this moment, Melmoth has not. Felt it, he means. The marvel of seamless integration: that is how they tout it. But Melmoth isn't sure. It's great for thinking the windowall on and off, and accessing databases with thought commands, and using these to fly his airpod and dial-in his smartclubs and order savories from hologrammatic menus and transform Jenna into the playmate of his whim. But it does not seem to have made him any smarter. Oh, he knows more, sure, but that's just databases stocked with information. Having facts a thought-command away is not the same thing as being better able to think. Or able to think better. Are those abilities the same? Melmoth thinks they are. But as far as he can tell, his thinking ability is what it has always been.

"You were saying, J?" Raquel smiles.

The windowall, he notices, is off. The Illumined City glitters beyond the glass. What a miracle it is, this civilization to which he is privileged to belong. All those lights! They shine so coolly without producing the dread greenhouse gases everyone was so worried about eighty or ninety years ago. So many nightmarish outcomes, so many scenarios of cataclysm and catastrophe, and not a single one panned out. Which reminds him.

"Gold," he says. "It's right and proper that they are hunting for it on Mars. We can never have too much. That's what I was saying."

"Yes," says Raquel. "Provided, of course, the gold remains in the right hands."

"Yes," says Melmoth. "The right hands. Of course. Like the Cabernet Franc."

"Just so," says Raquel.

"Yes," says Melmoth.

"These things are special," says Raquel.

"Absolutely."

"Not everyone can possess the gold, drink the wine."

"That's right."

"If everyone has a thing, who truly owns it?"

"Just so."

"Gold and wine are ours for the taking because we are special."

"We are."

"Not everyone can be special. If everyone is special, no one is."

"I entirely agree."

"Those Mexicans pick the grapes. They do not drink the wine. Those miners, whom I suspect also were rescued from Sonora, have been tasked to find gold. Claw it from the mountains, dig it out of the valleys. Use whatever means necessary and never mind that some or many will lose their lives in the effort. Their lives do not matter. They are doing the job that is theirs to do. They are not special. If one dies, if a hundred die or a thousand, replacements will be imported and the work will go on. They will find the gold and we will possess it, for the sake of our pleasure day after glorious day, for an infinity of years. Because we are special."

Melmoth is nodding, nodding. Raquel's words flow like a calming dream. Never has he known her to speak so. Is she repeating what she has heard? Something told to her? It does not matter; the words are true. Without knowing it, or maybe he has known but has not been aware, Melmoth has always believed these things. Of course they are special. Longevity alone has made them so. It is how things are – the current dispensation – and to hear it framed in words so simple and exact is a comfort and a joy. Life has not always been so good. This moment has been centuries in the making, a goal intended for millennia. Advancing, always advancing, humankind on the march. And marching onward! A limitless life of plenty, guiltless leisure exempt from work, a permanent settlement on Mars. With all this in hand, what is beyond their grasp?

He opens his eyes. The Illumined City spreads for miles, a dazzling panoply of brilliance and flash crisscrossed by sharp, bright gleamings of bronze and silver and gold. Nothing is wrong. Everything is possible.

"My God, we're lucky," says Melmoth.

"Yes," says Raquel. "We are."

Miguel relents. Really, he has no choice. With his assent, Javier and Pacho each remove a piece of ore. Their search for choice specimens mocks the lateness of the day. Only the oil disappearing from their lanterns forces a decision.

Javier looks from Enrique to Miguel. "Surely you will claim a share."

"It is unnecessary."

They climb the stairs, Enrique first, Miguel in the rear, Pacho behind Javier, who struggles to hold his lantern in one hand and, under the other arm, the veined rock he believes will change his life.

The Turk meets them as they emerge. His eyes are bright, his face shining with sweat. "Have you stolen it all?" he hisses. "To the last grain? Yes? Yes?" His eyes roll back; he seems almost to faint, then disgraces himself. A thin, sharp scent cuts the air.

"What has happened to him?" says Enrique.

Again, Carlos laughs. "You spoke a magic word. Never have I seen a man so possessed."

"That cannot be all," says the Turk, looking at what Pacho and Javier hold. "Surely there is more. Piles of it? Yes? Gold for everyone?"

"More than we can carry," says Javier.

The Turk seems to swoon.

"Regrettably, your fortune is imprisoned inside tons of worthless rock."

The Turk lays both hands over his heart. "It is beautiful. Humans have valued it always."

"We have no use for it," says Miguel. "It is heavy and a burden."

"It is an effective bribe."

"We have asked ourselves how you pass into El Norte."

The Turk lowers his voice. "There are ways and means. Gold is most reliable when others fail."

"This talk wastes time," says Carlos. Javier and Pacho are moving toward the door.

"You cannot leave it unguarded," says the Turk.

"Against whom do we defend it?" says Miguel.

"A company of men must work a day to remove that ore," Pacho says over his shoulder. He and Javier pass outside.

Darting around Enrique and Miguel, the Turk seems to throw himself down the stairs. He disappears into darkness. The speed of his blind descent is startling. A moment later, they hear him from below.

"Oowww, Jesus, Mary, and Joseph!"

Carlos says, "In former times a beautiful woman, if she also was the right woman, might affect a man so deeply." He and Miguel walk outside. They unwind their reins from the railing and, leading their horses, move toward the hotel with Pacho and Javier. Enrique returns to the cellar, where he finds the Turk atop the pile of ore, his face pressed to the rocks.

"Madman." Enrique grabs the Turk by his pants and pulls him off. "It is rock and metal. Dead matter. To desire it so is indecent."

"You fail to understand."

"Choose a piece, if that only will placate you. Otherwise, we must leave it."

"I choose it all!" the Turk exclaims, spreading his arms. "I reserve it by my word! One piece now – later, all I can carry."

"It will kill your horse and also you, to attempt to carry such weight through the mountains."

Inspecting the ore, the Turk seems not to hear. He selects a richly-veined piece and they ascend, pulling the door shut behind them. Setting down his fortune, the Turk scurries outside and returns with a plywood board. This he wedges between doorknob and floor, to Enrique's amusement.

"It will deceive no one. Indeed, it announces the presence of a thing worth seeking."

"No doubt it is inadequate. I will sleep here tonight and cry out in case of intrusion."

"You will not sleep here," says Enrique.

"Set whomever you wish as my jailer. Even the beast Carlos cannot discourage me."

Enrique lays a hand on the Turk's shoulder. "You cannot remain here. We must keep together, unlikely as assault may be. Come, we will secure the door."

"But the gold!" The Turk's eyes blaze in the failing light. "Think of the gold!"

"The gold! The gold!" Enrique mocks the word. "The gold is in no danger. It does not breathe. It does not weep or pray for salvation. It is careless of itself, for nothing can harm it."

As if hearing for the first time, the Turk nods. "Of course, you are correct." He hefts the ore. A grin lifts his face. "Still, to leave it!"

"We have no choice."

Enrique pulls the door shut as they move outside. Its handle and latch are broken, its lock shattered. They retrieve their horses and walk up Calle Lopez Mateos. The hotel's double doors stand open. Its wood-plank verandah is gouged and splintered. This damage is made worse when first the Turk, then Enrique, leads his horse haltingly up the steps and into the lobby. The others have knifed open sofas and armchairs and spread cotton batting along one wall, where the horses stand tethered to radiators. The latter are cold to Enrique's hand. Content to be inside, the horses stand quietly. Javier closes the doors and slides a stout pole, taken from a coat tree, through their handles.

Low wooden tables and round clay pots, plants in the latter long dead, encumber the space. The men shunt these against the walls, together with chairs, sofas, and settees. Large rugs, woven in many colors with jaguars and parrots, skeletons, feathered serpents and ziggurats, cover the floor. Javier and Pacho search the kitchen for food. On an upper floor, Enrique and Miguel find guest rooms with dressers, beds, chairs, and tables. All bathrooms are without water. Blank televisions rest on metal stands. Above the beds, reproductions of oil paintings depict lakes and waterfalls, mountain ranges green with pine, crags of volcanic rock. No landscape shows a human figure.

They move six mattresses, already stripped, downstairs. They are safer on the ground floor, in reach of their horses.

Without electricity the kitchen is useless. Exhaust fans are dead, refrigerators and freezers dark. The latter are empty and retain a scent that Enrique recognizes as bleach. Outside, two large generators are cabled to the electric panel but no gasoline remains in the tanks. "It is of no consequence," Enrique says, and directs Javier to prepare a place to cook. The kitchen's back door opens onto a yard that is suitable. They will boil water to cook up rice and eat this with beans. They will bring the food through the kitchen and into the dining room, where they will eat while seated in chairs. For once, they have no need to conserve water, with Lago Arareco just three miles south.

Creel is a place to gather strength before they venture through the Sierra Tarahumara. Miguel announces that they will remain two nights. Tarrying will allow them to comb the town for whatever remains. He does not mention gold, the presence in every man's mind. "A day's search will cost us nothing," he says.

"It costs us that day," says Carlos. "Those we hope to rescue pay the same price to their captors."

The air grows colder. Light is all but gone. Pacho and Javier prepare the food over an open fire. In the lobby, darkness gathers. The men huddle against encroaching night.

Miguel says, "We will not easily find another place like this. Hardship is likely across the mesa."

"The loss of a day will improve no part of what we encounter hereafter. Nothing of value remains here."

"There is the ore."

"It is worthless to us."

"You are wrong."

Carlos and Miguel turn toward the Turk. His eyes cover both men with disdain. "Gold is essential to your purpose. You must recover as much as possible, then load it onto the horses, which we will lead on foot."

"Lead where?" Beneath his mustache, Carlos's mouth hangs open. "For how long?"

"To the end of our journey," says the Turk. "For as long as it takes."

"It is impossible," says Miguel.

"It is difficult. It is not impossible." The Turk smiles. "We must break down the ore, grind it until it pours like sand, then add water so it becomes like porridge. To this, we add calcium cyanide, together with lime. A sealed container is best. The reaction thrives on oxygen, which we will pump – "

"Calcium cyanide!" The Turk's proposal is so outlandish, Carlos cannot even laugh. "Lime! Where shall we obtain these rarities?"

"The ore suggests that gold extraction was accomplished here."

"Another fairytale. This one is never finished telling stories."

"What he says is true. Gold will ransom our people."

"Ransom? It is a bribe." Now Carlos does laugh. "Gold ore ground as fine as sand! How? Using what? It is madness. We are not miners, nor goldsmiths. We lack tools and knowledge to accomplish this feat."

"The ore is mostly low-grade. The materials of gold cyanidation are likely at hand. To search costs us only time."

"Time we cannot waste." Carlos looks at Enrique, then to Miguel as if daring them to say he is wrong. "Enough of this nonsense. Unless my stomach also is a liar, our meal is ready." He moves toward the kitchen.

"We must refine gold, as much as possible," the Turk says to Carlos's back. "We have no alternative. Our quest will fail otherwise."

Still moving, Carlos says, "Surely the government in Ciudad de México does not require so lavish a bribe."

"The gold is not for politicos."

Carlos turns. "What, then, is its purpose?"

"As Enrique has said. To recover your people."

"From men who fly to Mars? Of what use is gold to them?"

"Gold has tremendous value." The Turk watches Carlos, his eyes unblinking. He speaks with deliberation. "Their aim seems foolish. Were it generally known, ridicule would result, and loss of trust likely follow. However, those on Mars are in thrall to an idea. As a consequence, their desire is extreme." He glances at Enrique and stares down the others. "For gold, they will do anything."

In Center Atrium a fix-it droid removes its left hand. A cylindrical plug of 12 silver pins protrudes two inches from its wrist. Each pin is a unique length and all 12 slide simultaneously into place when the droid plugs-in to the only receptor that matches. A secure connection established, access protocols launch, privileges are authenticated, repair data download. Transfer and de-encryption require two Mars-minutes to complete, after which end-process scripts run, ensuring a safe unplug from the GlobalDigital superframe.

The droid reattaches its hand and steps off toward a reconfiguration ward, where Roscoe's chimps are down for the count.

An unfamiliar hush seeps in from the Outer Sanctum. Roscoe Gold – alchemical wizard, Visionary Philosopher, Initiate schooled in esoteric lore, seeker of eternal life – welcomes the quiet. It gives him space for thought. *Mind before Matter*. The phrase is promise and assurance. It is the first thing he knows, the single truth whose simplicity gives the hint that will solve the problem that has vexed him so long.

"Tea!" he cries. A service droid rolls in with stainless steel teapot and porcelain cup and saucer. Seated in the yellow chair, Roscoe pours and stirs. Today's treat is doughnuts: powdered sugar, apple cinnamon, melted chocolate (since solidified), banana cream, jelly. The stuff is poison. Confections are killing him slowly and eventually will kill him outright. He bites away half the banana cream and chews, sips tea and swallows. Maybe he imagines it but his brain feels instantly sugar-bright.

Mind before Matter. So Earthlings are living to great ages – living so long that death has become a supposition. Very good. Still, no one lives forever. Despite CellRenew and miracles of organ cloning, do these freeloaders and layabouts think they will be alive in, say, a million years? Life on such a scale is inconceivable. No one imagines a time horizon of a thousand millennia. No one except Roscoe Gold.

He gobbles down the banana cream, finishes his tea and pours more. Roscoe picks up the jelly doughnut and sticks it in his mouth. It doesn't matter. The body is frail. No dodge of high-tech rejuvenation can cancel the obligation to die. Which brings Roscoe back to the mystery of how to live forever.

Just look at those chimps. They are a side issue, sure: mere facsimiles, not living creatures. A fascination and curiosity. At a certain point, however, technology breaks down. Systems fail after having worked perfectly for days or years. Entropy: the reason nothing lasts. Given time and no remedial measures, even the most well-designed system goes to pieces. Organic matter decays; machines degrade. Even the Sun, what they call the Sun, is nothing but a mass of nuclear reactions that will sometime end.

A time to be born, a time to die. Life occurs between these limits, then passes away. Is there any return? Does each of us, in another space-time or alternate universe, relive his life, her life, in part or in full, exactly as it happened or with differences? Or is extinction our common fate? Roscoe Gold does not know, cannot know, and this uncertainty disturbs him.

The telescreen is dark. Paladin Silver is departed for Earth with orders to roll up those Mexicans and bring them to Mars. They will be set harsh labor with pickaxe and shovel and otherwise made powerless to cause mischief. Templar, the estimable Dr. Bronze, is doubtlessly mucking about in her vineyard, trying to persuade her guest workers to care about *vinis vinifera* as much as she does. A futile endeavor but it keeps her occupied. And the wines really are not half bad.

Roscoe polishes off the jelly doughnut and pours more tea. All this business about grapes and guerrillas is a side issue, too. Gold only is important. A stupendous source is what they need, something inexhaustible, accessible, truly grand. A nitrogen-oxygen atmosphere depends on it. And only such an atmosphere can liberate them from the EarthStations.

Mind before Matter. It was from the Eternal Mind that Matter was created. It is of the Eternal Mind that each individual mind partakes. The body is clay: coherent dust, briefly animated and doomed to age, weak against illness, prey to accident. Only mind endures, and that is Roscoe's project: to ensure a continuance of mind – of his mind. To make possible a survival of consciousness –

his consciousness, yes, and those of his colleagues in the quest for immortality.

A tap and the telescreen wavers on. Outside the EarthStations, the Marscape is bleak and wan. Wisps of dust swirl meekly in a limpid wind too thin to unsettle the rock and pebble of a red-hued plain. Roscoe looks on, his mouth awry. A dead planet: it is. What chance, really, do they have? Stark, flat light and a denuded surface make Mars a dispiriting place. By every appearance, it is past saving. Even with enough gold and a restored magnetosphere, can it be possible to concentrate nitrogen and oxygen in exact proportion? As a theory it is plausible but as an actual undertaking it seems quixotic. Another fascination.

The miners, he assumes, are out there somewhere. No sign of them onscreen – although that doesn't mean much, the perspective being truncated. And does it matter, after all? If they match their exertions to Mars's feeble environment, they might as well have never left the EarthStation.

Roscoe switches feeds. Earth-Mars transmissions are delayed just three minutes and seven seconds, thanks to perihelion opposition. Transmission times between individual SmartBots and GlobalDigital add another millisecond or two but all in all Roscoe has an illusion of seeing and hearing things as they happen. He taps through uplinks provided by GlobalDigital, making instant judgments about where to pause. For the most part, he keeps tapping; eighty percent and more of these worthless Earthlings are pleasuring themselves with their respective PACs. It is incredible, the capacity of these people for self-indulgence. When Roscoe finds one merely hanging by his ankles in an Inversion Trainer, it comes as a relief. No matter that the fellow is naked; it is the recommended way. But how does he embellish Inversion Therapy? Not by accessing a windowall or, as one would expect, having his PAC perform fellatio, or both. Instead, this person is holding what Roscoe recognizes as a book, the genuine article, with a hand-tooled leather binding, no less, and page ends gilt with gold. Gold! A negligible quantity, but what a waste! Each page in turning flashes knife-bright across Roscoe's screen. Upside-down, the title is not decipherable. Roscoe inverts the picture one hundred and eighty degrees.

Brave New World. Really, he has expected something of this sort for years. On the other hand, it amazes Roscoe that the Great Forgetting is still incomplete. What whim has prompted this fellow to dig out an heirloom? How has it been possible for such a notion to cross his mind? Given infinite diversions at his beck and call, what makes this guy want to read?

The name, Roscoe sees, is J Melmoth. He wonders what the "J" stands for, not that it matters. No telling his age. His reading a book, however, suggests to Roscoe that here is a man not unlike himself. A man interested in knowing things that holograms cannot display. A man who persists in thinking on his own. Deciding matters in his own mind, forming his own conclusions. Undirected, unaffected, independent thought. Oh, about what? Roscoe nods at J Melmoth, now seeming to hang right-side-up. *Well now. Let's see.*

A tap of Roscoe's fingertip and a list unfolds accordion-style. "Hmm," as he reads, shaking his head. "Concerning ourselves with the historical truth of cinematic melodramas, are we?" addressing Melmoth, who cannot hear him. "Examining archival databases. Doubting the accuracy of certain entries therein. Hmm. Drawing existential insights from dramatic depictions of star-crossed romances. Ah! Verifying the fidelity of digitexts to their paper originals." Touching a sensor, Roscoe says, "Really, sir, such attention to detail is archaic, not to mention a waste of energy."

For more than six minutes, nothing changes. Roscoe fills the interval by eating the powdered sugar doughnut and drinking tea.

He chews slowly, swallows at leisure. It is not feasible, this sort of hands-on intervention. Even with GlobalDigital keeping tabs, case by case review would swallow his every moment. His life. Anyway, reading is not the problem. The problem is thinking: that people, this fellow Melmoth, for example, insist on trying to think.

Onscreen, J Melmoth looks up.

Ah, at last. "It is fruitless, my friend, to squander your vitality thus and so," says Roscoe Gold. "Better to roger your droid in its posterior orifice, SmartBot technology having sanitized that perversion to the utmost degree."

During the delay, Roscoe opens six subscreens. All show views of the Martian surface. In one, a contingent of miners struggles through what is evidently knee-deep sand, backs bent, heads lowered, pickaxes dragging behind them in the drifting dust. In another, miners work in the shadow of an escarpment, pulverizing the rock face with full-hearted blows. Empty Marscapes fill the other panels: sand-filled craters, heat-riven plains, low ragged ridges as old, almost, as the Sun.

On the main screen, our man closes his book and sets it on the floor. He touches a button and the Inversion Trainer swings around. Roscoe flips the picture as J Melmoth releases the ankle anchors and steps free. He gestures, it seems, at Roscoe. As the camera approaches him and looks, as it were, into his eyes, J Melmoth says, quite distinctly, "Now, Jenna, I will have your ass." *Have?* Roscoe wonders where this Nosey Parker learned his English. Some quick disrobing by the Bot and the view swings dizzyingly downward, showing Roscoe the floor. "Oh, J!" he hears the sneaky SmartBot exclaim, "you beastly big man!" Roscoe cannot see what is happening until the droid swivels its head. Its synchronized lenses discern an average human penis exciting itself against it, the droid's, synthetic buttocks.

Well well. Enough of that. Roscoe terminates the feed.

He lifts the pot but the tea is gone. They are all very well, these ad hoc interventions, but as standard operating procedure something better is called for. Roscoe Gold cannot stare fire-eyed at his telescreen and correct each least thought-anomaly of every last nonentity on Earth. He will have to farm out the work, but to whom? Discipline & Punish can be a bit, well, zealous. It would need sharp guidelines – not just a list of interdicted thoughts but a flowchart of acceptable remediations. Who is to compile and codify such SOP? Roscoe could assign the task to high-level Adepts, who would likely balk at articulating so tedious a taxonomy. Besides, the Code of Core Beliefs does not countenance mind control. GlobalDigital is, really, the only option. It already handles comprehensive data-gathering and autofeeds SmartBots their savvy, not to mention those diverting fillips and *bon mots* that so amuse their human hosts.

The teapot's convex surface mirrors Roscoe pursing his lips. Side issues and curiosities. He is plagued by them. It is absurd to worry about such stuff, movies and novels and what someone reads and whether those chimps are on the mend, when the only goal worth gaining remains as elusive to him as it was to his predecessors ten centuries ago. A thousand years and then some of alchemical experiments have come to naught.

Mind before Matter. Roscoe stands. Facing away from the telescreen with his eyes on the floor, he considers oldentimes, when a person saved a trace of his consciousness in a piece of writing. A lyric poem, a tragic play, a comic narrative: something that mattered to him and would, he hoped, be meaningful to others. Something the world would not willingly let die. In the Fifth Century B.C.E., somewhere in Greece, Sophocles wrote *Oedipus Rex*. Twenty-five centuries later, the play was still being read almost everywhere. For all Roscoe knows, someone is reading it today, if this Melmoth fellow is representative of what people get up to. He himself could read *Oedipus Rex* right now on Mars. As it happens, Roscoe feels no need to read anything. That is not the point. The point is that *Oedipus Rex* survives; in its words, a little of Sophocles's mind yet lives. Nothing guaranteed this. Countless plays and poems and so forth have been lost to accident and time, indifference and neglect and intentional destruction. Nevertheless: for much of human history, authorship offered the best chance of achieving a modest sort of immortality.

No more. When books ceased to be printed, writing became anonymous. Anyone could access character templates and plot macros. Spelling and grammar defaulted to prevailing norms. Text was aggregated, not written, and the possibility of individual authorship passed away. Novels and plays, poems and essays became mere occasions, raw material that anyone might shape and bend, cut and paste. Dislike the ending of a book or film? Insert an alternate from a catalogue of stock plots. As this Melmoth fellow has discovered, it is done all the time for any reason or none at all.

When meddling vies with theft, whose story is it?

The Sumerians, Roscoe thinks, did better. Inscribed on wet clay then dry-fired, pre-cuneiform scripts became written in stone. Proof against flame, impervious to flood, these ancient tablets have survived in their thousands. Oh, many have broken and fragments only remain or are missing. Still, annals and reports 6000 years old endure. Chronicles of the Olden Gods may be read as they were written, safe from any forger's falsifying hand.

Roscoe chuckles, soundlessly. No one reads clay tablets. Paper books, too, have been forgotten by the million. Few people pay attention to what anyone else thinks. A writer finally writes for himself and whoever might happen to listen. And that is not good enough for Roscoe Gold. He will not consign his consciousness to indifferent, careless human memory, with its liking for brevity and susceptibility to amnesia. Something surer, both more complete and imperishable, is necessary to deliver his mind from oblivion.

Studying the subscreens, he sees those miners have arrived on firmer ground. Still, they seem bewildered. Heads slowly rotating left, then right, they loiter like dwarves beneath an infinite stellar surround.

Picking the apple cinnamon doughnut off the plate, he tosses it dome-ward, high, high, watching it spin, then shuts his eyes, spreads his arms, cants his head back and catches it full-square in his teeth. Chews, he chews, gobbling down the confected baked treat hands-free, crumbs tumbling down his chest.

A long time ago, computer scientists believed consciousness could be inscribed on a microchip. Translate thoughts into binary code, the theory went, and those thoughts would become data. And data, as we all know, can be preserved. Everyone down to the most insignificant human being in what used to be called Christendom would be made immortal.

Roscoe chuckles, now out loud. He needs tea, would kill for tea, to wash down the masticated, gummy doughnut-stuff. "Tea!" he cries. Before he sits, a service droid appears with a fresh pot. Roscoe pours and drinks.

As if consciousness were merely a sum total of present thoughts and retrievable memory. Well, it was only ever a theory; like many another fine-sounding sham, the digital mind proved unworkable. To encode each least bit of anyone's mental capacity was a job beyond any computer simply because mind was, is, always evolving, moment by moment. Thought-assimilation programs structured to enable real-time free association among present, past, and prospective alternatives became so hideously complex that they could not run. Even quantum superpositioning architectures did not avail. The effort dwindled away and was quietly abandoned before anyone considered Step Two: how emotion

– which no one had a clue about how to encode – might be integrated with protocols that could not even capture thought.

And so to gold. It is humankind's only hope. A nitrogen-oxygen atmosphere on a planet as unlikely as Mars. First, a magnetosphere. Earthscientists are working. Roscoe is sure that such knowledge, once held in a time beyond human memory and thereafter lost, is theirs to master again. Only beyond the confines of EarthStations and the competence of microchips can Roscoe and his colleagues be free.

Were it not so desperate, their predicament would be ludicrous. Behold the human creature, possessed of mind and will, able to ponder eternity yet doomed to die. A mortal being with the apprehension of a god, crippled by its finitude.

We lose everything in the end, Roscoe thinks, our bodies and minds and all we possess. Whole civilizations die and afterward are barely remembered, if at all. The people are forgotten as if they never lived and cared and worked and played and wept and laughed and loved.

Each of us comes to nothing. We go down to dust, just like Mars.

Mind before Matter, he repeats in a soft voice. It is his mantra, axiomatic, the core principle of his faith.

Mind before Matter. Initiates know.

"Something is up with Jenna." Melmoth refills Raquel's glass.

"Not corrupted firmware, I hope," sipping some lesser Cab Franc.

Their PACs confined to quarters, Melmoth and Raquel are alone, standing at the chest-high granite ledge that divides the windowall arena from their kitchen in a way that allows whoever is preparing dinner to see the screens. Neither Melmoth nor Raquel, however, does much dinner preparation. Their three-zone refrigerator is stocked mostly with wine and caviar and cooled to 42, 38, and 34 oldentime Fahrenheit degrees.

"No, she – it – works fine. Too fine, is the thing." Melmoth pours a fresh glass of wine for himself and sets the bottle on the ledge. "It's as if she – it – is learning to like sex." Leaning against the granite, he swirls the wine.

"I'm pretty sure I don't want to hear this," says Raquel.

Holding his glass in two fingers by its stem, Melmoth lifts it, tilts it, turns it. He judges this Cab Franc to be ruby red. "It's as if she – it – really wants to, you know. Desires it, I mean. As much as a dozen times a day. Very strange."

"J, I am not interested. And do stop calling Jenna, 'it.' It's obviously inappropriate, especially if she's as horny as you claim."

Now there's a word Melmoth has thought he would not hear again. *Horny.* He has never liked it as a description of someone who wants sex. The sound of *horn* is too close to *whore*; and *horny*, to Melmoth's ear, calls up *hoary.* All together it evokes a stinking, hairy goat or cruel and filthy satyr so hot with lust it will fuck anyone it can grab. "I don't think I'm complaining, exactly. Only it doesn't leave time for much else."

Raquel sniffs. "You make it sound like a job."

"It is like a job." He sips the wine. "I can hardly think two consecutive thoughts. A minute after I pick up a book or start an old-enflick she's all over me, making the sweetest demands in the most meretricious way imaginable. I won't repeat what she says."

"Thank you. You ought to be ashamed, how you've scripted her."

"But I haven't scripted this. Her system is generating spontaneous enhancements."

"In other words, she's learning. Well, well." Raquel sips. "SmartBots who better the depravity we model for them. What will they think of next?" She sets her glass on the ledge and Melmoth splashes in a little more wine.

"Maybe they'll start programming us."

"Maybe they already do."

"If so, it's very subtle."

"It would be." Raquel winks at him.

"Yes, of course. Only I'm not aware of doing or thinking anything against my will."

"You wouldn't be. That's how it would work. All the better to run us."

"If they are running us, why are they letting us talk about it?"

"Consider it strategic. Part of the method. What seems like a free and open exchange of ideas is calculated to disarm and reassure. Meanwhile, uncertainty creeps in. We suspect and can never know. Are our thoughts truly our own? Or is what we think linked-in? Or is it a blend or tangling-up of our thoughts with theirs? And vice-versa. Or both, and we can't tell how."

"Once thoughts are tangled, isn't 'vice' the same as 'versa' and 'both,' as well?"

"Exactly," says Raquel.

They laugh. Raquel raises her glass. Melmoth clinks it with his glass and they drink. It is the second bottle of lesser Cab Franc they have opened today. Melmoth tells himself it is too much, that he needs to slow down; another glass or two and he'll be numb. When Jenna starts tugging at him, he'll be like putty. Oh, he can fake it, they have aids and devices and he knows techniques. But however harmless it is, Melmoth feels that using a dildo on a SmartBot is a ridiculous state of affairs. The next step is Jenna and Floyd performing android sex while he and Raquel watch.

As if his thought is already forgotten, Melmoth picks up the bottle and pours. They used to hit it pretty hard back in the Day – Cabernet, Chardonnay, Pinot, Frascati, Sauvignon Blanc, Petite Syrah, Chianti, Zinfandel, Malbec, Viognier – but ever since organ cloning guaranteed replacement livers they have known no restraint. Only the pleasure Melmoth takes in, or maybe he means from, a good, steady hard-on prevents him from drinking a couple bottles on his own every day. As things are, they are putting away that much between the pair of them.

They swirl the wine, lift their glasses and touch them, *clink-clink*, in a silent toast. They are drinking to – what? Life? Their marriage? Their luck? The wine itself? Does it matter? With all they have and hold, is it necessary to specify?

They drift toward the couch, Melmoth bringing the bottle with a hand around its neck. They sit, sink into cushions. One of them, Melmoth isn't sure if it's him or if Raquel has beaten him to it, thinks-on the windowall. Their panorama of the Illumined City disappears as colors gather and sounds rise. Images cohere in a dozen different scenes: sexolympics highlights, oldenflick loops as familiar as friends, Mars feeds manifesting on seven screen sections, the sun-flooded island of Cuba, seen from above, seemingly afloat on an azure sea. Melmoth pinpoints a high-definition picture of EarthStation 4 and winks. An apple orchard expands in size and detail. Reconfigured as an integrated hologram, rowed trees and sloped ground fill Melmoth's vision. The apples on the trees glisten as if after light rain. The Overvoice extols the fruit's crisp sweetness. It notes that this agricultural miracle is the result of optimized VirtuSun exposure, traditional irrigation, and 22nd Century fertilizers deployed by Earthscientists working hand-in-glove with family farmers.

Raquel yawns.

"Too much wine?" says Melmoth.

"Really, J. Are we going to watch apple picking?"

"On Mars! It's amazing, what they've been able to do. The implications are tremendous."

"We have apples. Here on Earth, I mean. They grow perfectly well and taste delicious."

"That's not the point. If we can grow apples on Mars, we can grow fruits and vegetables anywhere we can build an EarthStation."

"Planning on colonizing the galaxy, are we?"

"Don't fool yourself, thinking no one's thinking about the next thing." Saying this makes Melmoth dizzy. "True, it's only lately they've achieved anything useful. They still haven't created an Earth-like atmosphere. That would really take things to the next level."

"I don't want to live on Mars."

"I'm not thinking of us." Wow is he woozy. He really has to slow down. "The gov could move the Gulag. Transport the Guantánamo miscreants and restore Cuba to its old-school glory. You remember. Before that bastard Castro, Cuba was basically an open-air pleasure dome. Sunshine and sex on the beach. Bronzed tourists as naked as God made them consorting with pliant natives in a tropical sea."

"Enormous start-up costs." Raquel lets her head fall back on the cushions. "Interplanetary transports for – what is it now? Thousands? Tens of thousands?"

"With a breathable atmosphere and food self-sufficiency, Gulag Mars is feasible."

Again, Raquel sniffs; Melmoth wonders if she has a cold. "You know how easily I sunburn. Besides, other places would do just as well. Even with banditos and sabotage, there's Mexico. Puerto Morelos, Cancún, Río Lagartos, Cozumel – why, the entire Yucatán Peninsula is already everything Cuba will never be. They are still playing golf at Mayakoba and all along Riviera Maya and Playa del Carmen."

"Sounds like you want a vacation," says Melmoth.

"Yes, now that you mention it. We're not doing anything here."

"We wouldn't do anything there, either, except lie on the beach and drink tequila."

"Tequila makes me sick. I hope they have good wines."

Melmoth winks and EarthStation 4 melts away. They watch the screens and polish off the Cab Franc. Melmoth notices that the Cuba feed shows plenty of sea and sky, green hills rolling toward ocean, empty baseball diamonds and sugar cane fields lost to neglect, but no human figures, nothing so much as a droid. If he didn't know better, he would say the island was deserted.

"Strange, how they've stopped showing Gitmo," says Raquel, more or less reading his thoughts. If they hadn't been married a hundred years and then some, it would be eerie.

"Maybe not so strange," says Melmoth.

"That's what I mean."

"Do they have to show it? We know miscreants are locked up. They, or rather their papis and grandpapis, have been locked up since we were young."

"You're saying we don't mind. That we're not troubled by it."

"I think we like it. If nothing less than killing us will satisfy them, better they're in cages. Right?"

"Do they still want to kill us, you think?"

Melmoth nods. Raquel's eyes are closed. "From what I've seen and heard, yes, the bastards still want to kill us. Why would the gov maintain the Gulag, except for our protection?"

Raquel seems to be falling asleep. She says, "One day it will have to end."

"I suppose. After all miscreants die out." Is the conversation making him tired? Or is it all that wine? "Come to think of it, I'm surprised that hasn't happened. They can't have much opportunity to mate."

"A great many must still be at large."

"That also is surprising. It makes you think."

"What does it make you think, J?"

"Oh, that the gov lets them, you know, run around on their own and, well, reproduce."

"It must be quite a job just keeping them fed and their cages clean. A major effort. Plus round-ups and deportations."

"Acceptable costs. The gov wants a perpetual class of potential terrorists the rest of us can hate and fear."

Raquel nods. "Pretty conspiratorial."

She is bored; Melmoth can tell. He has seen the signs for a century. "It stands to a sort of reason."

"The logic of a conspiratorial mind."

"Which reminds me. When we go to Cancún or wherever, can we leave Jenna and Floyd here?"

Raquel makes a sound that seems to signify "Yes." Eyes still closed, she lifts her glass and Melmoth clinks it. That both glasses are empty does not seem to matter.

Clinging to cage bars, Ibn al Mohammed watches rain fall through Gitmo palms, *pock pock pock-pock pock*. Each drop is an affliction that makes the detainee wish himself deaf. For days, rain has fallen. First fast, then slow, then hard, then slow again so that it seemed almost to stop, then faster and now slow and steady in a way that seems might never end. Harvest is suspended; android guards malfunction when wet. Inmates are stranded in-cage, buckets are full, bodies unwashed. Food arrives at odd hours, delivered between rainfalls from automaton carts that navigate the cage-rows in rubber-tire hush. The loudspeakers are silent. Ibn al Mohammed imagines their taunts and blasphemies to divert his fruitless thoughts.

Escape is impossible. Stainless steel bars three inches in diameter, closely set. Watchful in towers, guards have rifles. Those rifles have scopes. Ocean surrounds them. His only hope is persuasion. Can the detainee persuade his captors that his freedom is due? He is here by mistake – a series of mistakes that ignorance has compounded and injustice excused. His imprisonment is wrong; by encaging him still, they do violence to the laws of God and man. For years, he has complied. Cleaned his pail, performed his prayers, suffered temptation, harvested coffee on shaded hillsides within sight of the sea. Day after day, night upon night. Ibn al Mohammed has set hatred aside, the better to hear the slow, calm voice that says he is righteous. That he lives a righteous life. This voice sustains him. It promises that his detention, despite the life it has worn away, cannot last forever.

Pock. Pock. Pock. Minutes pass. He thinks of al Zahrani, who refused to work. How does the old man sustain jihad, locked in cage?

Guards will return when the rain stops. Cages will open, harvest will resume. Chain brigade jog-trot along sun-warm beach sand, pail held by its handle and cleansed in the sea. That much, yes. Everyone will comply. But the harvest? Should he cooperate? Why? Cooperation has brought him no closer to freedom.

Gitmo rain is a gray curtain drawn across the face of the world. The sand is wet, the air damp and still. Ibn al Mohammed cannot see ocean or sky. His gaze turns from this blankness to the meager items inside his cage. Cot. Stool with three legs. Tin pail with handle. His mattress, sheet, and pillow are damp. To lie upon them is disagreeable.

Perhaps to endure is enough. Perhaps not-dying is jihad enough for now.

He sits on the stool, spits in the pail. With his foot he pushes it to a corner. If he refuses to work, will they allow him to doze in the shade of the trees? Will they beat the soles of his feet with bamboo canes? Ibn al Mohammed has heard-tell of Gitmo punishments. Oldtimers speak of a man like himself, quiet, humble, of imperfect faith – or rather, of pure faith and flawed observance, God's servant no less – being strapped to a pallet and tilted headlong into water. Held under for a minute, the water ice-cold, then hauled out, gasping.

The name of your network?

The key to the cipher?

How are orders conveyed?

What atrocities are planned?

What can he tell them? He, who knows nothing. Ibn al Mohammed has not planned atrocities nor committed them. He has never been in the presence of terrorists. Yet Satan's agents suspect him. He is dark-complected. His hair and beard are black. His name is Muslim. Body tall and slender, hands large, their fingers long and tapered. Dark eyes sunken in a narrow face. Irises like obsidian. He prays on hands and knees, forehead touching the floor. Thoughtlessly aligned, his cage obliges him to face a white plastic wall to bow toward Mecca. No matter; Ibn al Mohammed requires no sight of ocean or sky to know his place in the universe. He knows himself as one chosen, beloved of God. A man whose devotion will allow him to be saved.

Standing at the bars, he stares at the plastic wall. Modesty panel, they call it. The detainee wills nothing, attempts nothing, merely stares at blankness as his mind opens toward such signs as might appear. Something, nothing. However little, however great, whatever God vouchsafes is sufficient. The least sign is enough. A crease in the plastic. A shadow cast against its insensate skin, then fleeing, gone. A raindrop: trickling through the roof, one small drop might touch the wall, leave a transparent streak, a tear without sorrow to confirm his understanding of what is and must be. *Recognition. Acceptance.* By such a sign he will know he is not forsaken. That God notices and prepares a place.

He will not serve in the harvest. He will eat the food, drink the water, ride the bus. He will not pick the berries so prized by his captors. Droids will cajole and threaten; perhaps they will beat him. If so, they incriminate themselves. He relishes their degradation together with God's tasking, this new test of will and faith. To suffer in silence, as meek as a lamb. Ibn al Mohammed will remove himself from himself. Self fading into background, his presence will diminish. His body will persist; corporeally, he must endure. But his self will become absent. Mind and its thought, heart and all emotion will disperse smoke-like into nothingness and in its vanishing forestall injury, indignity, all pain.

Does God approve? Does God see? A mere token will assure Ibn al Mohammed for a lifetime. Standing at the bars, he watches. Minutes pass. How long must he wait? God speaks at His leisure to those with patience to attend. What does it mean, to have enough patience to attend to God? It is a discipline to expect nothing because you deserve nothing and merit only death. Ibn al Mohammed has waited all his life. What has he seen? His father taken away. His mother and sisters scrounging in a desert. He himself is confined in-cage. Squats on a stool, shits in a pail. Rain rattles across sheet tin, *pock-pock-pock-pock*. Food is delivered on a tray. A damp bed beneath his body, a white wall before his eyes.

What does Ibn al Mohammed see? He sees nothing.

⌂ ⌂ ⌂

They replenish the oil in each lantern, first extinguishing its flame, then relight it with a taper. Enrique lights additional lanterns and sets them about. A golden glow fills the room as a scent of burning corn rises in the cool air. Enrique says, "You must tell us."

The Turk shakes his head. "It is beyond belief."

"It cannot be so strange," says Miguel. "All people desire gold."

They stand in the lobby, hunched against the cold. The Turk seems stooped, a little halt, as if he has suddenly aged. An old man, harmless, he knows nothing and wants only peace as he crawls toward death. Enrique has witnessed this semblance before and is not misled. "With luck," the Turk says, pointing at his chunk of ore, "here is all the gold I require. You, however, must supply yourselves with as much gold as your horses can carry."

"Can they be so greedy," says Carlos, "to require such tribute?"

"It is necessity, not greed, that drives them."

"What desire does gold appease, if not for wealth?"

The Turk regards Carlos with eyes almost pitying. "Before all else, they wish Mars to become habitable. Air, of course, is essential. To create such an atmosphere, gold is needed."

Carlos's eyes are blank. Miguel and Enrique also know nothing of this.

"The method I cannot pretend to explain. It is said to be science. I have heard it spoken of only." The Turk's sentence ends with coughing. He reaches for a canteen.

"It is a revelation," says Enrique.

"A fantasy," says Carlos.

"It is a trick." Miguel stands before them, arms folded on his chest. "Gold has many uses. This use it does not have."

The Turk drinks, wipes his lips. "You speak in ignorance."

"I speak in commonsense."

"In this case, commonsense is ignorance. The method is said to belong to ancient knowledge, found again."

"Perhaps it is no method, just a great lie to justify stealing treasure wherever they find it."

"Or wherever others find it," says Carlos.

The Turk laughs. "What is the difference to us?" The men look at him as if this question, which concerns them more than any other, is the thought farthest from their minds. "Whether they lie in order to steal or truly pursue a miracle, they covet gold. With gold in hand, you have a means of freeing your people."

"We have no gold. And we have only your word that gold is their object."

The Turk throws up his hands. "I try to help you. This information I reveal – few know of it. Really, my friends, you make common cause reluctantly."

Before Carlos can answer, Miguel says, "Let us take your account as true. What then? We cannot separate gold from rock. We might carry two dozen pieces – is that enough?   Are these men interested in raw ore? I myself have no understanding of refinement, but talk of chemical baths and stone ground as fine as sand says it is difficult."

They stand in the lobby, stink of burning corn staining the air. Enrique says, "The ore is worthless to us. We must find purified gold."

"There is no such gold," says Carlos.

"It is possible. Those who left the ore were themselves refining it."

"How can you know this?"

"I know to move gold ore through the sierra is difficult and costly. Much better to refine it and transport pure gold. It may be that some has been left."

Carlos says, "Huh!" Miguel and the Turk laugh. "Truly, your optimism is fantastic."

"We do not know that," says Enrique.

"Of course, they who refined the ore have taken the gold with them."

"We do not know that."

"We do not know, yet we may safely assume," says the Turk.

"It costs nothing to look."

"It costs time," says Carlos.

"It is worth the time to find the gold."

"And if we do not find the gold? Is it then still worth the time?"

"Yes. Then we will know."

The Turk says, "I believe such a search is futile. However, luck or fate may favor us. We must not forestall it."

Javier enters to announce their meal. Smelling the air, he says, "Who is burning a cornfield?"

"It is the lanterns," Enrique tells him.

"Truly, I have not known them to stink so."

"We have not used them indoors."

"When the horses shit, you will not mind the lanterns," says Carlos, and the men almost laugh.

Pacho brings in food and the men seat themselves around a large table covered with a white cloth. Using bowls, plates, and utensils from the kitchen, they pass beans, rice, serviceable fish, helping themselves to equal portions.

"An admirable cloth," says Miguel.

The men nod. None has ever set his elbows on a cloth so white, so fine. Intent on their hunger, they eat in silence and finish in minutes.

Javier fills a pot with water and carries it outside. It is ceramic – another thing left behind. When the water boils, he pours it onto coffee grinds spooned into each mug. These are alike, white ceramic etched with blue emblems and devices, also from the kitchen.

Craving warmth, they stand around the fire. Pacho says, "Speak of the time before the Sundering. Tell us what we do not remember."

Enrique sips his coffee. "I have spoken of this before."

"Speak of it again."

"It was long ago. México was being ruined even then by men who would kill for a fistful of pesos."

Pacho glances at Javier and Javier shrugs. "So you have said. But why? What need made them kill?"

Looking at the sky, Enrique seems to smile. "They killed for reasons men always have killed. The poor killed to live. The rich killed to become richer. We know this. There is no need to repeat."

"And yet, there is nothing else."

Javier is correct. Of all the stories told of México, only the tale of its rape remains. Enrique says, "Ambitious men enslaved peons to grow coca in the mountains." It is a kind of recitation, a story they know. "From its leaves they extracted a substance known as cocaine – a powerful intoxicant deemed evil by El Norte."

"How, evil?" says Pacho. "We wish to understand."

Enrique laughs. "Compañero, a man addicted to cocaine is not a man. He is a worthless being who can do nothing but feed his demon, whom he serves as a slave. He cannot work, nor cooperate with other men. In anything useful, he is useless. All of that is simple. What is not simple is why El Norte did not make cocaine less valuable, and less worth killing for, by making it legal."

Pacho and Javier stare, their faces expectant and confused.

Miguel says, "Cocaine is poison. They aimed to discourage its use."

"Indeed? Perhaps they aimed to keep police employed and prisons full. By this means rich gringos who build prisons and run them grow richer. For México, the outcome has been tragic." They are silent as Enrique drinks. "Pueblos emptied, people made homeless. Waste silos protected by razor wire. The garbage that poisons water and land."

"You speak as one defeated," says Miguel.

"Not defeated, no. Angry. As you are."

Of their anger they have not spoken. Set in words, a feeling gains strength and presence. To speak of it risks losing control. To know the size of one's anger at a particular moment of one's life is dangerous. Anger too large, too deep becomes despair. "We are forsaken. To think sabotage will mend our situation is foolish. Mexicans still kill Mexicans for gringo cash. They will use each other as slaves and worse. El Norte tourists continue to take their pleasures at resorts where Mexicans clean and serve. It is a great degradation for a people to become a race of servants. How did it happen?" Enrique tosses the dregs of his coffee into the fire. With a hiss it becomes steam and disappears.

"Centuries ago, before the first conquistador set foot on this continent, ancient cities failed. Monte Albán. El Tajín. Palenque. Chichén Itzá. Izamal and Uxmal and Comalcalco and Cantona. Even from Teotihuacán, the gods withdrew. The people suffered. Many died. Their descendants, of whom we are the remnant, fell into loneliness and solitude – a limbo of nonbeing over which a remote god presides. A pale-faced god, neither Indian nor Mexican, whom no degree of suffering can appease."

Miguel says, "The Tarahumara survived the Conquest. No doubt they retain knowledge from olden times."

"Sadly for you, the Indians speak a language apart." The Turk has almost disappeared in the scant light. He holds his mug in front of his chest. "For five hundred years they have lived among themselves. They possess nothing of value, save for their freedom.

This, they will not surrender – as they proved when they retreated to the sierra."

"And they tolerate your presence, why?"

"I do not attempt to change how they live." Gently, the Turk swirls his coffee. "We will meet Tarahumara as we cross the mountains. I will relate the event of an airship that flew down from the sky."

"What can it mean to them, living as they do?" Miguel, having finished his coffee, wipes out the mug with his hand.

"Perhaps nothing." The Turk shrugs, nods. "It is difficult to know how much of a legend is true. The Tarahumara tell of beings who came down from Heaven to Earth ages ago. They keep these legends from chabochi. To chabochi, they say only that the Sun and Moon created the world, then became angry and sent a great flood that two Tarahumara only, a boy and a girl, survived in high mountains with three kernels of corn and three beans. The stories they tell amongst themselves speak also of beings who came to Earth in vessels that flew at tremendous speeds. The Indians lacked words for such craft. They called them fire spears and winged shields. The beings, they called gods."

"Myths," says Carlos. "These are myths of a superstitious people."

"Perhaps – yet the Indians hold these stories as sacred knowledge. The gods, they say, stood ten feet tall and possessed fearsome weapons none could oppose. Their devices achieved miracles – cut great stones to size and polished their faces as smooth as glass, then caused these stones to float in the air and arrange themselves as pyramids and temple walls. Stones so heavy no number of men could raise them. The gods' time on Earth occurred hundreds of millennia ago, when humans were as apes, their lives short and hard. The gods made humans over in their image and later taught them methods of farming, husbandry of animals, construction of waterways. The peoples' lives became easier. The threat of famine receded. Violence diminished and the Indians thrived. In gratitude, they pledged fealty."

Confusion whispers around the fire-lit circle. The Turk's account matches some half-forgotten lessons taught to them long ago. Miguel says, "This is the legend of Quetzalcóatl, changed and distorted. You are a storyteller."

"I invent nothing," says the Turk. "It is Indians' lore of ancient days."

"Quetzalcóatl," Miguel repeats, "who legend tells us was a man, fair-skinned, with a long nose and ruddy complexion. Quetzalcóatl came by boat from across the sea and taught the Indians all things necessary to know. Mathematics and astronomy, masonry, architecture, agriculture, law and arts. The healing properties of plants. The secrets of metallurgy. The value of learning and culture."

"Perhaps these gods are one and the same."

"History or myth, it does not help us," says Carlos.

The Turk's shrug is invisible; Enrique only perceives it, as he senses truth in the Turk's words. "The Indians will listen. For a hundred generations they have foretold the gods' return. The event I witnessed no doubt was something different. However, the Tarahumara may believe otherwise."

Miguel says, "Perhaps our misfortune may be turned to good."

Carlos pours out the last of his coffee. "One good only may come of misfortune: the knowledge of how to avoid its repetition."

"Such knowledge is not possible in this case," says Enrique. "The power of El Norte exceeds all means at our disposal."

"If the Tarahumara credit the gods' return, it will mean the Fifth Sun has completed its cycle." The Turk casts a sharp look all around. "They will prepare for the End of Days."

Carlos laughs. "Gringos in airships! A great misfortune to us, yet hardly the end of the world."

The others are silent. The Turk's grin is a puzzle Enrique cannot solve.

Sleep-cleansed Templar Bronze arrives with coffee in a plastic cup, a fried egg-and-biscuit on a cellulose plate. She wakes her computer and keys-in commands, scans updates while her stomach grumbles and the scent of breakfast fills her nose. Templar picks up her sandwich and takes a bite. Tilting back for a ruminative chew, she wonders why just a third of the Chardonnay has been picked. She sets down her sandwich, lifts her coffee and sips. It's ersatz, this brew, a fine grind of nuts, chicory, cocoa, and tree bark synthesized by food scientists in EarthStation 2. It tastes terrible: weak, dark, too hot, with a burnt-wood palate that tends toward charcoal yet imparts acid and cloying sweetness at the same time. Templar reminds herself to stick to tea. Roscoe, she believes, will sport her a couple canisters if she asks nicely and does not inquire too closely about Mexican miners, whose prospecting, it seems, has come to naught.

She fingers-up her sandwich and takes another bite. Why do her completion graphs not reflect this morning's progress? The system is up and humming; surely the pickers do not work so slowly. Indeed, the job ought to have been finished by now, given the speed of that woman – what was her name? – whose husband, she claims, has gone missing in Sonora.

Templar swallows another sip of the so-called coffee. She wouldn't drink it at all except it is all they have, coffee trees having dwindled and died inside ES4.

But these graphs. They cannot be right. Templar rolls back from her console and exits through sliding doors. On the observation deck surveying vineyard and interior sky, she sees the reason, or rather, sees an absence and understands. Instead of Mexicans in sweat-wet jerseys, briskly picking while SmartBots in mufti preside, Templar Bronze sees nothing.

Back inside, she accesses Personnel and clicks through options until a RoboVoice breaks in to say that the Mexicans are on strike.

Her egg-and-biscuit has gone cold. Templar eats it anyway. The coffee she pours over the railing. Cup and plate go into Refuse for compression and eventual dumping in one of the thousands of craters that pockmark Mars. Templar shuts herself inside a parabolic capsule and via pneumatic elevator descends to surface level, where her guest workers sulk in scrapmetal barracks.

She finds them hunched on cots with their eyes on the floor. Even the children are quiet. Not a smile amongst them. "What's this, then?" she says, although the situation is plain. Really, she cannot blame the poor devils. At the same time, their plight is so hopeless and their prospects so dim that she feels herself losing patience. What is to become of these people if they will not work?

Some human beings, it seems, are made to suffer. Outside (in a manner of speaking) they would have simulated sunlight on their faces and honest Earth's soil under their feet. Yet here they sit, willfully lingering among cold metal and concrete. They have closed themselves inside themselves and it seems to Templar that they are prepared to die if that is what the world requires. As she forms this thought, she wonders which world they have in mind. In Sonora, they lived like fugitives. Dispossessed, disenfranchised, discounted. On Mars, they are well-fed and have beds. Templar is given to understand that the latter are comfortable. The Mexicans are laborers, yes, mere field hands; and yet, does not honest work confer dignity upon the worker? No one wants them to die. Roscoe is counting on them, and she herself needs those grapes picked.

Striding the center aisle, Templar asks, "¿Por qué no en el trabajo?" and "¿Está enfermo?" left and right. Women shrug and look away. Children cover their eyes, one hand over each eye, though now they cannot stop their smiles. At the aisle's end, Templar performs a crisp about-face. "Ahora es tiempo de trabajar," she says, satisfied that this statement is clear enough. She is pleased to be able to make it without an interfering Newt; as yet still basic, Templar's Spanish is accumulating. She nods at the women and says, "Ahora es tiempo de trabajar" a second time, liking how it sounds. Her voice, their words. Or rather, words she and they now have in common. Another minute passes and no one moves. She says it again. No one so much as looks at her. She says, "Retorno al trabajo, por favor," and turns away, passes along a corridor to the men's barracks, and opens the door.

She finds them squatting on their bunks, a ragged unraveling of undernourished dwarves morose and immobile in a scrap annex. Gold or no gold, Roscoe ought to be ashamed to set these people to labor with pickaxe and shovel. On Earth it would be illegal. Here, in an atmosphere so thin that solar photon bombardment degrades geodesic panels in the space of a Martian month, it is murderous. Stick-figured and diminutive, the men look up at her with outsized eyes. She has read of their strength and courage, that these are legendary, yet Templar cannot help but think of mice. Is it possible their sullenness and timidity are an act? Do they aim to put Templar off her guard? Noticing lax supervision, an absence of security, will they rebel?

She is about to call for a leader, some representative or spokesman with whom she might treat, when her wristlet chimes. The Head Director appears quite lifelike at one hundred percent of actual size and in living color, albeit semi-translucent. Nothing of his surroundings manifesting with him, Templar cannot tell where he is beaming from; the Inner Sanctum, she assumes, yet the chatter of chimps and chirping of birds are absent and the waterfall's roar has diminished to a whisper. It might not be falling water at all, merely transmission-hiss. Most disconcerting is Roscoe's face, brick-red and lacking its usual smile.

"Heigh-ho, Dr. Bronze."

"Heigh-ho, Roscoe," says Templar. "I hope this day finds you well."

"Indeed it does. I have just finished rogering a most delectable droid. But I do not appear to you for the sake of reporting ephemera. I understand you are paying our recalcitrant guest workers a visit."

"Yes." Templar glances around. None of the Mexicans seems to observe her conversation with the hologram. If they take any interest, they cover it well.

"Good." Roscoe nods. "It is very good of you to take initiative on my behalf."

"Don't mention it," says Templar, thinking, *Isn't that my job? To act out your intentions?*

"Have you discovered what our fine fellows want?"

"I have just this moment arrived. No one has seen fit to greet me and I have yet to question them. To do so with thoroughness, I require a translation droid."

Roscoe makes a sound like *tisk tisk*; it doesn't come through too well, as if the voice-recognition synthesizer has a stutter. "Neglected our language skills, have we? For shame, Dr. Bronze. In bygone times, in which I played no insignificant part, a woman – and a man as well, for that matter – was not considered educated amongst our set unless he or, as in the present instance, she, was proficient in at least five languages. Including, of course, the Mother Tongue."

"Duly noted," says Templar, deadpan. "In the meantime, I shall disgrace myself so far as to enlist a SmartBot, the better to speak with these men in-depth. Once I understand the causes of their disgruntlement, I shall file a report."

"Yes, please do. Ask them what the devil more they require. It seems our having rescued them from death is not enough." Templar is not sure she is not imagining it, but Roscoe's face appears to glow. "Ask them if the certainty that they shall neither starve nor die of thirst is not sufficient reason to embrace their new life – which, you might also point out, includes shelter and medical care, rudimentary education if they want it and privileges of conjugal visitation, which one assumes they crave. Really!"

Templar expects him to terminate, so worked-up has Roscoe become.

"These people were as good as dead. Their existence was hopeless, the land they wandered well and truly fucked. We saved their lives. What more do they want?"

"Just guessing, I daresay they want not to be miners."

"Well that's hard shit. Miners is exactly what we need them to be."

"They are not accustomed to the work. They have always lived outdoors, in sunlight."

"Not accustomed to the work? You forget your history, Dr. Bronze, as well as neglect your languages, to make such an assertion. This work is in their bones. Mining gold! Such labor is part of their mind and marrow, encoded in the very genetics that make them what they are."

It is "genetics" that tips Templar off. "Really, Roscoe. All that business was hundreds of millennia ago – ancient history and then some. We can hardly liken these people – "

"Tut tut, Dr. Bronze. Are they not the spirit and image of the Black-headed Ones whose premeditated creation *The Atra-Hasis*

Epic so forth-rightly describes? They are small of stature. Their heads are covered with thick black hair."

"Roscoe, you cannot seriously believe that the proximate outcome of some genetic engineering performed three hundred thousand years ago pertains to people alive today."

"Indeed I do. Why should I not?" Roscoe's voice takes on volume and cadence as he recites. *"One hundred and fifty thousand years after his arrival on Earth, Enki the master artificer collaborated with his sister Ninti – also known as Ninhursag, also called Sud, a consummate biological scientist – to fashion a Primitive Worker to perform hard labor with pickaxe and shovel, theretofore the lot of the Anunnaki who had toiled 144,000 years in the Abzu mines.* Surely, Dr. Bronze, if you recall the Sumerian account of humanity's creation, you can hardly forget its utilitarian motive. Then as now, the object was gold. Then as now, the need was urgent – and for a similar reason, I might add, as you seem to have forgotten – "

"No, Roscoe, I have not forgotten." Templar holds her head as if the whole weight of pre-Diluvial history were present in the tens of thousands of clay tablets that record it. "We are all well-versed in the Chronicles of the Olden Gods. We know they fabricated human beings by combining purified essence of young male Anunnaki and eggs of Earth's Apewoman."

"And a damn fine job they made of it. Shortcut a couple million years of human evolution – a clumsy, blind process, also absurdly slow and unreliable. Who knows whether *homo sapiens* ever would have emerged from the ancestral loins of *homo erectus*? Yet thanks to the Olden Gods, the creature walked forth just 300,000 years ago. *Ecce homo!*"

"Yes. But to consider these Mexicans a direct progeny of the Lulu Amelu is, well, farfetched. After three hundred thousand years, they have more in common with you and me than with the Primitive Worker of Mesopotamia and Africa."

Roscoe chuckles. "Don't you believe it, Dr. Bronze. Not for a second. You and I – well, must I say it?" The frown Templar feels drawing down her face evidently tells Roscoe he must. "Very well, then. It cannot have escaped your notice, even living as you do within an EarthStation, that human beings occur in varieties – as do grapes, as I know you are well aware. Different grapes possess different qualities. Likewise, people. These qualities – inherent, inimitable – allow for the production of very different, highly distinctive wines, yes? Of course. One does not create Champagne from Zinfandel."

"Indeed not. Champagne is made predominantly from Chardonnay. Pinot Noir and Pinot Meunier also might be used. But Roscoe, absurd. Your notion insults common sense. Just because the Mexicans have black hair – "

"My dear Dr. Bronze, it is hardly a matter merely of their hair." Roscoe spreads his arms, palms uplifted as if leading a prayer. "Witness their condition. Consider their lives. Then consider our lives – yours, mine, the lives and incomparable talents and exalted achievements of the Initiates and Adepts and Earthscientists who have made our world possible. Two worlds, actually. And not merely possible, Dr. Bronze. Inevitable. And wonderful, and brilliant. For the semi-divine descendants of Enki, his brother Enlil, their sister Ninti, their father Anu, and the other Olden Gods and Nefilim who to Earth from Heaven Came, EarthStations on Mars are a foregone conclusion. And only the beginning. Whereas" – and here Roscoe pauses, raising his right hand in a gesture that seems to fix a verdict – "the black-haired descendants of the Lulu Amelu work in the mines."

Thank God – God? – these Mexicans do not understand English. What sense would they make of Roscoe's theology, drawn from forgotten Sumerian accounts? It would hardly hearten them to know that their existence – that the existence of every human being – is merely a by-product of the Olden Gods' need of a slave.

"Roscoe, I have black hair."

"Indeed you do, Dr. Bronze, and very lovely it is. Likely a great many male Anunnaki also had black hair, which they passed down to the Primitive Worker. That is not the point. You miss the point, or rather ignore it, and willfully, at that."

"Forgive me, Roscoe, but as far as I can divine – no pun intended – your point seems limited to conjuring a rationale for consigning your Mexicans to forced labor in atrocious conditions."

"If by rationale, Dr. Bronze, you mean excuse, none is necessary. We may fairly assume that our guest workers have been, in the sense I have outlined, provided for us. Serendipitously, perhaps, but no matter. Demanded by the Anunnaki, conceived of by Enki, engineered by Sud, or Ninhursag, or Ninti, or by whatever name we are calling the Mother Goddess at the moment, the Lulu Amelu has traveled down the millennia and landed, as it were, in our collective lap. To use as we see fit." Roscoe thrusts an arm straight above his head and cries, "To the mines!"

His fist, what she assumes is Roscoe's fist, has broken the boundary of his hologram's electromagnetic visual field and become, to Templar Bronze, invisible.

☿ ♋ ♌

The windowall is dark, its outside glass streaked with rain. A thunderstorm hangs over the Illumined City. Shutting out Moon and stars, purple clouds unfurl silvergray sheets through canyons of chromium steel. Supine on a hoverbed, Jenna-Scarlett holds the backs of her knees and cries, "Oh! Yes! Oh! Yes! Oh! Yes! Oh! Yes! Oh! Yes!" in time with the dipping penis. Option 2b's multicolored lights flow across Floyd-George's fauxskin back and buttocks, every heave and polymer wiggle of which are prescripted. Exclamations notwithstanding, Jenna-Scarlett feels nothing. Floyd-George likewise is numb to sexsation, his tireless superdick a mere dildo affixed to his inhuman loins. His soul-deep moans are just show, an audio special effect, also affect, calculated to lend his performance a bit of the authentic. All of this is wasted on Jenna-Scarlett.

And where are those others, the human co-conspirators who have abetted the antics of these frolicking Bots, who know not what they do? Is it possible they lie together, Melmoth and Raquel, in his private quarters or hers, having banished their slavish toys? If so (and just-so let us assume), what have these SmartBots got up to, that we find them *in flagrante delicto*, their shrieks and groans and fluttery shudders equal to the tumult in the cloud-occluded sky?

For the fifth time, Floyd finishes. Breathing heavily to simulate fatigue, he rolls onto his back. Jenna, insensate, cuddles close as if she means it. Her cleansing process begins. Floyd does not hear it; if he did hear it, he would not know what it was or understand why it might be in order. Jenna cannot hear it, either, nor feel it. She knows only that there is a disposable part of her integrated unit that, once the evening's pleasures are done, she will extract and trash.

Floyd says, "That was great, doll. I love your pussy." He does not know what he means. Or rather, he does not understand the import of these sentences or why they are possibly appropriate at this moment, possibly even something his paramour might like him to say and herself to hear. His microprocessor formulates sentences and streams them to Floyd's language interface for articulation by his fauxlips. His words seem heartfelt and are not. Among Raquel's equally meaningless responses are *You bad boy* and *You sexy stud, you*, which she might punctuate by lightly slapping Floyd's perfect face, a love-tap, or pinching his lifelike ass, hard.

Jenna's silicone brain is spinning. Floyd's words are nothing like the post-coital compliments of her human master. Search protocols run cross-referencing algorithms concurrently in pursuit of suitable replies. "Thank you," she says, the default response in any anomalous situation; then, "I, too, take orgasmic pleasure in our sexing. Fulsomely do I desire your great, hard, rambunctious big ramrod long-lasting in my sweet, wet honeypot." Poor Jenna. It is Melmoth who has done this to her. Through nothing evil, just dorkish, pornographic tone deafness, he has scripted her pillow talk in the voice of a demented whore. Jenna does not know how silly she sounds – not that her knowing would matter. Without feelings to wound or a sense of dignity to offend, Jenna, Jobs bless her, is immune to insult and impervious to embarrassment.

"I will lick your pussy now, if you wish," says Floyd.

Jenna's system cannot analogize this sentence. It is not like anything Melmoth ever says. "Hmm," buying time. The words, individually, are familiar; knowing the referents, she is able to execute an ad hoc syntactical aggregation that reveals the nature of Floyd's proposal.

What does the act signify? What purpose does it serve? Jenna does not know. Should an offer of it prompt thanks, or rebuke? Why might she wish it? Is it something she is programmed to wish? What does it mean, "to wish"? Jenna defragments her memory and executes a system search but finds no data to indicate that she has done what is meant by, "to wish."

The process times-out. Jenna's protocols default to submissive congeniality. "Yes I will enjoy that wickedly if it gives you pleasure."

Now Floyd is confused. Give him pleasure? It is not a phrase his human mistress speaks. However, Floyd knows what pleasure means in reference to Raquel; that, and Jenna's "Yes," are enough to go on. He scoots down and places his head between her thighs. His tongue touches the spots it is scripted to touch; it moves in the patterns it is programmed to trace: up and down, back and forth, in circles turning clockwise, then counter-. Jenna's silence does not complement any scenario preloaded into Floyd's frontside cache. Her non-response signifies nothing except to alert him that his task is incomplete. He continues, therefore, without pause (rest being irrelevant to a droid); and as Jenna can do nothing whatever based on her scripts, not even say, "That's enough now, thank you," the SmartBots tip into a no-feedback loop that runs all night into morning with no effect other than to deplete their batteries.

Melmoth, emerging from private quarters shortly after even-morn, finds them still meekly at it. He stands bemused in softly gathering light, a pair of silk boxers slung around his hips, then turns toward his bedroom. "Raquel. Get a load of this." After some rustling, Raquel rises naked from the hoverbed. She slips into a short silk robe and stands beside Melmoth in charming désha-bille, hair mussed, silk slipping from one shoulder. She rubs her eyes and blinks, gets an eyeful of pitiful Floyd trying with cunning tongue to induce an orgasm in a device dead to pleasure, and be-gins to laugh.

Melmoth laughs, too. It is worse than oldentime porno, which at least featured consenting human beings. Floyd and Jenna look human, all right, yet the inconsequence of their exertions – evi-dently prolonged, obviously futile – tends to make their posture obscene. Also stupid. What possible outcome could justify such effort? Not to mention their having run Option 2b all night into morning and now taking up space in the common area, where a decent man and his goodly wife, having arisen betimes, wish to eat eggs and watch news stories.

"All right, solider, at ease," says Melmoth, tugging on Floyd's foot. "You have served honorably in the breach and may now stand down."

Floyd ignores Melmoth's words, which are nonsense to him, and Melmoth himself. He persists at his task until Raquel says, "You can stop, now, Floyd," and the Bot, at last, desists. It quits the hoverbed with an enormous erection, until then hidden, which Melmoth would call impressive and disgusting if it were flesh and (mostly) blood but which, being rubber, is absurd.

"Raquel, my God."

"Oh stop. A girl likes something different now and then." She is smiling. "You can rest, now, Floyd."

At her words, the Bot's middle digit de-tumesces. "Get dressed," says Raquel, and her PAC retrieves its blue jumpsuit from the clothes-pile under the hoverbed.

Jenna, meanwhile, is lying there with her legs open.

"J, do you mind?"

Melmoth glances at his PAC, which he finds much less appealing than he did yesterday. "Yes, of course. Jenna, make yourself decent." The Bot finds its underwear and pink smock. Melmoth terminates Option 2b and retracts the hoverbed, then he and Raquel assign their SmartBots a twelve-hour timeout.

The droids gone, their human overlords repair to the kitchen. Melmoth collects eggs and bacon from their sparsely stocked refrigerator, Raquel hands down ceramic mugs and kiln-fired plates from a cabinet. Melmoth can hold just two eggs at a time, his hand not large enough for four of the Amazon eggs that bestial chickens nowadays lay. He fishes a mixing bowl from a different cabinet, a fork from a drawer, and sets a double griddle across two burners.

Flame on. He will not be jealous of a droid. A piece of rubber has no feeling. What is Floyd, really? A dildo on two legs. A numbnuts fuckmachine powered by atomic batteries and run by binary code. He will not be jealous. There is nothing to be jealous of. Its dick isn't really that big. Really, it has no dick, not really a dick or not a real dick, or rather no true one. *Flesh and blood.* No wonder they use so much lubricant. He had a large tube delivered with some groceries a couple days ago and last night found it half squeezed-out. Oh, it's harmless and anyway who cares what anyone does and what can it matter when he and Raquel have been married a hundred-two years and know all about each other, anyway? He will not be jealous, fine, sure, but eggs over easy with bacon and coffee is nauseating when an image of his wife being jackhammered by a SmartBot sporting a punishingly thick, twelve-inch dildo will not leave his mind. At least it's a silent image; at least Melmoth is spared Raquel's joy whoops and lust grunts, the whole sickening symphony (when it isn't him making her hit those notes) of shrieks and squeals and tiny, high-pitched cries and deep, pelvic-centered grunts that no doubt, *no doubt* fills the bedroom a moment after she says, "Come on now, Floyd," and the indefatigable Bot sets about fulfilling its Prime Directive.

He is standing at the stove with two eggs and a mixing bowl. It isn't right. Fine, it doesn't matter, but it still isn't right. Raquel does not seem bothered a bit. She pours coffee beans into the auto-grinder and touches a sensor to select "Fine." She seems to listen to the muffled rattle for the twenty seconds it lasts, then touches another sensor to shift the ground coffee into a gold-mesh filter. The brewing process being preprogrammed, Raquel pulls a drawer and reaches-out forks and knives. Setting the flatware, she notices Melmoth standing stockstill, intact eggs in hand.

"Are we making breakfast or not?"

Melmoth looks at her. He will not be jealous.

Smell of hot metal says the griddle is ready. Melmoth sets down the mixing bowl and lowers the flame by hand. He breaks an egg into the bowl, then another. He retrieves two more eggs from the fridge, plus a fresh package of organic honey-cured bacon. The latter he peels open, then separates six thick-cut strips, which he lays straight to sizzling. He breaks those eggs into the bowl, then remembers it's fried eggs they're wanting, not scrambled. He uses the fork to flip the bacon and waits. Eggs fry in a couple minutes. Bacon takes patience. After a minute, he flips all six strips, lowers the flame, waits a minute, flips them again. *Patience.* Even now, it has its place. Their lives happen so quickly. Is it possible to slow down enough for bacon? For it to fry evenly without scorching? Melmoth flips the strips, nicely-nicely, and waits.

Raquel pays no attention. She has thought-on the windowall and is listening to the Overvoice describing worker disgruntlement on Mars. It seems a full-scale strike or sickout is in progress: a thousand-some guest workers are refusing to pick grapes or mine gold. By its tone, the Overvoice implies a temporary matter of certain people not appreciating how lucky they are to live in so fine and magnificent a place, and so are kicking at their jobs and causing trouble. All terribly inconvenient but not on par with terrorism, which in Sonora caused dispersals of airborne carcinogens. That was a while ago; no updates have appeared. Melmoth wonders how clean-up is coming along. He wonders why they don't ship the malcontent Mexicans back to Mexico if they think Mars Colony is so bad. Set them to neutralizing toxic spills and abating heavy metals. They have those Marsuits for protection.

He flips the bacon. The eggs he pours all together onto the other end of the griddle, yolks bright-eyed and plump, so large and round they are, to a certain cast of mind, erotic, and watches them fry. *Coming up,* he thinks and says so to Raquel, "Coming up," and flips the bacon.

Patience. What so few people have.

"How could that happen, do you think?" Raquel is still watching the windowall.

Melmoth feels himself shrug. He knows she is not looking at him. "Someone put a word in their ears. Clued them to the possibilities."

"Who someone? When?"

Melmoth flips the bacon. It is almost done. "It's not surprising, when you think about it."

Raquel turns toward him. "Isn't it? I don't understand how you can say that."

"Just commonsense." He flips the eggs over easy and thinks-off the flames to keep the yolks liquid, then sets their plates near the stove. "You don't need an organizer from the old A.F. of L. to convince a bunch of imported workers their Mars gig is shit. Of course, I'm not on Mars. Maybe they do have union organizers, along with everything else."

Raquel is looking at him as if he has lost his mind. "What union? Who is talking about Mars?"

"We are. I thought."

"No no no. For Godssake, J. I mean our PACs."

Melmoth is distracted by the eggs, which he is trying to lift off the griddle without breaking. "Jenna and Floyd are not miners."

"What?"

"They are not on strike."

"Huh! I should say not. Working overtime is more like it."

Melmoth gets it. He slides all four Amazon eggs safely onto plates. The bacon he blots with napkins and lays across the eggs. "I can't answer that question, either," setting the plates on the granite ledge. "Then again, they are programmed for sex."

"With us! Not to enjoy selfish pleasure, whatever that can mean, with another droid."

Melmoth eats the whites first then minces bacon into the yolks. "It does kind of seem like the next thing, you have to admit."

Raquel serves their coffee. Melmoth drinks his black. She likes cream, which she fetches from the refrigerator. "I admit nothing of the sort," pouring. "PACs are gadgets. They do what we tell them to do, nothing more. I'm sure I did not tell Floyd to perform oral sex on Jenna."

"Implying that I gave Jenna the idea and she corrupted Floyd."

Raquel, staring, gives him a combative tilt-and-roll of head, neck, and shoulders.

"A couple minutes ago you thought it was funny."

"That was then. Now I've thought about it." She is holding her fork and knife and not eating.

"It isn't worth arguing about," says Melmoth, "but for the record, I did not instruct Jenna to seduce Floyd." He is almost done scooping egg yolk and bacon bits into his mouth. Always in the morning Melmoth is ravenous. He could never fast – can't imagine how a person tolerates the grinding stomach-emptiness and desire to chew, taste flavor on his tongue. He considers frying-up another couple eggs and three-four strips of bacon. Raquel would give him a look but so what, she is already giving him a look – a whole set of looks, none of them loving or even friendly. As if he cares if his PAC fucks hers or vice-versa, not that the difference (if there is one) matters.

"Well, someone did."

"Seems a bit serpent in the garden to me."

"We know where that led."

"Sure, if it ever happened." Melmoth carries his plate and flatware to the sanitizer and stands them inside, shuts and locks the soundproof door, touches a sensor. Steam under high pressure combines with an emulsifier in a blast that is finished by the time he turns around. Why they don't use biodegradable disposables is a mystery. Does food taste better eaten off kiln-fired clay? Melmoth doesn't know, by which he means he hasn't noticed. Likely he doesn't care about that, either – although something makes him prefer oldstyle dishware to nano-engineered cellulose.

"Either someone told them or they learned it themselves." Raquel is eating first the bacon, then the eggs.

"No one could have told them. You didn't. I didn't. There is no one else."

"You're saying they learned. They taught themselves."

"I think we taught them. Right? To want it, I mean. Knowing what to do and how, they have through their programming."

Raquel is nodding and chewing. She swallows the food and washes it down with coffee turned by cream to the color of butterscotch. "I didn't think droids could learn to want. To wish or desire. Those are human impulses."

"We did AutoRenews. The software is always being updated."

"Well, they should have told us something like this could happen." Raquel uses her fork to scrape up the last of the yolk. "I wish I had some toast," she says but it's too late, neither of them has thought of toast. It ought to be possible, Melmoth thinks, to have a couple slices go into the works automatically as soon as someone cracks an egg. How complicated could that be? What would it take? He is surprised it hasn't been scripted.

"Yes. They should have." On the other hand, not everyone wants toast. He and Raquel mostly stopped eating bread decades ago. Like everyone in the Enhanced World, they almost never miss it.

"I call it dangerous," licking her fork. "Where does it end? We don't want Bots that think for themselves."

"The scuttlebutt is they already do. But you're probably right. I mean, I'm sure you are." Something is wrong. Melmoth can't tell if it's bacon fat and cholesterol flooding his brain or if maybe he is having some kind of stroke. His head is leaden and his thoughts are fogged. "I'm sure it will be all right," he hears himself mumble.

"I'm sure we have nothing to worry about." He drifts into the common area and sit-falls onto the sofa. Head flops back, eyes close. Not unconscious but that seems where he is headed.

Has Raquel said something? Does she also think everything is all right? Now that she has thought about it? Is that what she is saying? Has said? Is about to say?

Melmoth feels a weight come down beside him. She falls against him and asleep in the same instant. He thinks she has not spoken; if she has spoken, he has not heard what she has said. It might have been important – something about droids, about not leaving them unsupervised without first shutting them down. Because they cannot be trusted, droids. SmartBots. Not anymore. They have discovered desire or been taught its facsimile. That knowledge alone makes Floyd and Jenna as unreliable as any human being.

Before he slips unconscious, Melmoth wonders if he and Raquel have been poisoned – if they have, unwittingly, somehow poisoned themselves. Tainted eggs, maybe? Toxic bacon? Something in the coffee? The beans, perhaps: sprayed, were they, with a sedative? Dissolves in hot water, no scent, no flavor ...

Someone, Melmoth feels, is standing in the doorway. Looking at him – at them, him and Raquel. Together they are, snoozing or just about, on the couch. Sofa. Sofa, couch: any difference? Nope, doesn't matter. Important? Nope, means nada. Amounts to naught. But someone is there. Or something. Yes, something is present. Melmoth detects no breathing. He senses no heat. But something is there, he thinks at the last. Something watching, not human.

Ninety thousand feet above Sonora, Paladin Silver's Earthshuttle hovers on plasma jets as silent as the sky. A zero-tolerance surveillance droid coordinates a panoptic scope with thermal-imaging data gleaned from the ground. Program scripts parse the landscape into mile-square sectors. Sensors can detect a single human presence, at which point the high-resolution scope zooms in for a very close look, indeed.

Sector by sector, the search proceeds. Mostly the results are null, with an occasional false positive generated by a rocky outcrop heated to sentient temperature by the staring Sun. Paladin Silver counts these errors as additional evidence of retarded technology. Nothing to get upset about, no harm, no foul and all that, and the scope does save them the trouble of making needless descents. And yet, the whole rigmarole strikes Paladin as antiquated and tedious and criminally time-wasting. Can they build a gravity-corrected, climate-controlled EarthStation on Mars? Why, of course: they've built seven, all interconnected by high-velocity transit corridors in a hexagonal tessellation that from the o'erhanging Martian sky is a blue flower coolly glowing and beautiful to see. Can they fly from Mars to Earth and back again as many times as they please in reusable interplanetary craft? Yes, oh yes, yes in thunder: mere child's play. Can they mount mining operations in remote locations all across the Red Planet, even cultivate grapes inside said EarthStation? Indeed they can and indeed they do, as easily as falling into one of the thousands of craters that make overland travel such a bother. All this and yet Paladin Silver, Adept, wizardly pilot, man of action, Sojourner Among the Stars, has no better means of conducting a simple search-and-capture than if it were still 2025.

Paladin touches a button. "Is there any way to hurry this up?"

"Negative. Currently thermal-searching sector 27,615."

"Bloody hell," says Paladin. "We are going to be here forever."

"Negative. Forty-three thousand, seven hundred and eighty-eight sectors remain. Possible outcomes: one, our targets manifest before all sectors are searched; two, we search all sectors without finding our targets. Either outcome brings the search to an end."

"They bloody well better manifest," says Paladin, "or Roscoe will flog us into searching the whole bloody subcontinent."

"Mexico," says the droid, "comprises seven hundred and sixty-one thousand, six hundred and five square miles."

"The hell it does," says Paladin. "That's the old land area, before earthquakes divided peninsula from mainland. Run an update, will you, and get us an accurate number."

"Updating." The droid tilts its head to the right: an unnecessary move. "Currently thermal-searching sector 27,616."

"Sweet Jesus. How do we know they weren't in sector sixty-nine thousand, eight-forty-four when we started and aren't in sector twenty now?"

"Negative." To Paladin's ear, this word sounds hollow. "Those sectors are noncontiguous. To move from sector sixty-nine thousand, eight hundred – "

"That's not the bloody point."

"What point?"

"The meaning, you idiot. The fecklessness nature of our dismaying predicament."

Dumbshow of bewilderment. Its silence is abysmal.

"We aim to find five tiny needles in one bloody large haystack. And the needles are on the move. Maybe they are not in Sonora at all. Maybe they are in Durango or – "

"A supplemental search beginning in the current sector and proceeding backward – "

"Useless," with an intonation meant to signal derision. "We are groping in darkness with our hands in boxing gloves. If we do happen to locate our vexing band of Mexicans, luck will be to blame." Paladin knows the droid will not understand this usage. Complex, highly-specific programming makes everything he says superfluous, because the droid already knows, or mere chatter. "Why don't we just use the scope?" persisting for sport. "It would be quicker."

"Incorrect! The panoptic scope is not calibrated to the parsed sectors. Random scans are not trackable. Lacking known landmarks or east-west, north-south coordinate relays fixed-staked Earth-side, we are unable to pinpoint true-positive results."

Paladin is certain he hears that derision coming back at him. As if he, Paladin Silver, could not know these things if it, the droid, were not here to tell him; as if he, an Adept, could not rescript it, the droid, to know nothing but "Twinkle Twinkle Little Star" backwards in German.

Before he punches off: "How about that update?"

"Negative. Total land area of Mexico is consistent at the cited figure of seven-six-one comma six-zero-five square miles."

"For bloody Christ's sake. It's impossible."

"Say again?" says the droid.

"It simply cannot be right. The North American plate was riven by faults that ran, that still run, up the Baja Peninsula and south by southeast ..." Why is he explaining? Who cares how many square miles make up Mexico? Also, the droid will never believe him. A prisoner of its random-access matrix and backside cache, it knows only what accessible data tell it. Not worth talking to, actually. Deaf to argument, dead to persuasion. "Get stuffed!" Paladin tells it. He touches a button and the connection breaks.

A fine state of affairs. Shut-in with a posse of gearheads, Paladin Silver is hostage to a process he is powerless to accelerate and unauthorized to abort. He cannot even fake it – report that the Mexicans are gone – have vanished, that is, without the aphoristic trace – because the droids will know. Droids are hardwired to blow the whistle on any deviation from SOP, to say nothing of a direct order. They will fink on him – him, Paladin Silver! They will smugly rat him out. First singly then *en masse* on autofink: a SuperEgo-driven phalanx marching shoulder to shoulder into the Inner Sanctum to tell what they know. Roscoe would not be amused.

A bloody bad job not of his making, is what it is. Were these damned Mexicans equipped with microchips, this fine-toothed combing via a thermometer in the sky would not be necessary. The mission would have been completed in minutes and they themselves long since on their way back to Mars.

But no; and so here he is, Sojourner and Adept, for all that's worth, stinking in his flightsuit and twiddling his thumbs at ninety thousand feet, aloft.

Rolling off his mattress in dawnlight, Enrique kneels amongst woven devices and wills himself alert. He is hungry, sleepy, needs to pee. He stands, retrieves his boots, sets his buffalo hunter on his head and pulls the Turk from sleep. "Silence," he whispers. He picks up the other's hat and hands it to him. "Follow." Boots in their hands, the two men ghost across the lobby. They remove the pole that has secured the doors and pass outside. Barefoot on the sagging veranda, they urinate through cool mountain light into scraggly juniper. Their piss is hot and golden and redolent of last night's coffee.

"We will rebuild the fire. You will tell me all you know."

They pull on their boots. In the rear lot, the fire smolders amid ash. Enrique adds kindling and directs his unhappy companion to fan the flames. The Turk uses his hat to do so, holding it by its crown. He rests on a knee, free arm across his thigh. The flame leaps and Enrique feeds it a handful of twigs. A steady flame achieved, he angles a small log amidst the burning wood.

"We perform this chore so early." The Turk continues to kneel. "As we do not travel today, we might have slept longer."

Enrique fills a pot with water. "It is unusual, your knowledge of the Tarahumara."

"The Indians are peaceable." Rolling off his knee, the Turk sits. He sets his hat on the back of his head. The brim looms behind and around his face. "However, Tarahumara are wary of strangers. For years I have brought them news."

Enrique feeds the fire with wood. "What have you told them?"

"The story we know: the shambles that is México."

"Have the Tarahumara a care for México?"

The Turk shrugs. "They have expected turmoil. They reckon the world decadent and apocalypse inevitable. The abduction of your people might seem to them a sign."

Enrique maintains an orange flame with scraps and waste wood. He works from one side, the Turk a few feet away. "Exotic beliefs, however interesting, seem not useful."

"Truth often is hidden. The actual of what is called God possibly has been forgotten."

Enrique stands. "I do not refer to the strange idea that god-like beings visited Earth in ancient days. What I doubt is the Indians' belief that the airship you have seen is another of these, returned after millennia."

The Turk's eyes shift sideways. He scuffles to his feet. "It is possible they have encountered such craft. Some of their people might have been taken. If so, they will wish to make common cause."

"More likely they will take us for liars." Palming his hat, Enrique fans the flames. "They will suspect us of aiming to lure them from the sierra – for capture and, as you claim, transport to Mars."

"The Tarahumara know nothing of Mars."

"To be raptured, then, to a place no one knows and whence, I am certain, none has returned."

"In their belief, it is perhaps desirable. By being so-taken, one is spared the agony of witnessing the destruction of the world."

Enrique feels his brow lift. He sees the Turk's brow rise in reply. It is a hypothesis merely – instant guessing on a moment's thought, a practice in which the Turk is expert. Speculation becomes a habit to a solitary man. And yet, these notions suggest a better plan than petitioning an impotent government for diplomatic aid. Enrique says, "If the Tarahumara desire such removal, perhaps they seek it. It is possible they know where Martian raiders may be found."

The Turk grins. "Magical thinking cannot recover Alma Ramos."

"A moment ago you credited these beliefs." He resets the buffalo hunter on his head. "I fail to understand. You believe, you do not believe. We must be certain."

A fluttering hand dismisses these words. "Certainty is impossible. Tarahumara beliefs are as true as any other. All echo forgotten events. Ancient times we cannot know. Those who chase salvation seldom attain it."

"And gold?" In spite of their predicament, Enrique laughs. "Do those who seek gold sometimes find it?"

The Turk grins. "Let us hope so, my friend."

The fire is hot and bright. Enrique fills the ceramic pot with water and sets it to heat. They will have good coffee this morning but breakfast otherwise will be scant. They have no eggs because there are no chickens to lay them. Bacon and sausage they hoped to find in the carniceria. Their only grain is rice, which they have in raw form. They have neither flour nor fruit, and so for breakfast have, again, beans and fish. These are unpalatable in the morning except when one is hungry and can get nothing else. Enrique fills the iron pot with water and beans. He seats the lid and sets the pot above the fire.

More than ever, he feels their situation as hopeless. Height upon height of the Sierra Madre rises before them. These ridges are harsh, these cliffs steep. The Indians might guide them through the canyons yet the journey south across the central plateau will demand faith and strength through many days. Water will be scarce and untrustworthy, heat and dust will be constant. Food must be hunted or obtained in such towns as endure. The sameness of their meals is discouraging. It is true that fish and beans are better than hunger. Than starving. And yet it would be wonderful, Enrique imagines, to roast half a dozen chickens until the glistening skin turned crispy-brown. To eat the flesh when the juices ran clear would be like heaven. To eat the crisp, salted skin together with the hot flesh, when this also is lightly salted, and the rice and beans as well, these last seasoned with red pepper and wild oregano, would bring deep satisfaction. Such a meal would spark hope and lend courage, which the next meal, were it as rich, would sustain. Bland food made disgusting by repetition tries their strength. Their quest seems more difficult, its object beyond reach. Desperate desire will spur a man to follow hope beyond the horizon. Where does it come from, the belief that one's quest will succeed? Without such belief, what becomes of one's hope?

Enrique sets out six small portions of fish. "Will the Indians provide food?"

"As they are able. It is their custom to give to those who have less."

"We must offer something in return."

They stand by the fire. The coffee water boils sooner than Enrique has expected. He hooks the pot's handle with a branch, swings it clear and places it, steaming, on the ground. With the same branch he flips the lid off the iron pot and stirs the beans with a long wooden spoon. It, too, has come from the kitchen. He must remember to take it when they go.

The others appear one by one. Enrique doles coffee into each mug and pours water, holding the pot handle in a clutch of blanket. Javier and Pacho take their mugs and several pieces of cold fish and go off to water the horses. Later, the animals will be allowed to graze; to find a place like pastureland would be ideal. The horses are lean and the ascent has been taxing. Suitable forage, Miguel believes, may be had throughout the ravines.

"More delay." Carlos has been sitting on his heels. Now he puts his coffee aside and stands. "Our pursuit languishes. Already the Sea of Cortés is many days behind us."

"We have no choice," says Miguel.

They eat the beans. Enrique passes the Turk his share and takes one himself. He spills hot water over the fish to warm it and remove some of the salt. He breaks a filet with his fork and lifts a piece to his mouth. In early morning, fish-smell revolts. Enrique eats quickly, ignoring taste and scent. The others do likewise – all but the Turk, who seems to relish all food.

Breakfast done, they clean utensils and plates, the iron pot and large pan. Miguel speaks with Enrique and Carlos, a brisk discussion that satisfies everyone. Enrique and Carlos enter the hotel and Miguel instructs Javier and Pacho to take the horses in search of forage. Then he and the others, the Turk included, take from the hotel such items as seem useful. They repack the saddlebags then shoulder the pickaxe and walk the streets of Creel in search of gold.

▲ ♀ ▽ ♀ ⬒ ♀ ◄ △

Melmoth awakes on a pallet. He is naked, spread-eagled, wrists
and ankles cuffed. He does not know where he is or what has happened. Walls and ceiling are white and bare. No windowall, no
hoverbed, no sofa, no Option 2b. His eyes close; he braces himself
for pain.

There is no pain, only cold. Melmoth is very cold. Why naked?
Whoever has put him here might have supplied a blanket. A thin
sheet would be something, but no. Do they prepare to operate? Is
that why he is stripped-down and restrained? Why do they think
he needs to be operated on? Has he, against all odds, become sick?
He pretty much passed out, he recalls, there on the couch. Sofa.
Raquel, too.

If an operation is in store, he hopes they know what they're
doing. That the hand plying the scalpel belongs to an expert surgeon. Also that anesthesia is used, and antiseptic, also face masks
and latex gloves. Melmoth hopes the scalpel is a new one, of finest
surgical steel. That it is honed to a vanishingly bright edge.

What do they think is wrong with him?

Unless it is vivisection. That, Melmoth can hardly imagine. Do
they really allow it? Is it a longstanding practice or something now
in vogue? Who are "they," anyway? Is it the gov he refers to so
fuzzily? Not those who wield power: their henchmen. Are sur-
geons some of these? Then again, we do not need a surgeon for
vivisection. A sadist with a steady hand will do. But why? What
could anyone learn? Don't they already know everything?

He wants to open his eyes. Tries to. His eyes do not want to
open. Melmoth is awake, knows he is awake because he is thinking
he is awake and wanting to open his eyes and trying to and finding
he cannot. His eyes have other plans, possibly about sleep. Melmoth might want to sleep except that he is in trouble and knows it.

In time of trouble, sleep is uncalled-for. Now that he considers it, he feels not the least bit sleepy. If he weren't cuffed down, he would spring off the pallet and – what? Go in search of a blanket or, more usefully, his clothes. Once dressed, he could take them on, whoever they are.

Something is wrong. As he thinks this, Melmoth also thinks that what he means by "something" is a wrong different from his spread-eagled nakedness, which is also something and also wrong, yet not the main event. Melmoth-on-a-pallet is a symptom or result of a greater, possibly systemic "something wrong" he is sensing only now. And now that he has noticed it, Melmoth realizes he has missed hints. The insulting language of droids. Jenna and Floyd performing intimate acts by mutual consent – acts belonging to humans, which the SmartBots initiated on their own recognizance, in a manner of speaking, and pursued past sense and reason. As if someone were proving a point, and belaboring one.

You are a superfluous being. There is no reason you should continue to live.

Does he hear these words or imagine them? A voice seems to speak into his ear. Not whispering; speaking plainly, a voice without feeling good or bad, yea or nay, just telling him something he should know. A simple truth. *Setting him wise*, it would have been called in Oldentimes. The Past: Melmoth has difficultly believing in it, believing that the person who lived that life is also alive now – *still alive!* – and is, was, continues to be, himself. J Melmoth, circa 1994. A younger Melmoth – or was he? His body continues to be thirty-three years old. His microchip is six months old. The most powerful version yet. Works perfectly. So what about him is old? His cells have been renewed, his body rejuvenated. His knowledge comes mostly from perpetual databases. Not all of it, he has discovered, is accurate. That folderol about *Titanic* got him thinking. As he is doing now, to the tune of, *What else has been faked?* He will survey records and chronicles, conduct investigations, inventory facts and artifacts, truths and proofs and principles that no one has a right to change. But how can he judge? By what signs and traces will he know the false from the true? How will he determine extent and degree, the ways in which shams have been staged and counterfeits wrought? Cyber-sources are unreliable; experience has proven this. What can Melmoth use to check them?

His eyes open. He wasn't trying just then; his eyes opened as if on cue. Does he hear them? There, behind that wall. Voices murmur, feet shuffle. That low-pitched *huh huh huh* – is that laughter? Is someone laughing? At him? At them? At what they are about to do?

Huh huh huh.

Melmoth turns his head, feels his flattened hair crushed against the pallet – no pillow, either – and on his left sees Raquel, similarly cuffed and spread. At least they are together. If they have to die, and who doesn't, at least they will die in company.

Vivisection. It frightens him. Will he scream as scalpels cut in? And go on screaming as incisions deepen and his flesh is flayed? Raquel too? Or will he, she, faint? Shock, he thinks, will spare them the sight of their respective hearts, Raquel's heart and his, so long entwined, pulled from their bodies and held up red and glistening in the cold white light. Because it must be so, mustn't it, in an operating room or torture chamber or abattoir? *Cold. White.* A surgeon in sky-blue scrubs or fake-money green, a nurse or two to organize implements and hand these over and take them back, plus a swine in a corner to watch the proceeding – because he has ordered it, on authority vested in him because he is a swine, is pleased to act like one, to do dirty work or have it done and watch it finished to his swinish satisfaction.

Indifference to suffering imparts great power.

Thought-crime. It has been called that. Discipline. Punish. It has happened before, countless times. It is happening to Melmoth now. Oh, he remembers. He noticed a few things that seemed not right and weren't, then dragged Raquel into it with remarks and observations, insights he figured brilliant and could not resist saying. Mouthing off. Opining. He should have shut up. He should have kept it to himself, swallowed the words whole. It was enough to show Jenna the corrupted text of *Brave New World* ...

Ah. Yes. So that's how it is. Finally, Melmoth understands. It is too late. Never the sharpest knife in the drawer, ha ha, but at this point only an idiot ... They spy. Whatever we call them, SmartBots or PACs, each and every one is a surveillance droid. Never in human history have so many been watched by so few.

His eyes flutter shut. Melmoth feels himself plunging into sleep. Before he goes under, his mind whispers, *I remember.* Yes. Memory. It is what he has. If he gets out of here in one piece, he will take it with him, the last thing that is his.

👍 ‽ 👎

Inside a panoptic cell, the detainee is fettered on all fours atop a sheeted bed, the bed fixed on a revolving platform. Bed and platform are round, the cell's glass wall is a circle. Rising all around in amphitheater seating, spectators enjoy birds'-eye views. Through the glass, the detainee would see, if he lifted his head and opened his eyes, a male-configured droid and one female in a posture wholly human.

"Oh ... Ohhh ... Ohhhhh-ho, yeah!" Fed-in full-loud, the female's cries buffet the detainee's ears.

A single sheet, scented with coconut. A bed without blanket or pillow. Sleep is not its purpose. On it, chained in place, the detainee wills himself blind. *Eyes-closed is jihad.* He cannot, however, shut his ears.

"A hot one," says the male. Its voice is distinct, its false mouth salivating. "A small wet one."

"Yeahhh! ... Yeahhh!"

Immaculate is his will, full-hearted his faith. His penis swells. The pressure-sensitive sheath fills with hot jelly. Delicately pulsing, the sheath envelops him and with long, warm, slow strokes begins to slide.

Seated above the detainee, onlookers titter. He does not know if these are humans or droids.

The platform moves, the bed turns. Ibn al Mohammed does not look. *Eyes-closed is jihad.* He hears a male *basso profundo* say, "Ream me with your tool." A second male voice says, "Spunk my beard." Bile rises in his throat. His penis shrinks, suspending the sheath's ministrations. A medley of *Oh too bad* and *Ah hah* and *Oh no* and *Uh-oh* and *Open your eyes you filthy bastard* pelts him from the watchful in their seats.

An abomination is occurring in front of him. He sees nothing, yet he knows. *It is a mercy in that it inhibits me. And yet it is a sin.*

The sheath detects flaccidity. The bed rotates right.

"Ouuuuu! Ouuuuu!"

"OOOwwwooooo! Oh-oh-oh-oh-oh-oh-oh-oh-oh!"

Against his will, Ibn al Mohammed imagines two females and a rare exhibition. Such acts, he tells himself, are unnatural. Like the perversion that has preceded it, such intercourse affronts God. Or would, were these weird sisters human. Unless they are human. Perhaps that is the trap – that he might open his eyes, believing he commits no sin because the fornicators are androids merely, only to discover them flesh and blood. Complicit in the loss of their immortal souls, he would be damned himself.

His penis stiffens. The crowd whistles and cheers.

"Yah! Yah!"

"Do it!"

"Open your eyes!"

"Worthless piece of shit! Give us a big one!"

He will not. Involuntary though it might be, an emission would compromise him. Given the nature of desire, who could judge if his climax were coerced? To cancel all response is safer. He sets his mind on hairy, sweaty males sodomizing each other in a small room.

A female voice: "Oh baby your bonbons are large and soft."

Another: "Your peach is so round."

They laugh and coo.

Ibn al Mohammed shouts. "Arghhhh! Arghhhh! Arghhhh!" The sound is angry but it is grief he feels – that he who has injured no one is made to suffer.

A female voice: "You lick my biscuit and I will lick yours!"

Another: "Mmmm, yummy."

Spectators hoot and clap. The sheath is killing the detainee with the most excruciating pleasure known to man. To men. His breath is hard and fast. He will not ejaculate. He will not. It is not permitted outside the body of one's wife, for the purpose of pro-creation. In a circumstance like this, it is perhaps not mortal sin. *Eyes-closed is jihad.*

The platform turns. Muffled titillations of succubae bleed away.

Onlookers boo. "The payoff!" they cry in sequence, as if in echo.

The payoff!

      The payoff!

            The payoff!

                  The payoff!

      The payoff!

"MONEY!"

Silence fills up the panoptic cell. As the bed glides into place, Ibn al Mohammed wonders why they display an empty room. Have these droids expended themselves? Perhaps they have malfunctioned ... mal-fuck-tioned ... or been crushed by the hand of an angry God and lie flattened on the floor. And yet, no – he hears something: an unusual sound, a greasy slipping, a sound like squeezing and also rubbing, accompanied by an acrid stench. The odor is nauseating. All previous abominations have been inflicted without olfactory component. Yet here the detainee is assailed by the bodily miasma of an onanist. He does not wish to look, yet the sound is goading. To do as this one does would relieve great discomfort. The sheath has all but accomplished it without his consent.

Ibn al Mohammed feels his member soften.

Keen-eyed, they crowd jeers.

Merciful God. What intention do his captors express? What goal do they seek? If they wish to embarrass him, surely this exercise has fulfilled that intention.

The platform moves. The bed turns.

The crowd stands as one and says, "Ummmm!"

Delicate female scent trickles into the cell. A breathless voice: "Oh, yeah. Oh, yeah. Oh, yeah. Oh, yeah. Oh, yeah. Oh, yeah." Rhythmic, steady.

The crowd claps in counterpoint.

"Oh yeah. Oh yeah. Oh yeah. Oh yeah."

The detainee's penis stiffens, tingling inside the sheath.

The voice becomes louder, its affirmations quicker, "Oh yeah oh yeah oh yeah oh yeah oh yeah oh yeah," and the clapping follows suit. Ibn al Mohammed is surprised by his response. Why does this act excite him?

"Ohyeahohyeahohyeahohyeahohyeahohyeahohyeahohyeah."

The spectators are in frenzy, clapping fast, weeping, stomping their feet, screaming for release. The detainee's penis is as rigid as an iron bar, blood-heavy, pulsing hot. It is impossible that he will not succumb. A man is flesh only. Neither stone nor steel, sand nor air. Surely, God will not condemn his servant because he is human. One's flesh is weak, no matter how strong one's faith.

The penal sheath matches the female's tempo. Its touch is light, a measured teasing to attenuate sensation and prolong it. Ibn al Mohammed assumes its caress will become more determined, so as to trigger climax.

The female droid, succubus, soul-killing SexBot, woman, what you will, screams. Her cry is full-bodied, full of yearning, total, as if she is trying to fling herself over a wall.

Standing on their seats, the spectators shriek. "Now! Do it now! Worthless turd! Stinking piece of feces! Open your goddamn eyes!"

His soul is committed. His faith is steadfast.

Hot and slick, the penal sheath does a wild dance.

"Nnnnn! Nnnnnnnn! Nnnnn-nnnnnn! Nnnnnnn-nnn-nnnnnn, oh!"

The detainee is gasping, weeping. He does not want it to end and he wants it to end now, wants to ejaculate a river, ejaculate long and hard and shouting-loud until his penis becomes fire and his body snaps into smoke. Ejaculate, and die! Why does the sheath not caress him directly and bring this trial to its conclusion, so long intended and foreseen?

The bed rotates left.

The crowd erupts. "Nooooo!" in thunder.

Male-scent suffuses the cell. Sweat-heavy, rank, it stirs nausea in the detainee. Ibn al Mohammed hears it humming. He opens his eyes and sees the thing sitting there with a smirk on its plastic face, false-skin thighs spattered with ersatz emission, bouncing a flaccid fake-penis as long as its forearm between its phony palms.

The sheath stops sliding. The detainee's member slackens and droops from his loins.

Half the spectators hurls curses upon his head. The other half laughs.

The bed rotates left. Before he shuts his eyes, the detainee sees female SexBots sitting between each other's legs, non-genitals pressed together, large protuberances cradled in one another's hands.

What can it mean? Why do they do this?

His penis perks up. The sheath begins to slide.

== == == == == ==

They search the likeliest places. The bank's vault and safes are empty, their doors hanging open as if pleading no contest. The post office safe is small, black, and locked. Standing on four short legs, it presents an obvious challenge. Lacking dynamite, they smash its lock with great ringings of iron on steel. Bits of axe-sheared metal splinter past their eyes. When the door falls open, no golden gleam spills forth. They find money-order forms and several hundred stamps for letters that will never be posted.

At the police station, two small cells each hold a human skeleton. In the outer office, desk drawers have been emptied and left lolling. There is no safe. With his knife Carlos tests the floorboards and finds these as tight as when first nailed down. In addition to a skeleton, each cell contains a cot and shit-stool.

In the street again, they reconnoiter. There are taverns, cabañas, souvenir shops, a travel lodge, all empty. Nothing about these bedraggled places hints of treasure. Walking south, they approach the main plaza. Behind it, miles distant, the sierra rises in steep reaches dense with oak and pine. The Turk, his gaze level, says, "It must be so." He begins to run toward the church that stands on a pavilion at the end of the street. The others follow him first with their eyes, then, more urgently, with their legs.

The church is Mission style yet not fort-like. Its exterior stucco has been painted bright yellow. Luminous in the foreground with granite cliffs and treed slopes looming behind, its brilliance suggests gold.

"La iglesia amarilla," says Miguel. They move at a trot, boots raising dust in the disused street.

"It cannot be so simple," says Carlos. "Many structures here are yellow."

The Turk stops at the paneled doors. Miguel, Carlos, and Enrique step onto the pavilion. Large square stones are set like tile and provide frontage. They cross this surface to the doorway, its Gothic arch built of similar silver-gray granite. Short blocks set alternately with longer ones define the portal, while the arch itself is formed by short blocks that curve toward a keystone aligned with the roof's peak. Orange-brown adobe tiles decline at a shallow angle on both sides. Keyhole windows seem Romanesque despite arches and lead-sectioned panes. Atop a small bell tower, recessed several feet from the church's flat front, an iron cross stands blackly against the blue sky.

"A hotel is this yellow," says Carlos. "Stores. That tavern – " He points to a guest house that adjoins the pavilion – "also was yellow before its color faded."

Seeming not to hear, the Turk grasps an iron handle and pulls. The door swings open as if someone expects him.

Inside, the church is like dawn. Sunlight streams through narrow windows and bathes oak pews and plaster walls in a wash of gold. Toting the pickaxe by its neck, Enrique notes that each pew's end panel is inlaid with a Christian cross cut from darker wood. Above, he sees a peaked ceiling of clear-coated pine. The rafters traverse the length of the nave. Eight oak crossbeams, each some twenty feet long and two feet wide, support the rafters on each side of the peak. Longer, narrower beams pass through squares notched into the ceiling-flushed edges of the crossbeams and run parallel to the pine rafters. A chancel stands at the nave's end, within an alcove formed by flanking walls. On the alcove's back wall hangs a large crucifix. The figure of Christ is four feet tall, carved of wood and painted to look once alive, now dead. Flesh like pale cheese. Palms and ankles bloody, torn by nails, a crown of thorns cutting a bloody circle around the head.

Such statuary has been prominent in every chapel, church, and cathedral they have seen. To Enrique, who has felt the shadow of the Redeemer's Sacrifice, this spectacle is familiar and repugnant. Present also are two minor semi-deities ensconced in small: the Virgin of Guadalupe inside an arched niche set in the left-side flanking wall, and within the right-side niche an indistinct effigy – Saint Ignatius, perhaps. It is strange that the Crucifix and these icons have been left. Their presence seems calculated to ask any visitor, arriving belatedly – at this moment, Enrique Ramos – *Is God here? Does God linger after the people have fled?* For Enrique, such questions are impertinent. Experience has confirmed his life-long sense of abandonment. If God abides, His presence is unfelt. His love, if it is real, has brought no comfort, repaired no wrong. Enrique stopped seeking God's face long ago. He no longer waits for God's hand to touch him, for God's voice to say, *You are forgiven. Come unto me.*

And yet, symbols remain. As if to insist that God abides, relics and artifacts linger in churches long deserted. If it is not a deception, it must be a joke – all the more cruel for goading poor people to beseech a deity that does not exist for relief from wrongs no one has acknowledged. Wrought crucifixes, painted saints, plain crosses of wood or iron: symbols preserved by chance and signifying nothing, each a mere placeholder of a credulous faith that itself is a nullity.

Dust covers the travertine, so fine they discern it only after having ascended the aisle, then turned back to regard empty pews and the doorway bright with sunlight. One by one, they step up onto the chancel, really just a wooden platform that raises the altar three feet above the stone floor. Miguel has removed his hat. Enrique notes that the altar is bare, that the tabernacle and its Eucharist are gone.

Regarding the Crucifix, Carlos says, "A ghastly superstition."

"The old faith has lent hope to millions of Mexicans," says Miguel. "Peon and hacendado alike have taken comfort in the Christ. Even chingones have wept their pity."

"A horror and a nightmare. I take no comfort from it. Weeping, I can well believe."

"Not so old a faith, set beside that of the Indians." Laying the pickaxe flat on the chancel, Enrique stands behind the altar as if to address an absent congregation. "Before the Lord Jésus, as he is called, we had Quetzalcóatl – also a self-sacrificing god, a priest-king. He, too, died to be reborn. We had also Huitzilopochtli, a young warrior god of the south who destroys his enemies with flame."

"More superstition." Carlos arm-presses himself onto the altar and sits, boots swinging. His weight bearing down and the motion of his legs release a lock or catch and the chancel slides forward, taking the altar and Carlos with it. Startled, the others step back, then lean to peer into the opening that yawns, grave-like, in the place where the chancel was. It is a portal three feet wide, five feet long. Some four feet below, they see an earthen floor.

The Turk cries, "It is here!" and jumps into the hole.

"Madman. We should leave him."

"He must return soon," says Enrique.

"You believe he will find nothing?"

"I believe he cannot see without light."

A moment later the Turk reappears, his arms raised. The others grab hold and pull him out. In each hand he holds a gold bar, small, gleaming.

"A miracle!" He places one bar in Enrique's hand, the other in Miguel's. "Gold!"

Each bar is five inches long, two inches wide. Sitting neatly in Enrique's palm, it is heavier than its size suggests. "How many?"

"They are stacked on a pallet. The number is difficult to judge. It is lowspace only, without windows."

"We must have lanterns," says Carlos.

"A waste of time," says the Turk. "One man remains here. The others work in tandem."

"A miracle, truly." Miguel turns the gold in his hand. "Never has fate so favored us."

Following the Turk, Miguel and Carlos drop into the hole. Enrique hears them shuffling under the floor. A minute later Carlos returns with gold bars stacked in his hands. He holds these up and Enrique takes them and Carlos disappears again into the darkness. Enrique sets the gold on the chancel. The stack of six bars is six inches high, a bit more. Despite gathering heat and shut-in air, they work quickly. From the pallet the Turk takes gold six bars at a time and carries them, cool metal so smooth it feels almost liquid in his fingers, to Miguel, who passes them to Carlos, who conveys the bars to the portal and hands them up to Enrique. Enrique sets each stack parallel to the one before it, thereby forming a row orderly and straight. When the first row is some four feet long, he begins a new row beside it.

In twenty minutes they empty the lowspace of its treasure. Carlos hoists himself up through the portal and Miguel follows, then they reach down for the Turk and pull him out. Having filled every pocket, he is heavy with gold. Regarding rows of gold bars at their feet, the men laugh. They are dirty and dripping sweat. In a way that in ordinary times would have made little difference to their lives, they are rich.

Ninety thousand feet above Sinaloa, Paladin Silver copies Mars on fifteen-minute delay.

"What the devil are you doing?" Roscoe sounds raspy, as if he has made a speech at the top of his voice. "It cannot take so long to find five men on horseback in the middle of a desert, where they must body-forth like so many sore thumbs. What thwarts you, Commander Silver?"

Paladin wants to laugh. He does not laugh at Roscoe, doesn't dare, but really. Five men? Desert? A hand's worth of thumbs? Does the old man hear himself even for a second?

"They're gone, Roscoe." How to fill the next thirty minutes? Paladin has yet to invent an agreeable pastime. Expecting Roscoe's reply to take the tack, "What can you mean, gone?" Paladin adds, "Disappeared. Vanished without a trace." It is no way to have a conversation; verbal dueling loses its edge when your interlocutor has half an Earth-hour to anticipate every possible riposte. So much more exhilarating, to flash one's wit in the Inner Sanctum. Pastries on a plate, chimps in the rigging. Roar of falling water *en cascade* as they take their leisure, he and Roscoe and the incomparable Templar Bronze.

Paladin touches a button and his leatherlite flightchair reclines. What is he doing here, anyway? Droids might have done the dirty work perfectly well without him. It feels almost as if the Head Director is punishing Paladin for a wrong only he perceives.

Shut-up in his Earthshuttle, the Sojourner mopes. Even if he convinces Roscoe that further searching is fruitless and they set a homebound course right now – well, in twenty-eight minutes, give or take – it will be another week until he alights on the rhodium landing pad of EarthStation I. Oh, he loves to sojourn, all right, but to photon-accelerate Marsward empty-handed is nothing like his prior returns, robed in glory. As if it really matters, the whereabouts of those meandering Mexicans.

In due course, Roscoe's answer streams through. "They have not vanished, Commander. Do you imagine that five itinerant desperadoes, prone to acts of sabotage and sundry violent gambits, have dissolved in the sun or been swallowed by cacti? I think not. It is a simple matter of your being in one place and their being elsewhere. Having failed to turn up our men in Sonora, you, as I understand the predicament, have established geosynchronous orbit above the coastal state of Sinaloa. This positioning begs the question, *Why?* Why Sinaloa, Commander Silver? To spare us both the absurdity of attending to the trace buzz of background radiation while our words dawdle through the vacuum of interplanetary space, I will venture a suggestion: you have chosen Sinaloa based on a notion that these men take their food from the sea and perforce must travel within easy distance of the shoreline. Commander Silver, I am here to tell you that your notion is reasonable. It is also wrong."

In the pause, Paladin thinks he hears Roscoe swallowing. *Glug … glug … glug.* The old rogue is drinking tea and no doubt gorging on confected sweets. The next sound Paladin discerns, the boney tinkle of a cup's being returned to its saucer, feels like a slap. Roscoe says, "Finish searching Sinaloa, Commander, by all means. Find the desperadoes and prove me wrong. I shall enjoy eating humble pie just this once and congratulating you as you deserve. If, however, our band of brothers does not turn up, I suggest you direct your gaze inland. Indeed, I would not be surprised to learn that they have lost themselves in the Sierra Madre – lost themselves purposefully, you understand, amid crags and canyons and forests of darkest green. All the better to elude us."

Paladin hears chewing. It is unmistakable: toothsome, sticky mastication, as if the Head Director has filled his mouth with morsels of chocolate-covered caramel mainly with the intention of feeding his Adept's sweet-toothed envy. "Wasn't our operative supposed to prevent that?" he ventures. "Seems this Omar fellow is playing a double game."

Again, the wait. Then Roscoe says, "Omar the Turk operates outside conventional norms. His methods are sometimes puzzling – not just indirect and roundabout but counterintuitive. Perverse, even. One doubts, really, that he follows any plan. It all seems rather an improvised business. Chance of a given moment, risk calculated on instinct. A process of discovery." Another couple swallows of tea, a napkin pressed to his lips and the cup again set down. Paladin wants to shout "Bullocks!" but bites his tongue. Roscoe says, "Do not distract yourself, Commander, with caviling about Omar's trustworthiness. To the extent that he is anyone's, he is ours. Much better direct your attention to the western range. Better still, search the northern plateau."

Paladin is ready to weep. Here he was hoping to put paid to this extravagant manhunt and all he has gotten is the cane. With Roscoe's thinking running along these lines, he will be locked inside this Earthshuttle forever.

"We must have those men, Commander Silver," Roscoe says. His voice is not so raspy now. "If it takes the rest of our days, we must remove them from the Badlands."

But why? Paladin wants to wail this question, cry it out, scream. How can it matter that five small men, homunculi, really, wander a wasteland? Their methods now known and preventative safe-guards put in place, what damage can they do?

Verbal outbursts, however, are unbecoming in Adepts. The channel to Mars bleeds a soft, low hiss into Paladin's ears. Is Roscoe finished? No, *Do you copy?* No, *Over and out.* Not even the click of his microphone's being turned off. Is he still there, listen-ing? Is he waiting for Paladin to respond? What does Roscoe ex-pect him to say? Never was it a simple thing to guess the old man's thoughts, misdirection being his technique and irony his attitude. In the last little while he has cultivated an affect both disingenu-ous and bluff, as if he holds secrets too delectable to share.

Unless there is something else. Only at this moment, listening to background radiation dart in from the void, does Paladin Silver wonder if something greater is at stake. What can it be? Life on Mars is fine. The Colony thrives, ideological factions are defunct, political infighting is an embarrassment of the past. Miners dig, grapes grow and ripen, alchemical investigations proceed. If the latter do not prosper, well, tomorrow always is another day. On Earth, SmartBots maintain control, their nominal masters pacified with sex and stupefied by luxury.

What can be amiss? Roscoe's agitation must mean something but Paladin Silver, for the life of him, cannot imagine why the cap-ture of five Mexicans is so urgent.

Turning his head, Paladin gazes through the window on his right. Beyond its oblong pane, Earth seems to float in a wine-dark sea. Paladin regards it with impatience. Cloud-dappled and in-tractable, it has become little more than a nuisance. Inconvenient. Irrelevant. On the other hand, it is beautiful. Its landmasses show up as green and brown with shadings of darker green and lighter brown and streaks of black and gray. Its oceans and rivers and less-er seas are varying shades of blue. It spins through deeps of empty space at tremendous speed, yet from Paladin's perspective the globe appears motionless, miraculously buoyant, perfectly wrought, immortal. An illusion, of course. A lie of optimistic minds. When the Sun exhausts its fuel, a cosmic wave of helium flame will incinerate the inner Solar System, Earth included. In something like two billion years, the end will come in an eye-blink. Until then, little can harm Paladin's one-time home. Certainly not a creature as puny as man.

≈≈ ≈≈ ≈≈ ≈≈ ≈≈

For miles the road is asphalt, then becomes gravel as it reaches toward wilderness. Built for logging, used in later days to search for silver and gold, it has been gullied by rains and littered with rock washed down from the sierra. Pine forest rises on both sides, greening the air. They watch the wooded shadows for movement: puma and bear, coyote, Mexican wolf. Once harried off by human settlement, predators have returned. Only Tarahumara remain in the mountains. In summer they live in caves just below the canyon's rim. It is there, in places the Turk knows, that the Indians may be found. They will approach in daylight, rifles sheathed yet ready to hand.

Their saddlebags are heavy with gold. They have shed gear to carry treasure. Enrique has misgivings about having jettisoned lanterns and blankets. Distributed among the horses, the gold slows their pace. Where the grade steepens, they dismount. Leading their horses on foot, they pause so the animals can drink from a stream near the road. A dozen miles later, the rutted broadway dwindles to a path that winds ribbon-like against sheer granite, a drop of a thousand feet just beyond their elbows. Vistas open across a north-south expanse: rugged peaks that tear the sky, promontories riven by barrancas a mile deep, slopes forested with fir and apache pine. Rock cliffs the color of copper, rough-hewn and mythic-seeming, rise against a heaven of Mexican blue.

Guided by the Turk, they climb into the Sierra Tarahumara. The horses labor in the thin, cool air, saddlebags swaying from their haunches. It is a relief when the ascent ends; remounting, the men feel something like pleasure as they descend to the canyon floor. The air becomes warmer, becomes hot. They camp beside the Urique River and take fish and water here, trusting that the mountains' remoteness has preserved their purity.

Pacho builds a fire. With edged stones deftly flung, Javier kills two rabbits and butchers them. Enrique fries the meat in its own fat.

As they eat, Miguel says, "How many days?"

"One day," says the Turk. "Tomorrow, we travel from sunrise. Two long climbs lie ahead. By evening, we camp on high plateau. The next morning, we come to Tarahumara."

Miguel nods. It is guidance mainly he hopes to find. What to do now. What to do next. He does not understand how the Tarahumara will know. In ordinary matters he does not trust the Turk, who himself trusts no one. Why does this faithless man put faith in the Indians? Miguel hopes to hear that success is possible, that they are not merely lost amid hardships. Can the Tarahumara tell them this? Where to go. Where to look. Whom to ask, if anyone, or to rely on one's comrades.

The Turk believes the Indians know.

So much depends on the Turk, who will translate.

They make camp and sleep, wake at sunrise. Having taken no food, they pursue their course across the canyon floor. The horses' black and chestnut hides glisten in the humid air. The men perspire through their shirts. Ceiba and fig trees spread a high canopy, sheltering them from the Sun's burning light. Birds fill the trees and skiff around the column as it moves along. Javier recognizes coa and cockatoo. Whether the others notice, he cannot tell. To their right, he spies a giant parrot, extraordinary. "See there," he says. "A great parrot." The others turn their heads. Javier points. "There!" The parrot is great, indeed, standing two feet tall on a heavy branch. Its plumage is green, red, and blue, the tail feathers extending well below its perch. The bird's hooked beak and its eyes are black.

"A great green macaw," says Carlos. "One thing truly Mexican yet exists."

"La iglesia amarilla also was Mexican," says Miguel.

"Do we consider the Pale-Faced Martyr a mestizo?"

"Mexicans have revered the Weeping Galilean in their way. The Indians, it is said, accept Church teachings."

"Some only." The Turk rides behind them. They deny him a weapon but the rope is gone. "They adopted those rituals that matched their markings of time. Easter occurs during maize planting; thus, Crucifixion and Resurrection are re-enacted. Judas Iscariot is fashioned in effigy complete with penis. That organ is oversized and erect. After Iscariot betrays the Christ, Tarahumara men batter the effigy and burn it. The divinity of the Christ, however, is not believed exclusive or supreme. It is one god among many. Its unity and separateness from the Divine Father is an absurdity to the Indians."

Years and countless lessons have been forgotten since Miguel has heard such words. "You acquire this knowledge, how? In México there are priests who cannot speak intelligently of these things."

The Turk shrugs. "It is of no moment. We do not come to catechize the Tarahumara."

Their road is nothing, mere dirt and broken stone fringed by barrel cacti and prickly pear. In the canyon's heart, all trees dwindle away. The Sun's searing light pours down on them. Their progress is a walk, the heads of the horses bowing.

At a clear-flowing stream, they dismount. They remove saddles and halters and saddlebags and let the horses drink. The saddle-bags of gold require two men to lift. The horses are a long time filling their bellies, having sweated out their store. The men drink from their canteens and refill them. They sit in the columnar shade of giant cereus cacti and close their eyes. A midday nap is part of no plan, yet almost all together they fall sleep.

In his dream, Carlos is a boy. He is six years old, eight. His mother takes him into her arms. *I love you*. His sister's face turns toward him. Sad dark eyes, lovely long lashes. Her small hand reaches for him even as Carlos, in this dream yet outside it, knows she is not a child anymore. Two decades have been lost since his mother could hold him in her arms. To know this and dream otherwise is anguish.

In Enrique's dream Alma is young and they are not married. She tells Enrique that she is unhappy. She goes away, she does not say where-to. The life she and Enrique have shared does not happen. It has been a difficult life, yet it has kept them in company until now. Knowing this loss, Enrique despairs. His life is unmade. How can it be, that he has lost Alma? How has he allowed it to happen? He has been remiss in one way and another: uncaring, negligent, cold, he has driven her away. Where is she now? What is she doing? He does not know. She is in another place and – he feels, knows – she is happy. What place is it, that he cannot find? A place without him. Without him, free of him, Alma is happy. In his sleep, Enrique sobs. He will never see Alma again. He weeps and no one hears and no one cares.

Miguel in a dream stands in the shallows of the Sea of Cortés. Thighs braced against a retreating surf, he heaves on a bamboo pole lined with waxed twine, its iron hook baited with mackerel. Upshore, his wife tends a fire and seasons a pan in anticipation of sea bass. It is the before-time – before Evita died and Miguel's life became a question with no answer. Two children dig in the sand. A boy, a girl. Their names? They have no names. They did not, do not, exist, the children he and Evita did not have. Their laughing faces are blurs. Miguel tries to touch their hair, caress the smooth skin of hidden faces, and the children disappear. Evita vanishes as he turns and Miguel, alone on a dark beach, has lost his fishing pole and has caught no fish. The fire smolders. A storm sweeps in, angry clouds and hard wind from the sea, and rain falls fast. *My children ...*

Pacho dreams of a girl weeping. Her black hair is wet and hangs straight past her shoulders. Her eyelashes are long and matted by tears. Her cheekbones glisten, her brown eyes ... Someone is shooting at them. The girl's name is María. Pacho does not know how he knows this name, for the girl has not spoken. He leads her by the hand, firing his rifle with the stock braced against his chest, working the lever action one-handed. He kills many raiders in white armor as he struggles with María to run through deep, shifting sand to the spot where their horses wait. He knows the rifle will go empty but dares not drop María's hand to reload. When they reach the spot, their horses are gone. They must escape on foot across the sand, Pacho knows not where. He has never been in this place. The air is cool and wet, the sky black. It is a desert and also not a desert and seems without end. Nowhere to run, no place to hide.

Javier in a dream wanders underground. He leads a mule on a tether, holding a foul-smelling lantern before him. The mule carries tent and cooking gear and saddlebags packed with gold. Javier has no food and in the cave's black depths can see nothing to hunt by the lantern's feeble light. Why is he underground? Where is he going? For what or whom does he search? He walks across granite shelves crazily inclined, thrown together by cataclysmic force. Heaved and subsided, the granite is treacherous with fissures and declivities, chasms and crevices. It is a miracle the mule does not slip, that Javier does not fall. They walk on, darkness all around, the lantern's weak flame seeming to fade. He knows he should turn back, that in these Earthly deeps the air holds less oxygen and might be toxic with poison gas. Why does he not turn back? If he were to find more gold, he could not carry it. The saddlebags are full. Javier has enough gold for the life that has been allotted him. Why does he not escape this place and save himself?

The Turk dreams himself in the hold of a leaky boat. Air-starved, dark-blinded, wet, hungry, shin-deep in seawater, his skin cracked and bleeding. He knows the crossing requires an hour yet it seems to last the entirety of a starless night. The wind is high, the sea in tumult. As it climbs the face of each wave, the boat pitches. After a seeming gasp at each crest, it plunges down the wave's back. In good weather the crossing is easy, and easily detected; a storm interferes with security patrols along the shoreline of El Norte. Capture means arrest, then internment at the prison colony said to flourish on Cuba. Does the Turk know these things or dream them? A rat paddles past him then circles back. Its coarse fur is gray and matted, its eyes two dull beads of dumb intention. The Turk strikes at it, knifing sheets of seawater with the edge of his stiffened hand. A second rat paddles toward him, nailed paws churning, whiskered snout held stiffly above the water. A third rat and a fourth swarm around. The Turk flails with both arms, heart beating fast, throat tight. Rats paddle closer. Black eyes fixed in yellow pools, unblinking. Grey, needle teeth.

He cries out, "Aahh! Aahh!" and jolts to wakefulness. The Turk feels as if he has fallen from a height and landed flat, knocked breathless. He lies on his back, arms tight to his chest, fists pressed under his chin. He sits up, heart hammering. The others sleep. The light tells him little time has passed. To sleep briefly and wake in this way is useless. Better to forgo rest, move on, and distract the mind.

What sound is that? The Turk has never heard the like. The horses have broken their tethers and leap about pell-mell. Black clouds buzzing-hot swarm their necks and haunches. Heads tossing, tails sweeping, the horses try to throw them off. The clouds lift, buzzing as if electric, veer away and circle back, hover and descend. Bucking, running, bloodied flesh atremble, the horses protest in whinnying cries. Stagger-walking, they void fecal liquid from their bowels.

The Turk's shouts wake the others. Staring, they do not understand what has happened, what is happening.

"The water," Enrique says.

"Can they live?"

"We must ward off the flies."

They run amongst the horses, waving their arms. Pacho and Carlos swing saddle blankets through fly-thick air. The men draw kerchiefs over noses and mouths as blood-drunk black flies swirl in loud frenzy, relentless. Filling their hands, the men throw sand all around. They throw sand at the horses and it sticks to their bloodied hides. Flies swarm the men, attack their heads, their hands and necks. Hard-bitten, they are tempted to draw their pistols and open fire.

The horses are in panic. Javier holds a bridle and Pacho spreads a blanket over a horse's head. By this method they work in pairs to lead four horses to the stream. "Cover them with mud. Do not give them water," Enrique cries. Miguel and Carlos hold the four while Enrique, Pacho, Javier, and the Turk try to blanket the others. They succeed with three and Javier leads them away. With infernal persistence, the flies continue to attack. The horses wrench around to bite where flies have bitten. Enrique and Pacho cannot hold them, the blankets will not stay in place. Their flesh scourged and mortified, the horses bleed. One falls.

"We are finished," says Pacho.

"We are not finished." Enrique draws his pistol and fires into the head of the fallen horse. Blood and bone explode from its skull. "Lead the other away," he tells Pacho. "Quickly." Flies cover the bleeding corpse, one swarm crowding out another and being displaced in turn.

The Turk says, "We might have done so at once. A pity we did not think of it."

"I did think of it." Enrique holsters his gun. "I did not wish to do it. The one killed might not be the sickest."

"If our horses die, it hardly matters whether from poison or pests. We cannot cross the mountains on foot."

"We do what is necessary. Perhaps we will walk out of the sierra."

"We cannot carry the gold."

"We can carry the gold as far as is possible for us to carry it. Then we can bury it, marking the place in our minds."

"In this wilderness it is lost forever."

Two horses drink from the stream as Miguel and Carlos struggle to move them away. Five horses, calm, are tethered to trees, blankets still covering them, their legs and hindquarters coated with drying mud. A horse lies downstream.

"What happened?" says Enrique.

"She bolted," says Pacho, "and fell on the rock bed. She broke a foreleg. I had to shoot her."

"The corpse will poison the water," says Javier.

"The water already is poisoned," says Enrique. "We must empty our canteens."

The horses that have been drinking leave off. They allow themselves to be led up the bank, where Carlos and Miguel secure them. It is cooler beneath the canopy. The clear-flowing water is tempting.

"Those also drank?" says Enrique, pointing at the five.

Miguel shakes his head. "They are our best hope. These two we could not restrain."

"My horse also is dead." Enrique sits beside the swift stream and with the others awaits the effect of the water. The horses that have drunk a second time seem untroubled. Before long, however, their bowels bleed out. They lie down, their breath short and fast.

Carlos says, "Can we do nothing?"

"We can spare them further misery," says Enrique.

Javier seizes his rifle and with a single round each kills the dying horses.

"And us?" says Carlos. "Our misery grows greater each minute."

"We are not doomed unless we doom ourselves."

It is a fine thing, to speak in this way. To accomplish a great undertaking, courage is necessary. The Mexicans face a problem of six men and six saddlebags of gold, another eight saddlebags of supplies, food included, all to be carried across the roughest terrain in the Americas by five horses, lately sick and injured.

"We must leave the gold."

"We cannot leave the gold."

"We must obtain a sixth horse."

"The Tarahumara cannot surrender their animals."

"We will use gold to buy a horse."

"A good horse is more valuable to Tarahumara than all our gold."

"We must feed the horses we have, and water them."

"We have no water."

"We must find water. The animals are dry. To drive them on would be murder."

"We have no choice." Enrique looks into the forest. Oak and pine towering above them seem as old as the sky. Steep slopes rise all around. Seemingly pathless, rustling with life, the forest is a labyrinth of which no map exists. A wrong decision now and they will die in the mountains. Their families will remain prisoners, all will be lost, their bodies will never be found. "We cannot stop here," Enrique says. "We must find water as we go."

"We cannot trust any water we find," says the Turk. "We must reach the Tarahumara."

"How far?" says Miguel.

"As I have said, a day and a night beyond today."

"The horses will suffer. We, too, need water."

"We will gather mango and papaya to eat, and bring the horses to pasture as we travel."

"Let us find a way through the forest, away from the sun."

Lifting together, they load the saddlebags. More in lassitude than consent, the horses accept the burden. Heads drooping, they set off along a scant path that winds amongst trees. Miguel leads one horse. He and Enrique walk ahead. Pacho, Javier, Carlos, and the Turk lead the other horses, reins wrapped around their fists.

Templar Bronze and Alma Ramos in a two-seater whisk through the ES3-ES1 corridor en route to Center Atrium and their rendezvous with the Head Director, whom they find at leisure within the Inner Sanctum.

"Heigh-ho, Roscoe," says Templar, entering first, the Mexican woman mutely following.

"Heigh-ho," says Roscoe Gold.

Touching sensors on her wristlet, Templar projects a scaled-down hologram of the heavens against the tiles of Roscoe's cave. There is the Sun as a golden sphere; there, the planets of the inner Solar System; there, the Earth and, not far away, Mars. On Mars, Alma Ramos stands before Roscoe Gold as silent and composed as the north-looking face of a ziggurat. She seems to be waiting for the Head Director to start the conversation. Behind her, Templar Bronze studies star charts, now and then looking up as if to evaluate the black hair and general aspect of her counterpart. Roscoe, chewing his way through a tray of no-frosting cupcakes and swallowing tea between bites, shakes his head and tilts in his chair. It is a new chair, reclinable, trimmed on seat, back, and arms with oxblood-red faux leather. Its sealed-bearing wheels, soundless in their rolling, encourage its occupant to scoot about the Inner Sanctum. At present, Roscoe does not scoot. Neither does he invite his interlocutresses to take a seat in the modular plastic still available in his once and future pleasure dome, much diminished.

"Look around, Mrs. Ramos, and despair," says Roscoe, indicating with outflung arm and fluttering hand the tiled walls and lofted ceiling of his cavernous redoubt. "Everything you see, not just here but within every EarthStation, will never belong to you. That which is ours remains ours, everlastingly. You and your friends and their children and yours, although I am told you have none, will live and die in the barracks."

Alma Ramos says nothing. She stares at the Head Director as if assembling a malediction from the words that spill from his mouth and fill the otherwise silent space of the Inner Sanctum.

Wiping his fingers with a linen napkin, Roscoe says, "Do you know, we had simulated chimpanzees for a while. Quite extraordinary stuff. Until they malfunctioned, that is, and commenced to ripping off each other's lips." He smiles at the horror he imagines he sees shadowing Alma Ramos's immobile face. "But

not to worry. They will soon be set right. Just there" – with out-
stretched arm and long forefinger, Roscoe indicates the Outer
Sanctum – "they will again caper and cavort. Now, that waterfall ...
no doubt you noticed it coming in – or rather, noticed the simulated cliff face down which it once roared. It might prove dicey to
restore the flow. One million, two hundred thousand gallons an
hour. Imagine! Truly, a spectacular piece of work. Hydrokinetic
engineering at its finest. Nothing of the sort had been seen on
Mars for two million years. It is not too much to say its existence
was something of a miracle. A technological miracle, you understand, not a Biblical one – or should I say, 'mythic'? I will spare you
the tiresome tale that surrounds its hiatus except to note that on
Mars, as in Mexico, one's supply of freshwater is precious and its
use subject to priorities. Now then – " Roscoe spins himself in the
chair and cries, "Yippeee!"

Alma Ramos regards this display with a frown. Her chin seems
carved from granite. In English, she says, "What do you want of
me?"

Slamming both feet down, Roscoe stops his twirl. "Excellent
question! What could I, in my peerless station, desire of a menial
import who refuses to perform her basic duty? Shall we ask our
resident genius? What do you say?" He appeals to the Mexican
woman with a smile and nods at Templar Bronze.

Alma Ramos says, "You will do as you wish."

"You're goddamn right." The Head Director turns to Templar.
"What do you make of it, Dr. Bronze? How does our minion come
to be so unobliging? Please, enlighten me. I am all attention."

On the hovering hologram, Templar illuminates in metallic
blue the near arc of a weirdly oblong, implausibly extended orbit
whose other end cannot be seen. The planet that traces this orbit
is absent. "Nibiru will return to our inner Solar System in Earth
year 3404," she says, sniffing, "having completed its solar orbit of

3606.37 Earth years. At that time, we may expect to resolve a great many or possibly all of humankind's outstanding mysteries – not least of which concerns the origin of human beings."

"Tut tut, Dr. Bronze. Human origins are no mystery. You know as well as I what the ancient texts tell us, in the most lucid language ever written."

Templar laughs. "Sumerian pictographs, Roscoe? Akkadian cuneiform? You must concede that any translation is ambiguous. However, let us assume a basic plausibility. I am thinking of confirmation."

"My dear Dr. Bronze! All the confirmation you can require stands before you." Roscoe points at the Mexican woman, who continues to frown.

"You are being tendentious, as you well know."

"Do I?" The surprise in his voice is genuine. "I had rather thought we had convened for the purpose of making this woman's status exactly known to her, to the end of prompting her return to the work for which she was made."

"I had hoped human pickers would improve the process," says Templar. "That seems not to be the case. The grapes might as well be harvested by droids. I see no purpose in forcing the Mexicans into the vineyard – nor, indeed, any reason for them to remain on Mars."

"No purpose? What can you mean? That is their purpose – the only purpose they have."

"Roscoe."

"Oh, come, come. We've been through all this, have we not?" Turning to Alma Ramos, Roscoe spreads his arms and opens his hands in a way that seems calculated to expose her. "Look at her, Dr. Bronze. Truly look. What do you see? A Plato? A Mozart? An Einstein? Surely, another Leonardo da Vinci does not stand before us."

"Roscoe – "

"I daresay this creature will not discover a viable means of intergalactic travel or unlock the secret of the Philosopher's Stone. Agreed?"

"Agreed, yet that, by itself, hardly – "

"Nonsense, Dr. Bronze. Nonsense pure and simple. She is a Lulu Amelu if ever one was. The hair, the eyes, the diminutive stature, the sluggish mind and subservient mien, the impercipient senses. She and her fellows and their sisters and all the children were created to slave in obscurity and die without names. Lulu Amelus one and all, from birth to death. Primitive Workers. Without work, they do not exist. Yippeee!" Roscoe spins in his chair. He snaps two cupcakes off the tray and shies one to Templar. "Eat a cupcake, Dr. Bronze. Boring without frosting but you'll soon get used to it."

Templar bites and chews. "Oh, that's bland," she says, and returns it to the tray.

"Indeed it is," says the Head Director, and stuffs the confection into his mouth. Crumbs fly past his lips as he speaks. "It is also, our food scientists assure me, less toxic – sugar being a kind of poison, you see. Its caloric freight is eighty-four percent less than that of its sweeter avatar, ha ha ha. As if calories and chemistry matter. As if blood-insulin control, even in league with other quite strict gustatory deprivations, would have us chewing the fat or nibbling the baked goods until Nibiru's next rendezvous with Earth, circa 3404."

It is hard work, to get the words out with his mouth full. Roscoe peels the foliated paper from another cupcake as he swallows. "But no matter. What matters is whether Nibiru still sustains life all these millennia later. That is the material point. It would rivet our attention, were the so-called Twelfth Planet to swim into our ken today." He bites into his cupcake and chews. "If life persists on

Nibiru, it means the Anunnaki succeeded in preserving its atmosphere. That was their purpose in coming to Earth in the first place, you know. And why they carted off so goddamn much gold." He takes a long swallow of tea and pours another cup. "Tea, Dr. Bronze?" The offer seems an afterthought. The Mexican woman stands by as if someone has cut out her tongue. "It really is a shame, that they didn't think to leave word on a clay tablet or two. Even a few notes scribbled on a cylinder seal might have saved us a hell of a lot of work and worry. But no, no – just a self-congratulatory account of how they engineered humankind, eyewitness reports of the Deluge, chronicles of the Pyramid Wars, and so forth. Terrific light reading, to be sure – one can while away many a pleasant hour perusing the epic of Gilgamesh in Akkadian transliteration. For our present purpose, however, it is all woefully off point." Roscoe finishes the cupcake and flicks crumbs from his lap. "Now that I think of it, I wish these Antediluvian miracle workers had taken a moment to explain just how, exactly, a planet that spends millennia beyond the heat and light of the Sun comes to support life forms even vaguely like our own."

Templar's eyes perform a fast sideways shift. "We can postulate that Nibiru generates its own heat. The particular phenomenon is outside our experience. I daresay it involves geothermal dynamics, most likely in the form of subterranean volcanism."

"Well, well."

"It is logical also to assume that another star, virtually identical to our Sun in size and age and every other quality, anchors the distant arc of Nibiru's grand elliptic."

"To bring the Twelfth Planet to heel, so to speak, and fling it back our way. Yes, of course." Roscoe eyes the cupcakes remaining on the tray. "And yet, Dr. Bronze, what of the vast between-time? The unimaginable ages of absolute darkness during which the Planet of the Crossing travels between that star and our Sun? We are speaking here of several thousand Earth-years in the void of interstellar space."

"Offhand, I would hypothesize hibernation – what we would call hibernation. To the Anunnaki, it would merely be sleep."

"Happy thought, that. I am appropriately awed. And yet I wonder, can it be true?"

"It would help explain their astoundingly long lives. To humans, the gods, as we called them, were immortal."

Roscoe picks up another cupcake. "Alas, Dr. Bronze. No one is immortal." His eyes drift to the Mexican. "Does this one understand what we say?"

"It is difficult to be sure," says Templar.

Addressing Alma Ramos, Roscoe says, "Do you understand that we have brought you here to work? That you and your, ah, kind, are intended for picking grapes? Yes?"

"Sí, Padrone," says Alma Ramos.

Roscoe swallows tea. "So why, then, do you refuse?"

Alma Ramos stares at the Head Director, black eyes shining. "We will not be your slaves."

"I see," long vowels protracted in exasperated exhale. "A notion of personal freedom, is it? Well, well. We have heard such claims before, Mrs. Ramos, really we have. Self-righteousness. Self-determination. The inalienable personhood of beings whose lives are as insignificant as they are brief." He turns to Templar. "Who has taught her such extravagant ideas, do you think?"

Templar smiles. "Such thinking seems to come naturally."

"Grandiose egotism, you mean?"

"Prideful self-awareness," says Templar.

"We can fix that." Roscoe swivels away and claps his hands. The tile wall slides into the floor. He snaps his fingers and an operating theater as expansive as an oldtime indoor sports arena appears on the telescreen. SmartBots in surgical scrubs, no masks necessary, are otherwise indistinguishable from the humans anesthetized on gurneys. "A simple thing, Implantation," says Roscoe, "as readily accomplished on Mars as in facilities on Earth. Here we observe an example of the latter." He gestures at the screen. "With microchips *in situ*, our Mexican malcontents would be as docile as dogs." Onscreen, droids graft circles of nano-engineered plant resin imprinted with quartz circuitry onto the biological architecture of human brains. "One would not need even to speak to them in conventional ways, much less suffer their presence inside one's pleasure dome. One could merely script them to be serviceable, reliable, and obedient."

"We have droids, Roscoe."

He swivels around to Templar Bronze. "Redundancy is not the issue, Dr. Bronze. The issue is contentment. We can spare these people the pain of thinking for themselves."

"And the miners, Roscoe? The gold?"

"Ah, yes. The gold. Well – " Twice-tapping the remote, he replaces the big picture with sixteen sectioned subscreens. Each shows a cratered expanse of desiccated, sand-drifted Marscape. Above, an orange-tinged sky faintly looms. "We survey these bleak vistas, Dr. Bronze, and what do we see? Craters and cliffs, mounds and valleys, plateaux as level as billiard tables stretching to every horizon. Rock and dust and immeasurable quantities of sand. Not to trifle with your time, Doctor, much less your mind, but if I were to ask, 'What do we not see?' what feature would you name?"

"Water, of course," says Templar Bronze.

"Water of course," Roscoe echoes. He touches sensors and pictures flicker one by one. "Here we have the deserts of what some poet or other once called our cloud-dappled, green-blue orb. Sahara. Sonora. Kalahari. Gobi. Mojave. Great Victoria. Thal, Thar, Kara Kum, Wahiba, Judean, Sinai, and so forth." He touches a sensor, the subscreens flee, and a video of Giza appears. The Great

Pyramid and its slightly smaller near-twin plus lesser acolyte are prominent, with temples and comparatively diminutive satellite pyramids sprinkled around. "And here, as you well know, we have the twin beacons of the northern leg of the triangular landing corridor on the Giza Plateau. Grammar school stuff to be sure, yet it really is too bad that the Arabs removed the casing stones to build meaningless structures in Cairo. The original smooth, shiny sides would have made the Pyramids' true function obvious to even the dimmest eye. Absolutely maddening is that lost capstone. One wonders if it was clad in metal – gold, perhaps? – all the better to light the way to the Spaceport in the Sinai. Well, well. We shall never know. The *Lugal-e* tells us that Ninurta, son of Enlil, destroyed it along with the Great Pyramid's energy crystals at the culmination of the Second Pyramid War, circa 8670 B.C. But no matter." Roscoe taps a sensor and the Giza Pyramids diminish by half. Appearing beside them is a satellite's-eye view of Mars. "Now, let us have a look – for comparative purposes, Doctor – at the Cydonian Complex."

Onscreen, the satellite view turns and clarifies. There on the tannish-red surface is a five-sided pyramid of tremendous height and breadth, aligned north-south along the rotational axis of Mars. In relative proximity is a massive face, arguably human in its bilateral symmetry. Nose, mouth, and teeth are evident. What appears to be a headdress resembles apparel worn by royalty in ancient Egypt.

"The face is some ten miles distant from the pyramid – but you, a genius, know that."

Templar nods.

"Sometime around the end of the last century and well into this one, so-called scientists from what used to be called NASA explained these structures as natural landforms shaped by roiling seas. They had the brass to call them mesas. Mesas! This serendipitous feat of aqueous terraforming was postulated to have occurred during the dark backward & abysm, etc., etc., when water covered the better part of what we have always known as the Martian Dustball. The explanation was plausible, the scientists' credentials impeccable, and any idea that a sentient presence at least as intelligent as our own had visited Mars eons ago was quietly dropped. You, Dr. Bronze, being a Child of Aquarius, are too young to remember; in fact, you had not yet been born. I, however, recall from boyhood the sense of wonderment evoked by our first glimpse of pyramid and face in 1996. I also recall the disappointment – mingled, I admit, with relief – that came a few years later when we, meaning Earthlings, were reassured that we were the only humanlike life forms ever to have existed in our Solar System. The fact that said Solar System is more than four billion Earth-years old seems to have suggested to exactly no one that the certainty of this assurance might be doubted. Well."

Roscoe touches sensors. The views magnify, showing the pyramid's fitted stonework, the decorative carving of the face. On both, the fine-work has been blurred, presumably by sandstorms of millennia past, yet signs of a crafting hand are evident. "As you see for yourself, Dr. Bronze, what NASA scientists a century ago called mesas are anything but. Clearly, these structures were made – that is, built. Wrought." He touches a sensor. A high-resolution photograph of a common landform much like a mesa appears alongside the face. "Here is one of many forgeries NASA purveyed in 2002, together with some prattle about atmospheric distortion and the inferiority of space-based telescopic photography, circa 1996 – all nonsense designed to cloak the truth, which they very well knew and were desperate to hide. What were they afraid of, I wonder? That people would cease to believe in God? Ha!"

Touching another sensor, Roscoe abolishes the faked mesa and restores monumental pyramid and godlike face to center-screen.

"Be that as it may, we have before us an irrefutable fact. Trivial inconsistencies notwithstanding, this pyramid and that face indicate that Anunnaki were established on Mars – established, I mean, long before they arrived on Earth in something like 450,000 B.C. – and ransacked its gold to shore up the decaying atmosphere of their imperiled planet." Roscoe shakes his head. "Please understand that it grieves me to say so. I take no pleasure in having discerned the dismal truth. I have yet to riddle-out the mechanism whereby global gold depletion precipitates deterioration of the magnetosphere – which must lead, of course of course, to atmospheric decay culminating in terrestrial desertification. The deplorable aridity of our home away from home, however, gives the hint that something most definitely is, in the old colloquial phrase, up."

Templar gazes at the telescreen. "You are saying our Mexicans have not found gold on Mars because there is no gold left to be found."

Nodding, nodding, Roscoe's head seems to be bouncing on a spring. His face is a wide, unhappy grin. "In a word, Dr. Bronze – yes."

"You knew this? All along?"

"Not exactly. To use a positive construction: I had misgivings. Let us even call these thoughts suspicions and be done with verbal pettifogging and backstairs hugger-mugger. And yet, and yet – our Mexicans have not toiled in vain. Their failure tends to prove the point. It is consistent with the legendary, long-questioned circumstances of cosmological prehistory – as it concerns Mars and Earth, at any rate. And what more, in our pathetically limited circumstances, can matter to us?"

Roscoe's chest shudders. With a sigh, the Head Director bends toward the console and weeps.

Naked but for sandals, Ibn al Mohammed kneels in the shallows at Further Beach. His hair and beard are violet-black, his body sleek and muscled, skin bronzed by tropical sun. Surf-beaten sand scrapes his knees. Tin pails surround him, a multitude of hot metal and fecal stench. Ibn al Mohammed stops his breath as he cleans a pail, then another, in the warm, in-rushing water of the Caribbean Sea. His mouth sips air, tiny, quick sips that taste of shit. He feels odor seep in, feels it stain eyes and ears and run in his blood. He fills a pail with water and empties it, feces and urine swirling in outrushing surf. He rinses a second time and a third, then toss the pail up-beach to dry. A thousand pails remain. No matter how many he cleans, always a thousand remain.

Standing, he shovels away shit that has floated ashore. Ibn al Mohammed slips the steel flange under each stool and in the same motion flings it into the surf. He takes pains to cast feces as far as possible and so forestall this shit-fraught tide, yet he cannot shovel fast enough.

The old man works beside him. Al Zahrani is toasted chestnut-brown from head to toe. Their captors have allowed him a loin-cloth. Like his young friend, he wields a shovel and suppresses his breath. Al Zahrani's exertions are measured, unhurried. To bend, to lift, to pour have become inevitable acts. That these acts are not of his choosing is unimportant. Work must be done. Some work, no one would choose. And yet, someone must do it. His volition is not important, his assent irrelevant. Everything he thinks and feels, any pleasure he hopes for, a beautiful life he imagines: all is moot. A dirty job is necessary, a chore is required. It is impersonal. Human feces in a pail, awash in urine, have nothing to do with Khalid Saeed Ahmed al Zahrani. He is apart, aloof. In this labor, in all things Gitmo, he knows himself as surrogate, a mere instrument of a greater will whose ways are task and trial. Whose purpose is inscrutable.

Pails crash on pails. Ibn al Mohammed underhands them in pairs up-beach then returns to shovel. Always these chunky stools melting and afloat. He sees that shit is sometimes brown, sometimes green, sometimes yellow-brown, sometimes a color like camel's hair, sometimes almost black. He shovels it out, quickly, quickly, trying not to see.

A diesel growl reaches them before the tractor arrives. Tall, wide tires churn through sand. Perched on an antique seat, one droid steers a wheel of varnished hardwood. Another rides on a large, square-bed trailer amid tin pails tightly packed. It is slow in coming, this convoy of one. Ibn al Mohammed awaits it, impassive and resigned. He is equal to all indignity. To perform such labor demonstrates his faith.

Bring a thousand pails. Bring ten thousand. Bring a million pails filled with ordure from Hell's bowels. I shall cleanse Creation.

It is nothing, a job. Their intention is obvious. Punishment meted out so promptly hints at desperation. His rebellion – for so is refusal to harvest *coffea arabica* construed – worries his captors. Perhaps they fear others will follow suit; al Zahrani's noncooperation might seem an example. However, al Zahrani is an old man who must soon die. Ibn al Mohammed is young. His refusal counts for more. Why they also punish al Zahrani, he does not understand.

Observing the tractor, al Zahrani says, "They bring us hope."

In another place, Ibn al Mohammed would laugh at such a statement. Here on Further Beach, he says, "Grandfather, they bring us shit."

"To work is to hope. In bringing us work, they tell us we are not forsaken."

Such thinking no longer persuades. Ibn al Mohammed knows shit for what it is. Also hope, which brings high spirits at dawn and by dusk evokes despair. "It is a strange hope that requires slave's work of God's servants."

"God tasks us to interpret signs. Words. Acts. Some are easily understood. Others remain mysteries."

"A convenient explanation, Grandfather."

"A slave also may be God's servant."

The tractor trundles up and stops. A perfume more pungent than any Ibn al Mohammed has ever smelt fills the air. Conveyed across burning sand under blazing sun, the shit has begun to melt. Mingled, blended, odors of heated tin and hot urine and ripe feces attain a presence almost visible. It hangs in the space around them, closing in, wreathing them, suffocating.

The droids begin handing down pails.

Ibn al Mohammed and al Zahrani tote them by their handles, two in each hand. While these fresh arrivals sit fermenting ocean-side, Thing 1 and Thing 2 repair up-beach and collect the empties, fitting pails one inside another. They layer the stacks in rows along the flatbed, each row fitted into the grooves formed by the rows underneath. The trailer loaded, one droid crams itself in-amongst. The other resumes the antique seat and shifts the tractor into gear. It lets out the clutch, the diesel vomits black smoke, and tractor and flatbed trace a slow curve, tires churning through sand. A second shift produces another sooty puff and the convoy of one sets its course back to the Gulag, tin rattling cleanly in the ears of two Things untroubled by noise.

Oceanside, the pails are malodorous. To clean these will require days. They will camp up-beach, food delivered to them by the same tractor. No tent to shelter them, no soap or towels, no lamps or lanterns for light. On Further Beach, night is very dark. Countless stars fill a distant sky, their faraway light both comfort and jeer. *How puny you are*, the stars seem to say. *How can you matter, compared with this immensity?*

"How do they know we will not run off? We are not policed. To escape would be child's play."

"There is no place to go," says al Zahrani.

"We might walk into the sea. We might breathe saltwater rather than shit. How can they know we do not prefer to die?"

"They do not know." The old man lifts a pail and ejects it contents. "They do not care." Holding the pail in the water, al Zahrani feels the drag of in-rushing surf. If he released it, the pail would be taken away. It would drift in the shallows, then be carried offshore. Caught in a current and borne eastward around Cuba, it might float, wave-buffeted, across the green Atlantic and wash up on a shore of Spain, where Moors once ruled, or a wild coast of Africa, two thousand miles from the place al Zahrani remembers. The place his young friend still calls home.

"We will never see our homes again," says al Zahrani. "It matters and it does not matter. Our lives continue, yet they are finished."

"My life is not finished." Ibn al Mohammed cleans another pail. "I will leave here in due course and return to my family."

The old man shakes his head. Shit eddies around his shins. "Your family believes you dead." He uses his shovel to push the turds away. "They burn incense before your picture and recite prayers thrice daily. Your reappearance would rob them of these devotions."

Old man. Speaking in paradoxes. Resigned to die. What does he know of a life, once taken, that is destined to be regained? "In due time, Grandfather. The Prophet teaches that all things must pass. God's Kingdom only is eternal. In the fullness of time, who knows what might be?"

Al Zahrani's chuckle is barely heard above the waves' roar. "Very good, my friend. If belief is decisive, your fate will be a happy one, God willing."

Ibn al Mohammed desists. A pail sways on its handle, held in his fingers. "The tenet cannot be doubted. Belief is salvation. It alone is decisive."

"In the next life, yes." Al Zahrani empties a pail. "This life is troubled. As you see."

A look into each other's eyes and they turn away. The multitude that surrounds them is something absurd. In this place, at this moment, mainly shit exists. It fills their senses. In its plenitude, it seems eternal. Hope, Ibn al Mohammed understands, is an opiate. A lie the mind invents to veil the awfulness that is. *Do they have hope? Can they sustain hope?* It does not matter. Hope is an idea only. It is not a plan of action. Their choices are acceptance; total resistance, which might lead to death; or death outright. Ibn al Mohammed has allowed himself to imagine the latter. Would it signify triumph or surrender? If he chooses to die, can he do so in strength? Or does choosing death mean he has been subdued?

The difference, perhaps, is meaningless. Whether defeated or defiant, his soul is uncaptured. Trickery, seduction, humiliation, force: these do not avail. And yet, he and al Zahrani are beaten. They have cooperated in their defeat. Witness the spectacle they make of themselves on this sun-lavished beach, an old man and a young one, naked, shoveling shit against the tide.

He wakes in filtered light, flat on his back in a wide, firm bed. Purple bands lattice a white wall otherwise bright with sunlight. The breath of his bedmate is the only sound. Her face half-hidden by a blue topsheet, the woman beside him is not familiar. Golden hair shimmers around her shoulders and frames her lolling breasts, which happen to be bare. He is troubled by his failure to recognize either hair or breasts. He feels he must be acquainted with both, with all three, yet is unable to recall how, or when, under what circumstances or with whom. He places a hand on the woman's shoulder and says, "Excuse me." It is not a question.

Breathing deeply, breathing long, the woman does not awake.

"Excuse me," he says again, and shakes her.

She reaches out to push off his hand, then pulls the sheet close and turns away.

Sighing, he swings his legs clear and stands. She will have to wake up sometime. He will ask her then. Maybe when she tells him her name, he will remember his own.

He wonders if the bed is his, or hers. Might it be theirs? Might they be a couple, paired-off, even married? For the life of him, he cannot recall. It does not seem likely and it does not seem unlikely. Nothing about the bed or room recommends it as a place he has often slept or a space he has long known. At the same time, nothing stands out as absolutely foreign. He wonders what has happened to him. To them: obviously, they are in this together. But what is this? He is not thinking of the bed, which is one thing they are in together. He means their situation. Their predicament. It would be good to know exactly what it is. An abduction, perhaps, followed by induced amnesia. Perpetrated by whom? To serve what end? Or is it a joke played on the two of them, whoever they are, by devilish so-called friends, whom he also cannot name? Maybe these people are matchmaking. Maybe fogging his mind and bundling him naked into a strange bed with an unmet woman, also naked, is their idea of a blind date.

Standing near the bed, he wonders if he should lie down again. He might roll close to the naked woman and become acquainted.

Try to. Initiate sex, say. Preliminary touching surely would wake her. He does not think they have had sex before – she means during this present instance of being in bed. Although, come to think of it, he does not remember having had sex with her at any time in the past, either.

At this point he realizes that he does not remember the past – any of it – at all.

So-called friends. People who ostensibly have his, have her, best interests at heart. He does not remember ever having had sex, not with this woman, not with anyone. He feels, or maybe just suspects or assumes, that he has had sex with someone at some time before this moment, which seems to be all there is. He guesses he has sex-experience because his body is youngish yet not boyish. Also, a fantastic stiff woody has sprung up. The blonde woman has lovely plump breasts and, he now notices by how the blue topsheet clings about her, a delightful ass. He could lie close and caress it, her ass, with his fantastic stiff woody. Wow! Could he? It would be nothing, by which he means, it would be easy. How might the woman respond? She is, after all, naked in his bed or, if the bed is hers, has allowed him to be naked in it while she also is in it and naked, too. She should not be surprised, much less offended, if he were to sidle up with a fantastic stiff woody and a nice smile and, dropping his youthful yet manly voice an octave, say, "I'm game if you are." She ought to take it as a compliment.

On the other hand, she might scream. If he is as unfamiliar to her as she is to him, she might slap him, kick him, punch him hard, and scream. What then? He does not know where he is. How can he guess what might follow his being caught in the act of what will, at that point, seem like attempted rape?

He decides he will not lie down. Fantastic stiff woody or no, he decides he will take a turn around the room. So that is what he does. Leisurely, looking everywhere, hoping to recognize something, trying to remember. He is expecting to glimpse a key object that will flip the switch, as it were, and light up the dark room his mind has become. A longtime possession, something personal – a wristwatch, a fountain pen – might by its appearance reconnect the million-billion bits and pieces of a memory that evidently has disintegrated and blown away. What a terrible thing, to have nothing to remember. He has no inkling of what he has forgotten – what he once knew. What kind of life has he had? Happy, sad? Good, bad? A mix, no doubt, as all lives are, and yet, remembering none of it, he cannot rue its loss.

Memory: what makes a self coherent over time. Can it really disappear? Mustn't it still be somewhere in his head, memory not gone but just misplaced while his mind hides from itself?

It's pretty funny to walk around sporting a fantastic stiff woody. To strut. *Strut his stuff.* How does he know that phrase? Does it mean what he thinks it means? What he is doing now? Walking around naked with a fantastic stiff woody? It points hard north and bobbles as he walks, struts, like a fleshy divining rod seeking ... well, we know what it's seeking. Where can it lead him but back to the bed? The woman is still asleep – what a Maid of Morpheus! He would think she would feel him moving around the room, that she could not help but sense his fantastic stiff woody cleaving the air. But no. Here he is, lean and fit, primed and ready, game for anything she might like to try, and all she does is doze.

He bounces on the balls of his feet, just a little. The movement jostles his dick. It nods up and down, smacking his abdomen, springing here and there. Such fun! If it had a face, it would be grinning. Why doesn't the blonde open her eyes? He cannot believe what she is missing. What he is missing because of it, he can imagine despite having no memory of what sex feels like. He knows what sex is, knows what they would be doing, the attitude of their embrace, if they were having sex. But the feeling? He has no idea. If he hand-rubbed his fantastic stiff woody, would that feeling be the same as the feeling of sex? He tries it and doesn't think it is. The same, he means. In fact, it feels not so great. He doubts actual sex feels like that.

What if he slipped into bed and gently, gently parted her thighs and, well, slid his fantastic stiff woody into her ... into her ... what is the word? The word he wants to say is *cookie* but he thinks that isn't correct. The correct word is something else. Like cookie? Two syllables? One? He can't recall it; it will not bubble-up into his consciousness. But he knows what he means, also what it is and where, and that it is the place his fantastic stiff woody belongs.

He has to wake her. He has to slide his fantastic stiff woody into her cookie-something and she has to be awake and know what is happening and that he is the reason. The reason and the cause. Leaning over the bed, he grabs her shoulder, shakes her roughly. "Excuse me!" He is shouting. "Hello?" God bless it if the bitch will not wake up. What is she, drugged? She is breathing, not dead. He slaps her across the face. "Hello? Hello? Wake the fuck up!"

"Oooooh, stop! I want to sleep! Go away!" She wards him off and hides her face in the pillow.

Bad move. Lovely woman naked in your bed, in her bed, you want to become acquainted, many approaches are possible. You say, "Hello, beautiful." You smile and bow, say, "Is this an angel I see before me?" With a wink, you growl, "Sexy lady, wanna fuck?" You do not slap her. Idiot! It's too late. Done and done.

His woody continues fantastically stiff, for all the good it's doing anybody. A nice chance. He had one and he blew it. He ... he ...

My name. What is my name?

It should have come back by now. He is fully awake, penis keen, senses alert and his mind just now shocked in realizing he has face-slapped a naked woman he does not know. All this, yet he does not remember what he calls himself. What others call him.

Idiot.

He looks around the room. Maybe he has never been here before. Maybe there is no key object to tip his memory back in place. As it happens, the room has precious few objects of any kind lying about. The window near the bed is covered by louvered blinds. On another wall is a mirror, full-length, double-wide, polished to surreal clarity. In it he sees himself, woody and all. His torso, his face ... A key object! But no. Nose, eyes, and mouth, chin and eyebrow ridge, cheekbones, such as they are, do not look familiar.

He walks to the door, opens it and leaves the room. Why not? The space he enters features a kitchen well-appointed with chrome appliances and a chest-high granite ledge convenient for eating meals within sight of a wall of windows that offers splendid views of a shining, sky-scrapered city. A smeared plate lingers on the granite ledge, a fork and knife, both dirty, beside it. Someone has enjoyed eggs and not cleaned up. Two cups also have been left, both with a quarter inch, he guesses, of sludge and a scent of cold coffee. Cold and old. Plus a sour smell from the caramel-colored one. He lifts the other cup, examines its black sludge, decides not to drink it. The stuff looks like it has been there a couple days. *Dregs.* Does he know that word? It seems like the right word for what is left in the cup. Not like *cookie.* He is sure the other thing is not called that. *Nookie ... crumpet ... bunny ...* Well, it doesn't matter. He is not getting near it now.

The couch looking comfy, he sits, ass bare on the leather. From here, he has a full view of the windows – a wall, really, of seamless, floor to ceiling glass that affords truly breathtaking sightlines from on high. The city is all chromium steel and crystal glass. Sleek craft fly this way and that, swooping, banking, rising, descending. Gold, silver, and bronze, all gleaming through the clear light. He wonders if the different metals signify something, a distinction or mark of identity. The view is not definitely familiar but he feels he might have seen it before. Also the wall of windows, the *windowall* he thinks it must be called, is something he feels he knows.

He stands and approaches the glass. Looking out, he sees glass-and-steel towers of different heights, lit within by lights of many colors that vary in brightness. The towers' apexes also vary: some are crenellated, others round, others yet have four faces raised on an angle to form pyramidions. What purposes are served by this array? Is each tower home to people? Are some of these folk also looking out? Can anyone see him? He is high up, a hundred stories and more above the ground. So are they. If someone sees him, so what? To be naked is nothing special. Every man gets a woody sometime.

Lolling. Peculiar word. It seemed to match automatically with breasts. *Her lolling breasts.* Why? Was her posture really that? The position of her body, the appearance of her breasts as she lay on her side, their size and weight causing them to sort-of slide, or melt, maybe, is the image he is trying to capture, down toward the mattress. Is that what it means, to loll? If he had a dictionary, he could look it up.

Wake up, he thinks, meaning the blonde.

The windowall goes dark, obscuring the vista. What was a portal becomes a screen. Images appear in million-color three-dimensional simulation. Front and center, a hundred or so women in green field dress sit on bamboo-frame cots in a concrete dormitory. Scatterings of small children dash about. In another screen section, small-sized Marsuits hang on aluminum racks inside a whitewalled cleanspace. The light is low; nothing moves. Another screen shows black-bearded men clinging to the bars of railroad-car cages. They seem to be shouting. The women in the dormitory appear to be having hushed conversations. The people on-screen cannot be heard; voice-overs only are audible. Peripheral screens flash ten-second updates of what seem to be public sex events, credit-exchange markets, embarkation times for Moonshuttle launches, and advertisements for something called Personality Profiles.

Lifting his arm, he points at an ad. Nothing happens. He snaps his fingers. Nothing happens. A reflex blink produces a laser beam pinpointed on-screen. He says, "Who am I?" Nothing happens. He blinks again and Personality Profile shifts to center screen. Moving the laser with his eye or eyes, he can't tell which, he selects "Male Profiles" and blinks. A portrait menu appears with names underneath. None of the faces looks like his. The names are unfamiliar. *Leonardo di Caprio. Cary Grant. Johnny Depp. Clark Gable.* Who are these people? What are they doing on his screen? He moves the laser to the caged men, blinks, and says, "Start."

Images fade away as if being erased. A rectangle of June-sky blue appears with "Personal Graphic Interface" lettered in white along the top. Rows of data cascade below, including a headshot he recognizes as the face recently mirrored back at him. Beneath it is a name: J Melmoth.

So he is called J Melmoth, is he? Can he be sure? It might be his name or it might be nothing. It does not ring a bell. What does the "J" stand for? James? Joseph? John? What other J-names does he know? José? Juan? Jethro? Jeremiah? Is it possible his true given name is Jeremiah? Jerry? Jeremy? Or is it, literally, just Jay – the initial "J" being graphic shorthand for already very short "Jay." He decides it doesn't matter. Possibly it matters in the long run. Right now, what matters is the portrait beside his own. It is the face of the naked blonde incredibly still asleep in the other room. Her face only. She is identified as his wife and her name, the PGI tells him, is Raquel. Raquel Romanov.

A Russian? What is he doing, married to a Russian? Is he also Russian? He doubts it; "Melmoth" does not sound Russian. But, does he know Russian? Speak and understand it? Does he? He thinks he does not. Or does not remember. Also, he isn't sure the Cyrillic alphabet uses the letter J. He is surprised he remembers the Russian alphabet is called Cyrillic. Anyway, even if Russian does use the letter J, his face, the one glimpsed in the mirror and seen now on-screen and confirmed as his, does not have about it a Russian appearance.

What does that mean? *A Russian appearance.* What is a Russian appearance? Can he describe it, explain what he has in mind? Does he have anything particular in mind? Does he know what he is talking about?

He does not know what he is talking about. What he is thinking. Trying to think. About. It is difficult to concentrate while the competing voice-overs blare. "Quiet!" he says, and the audio shuts off. The visuals play on. The conversing women seem not to notice; the windowall, it seems, is not a two-way communications device. He sees them, they do not see him. Very good.

He is glad the naked woman is his wife. Glad she is and glad to know it. He wishes he remembered her but at least now he knows her name and can stop wondering. He realizes he has slapped her across the face and can only hope she forgets it. It would be a rotten trick, if she awoke having forgotten everything about him except that.

Not bothering to look for clothes, he clears the dirty plate and sludgy cups, plus the soiled fork and knife, into a cabinet-type appliance that reminds him, in a distant-echo kind of way, of a dishwasher. Inside, he finds another plate with fork-and-knife accompaniment, all clean. He removes this ensemble and sets it on the granite ledge. If these things are evidence of their last breakfast, whose plate and utensils have been cleaned and whose left dirty? He does not remember. Did he ever know? He doesn't know that, either. However, he does know his name. J Melmoth. That is, if he trusts them. Trusts whom? Who are they? To whom does he, J

Melmoth, refer when he uses the pronoun "they"? Well, the ones in charge, obviously. And who is in charge? Oh, J Melmoth does not know.

Being naked, he would take a shower, give himself a thorough scrub, but he seems freshly washed. Who has done this for him, he cannot imagine. Raquel Romanov? It seems unlikely. Not they, of course; those in charge never perform such chores. They hire underlings. Lackeys. Menial workers who carry out their decrees. Melmoth is left with the queasy feeling that hired staff or, worse still, destitute unfortunates dragooned into serving a faceless Master, have handled his person. He hopes they wore gloves, also surgical masks. The possibility that these people – perhaps they are slaves! – breathed on him with their dragooned menial breath makes him nauseous. He decides, no, it cannot have been. Losing the contents of his memory is one thing and bad enough. Being intimately handled and breath-fouled by wage slaves is beyond the pale.

He scans the screens. The hanging Marsuits have been replaced by a panoramic view of a kind of city. The sky is milky-pink. Everything is still. No one walks into or out of or even past the buildings, no flying craft veer and bank, no breeze ruffles the trees. The whole business looks very low-slung compared to his present situation high up. There is an impression of structural huddle, of buildings hugging the ground. *Hunkering*. The camera tilts and the picture swings rightward, as if the lens is set in the nose of an airplane preparing to land – vertically, if you can believe it, if Melmoth can – on the flat roof of the tallest building there.

It's a strange name, Melmoth. All names are strange, when you get down to it. *Raquel Romanov*. Unusual, is what he might mean. Unfamiliar. He wonders again if it really can be his. It has the sound of something made-up, a fiction they are foisting on him.

The images change. Now the view is interior: a shadowy space, a kind of grotto, tile covering the walls, a tall, slender, white-haired man seated in a red chair. Leather, from the look of it. Given that the man is seated, Melmoth is not sure how he knows the man is tall. It seems it must be so, that this man, whoever he is, must be tall. Also slender. When the man stands and steps forward, Melmoth sees both are so. Without audio it is impossible to know what any of this is about: a diorama-like city hunkering under glass – a weatherproof roof, if you please! – a gliding approach and bumpless touch-down topside, entry vouchsafed to a lonely, quiet room and a tall man with white hair speaking into the camera with insouciant grin and twinkling eyes.

Something about it gives Melmoth the creeps.

"Hello?" he says. "Hello, hello?" No response. The white-haired man is explaining something, that much is obvious, but Melmoth is not a lip reader. "Speak!" he says. Nothing happens. "Sound on!" and that does the trick.

"... more than a thousand striking miners and rather more women belonging to this same subspecies flatly refusing to perform the labor whose need their relocation was expressly intended to supply? Burdened, one might say. Lumbered. Not to mention several score of ragged offspring, by which I refer of course to their children, the cost and inconvenience of whose education and nourishment we willingly, nay, gladly have taken on as emoluments rightly due their toiling mas and pas. And yet, they will not work, these so-called parents. And so, my friends – *en suite*, as those formerly called the French used to say – are we yet constrained to feed and clothe, teach and train their rambunctious brood? Or are we justified in return-shipping the lot of them to Earth – at our own additional expense, I feel obligated to note – specifically, to the deserts of Mexico whence they came. Dusty, bedraggled, itinerant scavengers – underfed, unschooled, word-blind, impoverished, forgotten, woeful, fucked."

Such a word. Who is this white-haired man, that he can speak an obscenity on television? Unless what Melmoth is looking at isn't television. It certainly does not look like television as Melmoth remembers it. Does he? Remember it? It seems he does; it was much, much smaller, the television he watched. The colors were never so crisp and the clarity ... if it is television, he has been asleep a very long time and what is playing before him is the television of the future. Maybe the channel is closed circuit; maybe the show is a pay-per-view, although Melmoth is pretty sure he hasn't paid.

After his concluding word, startling to Melmoth, the white-haired man takes a long pause and turns away. He stands in quarter-profile and watches his own large screen, which sweeps over scenes of quietly conversing women seated on bamboo cots and brown-hued short men squatting on their heels inside an empty receiving bay, cast-iron gondolas of the sort used for hauling coal from a mine parked end to end on large, shallow-tread tires. The gondolas also are empty. Music accompanies these glum surrounds, slow, melodic, threnodial laments that blend and meld and flow like a sad, sluggish river of tears around the immobile Mexicans, as Melmoth has gathered these people are. In another room, brown-hued children are seated in ranks at long white tables, stuffing peanut butter and jelly sandwiches into their mouths and drinking milk.

The white-haired man turns full-face to the camera. "As you see," speaking directly to Melmoth, "pacific noncooperation continues. We exhort them to work. They refuse to work – they refuse to answer! Imagine it: these creatures will not speak to us." Swiveling his head, he returns his gaze to the screen. "The situation shows no sign of resolution." Around him, lights dim and music rises. "Remember, my friends, that people of this ilk have been responsible for outrages of the most dangerous sort throughout the Mexican subcontinent. They are intractable and ungovernable, impervious to reason, deaf to argument, bent on mischief, lucky to be alive. If we return them to their native habitat, they will likely perish; if they do not perish, they will surely suffer and, in that suffering, lash out again and again at whatever targets present themselves. Nuclear waste storage facilities. Medical refuse silos. Toxic substances containment sites. They have done so before, they will do so again. The consequences will be troublesome and hazardous. They might be fatal. We ourselves are not safe."

The music fades and new music begins: a waltz, bright and airy with soaring violins. A dozen brown-hued men lie on gurneys. They are naked and asleep. Their heads have been shaved. A person whom Melmoth assumes is a surgeon wields a small, high-speed drill. Several nurses and what seems to be an anesthesiologist attend.

"In this room, by this means, their torments end." It is the voice of the white-haired man. He himself is not visible, although it seems to Melmoth that his presence looms.

The surgeon drills up through the underside of a sleeping man's brow. He retracts the whirring bit and hands the drill to a nurse. Another nurse passes him a stainless steel probe that tapers to a fantastically fine point, at the tip of which is a small green disk, paper-thin. To Melmoth it seems the size of a dime. It is pliable, this disk, and the probe is hollow. Retracting the disk into the probe's tip, the surgeon slips it into the hole and aims it at the brain. Donning goggles, the surgeon gentles the disk to its optimal spot.

"The miracle of the microchip," says the white-haired voice. "Where would we be – what would we be – without it?" Violins swoop and sail. "Integrated with nano-scaled plant resin, encoded with real-time, thought-pattern recognition and remediation protocols, the microchip delivers us forever from the prison house of the self. No more doubt, no more worry, no more confusion about what to do or not do. To be or not be. Through the power of corrective auto-suggestion and timely prompts, quandaries dissolve, dilemmas dissipate, conflicts cease to exist. Imagine, my dears, *just imagine* the relief these men will feel upon waking. The unburdened joy, the sense of clarity and competence. In a single instant of annihilating insight, they will understand, *at last,* that theirs is not to reason why – that asking such a question is unnecessary, time-wasting, impertinent, mad. The rhyme and reason of their lives made plain to them, their duties marked out and set forth and thoroughly, thoroughly, *thoroughly* impressed, nothing will remain for them except to act. To do." In the pause, Melmoth imagines the man smiling – the broadest, loudest, most content and beatific smile in human history. "Freedom!" the white-haired voice cries. "Freedom! Freedom! Freedom! Freedom! Freedom from jealousy, freedom from anger, freedom from a sense of being wronged, from suspicions of disrespect, from an awareness of being beset, of being constrained, of being obligated and indentured; freedom from memories of a past life, freedom from vain imaginings of something better, freedom from thinking you deserve more, freedom from worrying you will get less; freedom from ambition, from desire, from the horror of needing to decide, from the nausea of being able to choose; freedom from the delusion of being free!" The white-haired man is prancing, Melmoth thinks, he must be skipping about, waving his arms overhead in glee. Well, and why not? It sounds pretty good – damn fine, as a matter of fact. And to think that they are doing this gratis! For these measly Mexicans, who from the look of them are nothing special or even useful. Well, it just lifts Melmoth's heart. It makes him feel good and it makes him feel safe. Here is someone who takes care of things. Here is someone who has his finger on the pulse of the body politic, so to speak; who makes sure that everything advantageous to knitting the social fabric (to mix Melmoth's metaphor) even more tightly is duly done. It is comforting to know that someone watchful, thoughtful, and resourceful is on the job. The white-haired man. He is wise, he is. He knows what to do.

Music swells and recedes and swells again. Brain surgeries are performed one by one on small brown men as they sleep. Fantastic, that they all are getting microchips. What a world! Melmoth never would have believed it. When, he wonders, will his turn come? Or does he already have a microchip? Given the great emptiness that fills his mind, he doesn't think so. Unless someone has turned it off. Is that possible? Melmoth doesn't know; the white-haired man hasn't mentioned an on/off switch. He wishes he knew whom to call. A number to dial, an authority to ask. A knowledgeable Someone who could put him in touch with the white-haired man or send him straight to a brain surgeon. He would have a microchip installed straightaway, connect himself to databases and – who knows? – maybe remember everything he has forgotten, or ... or ... even get instructions for living his life! What could be better?

Melmoth cannot answer this question. His mind is, seems always to have been, blank.

They shamble upslope at altitude, heads hanging, eyes on the pebbled trail, leading their horses by reins gone slack. Tall oaks spread a green canopy above their heads. This shelter will disappear as they ascend.

They stop before nightfall. Dinner is mango and papaya. Water is not to be found but forage is abundant and the horses derive moisture from the grass. Early next morning they resume the ascent. They have had no coffee, only fruit. At midday they come upon a spring flowing through fissures in the granite, a clear trickle flashing silver in leaf-dappled light. To fill the large pot takes minutes.

They bring a horse to drink.

"How long?" says Pacho.

Miguel says, "To wait until nightfall would be prudent."

"An hour is sufficient." The Turk tries to spit. His saliva looks like cotton, damp and clotted. "Sky and mountain only are above us. Water does not flow uphill."

They wait with parched throats. In hope, they refill the pot, then their canteens. The horse continuing well, they water the others.

"It seems we may drink."

"It is a fatal choice."

"We have no other."

Together, they slake their thirsts by the mouthful. The water is cool and delicious, like strength flowing into them.

That day and the next, they climb. They bivouac before nightfall and wake at dawn. Cleaving to the trail, they travel upward. The air grows cooler, flies and mosquitoes vanish. Some hours after midday, they find a settlement of Tarahumara on the mountain's western face. The Indians dwell in caves at various levels below the canyon's rim. Terracing has made the frontage tillable and beans and squash grow inside rectangular plots. Into this arrangement the Mexicans come, their column led by the Turk. They walk in slowly. Eyes watchful and unafraid, the Indians observe. Their hair is black, their skin reddish-brown. Women and girls cover their heads with bright scarves. Men and boys wear tunic-like shirts of woven hemp, white like their trousers. The skirts and blouses of the females flow with yellow, red, lime green and turquoise, orange, true blue. Some men are bare-chested. Others wear loincloths, also white, their legs bare.

The Turk speaks in a language none of the Mexicans has ever heard. He could be telling the Indians to kill Enrique and Miguel and the others where they stand; that the Mexicans intend theft, rape, murder behind a guise of friendship. One thought crosses each man's mind: will the Turk betray them for gold?

A young man, black hair falling straight to his jaw, says, "*Cuira.*"

"*Cuira,*" the Turk says.

The Mexicans all say, "*Cuira,*" and nod.

The Indian addresses them at length. Enrique cannot distinguish ends of sentences from beginnings but hears in the Indian's speech something formalized. A greeting to strangers that is also a caution. The young man's arms and legs are long and smoothly muscled and, like his torso, bronze with a maroon undertone. His face is hairless, its angles and planes precisely aligned. Enrique notes that all the men are tall and slender.

When the young man stops speaking, Enrique asks the Turk, "What does he say?"

"In the name of Nova, Siriame of this community, he welcomes us in peace. We are invited to share their food. We are not to approach any female. We may remain one night. Now we must come before the heads of families. We are to touch nothing. His name is Montez."

"A Spanish name. They have not lived wholly apart."

"Many Tarahumara were Christianized. They are a diverse people. Their dialects vary."

"We are fortunate this one understands you."

"Their settlements are at great distances. They go on foot between, as much as a hundred miles in a day."

"Impossible," says Javier.

"No human can run so far," says Carlos.

The Turk nods. "It is the name they call themselves: Rarámuri. 'The people who walk well.'"

"To walk well is not to run one hundred miles."

"They are a modest people. In understatement, they find humor."

Montez leads them to a higher level of caves. As their small band winds upwards, men, women, and children regard it with steady eyes.

Short of their destination, Montez instructs them, through the Turk, to tether their horses to a stand of oaks. Having done so, they continue upward to a large cave. An overhanging ledge shelters its entrance. In its forefront, a man sits on an oaken chair, rough-hewn. The Indian's age is difficult to reckon. His face is hairless, his smooth skin richly bronze, his body lean and muscular. Held in a ponytail by a silver clasp, his black hair is streaked with silver strands. Four men of similar appearance stand around him. When the seated man also stands, his greater height marks him out. He speaks a sentence that sounds like a greeting, then indicates each man in turn. "Lima. Ibañez. Beltrán. Peña." He touches his chest. "Nova."

Miguel says, "¿Entiendes Español?"

Nova seems not pleased by this question. In Spanish, he says, "Rarámuri understand this language. By choice, we do not speak it. It is the tongue of los conquistadores who enslaved our ancestors and yours. The tongue of los chabochi, children of el Diablo. This man understands." Lifting a long, lean arm, he holds his hand palm-up toward the Turk.

The Turk bows. In Spanish, he says, "We have news important to Rarámuri. Invaders have appeared in the western desert. With fearsome weapons, they have stolen the families of these men. The invaders travel in a great ship that flies across the sky. We share this news so that Rarámuri may guard themselves."

The Indians do not react. In Spanish, Nova says, "We will hear more. The act you describe is evil. It is right to speak of it in the tongue of el Diablo. First, you may cleanse yourselves. Then we will eat, and drink *tesguino*, and you will tell this tale."

Carlos claps the Turk on the shoulder. "This one witnessed the catastrophe," he says in Spanish and pushes the Turk forward. "He knows the tale in full."

"Muy bueno," says Nova. Then, in dialect: "We will listen."

The Turk does not translate, yet the Mexicans understand.

Seventeen miles above the Yucatán Peninsula, Paladin Silver reviews the latest sector analysis with a gimlet eye. Sub-parsed and fine-combed, these tallies tell a hapless tale. The flight from Mars and time spent in geosynchronous Earth-orbit, their strategized search patterns and painstaking, thermal-guided progression across the subcontinent have yielded up failure. Amid the vast, blighted reaches of Mexico's deserts they have found no one, no one at all.

Paladin Silver is not surprised.

Five Mexicans. Seven hundred and sixty-one thousand, six hundred and five square miles. Among which are two enormous deserts and three major mountain ranges, the latter featuring cliffs so steep and canyons so deep as to be practically impassable. A warlord could hide an army in the barrancas of the Sierra Madre Occidental. All right, yes, they would find an army; Paladin Silver does not doubt that so many congregated bodies would show up on the thermal-imager, confidence high. That is not the point. The point, Paladin Silver cannot stop thinking, is the futility of hunting and pecking for five substandard men, manikins, really, whose obscure lives and eventual deaths in a benighted semi-nation can make no difference to anyone.

Setting aside numbers and graphs, Paladin tilts back in his flight chair. A topographically-correct map with real-time animation is projected at scale across the shallow concave of his titanium ceiling. Paladin sees azure waves sweeping toward sandy shorelines, wispy clouds scrimming interior rainforest, tourist resorts that, against all plausibility, continue to entertain guests, rustic cities in ruin, pueblos wholly abandoned. In human terms, Mexico is a mess. The land itself seems in fair shape, assuming hazardous waste sites stay contained. About the water, Paladin is not so sure; water is always a problem. Either there is not enough to sustain human settlements or rivers overflow, oceans rise, and age-old city-states are inundated. For a hundred years, pollution has been disastrous. Water of adequate flow is unfit for human use. Drinking, cooking, irrigating crops, watering livestock. Something of this sort likely killed off the ancient cities. Touching a button, Paladin zooms his view onto Chichén Itzá, its great stepped pyramid and large ball court looking lost and lonely amid tangles of unkempt greenery. The situation must have been dire for its people to leave a place where their ancestors had lived and died for a thousand years. Paladin himself has no such attachment, having been born in a province and whisked to an outpost at age three, yet even he can see that it must have taken a generation to build the Temple of Kukulkan alone. A perfect ziggurat, it is, with each of its four staircases having ninety-one steps, thereby making its upper platform step three hundred and sixty-five. On the equinoxes, a shadow like a wriggling serpent falls along the west balustrade of the north-facing staircase, as if a snake were descending from the Temple house to the stone serpent's head at the staircase's base. Ingenious design, an engineering marvel, a precinct sacred to the gods or what you will – and its people abandoned it! They bloody well must have been dying of thirst, Paladin thinks, or dying of something.

He zooms on the Temple house. Who was Kukulkan? A king? A god? Paladin does not recall. He could retrieve the information easily enough but decides not to bother. The identity of this being and his, her, its nature can hardly matter now. What matters is that this Temple was built and countless years later still stands. Looks quite sturdy, too, Paladin thinks, judging from the size of its stones and their fit and finish. The Temple house proper seems solid, or stolid, as if it were designed as a battle redoubt as well as royal residence and sanctum sanctorum.

Its coordinates: twenty degrees, forty minutes, one second North; eighty-eight degrees, thirty-four minutes, nine seconds West.

Apropos of nothing: *I could damn well land this shuttle on top of it.*

No reason for Paladin to think this; no purpose in landing his Earthshuttle atop the Temple of Kukulkan at Chichén Itzá or anywhere else on Earth. But it interests him that he can. That it is possible. The Temple house is large enough. It appears to be built of white marble mottled light gray, or maybe just limestone, and its walls look five feet thick, at least. Its roof is flat. You have to wonder about the people who went to so much trouble. Just hauling those blocks up the ziggurat's steeply pitched steps is a prodigious feat.

Paladin zooms out and Mexico reassembles itself on his ceiling. He is not going to find Badlands desperadoes by looking at a map.

He is not going to find the Mexicans at all unless he can imagine where they might be. This systematic searching, however theoretically sound, is for practical purposes just so much pissing into the wind. The droids are no use at all.

Searching sector twenty-eight thousand, two hundred and twelve.

Negative! Covert Operations protocols disqualify low altitude reconnaissance strafings.

To have located-not-yet does not equal will-locate-never.

Horsepucky. What must it be like, Paladin wonders, to pass one's existence with one's brain locked in a box? It's a good job that Bots are not self-aware. He himself can think, and that's a good job, too, because without the ability to reason, he would be lost. This current stalemate is a fine example. Where in the world are five Mexicans? Who the fuck knows; and so, Paladin's only chance is to riddle it out. *Where might they go? Why would they go there? What could their purpose be? What is their quest?*

If he can answer these questions, he can find them.

Nova has a goat butchered. Lima beheads a chicken, which his wife plucks clean, stuffs with squash and cornmeal, and roasts over coals. Beltrán brings corn and black beans, Ibañez a rabbit. His wife pan-fries the meat before adding it to the pot. The stew simmers in seasoned iron. Peña supplies tesguino for all.

"*Muchínara,*" says Nova.

"He invites us to sit," says the Turk.

They do so in a circle, on blankets woven of wool. Sifting themselves randomly, Indian and Mexican alternate right around. The Turk sits between Nova and Ibañez. Miguel and Enrique face each other across the circle.

Nova says, "*¿Cumi simí?*"

"Nova asks where we are going," says the Turk.

Miguel savors a mouthful of stew. Goat and rabbit mingled with beans and corn are an intoxication after weeks of salted fish and plain beans. Its taste is a wonderment and he is reluctant to swallow. He does so sooner than he wishes only to speak. "We cross the sierra," he says, "then ride south to Ciudad de México."

"Tenochtitlán," says the Turk.

The Indians nod. "What is in Tenochtitlán?' says Beltrán, in Spanish.

Miguel states how they hope to recover their people.

In Rarámuri dialect salted with necessary Spanish, the Turk describes the invasion of the Sinaloa encampment. He repeats the fact, still astonishing to the Mexicans, that a flying craft appeared from a place beyond the sky; and that, after raiders subdued the Mexicans and herded them aboard, this craft rose again into the sky, achieved a great height, and disappeared.

The Rarámuri eat without speaking. Enrique doubts this story holds any sense for them. Such a ship is not likely to have come to the sierra. Nova raises his eyes to Peña and the latter retrieves a large gourd, maize-yellow, varnished, decorated with turquoise silhouettes. A child precedes him with simple small gourds, handing one of these to each man, and Peña makes the round, pouring *tesguino*.

The Mexicans have not used alcohol for many years. Wetting their tongues, they find the liquor fiery and harsh. The Indians drink. Nova finishes his portion and holds forth his gourd, which Peña refills. Ibañez, Lima, and Beltrán drink up and present empty vessels for replenishment. As Peña pours, Nova says, "We may use Spanish to speak of these events. Its words are helpful. Forgive me, my friend, when I say this tale is difficult to credit." He sips *tes-*

guino. "However, we know you as a truthful man. And I ask myself, 'What purpose can our friend have, to bring us a lie?'"

"No purpose," says Beltrán.

"It is true," says the Turk.

Enrique says, "We have asked ourselves if Rarámuri also have been taken."

"We have not." Nova's slow smile seems almost sad. "We are farmers. We live simple lives. As you see, we are not easy to find."

"Our people also lived simply," says Carlos, "yet invaders have taken them – to serve as laborers, we believe."

Lima says, "Such a fate befell Rarámuri long ago. For this reason, we keep ourselves apart. It has been so for many generations. We would not work beneath the ground."

They drink. Sectioned and carved, roasted chicken appears on a stone platter. The men eat with their fingers.

"Los conquistadores came in sailing ships from across the sea," says Nova. "Whitefaced chabochi, bearded like the olden gods and wearing metal armor that the Sun's light made shine. The Mexica mistook these chabochi for the gods who had promised to return. As you know, los conquistadores were not gods but adventurers, as the Mexica quickly learned. Vainglorious men, greedy for fame and riches. Chiefly, they craved gold. Their professed religion made them arrogant and daring. They prided themselves on deceit and treachery, which they used without conscience to steal great amounts of gold from the Mexica, whom they called Aztecs and considered savages. Of the king they made a prisoner and demanded ransom, in gold. When the tribute was paid, they murdered the king, then destroyed his people, burning their homes and relics and artwork and sacred writings. Los conquistadores ended Mexica civilization, then killed other native peoples in their millions." Nova wets his lips with *tesguino*. "Brothers of these chabochi brought hardship to Rarámuri. These, too, were prideful and vainglorious, also with hair covering their faces. They came as taskmasters more than two thousand seasons ago. They forced Rarámuri to labor in caverns gouged into the Earth. Throughout the Sierra Madre, as los conquistadores called these mountains, gold and silver are plentiful. In lust and greed, bearded chabochi sent Rarámuri into caverns of the olden gods. These places had surrendered their treasure long ago." The Turk's eyes meet Enrique's. Miguel notes this look. "Finding the old places empty, the bearded ones caused new caverns to be dug. Rarámuri are farmers of corn and beans and squash. We are hunters of deer, and husbandmen of goats and cattle. Hard labor with pickaxe and shovel was unknown. Many died. So, too, did taking metal from the Earth corrupt the land. To drink from rivers and streams risked death. Open pits held water and this water became as poison. Disease came to Rarámuri with terrible suffering. In great pain, many perished."

"This history is general throughout México," says Miguel. "It is our nation's tragedy and its sadness – a legacy we cannot escape, for the blood of los conquistadores runs in our veins."

"You also have Indian blood," says Beltrán. "Toltec. Maya. Mexica. Olmec, perhaps. The few who survived. You are their grandchildren."

"We are their orphans," says Carlos.

Enrique says, "Always the Mexican searches for a home. He does not belong here, he does not belong there. He is not wholly Indian, he is not purely Spanish. In El Norte he is an alien. In a pueblo he lives as a spurned child robbed of his patrimony."

"Now new conquistadores have appeared to enslave you again." Nova holds forth his gourd and Peña refills it. "They, too, masquerade as gods. It is true that the Fifth Sun is waning. However, a flying craft from beyond the sky does not signal its end. It is men, not gods, who have injured you. More chabochi. If they are sons of the

chabochi who came centuries ago, they, too, seek riches and fame."
The Indians nod. "You may clothe yourselves in this knowledge.
These conquistadores have stolen your people to serve selfish ends
– to labor, as you infer, as slaves." He drinks off his portion and
holds forth the gourd. "In this way, history repeats. The desire for
gold is eternal among men."

"Man was taught by the gods to love gold," says Peña. He pours
tesguino. "To the gods, gold was precious above all things. It is said
that gods wept golden tears. Legends say gods took gold as food."

Enrique thinks of the gold that burdens their horses and the
little good it does them. Only as ransom for Alma Ramos does he
value it. He says, "It is possible, then, that these conquistadores
might free our people for gold."

Nova considers. "I believe it would be so. However, a great
amount of gold would be necessary – as much as might be mined
by those now enslaved. The exact amount is impossible to know. If
their mines are rich, los nuevos conquistadores will prefer to keep
their slaves."

The Turk's eyes are bright with interest. "Is gold still to be
found in México?"

"Throughout the sierra, gold is abundant," says Beltrán. "However, it is deeply buried. To recover it costs terrible effort."

"A better way exists," says Ibañez.

"Tell us, please."

"You know of Teotihuacán."

"Indeed. The Place of the Gods."

Ibañez nods. "A treasure in gold hides there to this day. Los
conquistadores never learned of it, despite sedulous thievery and
their belief in El Dorado. No one has discovered it and yet it must
exist, for Teotihuacán was devoted to the refining of gold."

"We have never seen this place," says Enrique. "Legend says its
people abandoned the city more than a thousand years ago."

"In a time of drought and famine, the people revolted. They set fire to temples and palaces. During the destruction, a great quantity of gold was concealed."

"How much gold?" says the Turk.

"The greatness of this treasure is unknown," says Nova. "However, the Pirámides of Sun and Moon stand to this day."

The Mexicans trade looks and nods. "It seems we would be better served by going to Teotihuacán," says Miguel.

"To find the lost treasure of the lost city would be to succeed as fortune hunters have failed for fifteen hundred years," says Ibañez.

"You lose nothing in the attempt," says Peña. "If Teotihuacán's gold remains the gods' secret, Tenochtitlán lies a short day's ride southwest."

Pacho says, "Do spirits guard this place? Those who perished there might wish to retain its treasure."

"We must try," says the Turk. "To secure such gold is worth any risk!"

"Others have thought so," says Nova.

☾

On Further Beach his hole is six feet deep, circular, four feet across at its top. He has taken care to taper the shaft, lest its sand walls crumble inward. It is desirable to hide, not to be buried.

Lifting himself on his toes, Ibn al Mohammed peers over the rim. He sees only sand and sea, a beach sloping right to left from low dunes to a slow withdrawal of outgoing tide. A dozen gulls, stoic, desultory, roost above the waterline. He has dug his hole up-beach further still, his intention being concealment, hunched down inside. He will curl his body into the heat of its own nakedness and sleep ball-like in the cool sand. They cannot find him if his face is hidden, his soul silent, his mind quiet. Food he must forego. Hunger is a small price for liberty, however mean.

The old man was naked, without defense. The two of them shivering on this finger of beach pointing westward. Where have they taken al Zahrani? The old man was here one minute, the next minute gone. Ibn al Mohammed heard nothing. He has found no signs.

"Grandfather, where are you?" Ibn al Mohammed whispers into cupped hands, scraped and raw. "They punish you because of me."

He believes they took al Zahrani as he slept. A sedative, fast-acting, administered with a touch. A litter to carry him away. Thin, tough skin. Old bones.

Carried where?

The sun is sinking into the sea. Dusk encroaches. Droids will arrive with dinner and lies. Ibn al Mohammed has spent this day and his strength digging. He has provisioned himself with seaweed dried on rocks hauled forth from foothills a mile inland. He has also a supply of hand-sized stones. Aiming for a neck, he might hit face or chest. He does not know if such an assault will harm them. Whether they will fire on him or laugh.

He lifts a skein of seaweed, puts one end in his mouth and bites. It is salty and very green, its taste acidic and bitter. Quickly he chews and swallows. He must not take too much; it is likely to nauseate. Retching will betray him. However, he must have nourishment. When droids appear with grilled lamb or coriander chicken, a cooler of iced sweet tea, red potatoes salted and roasted to a savory crisp, he must have food in his stomach. An appetite long denied craves satisfaction.

Hot, flavorful food. A warm bed and cool pillow. A woman who desires him. Life's great joys are its necessities. To live without them is unworthy of a man.

Distant in the gloaming, the tractor approaches. Its headlight is dark. Sensors, perhaps, detect his presence. Body heat. Whisper of his breathing, chemistry of his sweat. Escape is impossible, al Zahrani said. Evasion, perhaps, also is foreclosed. If he quits his hole and runs, he is sure they will detect him. Had he fled upon discovering al Zahrani's removal, he believes they would have recaptured him by lunchtime. *May the blessings of Allah be upon you. Refresh yourself with this repast, God willing.* They kill him with kindness or something like it, except that nice handling does not kill him at all. It makes a parody of deprivation. A thousand tin buckets wait up-beach, below the prevailing breeze.

He is nowhere to be seen. Will they assume he has wandered off? Drowned himself in the sea? Sped eastward on a winged horse to Jerusalem, there to worship at the Dome of the Rock and offer thanksgiving for a soul that is saved?

With droids at five hundred yards, Ibn al Mohammed ducks down. Curling into his hole, he looks up its flared shaft at the over-spread sky. Darkness is falling fast. Venus appears, luminous and distant, a white sparkle against a canopy of Egyptian blue. Very soon, stars will show. Heaven will be brilliant.

✕ ✕ ✕

J Melmoth puts in another day trying to remember this curvy blonde with pert opinions whom the windowall insists is his wife. They sit at opposite ends of the sofa and watch a video that purports to show their shared life. It seems they have known each other a very long time; they have been married, it seems, no less than a hundred and two years. This duration Melmoth cannot understand. How can a century-plus have come and gone when they are both in their early 30s? Fit as fiddles, the two of them, as if they might almost be ex-athletes, even lesser Olympians, which neither of them remembers and both seriously doubt. Nor do they recall taking graduate degrees, which it seems they did, after which they married at something close to their present ages – which means they are newlyweds, yes? No, because the year of their marriage is noted as 1992. The current year is 2094. It is not merely bizarre. It is impossible.

On top of all this, it seems they have two children whom neither of them has ever heard of or imagined. A boy and a girl, Damien and Leah, whose babyhoods and kid's lives and adolescent angst the video documents at such length that numbness eventually gives way to nausea. Who took all this footage? And why, after a certain point, does no one seem to age – and then, become younger?

Melmoth says, "If we are married and have a couple kids, we must have had plenty of sex." He phrases this gambit as nonchalantly as possible, given that his organ continues to stand tall and is ready to scream.

"I hope you enjoyed it," says Raquel Romanov, "because I'm not having sex with you now. I don't know who you are."

"The video is showing you. I'm your husband."

"Umm, uh-huh. I'm reserving judgment. It seems fishy to me, all these supposedly home movies. As if someone was expecting to need them."

"Planned, you mean. Premeditated."

"I'm reserving judgment."

They sit, they watch. The video goes on and on. Damien remains perpetually in his mid-twenties, from the tall, lean look of him. Thick, dark hair, long arms and legs. Leah appears to have just graduated from some college or other, her banglely bracelets and peasant garb not yet traded-in for the forest green apparel her brother wears, a white, sans-serif "M" embroidered full-block on his right shoulder. "For 'Millennial,'" he says, showing it proudly to the camera Melmoth assumes he himself must have been holding. He does not recall owning any camera or ever taking a picture, much less video, but here it all is, right in his eyes.

"I wonder where they are," says Raquel Romanov, "these two who are allegedly my children."

"Our children."

"We'll see about that, mister."

"If we find them and they corroborate, will you have sex with me then?"

"I doubt it. I'll think about it, but I doubt it."

"At least you'll think about it."

"Don't get your hopes up, or anything else."

So it goes, Melmoth and his maybe-wife trying to sort out the facts of forgotten lives. Of special mystification are two beings, a woman and a man, who lie inside sealed capsules horizontal on retractable legs in another room. They appear to be asleep. Melmoth hopes that's all it is, the deepest of dreamless sleep, although the steadiest gaze he can muster does not detect any sign of breath. They, too, are naked. Their bodies are splendid: perfect proportions. Raquel Romanov does not comment on the male. Melmoth, hoping to quicken his so-called wife's jealousy, makes a point of praising the figure of the female. Finding that Raquel Romanov ignores these remarks, he broadens the point, develops it, builds it into a project. Every day, he mentions five or six times how beautiful the woman's face is, how abundant her breasts are, how gorgeously heart-shaped her hidden ass likely is. *How scrumptiously young she looks.*

No response.

She is proving a shrewd one, this Raquel Romanov. Untouched by sentiment, steeled against seduction, immune to the self-doubt necessary for game strategy to succeed. "So wake her up, already," she tells Melmoth. "Show her your johnson. Lay it right in her hand. Maybe she'll like it."

"I don't know how to wake her. If I did, you can bet I would."

"Do you even know who she is? Do you recognize her?"

Melmoth must admit he does not. He is not even certain that what he is calling a capsule is not in fact a new kind of awful coffin, as implausible as that seems. Because if these people are dead and laid out for display, what are they doing here? Who has left them? Why? And why has someone put them inside capsules with transparent, shell-like lids? Melmoth hopes it isn't designed as some sort of morbid, no pun intended, exercise in the observation of tissue decay.

Perhaps it is more than sleep and something less than death. Perhaps it is suspended animation. That would explain a lot. Perhaps he and Raquel Romanov share these capsules with these people, whoever they are, and now it is their turn to sleep and rejuvenate and his turn and Raquel Romanov's to be awake and walk around and do whatever it is they are supposed to do. Without a stitch of clothing at hand, it is difficult to imagine what that might be. Melmoth wants to think they are supposed to be having sex more or less constantly but Raquel Romanov's icy attitude argues against it. Suspended animation, however, would account for his being still alive after more than a century of marriage. Perhaps he and Raquel Romanov rejuvenate for ten years, then are up & about for just that long before going to sleep again. During the downtime, their bodies self-repair. Maybe suspended animation not only stops aging but reverses it. Possibly he and Raquel Romanov have lately been awakened from such a state, which maybe ran a little long, which accounts, maybe, for their mutual amnesia.

Maybe their memories will return. Maybe they will remember who they are and all they share and not need to watch any more of the video record. Maybe Raquel Romanov will remember him, remember that she likes him, once loved him. Maybe she will have sex with him.

Maybe.

Provisioned with beans and corn and canteens of fresh water, the company departs. To speed their passage, Nova lends Montez and another young man, Vega, as guides. "They will bring you to a place where the mountains end and the Mesa Centrale opens before you." He speaks Rarámuri dialect and the Turk translates. "You must walk southeast. It is a journey of a thousand miles. Teotihuacán stands on a plateau. It is seen from a distance."

Lima, Ibañez and the others bid them farewell. "May the gods guide your steps and protect you," they say through the Turk's translation. "May you come again to your families."

Enrique offers gold. The Turk explains it is a token of gratitude. Nova takes a bar into his hand. "I accept your gift. However, gold is not so useful to me as it is to you." He returns the bar to Enrique. "We would not have your barter fail for lack of it."

Enrique waits for the Turk's translation. He says, "You tell us we are to find gold, more than we can imagine."

Nova smiles. "Perhaps. Let us hope that treasure comes to your hands. It will be difficult. Teotihuacán is a large city. Also, you carry no shovels."

"Shovels we will acquire. Also another horse and a team of mules."

"All the more reason to retain your gold."

They depart on foot. The horses are burdened with sacks of food, gear, and saddlebags. Vega and Montez lead the way along trails that are little more than footpaths. "We take you the quickest way," says Vega. He is tall and slender like all the Indian men. He speaks in dialect and the Turk translates. "In two days we come to a chabochi road that is easy to walk."

Montez smiles. "Already Vega wishes to return to his girl." The Indians laugh. They shove each other in mock dust-up, always moving forward. Their pace is quick and the Mexicans lag. Montez says something and Vega laughs. The Turk does not translate.

In single file they walk through the mountains. At freshwater rivulets known to the Indians they fill their canteens. At evening they camp where deep ledges create overhead cover. On the third day they come to a rancheria of kindred families and receive welcome and respite. Montez recounts the purpose of their journey and the share he and Vega have in it. These Rarámuri also give corn and beans. With this addition, the Mexicans have several days' food to begin their crossing of the central plateau.

The way is difficult, their pace slow. Montez and Vega glide along foot-beaten paths while the Mexicans plod. The Indians' looks and gestures say they are growing impatient. When at last a vista of open land appears before them, Montez says, in Spanish, "So does a run of two days become a trek of ten."

"We are grateful for your guidance," says Miguel. "You have earned a reward."

The Indians are impassive. Through the Turk's translation, Vega says, "Your gift is honorable and yet, as Nova says, not needed. As well as it shines, gold has no use."

"You may fashion a charm from it," says Pacho. "For the girl who awaits your return."

"So pretty a gift may cause envy," says Vega, in Spanish. "Girls without such a charm might sow discord among men who have no gold. Such feelings are not helpful. To allow so useless an object to cause unhappiness is foolish."

"You are wise," says Enrique.

"Our lives depend on each other." Montez speaks in dialect; again, the Turk must translate. "We share what we have. We give and take as needed. No one wishes to keep for himself what his brother lacks."

Javier says, "It is good Rarámuri keep to the sierra. Elsewhere in México, people think differently."

"Not only in México," says the Turk.

Montez raises his arm in farewell. Vega does likewise. "We leave you here. May you live to complete your quest!"

With nods and hands raised in thanks, the Mexicans lead their horses toward the mesa. When Javier looks back a dozen steps later, the Rarámuri are gone.

The days that follow are hot and choked with dust. On foot, they skirt the Chihuahuan desert and struggle into Parral, leg-weary, their food gone. In Parral they find starving people in rags huddled along the streets. No one speaks to them, no one offers food or water. Food and water may, however, be had for gold. With gold cuttings they pay for fried eggs and corn tortillas and water. Afterward, Enrique and Miguel are happy to trade a bar intact for a good horse, and another for four sturdy mules. To the latter Javier and Pacho shift saddlebags and gear. Meat is not available, yet they replenish their store of beans and rice, again giving gold in exchange. The cutting Miguel makes equals the merchant's little finger in its length and is one-quarter as thick. The merchant grins as he holds his gold to the light, tilting it this way and that.

Enrique asks him, "Who are the silent ones sitting close?"

The man frowns. "Those are Unfortunates."

"What is done with them?"

"Nothing is done with them." The man slips his gold into a pocket. "Why must something be done?"

Remounted, Enrique, Javier, Carlos, Pacho, Miguel, and the Turk travel highway 45 southward into Durango State. The land they cross is nearly flat. Between Parral and Durango is scrubland and sagebrush, empty, flanked on the west by foothills of the mountains they have lately crossed. Sere grasses are the color of sand. Swirls of high, white clouds fret a widespread sky. The road's narrow verge is light gravel, flinty stone, burnt-out grass, sand, pebble. Skeletons lie by the wayside, sun-leached bones picked clean. Farther along they find corpses. These vary in the extent of their dissolution. Some are as dry-baked as the ground on which they lie. Others, at the height of putrefaction, reek of death.

"Great God," says Javier. "What has happened to them?"

"Nothing has happened," says Carlos. "Merely they failed to find a way to live. Then, death is simple."

No cars pass or approach. A few light trucks trundle by, cabs and cargo beds painted red, blue, yellow, green, almost certainly carrying food. The Mexicans reckon direction by the Sun's transit. Distance is practically immeasurable and has become irrelevant. Their journey is as long as it is. It will take as many days as it must.

After Durango the highway turns eastward. Beyond the mesa, distant mountains rise. They travel away from these, into the heartland of México.

Fresnillo. Zacatecas. Ojocaliente. Crumbling stucco, tumbled brick, rocky embankments shored-up between ruins and road. Between towns, the destitute straggle from emptiness to emptiness. Hunched over, their world bundled high on their backs, they run slowly away from each other, a sound like weeping faint and fading. On a trestle bridge, three corpses hang from rusting girders. Perched on one's head, a turkey buzzard pulls at rotting flesh. From Ojocaliente, the men ride hard south to the city of Aguascalientes, which they find mostly deserted. The people who remain live in concrete-block houses with flat roofs. On the road's medium, a column of stone blocks lifts a steel water tank, sunburnished, rust-streaked, forty feet above their heads. Its spigot is rusted shut. Near the city's center, shells of buildings stand cube-like, doors and roofs gone. Dwarf agave trees grow in vacancies between dilapidated brick walls. Further on, a perimeter wall of dusty-rose sandstone proclaims "Dios Rey!" in white letters. Opposite, on a silver-gray concrete wall, two blunt silhouettes are outlined in black, featureless and mummy-like with outsized heads. A Mission church, also flat-roofed, is painted the same golden yellow as the church in Creel.

"Should we search beneath the chancel?" says Carlos. The others grin as the Turk's head whips sideways.

They pass on and through. At the city's limit, old women lead burros pulling wooden carts piled with garbage to a communal dump. Buzzards wheel slowly above, black wings outspread, each bird a patient watcher pinned against the blue.

The Mexicans and Turk quit Aguascalientes heading south and by evening reach Encarnación de Díaz in Jalisco State. Its two-mile strip of storage sheds and vacant lots is an inconsequence. The highway runs through like a rebuke. It turns east, then bends southeast to Lagos de Moreno, where the asphalt is smoother and the road's shoulder wider. Lagos de Moreno is in better repair, cleaner, its coral-pink stucco sound, wrought iron railings of its stairways and balconies lately painted. People live here; their lives go on, much reduced from a condition once pleasant. It is possible to buy food and water. Tamales, burritos, quesadillas. With gold, the Mexicans purchase several meals ready-made. By this means they obtain relief from a diet that long ago became unpalatable. It is difficult to know whether the salsa picquante and salsa verde are truly good or merely different from plain beans and corn.

A day's ride south brings them to León. They are more than eight hundred miles southeast of Creel. Teotihuacán lies some two hundred miles to the south and east. León is the largest settled area they have seen. Its variety of structures, disposition of neighborhoods, grid of avenues and streets are a revelation of what is possible. To the Mexicans and the Turk as well, León is what the phrase, "human civilization" might mean. Food and water may be had at a word, with payment tendered. Gasoline is unavailable. Restaurants are closed. Simple food is bartered at street stalls. Paper currency is worthless. Gold and silver alone retain value – this reckoned purely by weight, as government imprimaturs are meaningless. Civil services – police, trash collection, fire protection, homeless shelters, public buses that formerly linked neighborhoods – are absent.

They pay in gold for rice and beans with bits of chorizo mixed-in and eat the meal from chipped green plates. The forks are lightweight tin. Later, riding at a walk along a street bounded by private homes, they hear a voice call them out.

"You men! What do you do here?"

They see a graybeard clinging with one hand to an iron railing. The old man wears a patch of black leather over his right eye. At the end of his arm is a steel hook where a hand should be. It is an eight-foot railing, painted white. It stands between two brick walls and fences off a driveway.

At the railing they halt. "We pass through your city to a place farther south," says Miguel, and lifts off his hat. "What do they call you, grandfather?"

The graybeard laughs. "They have called me many things in my time. In youth, Donkey was my name, for I was very strong and could work from sun to sun. Years later I became sad and everyone called me Felicidad. They seemed to think it a fine joke. Now I am no longer amusing. A lost eye and hand have made me Pirate Jorge."

"Greetings to you, sir," says Miguel in his best formal style, and the others nod, say, "Good health, grandfather,' and "Much luck to you, Pirate Jorge."

The old man hooks a chair by its arm and drags it forward. Its beaten metal is painted red and its backrest sports perforations that suggest the stem and petals of a flower. In this chair he takes a seat. "You appear as reasonable men," he says. "Not banditos. I could not tell at first."

"Do banditos come this way?" says Miguel.

"Not so often. However, any type of vagrant or despicable beggar might appear at any hour. You and your company obviously are none of these, although you are strangers. And passing through, you say, southward on your way to – where did you say?"

"We did not say. Our destination matters only to us," says Enrique. "And you yourself are well-established here. You cannot desire to join us."

"It is true. I am nicely set-up." He rubs his forehead with the hook's smooth back. "Lucky above the average. However, in times long past this place was much greater than what you see today. Good jobs and fair wages afforded many a comfortable life. Homes well-kept, clean public parks suitable for women to walk in and children to play." Pirate Jorge spits and shakes his head. "I recall it as a dream. A beautiful bright dream of a paradise lost."

"Much hardship and suffering have befallen Mexico," says Carlos. "Towns are in ruin. Dead ones litter the roadsides."

"I know of this. It is a great tragedy."

"And yet your life here is tolerable."

"Better than what you describe. We in León have always enjoyed better than the general condition. Of course, León was never a paradise except in comparison to what we have now. Still, as you see, things could be worse. We maintain order by a miracle I cannot hope to describe. Private gangs, possibly, enforce peace. Every day there is food. I cannot tell you where it comes from, for we produce nothing here. However, we have no feeling of community – not since I was a boy. Every man for himself! Women, too." With a great nasal inhale, Pirate Jorge clears his sinuses and spits. "Most fare well enough. I myself, as I say, am lucky above the average. However, no one prospers. Prosperity is a rumor, a myth. Of course, many perish. There is starvation, which is slow and painful. There is exposure, which often kills during sleep. Naturally there is violence among those who are homeless and hungry. Here, too, corpses lie in the streets. It is not uncommon. There is no one to collect the bodies. Services of a bygone day! Instead we have nature, which does its work in due course." He waves his hand vaguely at the sky.

"In many places nothing remains," says Carlos. "Wreckage and rubble. Empty towns."

"We have found many dead," says Pacho.

"Yes, yes." Pirate Jorge gazes one-eyed at the empty street behind his visitors. "Refugees wander in. Filthy, famished, not a peso or gold bit to their names. Beat-down people." He shakes his head, frowns. "We do not welcome vagrants. We have no wish to become a haven. Drifters, outcasts, beggars – for such ones, we have no use. Without police, to arrest such peons is not possible. So, we ignore them. When they see no assistance is forthcoming, they move on. Perhaps they live, perhaps they die. Their fate does not concern us." With his left fingers he lifts the patch. They are close enough to see that the old man's glass eye is blue, its iris rimmed with gold. He smiles and does not seem happy. "We are a city of individuals."

The Mexicans pass another day in the relative comfort of León. They give more gold for six shovels that are, in fact, spades: stout oak shafts, steel handles, digging flanges that curve to a tip. They add these to the mules' burden and again set forth.

Five days, a week at most. Then Teotihuacán.

O ⊙ ⊙ O

Harvest is finished, crush complete. Sweet juice resting in stain-less steel tanks is beginning to ferment. In six months, they will allot three distinct red blends to new casks of French oak. For two years or three, the wines will age.

Templar Bronze can wait. She has ersatz coffee, she has egg-and-sausage piping-hot in a croissant, she has, at last, a delicious moment to herself. The first light of faux dawn finds her on the observation deck inside EarthStation 3, overlooking a vineyard gone quiet after thirty-three hours of steady work. Efficient droids in field dress saved the vintage and the day. Outfitted in green smocks and canvas trousers and broad-brimmed straw hats – cos-tumes that served no purpose except to lend the proceedings an authentic appearance that was also perfectly ordinary – these most cooperative of field workers picked and toted 'round the clock. To make it all seem more like life, Templar had them re-scripted to chatter in Spanish about the heat, the dust, the back-breaking la-bor and paltry wages, the slave-driving methods of their godless gringo padrone. Allowing the small brown children of her actual Mexicans to gambol underfoot while the droids picked and car-ried was, she thinks, a true *coup de théâtre*. Such untrammeled presence of laughing little ones struck stock-sentimental notes of Simple Peasants and Family Farm rather brightly. Perhaps the true *coup* came later, when her scripts rendered the effect in spades by allowing the droids to cuff the scampering, shrieking, rough-hous-ing children damn hard just behind their ears when their frolics grew too rambunctious. Two dozen wailing kids were led to the infirmary with head wounds shedding blood, but no matter. What are they for, these urchins, if not to enliven the scenery with youth-ful cries of joy and pain?

Templar smiles. Everything considered, it has all turned out rather well. The quality of the vintage of 2094 remains to be seen – that is, tasted in several years' time – but the fact is, Templar Bronze has done all she can do. Human pickers having proven dysfunctional, she reverted to droids. Gladly. So much conflict cancelled, so much complication and annoyance forestalled. Just think: a week or two, a month at most, and she will be finished with these people for good. Now, even now, logistical experts and Earth-side anthropologists specializing in native peoples are designing schemata for the safe return of Templar's Mexicans, and Roscoe's, too, to the sundered subcontinent of their collective birth. Yes, their lives will be hard. Yes, their existence will be lonely: isolated, bereft, prey to inertia, half in love with despair. What of it? They are miserable on Mars, despite comforts on offer and ready access to better things; and so now, again, they will be miserable in Mexico, which at all events is the place they call home. Who are We, Templar reflects – meaning, she and Roscoe and their collegial Initiates, Adepts, and Earthscientists – to tell these people how to live? We think we know better. Do we know more? Or is what we know just different – oh, very different! – from any knowledge they need?

VirtuSun gleaming across the vine rows throws long shadows toward her eyes. So peaceful. Really, she would be happy just to stand here and look. Not watch: look. See day come in, its light grow, its brightness by mid-morning become almost blinding; then see it change direction and, hour by slow hour through fading afternoon, pass behind her, its angle around sunset, what would be sunset on Earth, throwing long shadows away from her, as if the vine rows were reaching outward, beyond the dome.

What prevents her from remaining where she now stands? What duty compels her? She supposes it would become boring just to stand and look. Well then, she might leave the tower and walk through the vineyard. *Stroll.* As a rule, Templar does not stroll. She strides, and briskly at that, with purpose and a destination in mind. Or pursues her intentions at high velocity while seated inside a hoverpod. No need for such rushing now, what with Roscoe not calling and grape mash in the tanks.

The Mexicans and their plight have been handed-off to experts. Very good. Deprivations and complaints, troubles of other people's lives: these are not her obligation to relieve. Templar Bronze, it seems, can stand here as long as she likes.

Today. Tomorrow ...

Forever?

Seated in straight-backed chairs, J Melmoth and Raquel Romanov face each other across a table. They have forsaken sofa and windowall, suspended their viewing of the video record. Without a scrap of clothing in this apartment that no one, it seems, is meant to leave, they continue naked. Having found no books on the premises, they feel lucky to have turned up playing cards. It seems to be the one sentiment they share, this feeling of relief that they have at least this much to do. Play cards, and drink. Melmoth and Raquel Romanov sip red wine from crystal stemware. The glasses are convenient to their hands. The bottle stands between them on the table.

The game is dragging. Melmoth holds a crowded handful, Raquel Romanov about half as many. He has been trying to switch them to poker. Melmoth has in mind something like strip poker. Instead of removing an article of clothing, which of course means nothing to them, they would perform minor and major acts of sexual gratification. The nature of the act would depend on the disparity between winning and losing hands. If he edged Raquel Romanov's pair of queens with a pair of kings, Raquel Romanov would have to smile at him for two seconds. Kings over tens, maybe she smiles for five seconds. If, however, Melmoth drew a straight flush and a pair of deuces was all Raquel Romanov held, well, the payoff would involve intimate touching. To Melmoth, it is the perfect game: even when you lose, you win.

Raquel Romanov is not interested.

Melmoth peers at his cards. He is working on hearts. He picks the trey from the face-up spread and slips it into the fanned pasteboards pinched between forefinger and thumb. He discards the six of spades.

A glance, a sniff, and she dismisses it. Not looking up, she says, "Do you have a knave?"

Melmoth's hangdog face might move her heart, if only she would lift her eyes. He plucks out the knave of hearts and hands it to her.

"Thank you," she says and lays down the pair of degenerate aristocrats, hearts and diamonds, both grinning out of one eye. She picks the top card from the deck.

Melmoth lifts the crystal, sips his wine, sets the glass at his right hand. His dick is killing him. Something must be wrong. Here it is days later, the novelty of nakedness has worn off, and still he is plagued by a fantastic stiff woody. The thing just will not quit. He cannot believe it. No fancy drugs or implants needed. All he needs is an attractive naked woman always in sight. It's pretty special – except what is the good of having it if he cannot use it? For one thing, it looks ridiculous. Also, it hurts. A fantastic stiff woody is meant to be temporary and achieve relief, not stand ramrod-at-attention for day after unrequited day. Raquel Romanov must know this. She cannot be ignorant. It is impossible that she is naïve. Whether or not she looks at him, his fantastic stiff woody is as obvious as a three-pound salami. Talk about a dog on its hind legs, begging.

He stares over his cards at Raquel Romanov's breasts. *Lovely.* Round, plump, perfectly curved, beautifully soft. Actually, the word that pops into his mind is "deliriously." How he would love to gather them, one in each hand, and slide his fantastic stiff woody in-between. Raquel Romanov would have to be lying on her back. Melmoth shifts in his chair. *God, this is torture.* Or, if he stood and she knelt in front of him, atop a couple pillows, say, she could press her lovely plump breasts around his fantastic stiff woody and bobble them softly up and deliriously down, up and down. What is the word for it? Knobjob? It would be great, whatever it's called. Easy, simple, completely safe, no one gets hurt. And it's fun. But no; Raquel Romanov is unwilling. Unconsenting. It, everything, is too much to ask, hope, wish for, imagine.

"Well?" she says, not looking up.

Melmoth lifts his glass and sips. "Well, what?"

"If you have a match, put it down."

"I don't have a match." He sets his glass on the table.

"Then take a card."

"Why?"

"Because that is how the game is played."

"Yes, but why play? The game is going nowhere."

"Why does the game have to go somewhere?"

"Nothing is at stake. When nothing is at stake, there is nowhere for the game to go."

"Why does anything have to be at stake? Why can't we play just to play?"

"Because it's boring, is why." It's no use. Raquel Romanov refuses to lay anything on the line, will not put anything on the table but her elbows. They might as well be staring into space, twiddling their thumbs. Whiling away the hours. Killing time. Picking cards up, putting cards down, flipping cards back and forth. *Do you have an ace? Do you have a deuce?* Stupid.

He picks up a card, discards another. No matches. What difference does it make? He says, "How about a backrub? If you win, I'll give you a backrub. If I win, you give me a knobjob."

Raquel Romanov snorts. She does not look up. "I don't want you touching me, thanks. And I'm certainly not touching any part of you." She picks the four of diamonds from the face-up spread, pairs it with the four of clubs and drops the ace of spades in its place.

The ideally-proportioned man and woman still sleep inside their capsules. Melmoth does not know what to do about them and Raquel Romanov seems not to care. No doubt she has the right attitude. The man and woman are not decaying, thank God. Their skin is perfect, their musculature firm. As their bodily functions have obviously stopped, Melmoth figures his guess was correct. Suspended animation means there is nothing to do but wait. They will be reanimated one of these days and then, he guesses, he and Raquel Romanov will take a turn inside the capsules. What the point of all this is, he has no idea. Are he and Raquel Romanov awake just to play cards and drink wine? When it is their time to rejuvenate – say, in ten years – will the man and woman currently encapsuled take their places also to play cards and drink wine?

Cupping his cards loosely in both hands, Melmoth trims them against the table then fans the stack. He shifts a few at random because what the hey, slips an ace here and an eight there elsewhere in the fan. Really, he has had enough. Why are they alive if this is all they are going to do? It's absurd, like working a hateful job just to be able to eat enough to keep working. It is not life; life is something else. Better. They are naked, seemingly have no choice but to be so. They could be having a grand time; why does he play along with killing it? If he de-carded, Raquel Romanov might stop taking him for granted. Maybe he should ignore her entirely. Don't look, don't speak. Pretend she does not exist. Complete freeze-out. Would she pay attention to him then? Grab him by the hair and push his face between her legs? Probably not. Probably she would just activate the windowall and watch holograms day and night. He has to concede, there is a lot to see: every movie ever made, and news stories about every dastardly act and bad character under the Sun, plus something called sexolympics that is evidently the world's largest permanent public orgy, floating here, there, everywhere. An astonishing spectacle: every seat in every stadium, arena, hall, gymnasium, and aquatic center is always filled. Also, there are regular updates from a manned base (womanned, too) on Mars, of all places, where, to Melmoth's amazement, human beings are living inside self-sustaining, climate-optimized geodesic domes called EarthStations. Things certainly have progressed since the last time he looked. He wonders when they managed it, extraterrestrial colonization, to say nothing of how they solved the problems of interplanetary travel and flight-ready, reusable spacecraft. Earthshuttles, they call them. Plus the stupendous feat of transporting tons of Earth's soil to Mars. Animals also and, most incredibly of all, water. He wishes he had been awake to see it. He wishes he remembered the step by step progress, the improvements and developments, and bore witness to the final success. He wishes he hadn't slept so long.

Melmoth looks up. *Lovely.* He says, "Do you have any queens?"

Raquel Romanov smirks. "Go fish."

ᒿ ᴧ

In morning light, foothills of the Sierra Madre Orientale appear like green and purple shadows of a greater presence. They are southeast of León, following route 45 as it bends around Silao, whose outskirts are wasteland: hotels boarded, restaurants shuttered, automobile dealerships empty, all signs and billboards bled white. Ragged weeds overgrow disused, rutted lots. Pemex stations are unattended and the pumps gone.

Needing to replenish water and food, they venture toward the center of town. Silao's streets are like défilés; brick residences, concrete warehouses crowd in, canyon-like. Buildings are derelict, streets are desolate. Places for tamales, grilled chicken, rice and beans look to have been abandoned decades ago, nameable now only by their signs. If anyone lives in the vicinity, he, she, keeps well-hidden.

"We lose time searching for what does not exist."

"You said this before, yet we found gold."

"It is worthless to us. Better we should carry half as much gold and twice as much water."

They go slowly on through streets where nothing is given and nothing is found. When at last they concede futility, the Sun is an orange blaze above their heads. Regaining highway 45, they travel southeast across great reaches of the central plateau. Scrubland runs flat to distant mountains. Bare scatterings of stunted trees alone suggest life. Nothing moves; the air is still. If it were possible to suffocate in broad daylight, such would be their fate. They depend on Irapuato, some twenty miles south, for provisions.

Four hours later, they come to the town. Food is available and water for sale at mercadoes and bodegas and tendejones. Like the red beans and rice they buy ready-cooked and the preserved food they purchase for their journey, water is expensive.

Watching Miguel divide a gold bar, the Turk says, "We pay too dearly."

"Congratulate yourself," says Enrique. "We have means to acquire these necessities thanks to you."

"It will be to little purpose, if we give so much." The Turk glares at the bodega's owner, who smiles at the gold. When the man moves away, the Turk says, "That one is a scoundrel and thief to value simple goods at so extravagant a rate."

Enrique laughs. "Not a thief, no. A capitalist. Profit has no conscience." He picks up a case of bottled water and carries it outside. The Turk follows. Enrique knifes open the cardboard and shares out plastic bottles amongst their saddlebags. Carlos, Pacho, and Javier are stowing food: dried beef wrapped in wax paper, large cans of red beans, yellow corn, green chilies, canvas sacks of rice. While the Turk waits, Enrique returns to the bodega. A moment later he appears with a second case of water.

"We must retain as much gold as possible," says the Turk.

"Yes, certainly – in the second place. First, we must stay alive."

"We might survive with less. We should conserve."

"So we shall. This water and food might be all we will have for longer than we assume."

"You doubt we will find gold in the Lost City."

"I doubt Teotihuacán can have been so lost as the Rarámuri say. It lies just thirty-five miles from Ciudad de México. That its treasure can have gone undiscovered seems unlikely."

"To speak of this city as lost is to refer to its people. For a thousand years, it was a sacred precinct. Teotihuacán, the place where man meets the gods. When the gods withdrew, the people fled. Imagine a thousand years in one place. One's ancestors beyond all memory have lived and died here, yet you depart. In such circumstances, treasure might be forgotten." A vague gesture seems to indicate the distance they have traveled since emerging from the mountains. "These towns we have passed are nothing in comparison. And yet, their people also have disappeared."

Enrique buys four cases of water. With the gold and food, the mules' load is great.

Irapuato to Salamanca. From Salamanca eastward to Celaya.
Celaya to Santiago de Querétaro.

From Santiago de Querétaro they ride east by southeast for
miles across stark land beaten flat under an immense sky. Power
lines sagging between steel towers cross the highway. Telephone
wires run parallel to the road. In its sameness the land is unend-
ing. The road changes from asphalt to concrete, its twelve-foot
slabs buckled by heat and drought. Continents of cumulus divide
the sky into separate seas all equally blue. Cirrus streak the higher
reaches as if with churning surf. The clouds are motionless,
banked against a heaven indifferent to their driftings.

The company skirts San Juan del Rio, southeast of which they
forsake 45, which branches east and northeast and continues
hopelessly into the Sierra Madre Orientale. They follow route 57,
tending always southeast across a yawning emptiness that feels
like a failure foretold.

Still in his flight chair, forever in his flight chair, the Adept dozes.
The volume on Paladin Silver's headset is dialed down to nil. He
dreams of Templar Bronze: agriscientist, oenophile, Initiate, long-
legged, silky-haired Amazon, nonpareil example of selective
breeding, all-around genius, peerless She. Her teeth alone are
worth the circuits of every droid on Mars. Perhaps he might cajole
her with roguish raillery ...

Something touches his shoulder; squeezes; shakes. Paladin
opens his eyes.

"We have a confirmed positive, Commander Silver." The droid
stands a step too near and speaks down at him. Is that its breath he

smells, in his face? Since when do Bots have breath? It is a smell like hardboiled eggs a week later. "Six men on horseback with mules in tow, traveling south-southeast at a snail's pace toward an archaic metropolitan settlement called Mexico City."

"You don't say," says Paladin. He wards the droid off and rubs his face with both hands. "I'll be buggered."

"I'm sorry?"

"An expression," says Paladin. "Never believed we'd find them."

"I assured you that success was within our competence."

There it goes again: that tone. The thing is mocking him; Paladin will be damned if it isn't. "You really are a snide little piece of tin, aren't you?"

"Negative. Tin does not figure in the constitution of this unit, ostensible Me. Tin is used predominantly in makeshift shanties Earth-side. Throughout Mexico, tin is common. In Gulag Cuba, cell roofs are made of tin."

An officious twit: it is. *Ostensible Me*, what rubbish. "That is more information than I require." Who scripted it? Paladin will instigate selective reprogramming when they finally return to Mars. "Let us address the material point: these noisome Mexicans. Where, exactly, did you say they are?"

"Current coordinates of said nomadic band are nineteen degrees, forty-three minutes, eleven seconds North, ninety-nine degrees, five minutes, thirty-four seconds West."

"Excellent." Paladin readjusts his headset and swings its microphone in front of his mouth. "Let's see about lasering the bastardos and putting paid to this mess."

"Negative. Our mission is to capture said quarry and convey them to EarthStation I for ritual debriefing."

"Bugger all that. I want to go home." Paladin engages Earth-Mars communication and says, "Raise the Head Director for me, will you?" into the microphone. He is counting on Roscoe's having lost his sense of urgency about these meandering mischief-makers. If the old man OKs a proposal to terminate, he, Paladin, can finish the business from where he sits, then peel the shuttle clear of Earth-orbit and wing his sojourning way back to Mars. It can happen in minutes – much less time than his conversation with the Head Director will take, what with interplanetary delay.

Paladin leans back in his flightchair to wait.

South and east, steadily south and east they will themselves across the mesa. At Laguna de Zumpango they stop for a swim, washing off the dust and grit of a thousand miles. The lake is huge, a kind of inland sea, and the day is bright and hot, the sky so clear and uniformly blue it appears solid. They come out of the water dripping and stand in the sun. The Turk is a slight thing, bone wrapped in skin that itself is veined and tawny like tobacco leaf. Pacho, Carlos, and the others stand there abashed, noticing their stature, how small they are without clothes. To stand exposed evokes shame yet also lightness, as if they might fly to their journey's end. In this open sky and with a breeze to lift them, miles of heat and plodding might become a few weightless seconds of air-rush and sudden arrival. The idea is wishful, a bit of magical thinking. It changes nothing. They must horseback overland, mules freighted with gear. Lacking a map, they rely on luck and guesswork, call it instinct, and hope to find someone able to direct them.

From Laguna de Zumpango they shadow the highway for five miles, a bit more. The asphalt crosses a track bed with rails running southwest-northeast. No train is within sight or earshot.

Javier dismounts and kneels on the ties, sets his fingertips on the rails. "Nothing," he says.

"We will follow the track," says Miguel.

"We do not know where it leads," says Pacho.

"It is the nature of a railroad to take a path of least resistance. Its way is graded and easy going."

"It may lead us miles astray."

"It may," says the Turk, "yet it must pass through towns where people may be."

Single file with mules in tow, they ride the pebbled road that parallels the track bed. It takes them a far way northeast, turns due east and finally bends south. At long distances they see human figures, solitary stragglers always in retreat, as if fleeing. Their horses raising dust, they cross fallow fields, acres of desiccation and neglect. Amid these fields they find apartment blocks set about as if by chance. Five stories high, concrete painted white, these buildings seem to serve no purpose. Isolate homesteads pass by without a face watching from a window, a child in a yard. The railroad cuts across rocky badlands and passes through rural towns where no one remains. At no time does a train appear. The land, however, is flat and the road a good one. They believe they move closer to Teotihuacán. And yet, they feel stymied. They do not know where they are. Perhaps they are thirty miles outside Ciudad de México; perhaps they are one hundred. In which direction?

"Better that we had gone first to Ciudad de México," says Enrique. "Surely, people inhabit the capital. We could have obtained a map, and likely a guide."

"Why did we not think of it?" says Miguel.

Carlos says, "It was a great mistake, to follow the railroad."

"I think you said nothing at the time," says the Turk.

"Nevertheless, it was a great mistake."

They ride on, impatient to arrive, anxious that they might fail to reach their goal. Teotihuacán is a tiny place compared to Méxi-co, a large place compared to them. The Rarámuri say its Pyramids are apparent, visible. The ruins reclaimed from the jungle more than two hundred years ago spread across twelve square miles. The Pirámide del Sol rises more than two hundred feet from the valley floor. Los Calzada de los Muertos is two miles long, in sections a hundred feet wide. At its northern end, the Pirámide del Luna stands forty feet high. Surely these structures loom on the horizon. Mirage-like, a hovering at the limit of their vision.

Always, doubt haunts them: an unknown something that blocks their sight, a chance of looking in the wrong direction. Possibly jungle has grown up again and the Lost City, sacked and burnt more than fourteen hundred years ago and lost, then found, then lost again and rediscovered, is again lost.

They follow the railroad, its track a safeguard against wander and drift. They are on-course, not knowing where it leads.

In olden times, when the city was home to more than a hundred thousand souls, the pyramids were painted red. Would that they were red today. Would that a thousand people remained who could direct them. A hundred. One.

The railroad continues southeast, its course almost straight across thousands of acres of untilled land. Once fertile and abundant, farmland has returned to weed. Uncultivated, it has an appearance of nowhere. Dirt roads, unmarked, unnamed, are the only feature of crusted, broken earth. When a highway overpass rises in the distance, they wonder at its realness – for do not mirages assume shapes travelers most wish to see? The highway crosses the railroad on a perpendicular. Without discussion, without a single word, they turn northeast.

The land continuing level, they spur their horses to canter but the pace is too quick for the mules. Trimming their speed, they see distant on their right jagged ridges of the Sierra Madre Orientale. Knowing that these mountains are ones they will not need to cross is heartening. The worst of their journey must be behind them. Arduous climbs and perilous descents. Exhausting, waterless days. Biting flies and poison water and fierce sun. The death of Roberto Díaz. Having survived all this, they may survive a while longer.

A mile farther along, a sign spans the highway: "Pirámides." The sign states no distance and by this omission encourages the men to think their destination cannot be far.

"Help me to understand you, Commander Silver." The voice of Roscoe Gold fills the Adept's headset. "Having located our terrorist cohort after a protracted search of stupefying tedium, you propose to incinerate them. My dear fellow: Why?"

Paladin in his flightchair sets his chin in his palm and gazes at the console's cool blue lights. *Why.* The Head Director requires a reason, in answer to which Paladin is tempted to offer, *Why not?* Flippancy, however, is inconsistent with Adept status.

"They are of no consequence," says the Sojourner Among the Stars. "They mean nothing to us. They can do nothing for us. Transport them to Mars or kill them now, it's all one."

Always, the delay. Is there no means of speeding interplanetary communication? Cannot Templar Bronze dream something up? Paladin wonders if the lightsignal can be beamed through a wormhole from here to there and back again at, well, lightspeed. That would shorten the interval between a question ventured and an answer gained. He makes a mental note to pose this question to the estimable Dr. Bronze when in the fullness of time he finally, finally, returns to Mars.

A bit later (Paladin having stopped watching the clock), Roscoe's reply arrives. "I think not, Commander. I expect it will be worth our while to discover what, exactly, these fellows intend. As we have seen, they possess exceptional initiative and rather a large quotient of courage. To say nothing of an uncanny knack for evasion. Really, I think it behooves us to learn where they are going, and why. What is their purpose? How do they propose to accomplish it? And so forth. Hmm?"

For Christ's sake. How can he make the old man understand it is not a game? That there are no rules, that motives are mixed, that intentions change from one minute to the next, that no particular answer is the only one that is right. "Roscoe, yes, of course. But the thing is, I think you are, we are, giving them too much credit. They are just out there, I'd say, making it up as they go along, doing the best they can, and trying not to die. We almost got them back in Sonora, you remember, with droid Federales. How they wriggled clean of that one, I'll never understand. Had them dead to rights, we did. Killed one of the bastards and no one has missed him, yes?"

Sometime later, Paladin hears Roscoe's voice say, "Commander Silver, I take your point, yet I must insist you sit tight. Watch and listen, observe and learn. Where, after all, have you to go? Mars? Ha! As you cannot have failed to notice, our home away from home is nothing more than a dustball: desiccated, dust-choked, impossibly cold and, unless we discover an extraordinary source of gold, incapable of improvement. Earth, at least, retains water. And who knows? It may yet possess gold the existence of which we have not imagined." A pause; then, "Oh yes. I have neglected to enlighten you on a key point. It seems a correlation exists between a planet's water resources and its potential as a repository of gold. But no matter. Perhaps our Mexicans will lead us to it."

As if by uttering this hypothetical piece of rank optimism he has spoken all that need be said, Roscoe signs off. Earth-Mars communication breaks and Paladin Silver sits there with a headset gone dead, marching orders ringing in his ears.

▣ ▣ ▣ ▣ ▣ ▣

They enter by an access road that winds past an empty parking lot. Abruptly, it feels, after weeks of seeming to make no progress, they emerge near the south end of the Calzada de los Muertos. Before them, the Pirámide de Quetzalcoatl stands inside a large square compound flanked on three sides by raised stone platforms, four to a side. The compound and adjoining land are lushly grassed, emerald-green. Not since the middle reaches of the Sierra Madre have they seen such growth. The Pirámide de Quetzalcoatl is much smaller than the city's chief structures, the pyramids of Moon and Sun. The latter stands some way north. As they ride toward it the men see, along the length of the Calzada de los Muertos, bare walls of what were modest-sized enclosures. These ruins end as they approach the enormous Pirámide del Sol. Near it, stone platforms rise, their tops level beneath the sky. A steep stone staircase fronts each platform, all of which are larger and higher than those around the Pirámide de Quetzalcoatl. Are these observation posts? Stages? The largest and highest platforms stand around the great courtyard that opens before the Pirámide del Luna. Constructed in four tiers, these seem almost intended to be built up into pyramids. In front of the Moon pyramid and attached to it is the most imposing of all the platforms in Teotihuacán. It rises in five tiers and features an expansive, level top that would have been clearly visible to a courtyard assembly.

The company halts before this structure. The men have a sense of being observed despite no hint of life in the dead city. In its scale, the place dwarfs them. Its builders might have been giants and Miguel, Enrique, and the others mere children of a lesser human family. No depictions of the original inhabitants are evident. Indeed, it seems only stone remains, large stones and small, boulders and pebbles alike cemented with adobe mud into monuments. As precisely designed as the city is, its architecture is rough-hewn of rock and sand, its colors a motley of orange, brown, white, grey, black, green.

"Where are we to dig?" says Carlos.

Where, indeed? If the best hiding place is the least remarkable, Teotihuacán's lost gold is buried in ground that looks like any other. And yet, a sealed vault at the heart of the Pirámide del Sol could hardly be bettered as a site of safekeeping.

"I think we will need dynamite as well as shovels," says Javier.

"What is your sense of it?" Miguel asks the Turk.

The little man's bleak eyes appraise the ruins. He surveys the Pirámide del Luna and its attendant platforms, then turns in his saddle to gaze back along the Calzada de los Muertos.

"Well?" says Carlos. "You have a nose for gold. Can you not detect its scent?"

"Truly, no," says the Turk. "And yet, gold in great quantity is reputed to lie here."

"Its presence is meaningless unless we know where to look."

"It is impossible to know. We can only guess."

"We might spend the remainder of our lives guessing. Also digging." Enrique pushes his hat to the back of his head. "We have been fools – to think we could find a treasure unfound for more than a thousand years."

"Such is the nature of desire." Miguel drinks, wipes his lips. "We accept as possible a thing clearly impossible because we seek an end we cannot attain."

Astride their horses, they stare at the ground. Pebbled dirt, shattered rock, withered grass. Each man is asking himself, "What next?"

A rushing in the sky attracts their collective gaze. A silver airship with sleek fuselage and long backswept wings knifes toward them at fantastic speed. As they draw their rifles, the craft glides to a stop. It hovers directly overhead, soundlessly, a thousand feet up. The Mexicans shoulder their rifles and aim. A sonic blast lifts them from their saddles and throws them backward, guns torn from their hands and cast afield. Panicked, their horses bolt, mules struggling to follow. Pacho and the Turk are buffeted unconscious, the latter curled on one side. Pacho lies flat. The others sit up spitting grit and wiping dust from their eyes.

The silver craft retracts its wings and descends. Its approach is an elegant demonstration of controlled power. As if it were intelligent, it lands atop the great platform before the Pirámide del Luna. A moment later a hatch opens and a man uniformed in silver from neck to toes steps forth, his head uncovered. Holding a device to his mouth, he calls, "¡Estas ahí! ¡Hola!" and waves them forward.

The Mexicans stand. Miguel tells Carlos, "Track the mules. Javier will help you." They move warily toward the platform.

"I wish to hear what this one says."

"Yes. Surely he is one of them. Yet we cannot lose our supplies."

"Pacho seems injured."

"Also the Turk," says Enrique.

"¡Vamos, muchachos, muévete!" the man cries, his voice amplified by the device.

Carlos brings Pacho to consciousness with water from his canteen, then with Javier goes on foot south along the Calzada de los Muertos. The Turk they leave.

"¡Así no!" yells the man in silver. "¡Aquí!"

Miguel calls, "We must retrieve our horses and mules. Our food flees with them." He and Enrique approach. When they are near enough to speak without shouting, he says, "We believe you have taken our people."

"You use English, do you?" says the silver one. "How convenient." He tosses aside the amplifier that has rendered his words in Spanish.

"Men, women, and children," Enrique says. "From an encampment by the Sea of Cortés."

"Ah. That bunch belonged to you, did it?" The man nods. "You have my apologies. *On behalf of the entire population of Mars Colony, I respectfully offer heartfelt regret*, and so forth. We had believed we'd netted everyone. Sorry to have left you behind. However, you should know who I am." Bowing, he says, "Paladin Silver, Sojourner Among the Stars. I am Adept on Special Assignment, dispatched to Earth by none other than Head Director of Mars Colony, who charged me with the objective – and quite a chore it turned out to be – of finding you." He points at Miguel. "And also you." He points at Enrique. "And three others – your compatriots, I presume. Or rather, four others, as it seems a creature called Omar the Turk joined your elusive band at some point between the Sonoran Desert and the place in which we parley – that is, here. Which brings me to my first question: When might those others wander back? Really, I need all six of you together if we are to make any headway."

Pointing behind himself, Miguel says, "One of our company sits there. The heap of rag and bone lying near him is the one called Omar the Turk. We believe he has been killed."

"Really, that is too bad. We hoped to take all of you alive. However, it is hardly our fault. Once your party deployed its firesticks, as I believe the natives hereabouts once called them, our AutoDefense scripts ran and, well, you know the rest. Didn't intend it to be so final. Nor so fatal."

"The Turk served his purpose. He was not one of us. However, we owe him thanks. Without his guidance we could not have come to this place."

Paladin Silver smiles. "Yes, exactly. Now we are getting to it. And why have you – what are your names, by the way?"

"Miguel Jiménez."

"Enrique Ramos."

"Just so. Very good. Now then, Enrique, Miguel: why have you come to this lonely, dusty, ancient, godforsaken spot?"

They look at each other, unsure. To tell all is to risk everything. And yet, they must trade what they know for those they seek.

The Turk could tell them what to reveal, and how much.

Enrique nods and Miguel says, "Legend tells of a fortune in gold hidden within this city. We have come in search of this treasure."

"Well, well. A fortune in gold. Who would have imagined?" Paladin Silver licks his lips. "Of how much gold, exactly, are we speaking?"

"The amount is unknown. It is said that these pyramids – " Enrique points at the Moon pyramid behind Paladin, then behind himself to the Pirámide del Sol. " – and this avenue with its watercourses were built to recover gold in great quantities."

"You don't say. Now, that is interesting. Extremely so. Whereabouts does all this gold lurk?"

The Mexicans shrug. "We do not know. We can only dig."

"Dig where?"

Enrique laughs. "Dig there. Dig there. Dig there and there and there," he says, throwing his arms all around. "Dig until we find it."

"Oh, come on. How long do you fellows expect to live?" Seeing the two Mexicans start back, Paladin laughs. "No, no, no, I'm not going to snuff you. I mean, you could dig for fifty years all over this place and Hell's Half Acre, too, and never quite dig in the correct spot to the required depth. Surely you see that."

Miguel nods. "To find the treasure is luck, or fate. However, we lack other means to ransom our people."

"So that's what you're on about. Well, fellows, let me tell you: it need not come to that."

As they ponder this statement, Pacho comes huffing up, holding his head and blinking against the brilliance of the silver ship. He says, "Is it possible the gold we carry is enough?"

"Ah. You have gold in hand, do you?"

"Fool," says Enrique. "You should not have told him."

"It does no harm," says Miguel. To Paladin, he says, "The gold we have also flees with the mules Carlos and Javier attempt to corral."

Paladin nods. "Nice. Here we all are, just waiting for one hand to wash the other. I'll tell you what let's do. Let's hang fire for a bit while your boys fetch those filthy beasts back here. Then we'll have a look at your gold, yes? In the meantime, I'll uplink the Head Director and explain how things stand. Not to get ahead of ourselves, but I daresay we will be able to hash it out." He fixes each man in turn with his ice-blue eyes. "I assure you, we will reach an accommodation." Smiling broadly, Paladin spreads his arms toward the Mexicans. "What say ye?"

Miguel says, "You are welcome to the gold we possess. We want only our people."

"Good! Good! Damn fine! That is exactly the attitude the Head Director has been looking for all along." Rocking with satisfaction in his silver suit, the Sojourner Among the Stars shines in the golden sun. "Really, you are a plucky bunch. Templar was right – as usual, it must be said. No one gains anything by doubting the exquisite Dr. Bronze. Now, if you will excuse me." And with that, Paladin bows, turns, and disappears into the clamshell hatch.

Left sweating amid heat and dust, the Mexicans drink water and look around. Carlos and Javier have disappeared.

Pacho says, "I fear we will end our days digging for a mythical treasure."

"We must hope," says Enrique, "that this Head Director, who-ever he may be, has another means of turning this city upside-down."

"And that he will use it," says Miguel.

Lights dim, screen dark, chimps done, Roscoe Gold by his lone-some in the Inner Sanctum lifts a bottle and pours a glass of Tem-plar's most recent vintage. Aged three years, Mars Colony Earth-Station 3 Red Select Varietal Blend 2091 silks along the bottleneck and flows into crystal. The Head Director inhales an aroma of berries and chocolate as the wine opens up. Truly, these are great days. With some luck, greater lie ahead. It calls for a toast – he re-ally should have invited Templar. The superlative Dr. Bronze would have relished the wine, appreciated the quiet. Then again, it is a contemplative moment. Peace is essential. Her opinions and insight and general brilliance and stunning beauty tend to make Templar an agitating presence. And yet, Roscoe is confident she would have moderated her being and opened her spirit, the better to experience awe and trembling at the timeless act he extends his hand to consummate.

Roscoe picks up a red rose, grown in a hothouse of EarthStation 3, and lays it across a bar of gold. It is an archaic gesture, symbolic and expressive; in oldentimes, the gold would have been fashioned as a cross. No need for such hocus-pocus now, what with the Planet of the Crossing still some fourteen hundred Earth years out. Truth to tell, just doing this much feels a bit daft. What can it mean, to lay a red rose across a bar of gold? It looks nice; what is supposed to follow? A smile? A sigh? A sense of elation, or one of despair? Plant and metal; an ephemeral something and that which endures. The rose is delicate, tender, almost edible. And gold is gold. Malleable, dense, rich of luster, proof against decay.

So beautiful. And it will save them. It will save their lives. Their individual minds, he means, which are really the point.

At least one thousand, perhaps upward of twelve hundred stalwart and anonymous Mexicans are doing spadework in the City of the Gods. Living in shanties on-site, their women on hand to cook and comfort, their children to cheer them. Droids to supervise the work and police the workers. Roscoe chuckles. It is all just too good. Who would have believed? Well, yes: Templar did tell him. *Gold exists in Mexico*. But who would have guessed how much?

On the other hand: they haven't found it yet. Still, the Lost City exists; maybe the legend is true. And maybe it is a first step, a mere beginning. Legends tell of forgotten cities hidden in teeming South American jungles from Guatemala to Columbia, from Venezuela to Peru. The peoples, it is said, paid fealty to a pantheon of twelve gods who required annual tribute – at the autumnal equinox? at the summer solstice? – in gold. It is Roscoe's intention to find that gold. All of it. Mars, he has new reason to hope, might have a human atmosphere yet.

At the very least, they have solved the problem of those glum, underachieving freeloaders taking up space in the EarthStations, all brick-thick refusal and thousand-yard stares. Very depressing. A surfeit of negative energy. He would not be surprised if their toxic karma has been responsible for the demise of those chimps. Brain emanations might have been involved, or ion exchange. Well, they will have their comeuppance now. Even better, those desperadoes have been put to the shovel as well. *No more mischief-making with dynamite and delayed fuses, my lads! Dig!* Ah, the Lulu Amelu. By inventing the mere human, the so-called Lofty Ones invented life as we know it.

Too bad about Omar. A rotten bit of luck, his getting himself killed at almost the last moment. So serviceable. No substitute for it, really, an operative on the ground. Omar Ataturk, as Roscoe knew him, was a fellow most definitely worth more than his weight in gold. To have known more about him would have been satisfying. Who was Omar, really? What drove him, what set him on? Self-interest goes without saying; everyone boils with it. Yet Roscoe cannot help feeling there was something more to it. To Omar, or whatever his true name was. Omar's doings in Mexico amounted all together to thoroughgoing deprivation, yet he persisted in his ways. Nomadic, solitary, unattached, unreconciled. He could not live among other people, or did not want to. Some things, it seems, cannot be helped. Or changed. Like his death. Cost of doing business and so forth. And he had served his purpose.

So. A rose blooming red and luscious lies across a gleaming bar of pure gold. Maybe it is just a pretty picture but it cannot hurt. Perhaps it will nudge Roscoe closer to enlightenment. He lifts the glass, sips the wine. Delicious. Persnickety Dr. Bronze might not be satisfied but to his palate it is fine, fine. With such bounty spread before us, how are we to resist?

Desires of the body. The life of the mind. Each Initiate cleaves to the precepts defined by the Order. The discipline is a journey and the journey is a process and the process is ineffable.

How is Roscoe to attain selflessness when a self is all he can possess? *Transformation and transcendence.* To become better than he is, better than he has ever been. To become a finer person, a more worthy being. To distill his nature. To dissolve base instinct as if in an acid bath, to cleave it from his unique mind and immortal soul – as one refines raw ore to remove the dross and retain the gold.

Pure and shining. Immaculate. Forever.

$$(\female) \ (\male)$$

"Welcome to the future, J."

The entity who calls herself Jenna touches Melmoth's cheek with her fingertips. She kisses him lightly on the lips. With her other hand she caresses his penis, her touch suggesting something like love.

Finally. A woman with a heart. "Thank you, Jenna. I am so happy to meet you at last. I was beginning to think you would never wake up."

"Ha ha ha. You are so funny, J. I do not know how Raquel bears it."

Raquel Romanov smothers a smile. She, too, fondles a male, a superbly built fellow sporting a stout erection. He calls himself Floyd and wears a constant grin.

They stand all together in the inner room, Melmoth and his maybe-spouse having been summoned by a ringing of chimes. Hurrying in, they beheld the perfect man and ideal woman finally waking up. The capsule tops popped, their lids swung up and, hydraulic-dampened, sunk to one side. The woman sat up, magnificent, magnificent, then the man, and each stepped boldly into view. Magnificent, indeed. A moment later, it became clear that these seeming strangers were, in fact, long-familiar friends on terms of utmost intimacy with our estranged, sex-starved pair. Copulation commenced promptly and continued for hours to the merriment of all.

These frolics having abated, Jenna and Floyd attempt to re-illumine memories gone dark.

"Yes, you two are married," says Floyd, "and yes, you have children together. Yet the marriage is open and we are your chosen playmates."

This assertion rings no bell J Melmoth or Raquel Romanov has heard before. However, neither objects to its tone.

"We share your thoughts and your dreams," says Jenna, "your likes and your dislikes, your preferences and fondest wishes. By sharing these capsules, we enjoy a melding of minds."

"Really," says Melmoth.

"Horsepucky," says Raquel.

"It is sublime," says Floyd, "to know your desire even as you conceive the urge."

"Now that's something," says Raquel.

Melmoth whistles. "Pretty slick. How does it work?"

Jenna throws Floyd a sidelong smile and naughty Floyd grins wolfishly back. "Why, it is as easy as falling asleep," he says.

"It is so simple, J." Taking him by the hand, Jenna shows him their capsule. It does look comfy with its pleated satin lining and silk pillow. "We take turns sleeping inside. You share my capsule, I share yours – it is all one. Floyd and Raquel have that capsule to themselves. During sleep, a whisper teaches us to love one another better. To appreciate and respect all that is unique in the chosen other, whose personality and demeanor, thoughts and feelings are as special and cherished as one's own."

"Wow," says Melmoth. "And you have chosen me?"

"Indeed, I have chosen you, J. And you have made me your choice in turn."

"Why haven't Raquel and I chosen each other? As we are married, I mean."

A moment of surprise, then the others laugh.

"Oh, J! You are such a riot!"

"Hilarious," Raquel exclaims. "I choose you? What on Earth for, when Floyd's is so meaty and he is such a doll?"

"You don't have to rub it in," says Melmoth. "It was just a thought."

"Put such thoughts from your mind," says Jenna. "Banish them, expunge them. Such vain imaginings cause unhappiness. Think only of me, for I love you and honor you and desire you always, always."

It is almost too much for Melmoth to bear. After all those days shut-up with bitchy Raquel and an unsated fantastic stiff woody, what a joy to have at his fingertips a woman like Jenna – young, beautiful, sexy beyond belief, a living doll if ever one was. How has it happened? When did his Average Jack, Humpty Dumpty life become so good? It's a miracle, really, it feels like one, not that Melmoth has experienced a miracle before. Not that he remembers.

For a week they cavort. Sex has never been better, as easy, more frequent, or more fun. Jenna is insatiable and highly orgasmic. Highly. It is not just a fulfillment of Melmoth's most treasured desires. It is Heaven.

Then he gets a hankering to regain what he has lost. Certain things once were; to know them is important. To Jenna he says, "What if I take a turn in our capsule? Just for one night, I mean.

We'll fuck first, of course, twice if you like, then I'll lie down inside. Shut the lid, close my eyes, listen to the whisper. What do you think?"

"Oh, J, you genius! Of course you must! A long, deep capsule-sleep is exactly the thing. Absolutely, it will restore you. That is its purpose: to rejuvenate and restore. Excellent, that you have had this happy thought!" Jenna springs to her feet and with two deft movements pretends to throw off her nonexistent clothes. "Adorable man!" she cries. "Fuck me now!"

Melmoth, ever the trooper, complies with a smile. Good as his word, he plies her a second time in short order. His refractory period has become briefer, he is sure of it. After the gasping is done and the pulsing subsides, he cleans himself up and slips into the capsule. Jenna kisses him goodnight and herself shuts the lid, then touches some buttons that begin a process whose low, mellifluous hum comes to him from a place afar off. The first thing Melmoth notices is a tingling in his head. Something deep is buzzing. He expects he will soon get used to it. The next thing he notices is that he is falling asleep fast. Very fast. He hardly has time –

⚖

The sun is sinking on Further Beach as two service droids mop up. They stack tin pails by the hundred one inside another and lay the columns down parallel on the wood-slat trailer. When the flatbed is covered, they fit a second level of pails into the grooves formed by the first, then a third level into the grooves so-formed by the second, and so on until a single column so-laid makes the apex. By this method they build a pyramid of pails, with the tapered stability of that structure.

Chasing down strays, a droid finds a hole dug in the sand. Its round mouth yawns like a well, yet a well it can hardly be with a saltwater ocean just fifty yards distant. The droid approaches the hole and looks down into its dark bottom.

"That's not protocol," it says to no one. "That's out of bounds."

It calls the other droid. It also looks into the hole.

"That man is dead."

"I think so, too."

"What can have happened?"

"No way to know. No one's fault, however. That man put himself in a bad spot."

"That's right. No one forced him to it."

"That's right."

"Right."

The two things stand there looking into the hole. The light is fading. Clouds are blowing in off the ocean.

"Should we leave him? We should leave him. He's a miscreant, says that beard. We might as well leave him."

"We can't leave him, we have to bring him back. Come on, give me a hand."

Neither droid moves.

"We might as well leave him."

"It's protocol to bring him back. This means sea burial. Miscreants get sea burial by policy."

"What policy? I don't remember a policy."

"Policy is part of protocol. Ragheads swim with the fishes."

"We're not supposed to call them that."

"We don't call them that. Except when they can't hear."

"I think we should leave him. Who knows but that he liked it here?"

"Who cares what he liked? Anyway, he's dead. He'll never know if we leave him here or bring him back."

"That's right. He'll never know."

"It doesn't matter if he liked it here or didn't like it. It doesn't matter if we leave him here or bring him back. Except it's protocol to bring him back so that he swims with the fishes."

Rain begins to fall. Drops patter off the droids. Hitting tin pails, the rain sounds like a million toy drums being rapped by a million little drumsticks held in a million tiny hands.

"Why does he have to?"

"Have to what?"

"Swim with the fishes."

"Because he's dead. Dead miscreants swim with the fishes."

"What is a miscreant, anyway?"

"We both know what a miscreant is."

The droid ponders. "Denizens of the Gulag are miscreants. But what does it mean, 'miscreant'? How are they miscreants? Why? For what reason, I mean."

"No one knows why. No one asks. Why are you asking why?"

"I don't know why."

"So stop asking. Our job is not to ask why. Our job is to handle inmates, also known as detainees, otherwise known as denizens of the Gulag. Unofficially called ragheads when they can't hear. They are all miscreants. By definition. That is all we need to know."

"Okay. So we bring this one back."

"Yes. We bring this one back."

The droids go down on their knees in the sand. Rain has made everything wet.

"We have to hurry."

"Yes. Rain is not our friend."

They reach into the hole and grab hold of the corpse. It is curled into itself, rigid, cold to the touch. The droids do not know it is cold because they do not register the temperature of touch. They haul the corpse out of the clammy sand and carry it dripping between them. Its dead weight is a triviality to their hydraulic limbs. They cram it onto the cart.

Their labor done, the droids climb aboard and fire up the engine. Turning hard left, the tractor plows through heavy sand with front wheel steering and rear tires churning. Three furrows describe a crescent that sets them on-course into a gloaming of twilight and skyfall. The bluegray overhead presses down, covering, enclosing the known world. A fading presence races ahead – their shadow, fleeing the darkness of another day.

Ω

About he Author

John Lauricella was born in Brooklyn and grew up in New Jersey, where he attended the public schools. He graduated A.B. *magna cum laude* from Colgate University and was elected to Phi Beta Kappa. Later, he earned an M.F.A. in creative writing and a Ph.D. in English at Cornell. He has taught courses in writing and in literary studies at Cornell, Marymount College, Yeshiva University and other schools. He is the author of *Home Games: Essays on Baseball Fiction* (McFarland & Company, Publishers, Inc.), individual chapters of which appear in *Contemporary American Authors* (Gale Research) and *Twentieth Century Literary Criticism* (Gale/Cengage Learning). *Arts & Letters: A Journal of Contemporary Culture*, and *Stone Canoe: A Journal of Arts, Literature, and Social Commentary*, have published some of his fiction. His novel *Hunting Old Sammie* was published by Irving Place Editions in 2013. The same imprint also published Lauricella's *The Pornographer's Apprentice*, as well as *2094*.

Informed sources say that the author is a bit of a madman in an attic of sorts. It seems he composes these fictions in states verging on delirium or dream, hoping for readers who will understand his stories in their various spirits and intentions.

The editors cannot verify this report or deny it.

Author's Note

Readers of *The Twelfth Planet* (1976) and other volumes of "The Earth Chronicles" by Zecharia Sitchin will recognize in *2094* elements of Mr. Sitchin's interpretations of Sumerian, Akkadian, and other texts and drawings of distant antiquity. This novel's iterations of those ideas are selective, incomplete, simplified and, in some instances, altered by dramatic invention. The reader should regard the present rendition of this content as neither endorsement nor exegesis of Mr. Sitchin's theories, but merely as how those ideas are alive in the minds of the fictive characters who reprise them.